MR. WOLF'S CLASS

LUCKY STARS

ARON NELS STEINKE

AN IMPRINT OF
SCHOLASTIC

For Marlen

All rights reserved. Published by Graphix, an imprint of Scholastic Inc.,
Publishers since 1920. SCHOLASTIC, GRAPHIX, and associated logos are
trademarks and/or registered trademarks of Scholastic Inc.

The publisher does not have any control over and does not assume any
responsibility for author or third-party websites or their content.

No part of this publication may be reproduced, stored in a retrieval system,
or transmitted in any form or by any means, electronic, mechanical, photocopying,
recording, or otherwise, without written permission of the publisher. For information
regarding permission, write to Scholastic Inc., Attention: Permissions Department,
557 Broadway, New York, NY 10012.

This book is a work of fiction. Names, characters, places, and incidents
are either the product of the author's imagination or are used fictitiously,
and any resemblance to actual persons, living or dead, business
establishments, events, or locales is entirely coincidental.

Library of Congress Control Number: 2018953582

ISBN 978-1-338-04789-9 (hardcover)
ISBN 978-1-338-04783-7 (paperback)

10 9 8 7 6 5 4 3 2 1   19 20 21 22 23

Printed in China   62
First edition, September 2019

Edited by Cassandra Pelham Fulton
Book design by Phil Falco
Publisher: David Saylor

CHAPTER ONE

Writer's Workshop

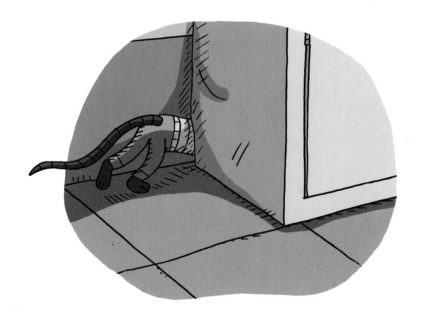

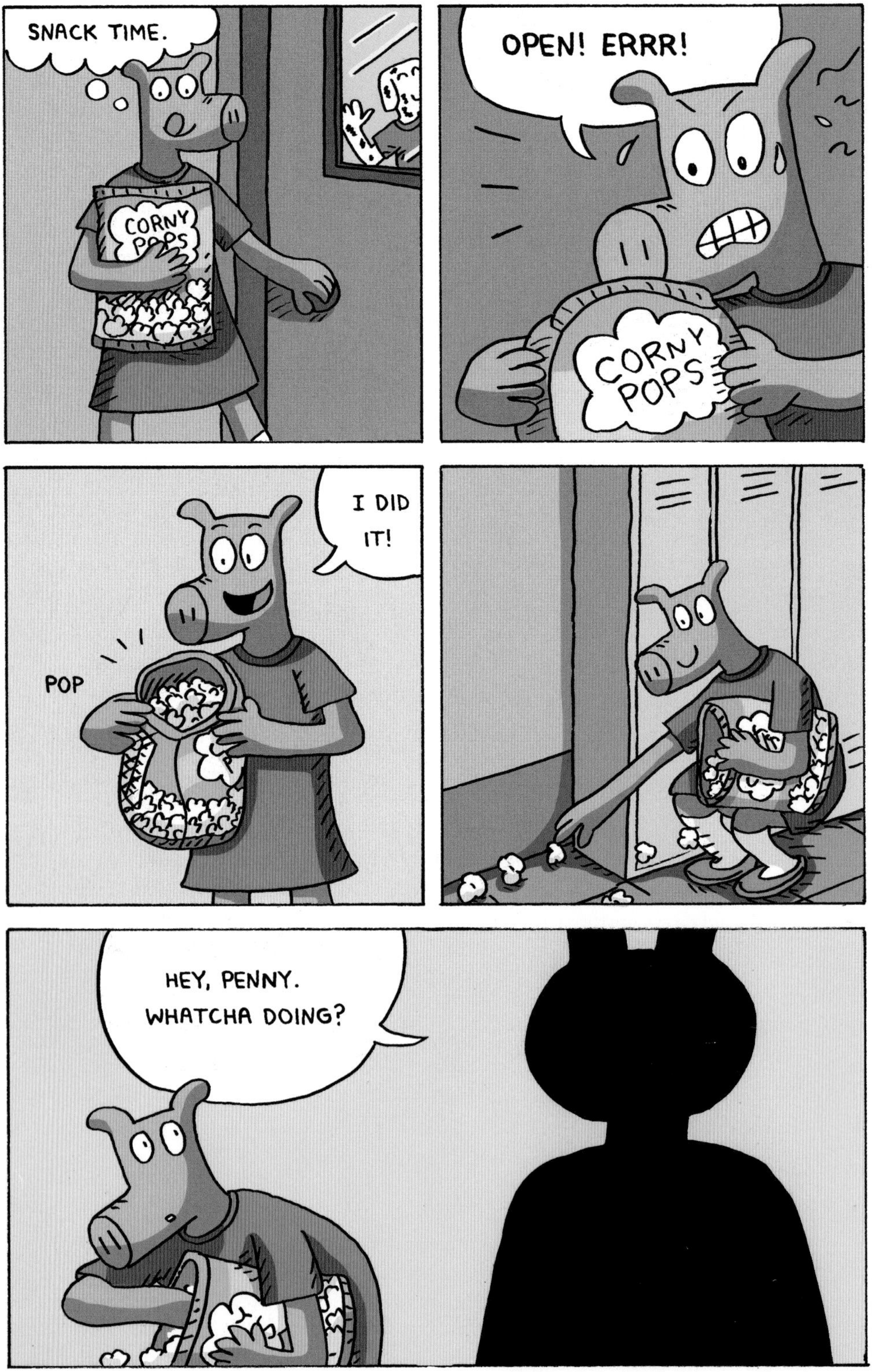
SNACK TIME.
CORNY POPS
OPEN! ERRR!
CORNY POPS
I DID IT!
POP
HEY, PENNY. WHATCHA DOING?

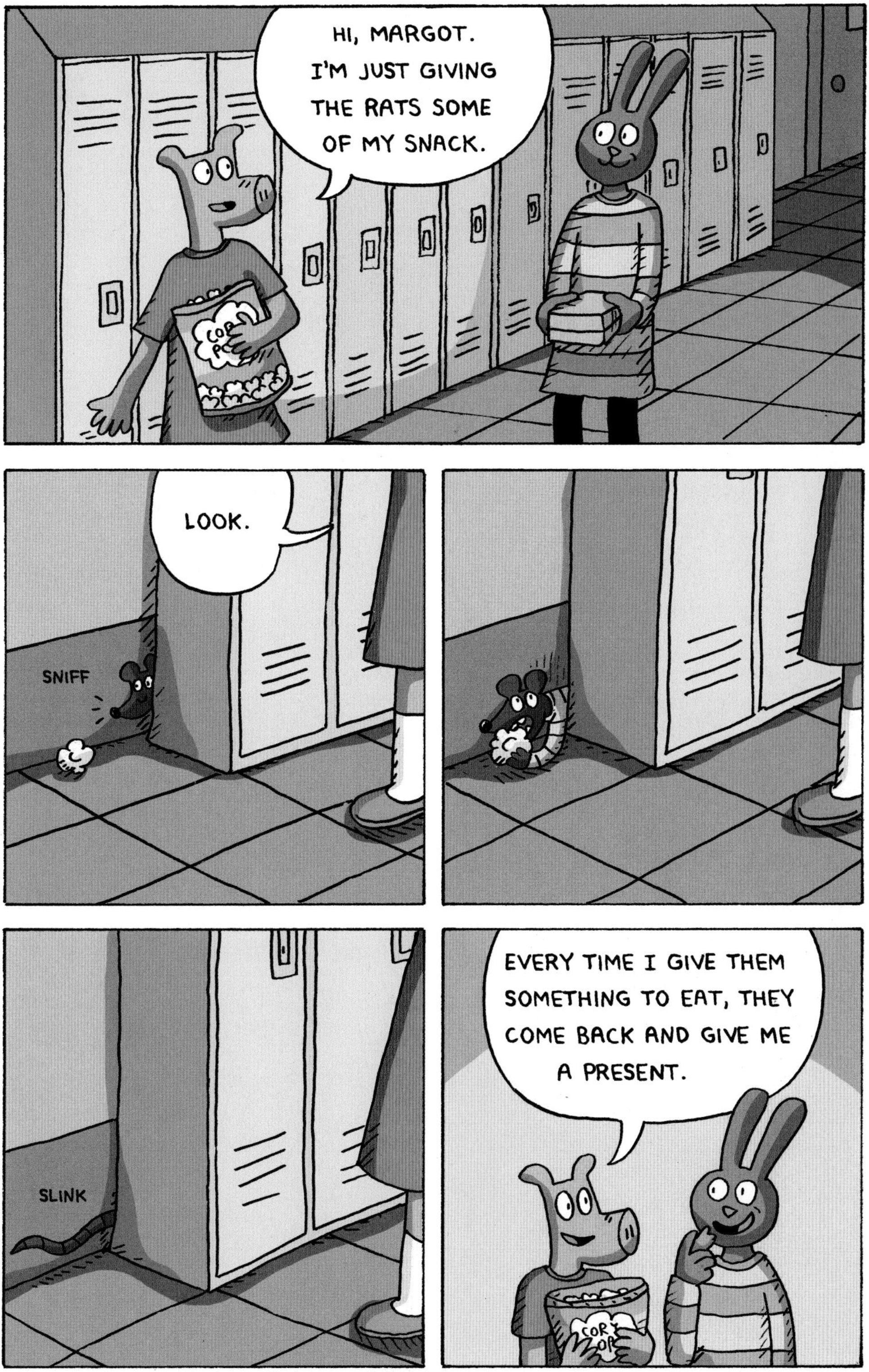
HI, MARGOT. I'M JUST GIVING THE RATS SOME OF MY SNACK.
LOOK.
SNIFF
SLINK
EVERY TIME I GIVE THEM SOMETHING TO EAT, THEY COME BACK AND GIVE ME A PRESENT.

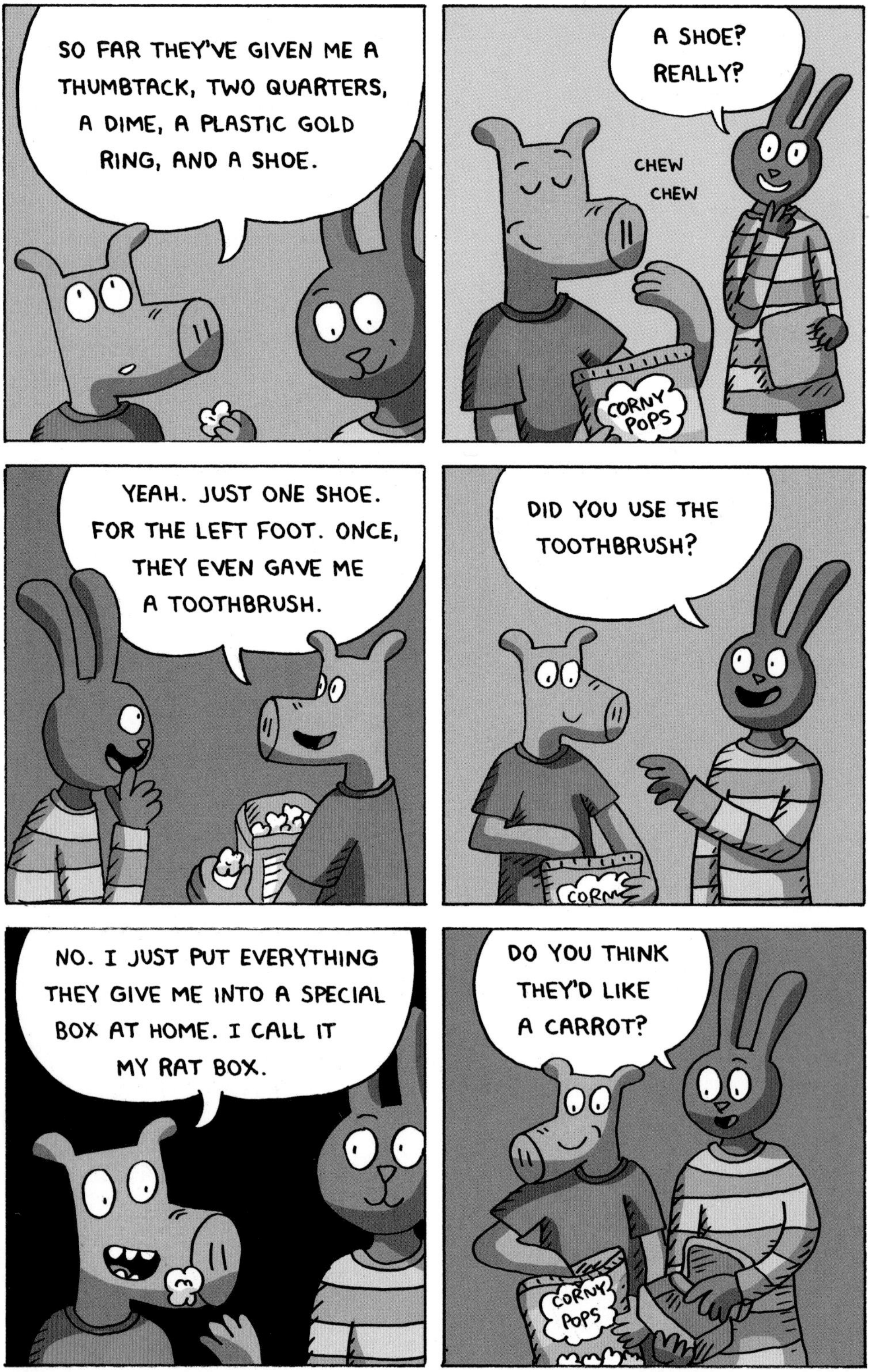
SO FAR THEY'VE GIVEN ME A THUMBTACK, TWO QUARTERS, A DIME, A PLASTIC GOLD RING, AND A SHOE.
A SHOE? REALLY?
CHEW
CHEW
CORNY POPS
YEAH. JUST ONE SHOE. FOR THE LEFT FOOT. ONCE, THEY EVEN GAVE ME A TOOTHBRUSH.
DID YOU USE THE TOOTHBRUSH?
NO. I JUST PUT EVERYTHING THEY GIVE ME INTO A SPECIAL BOX AT HOME. I CALL IT MY RAT BOX.
DO YOU THINK THEY'D LIKE A CARROT?
CORNY POPS

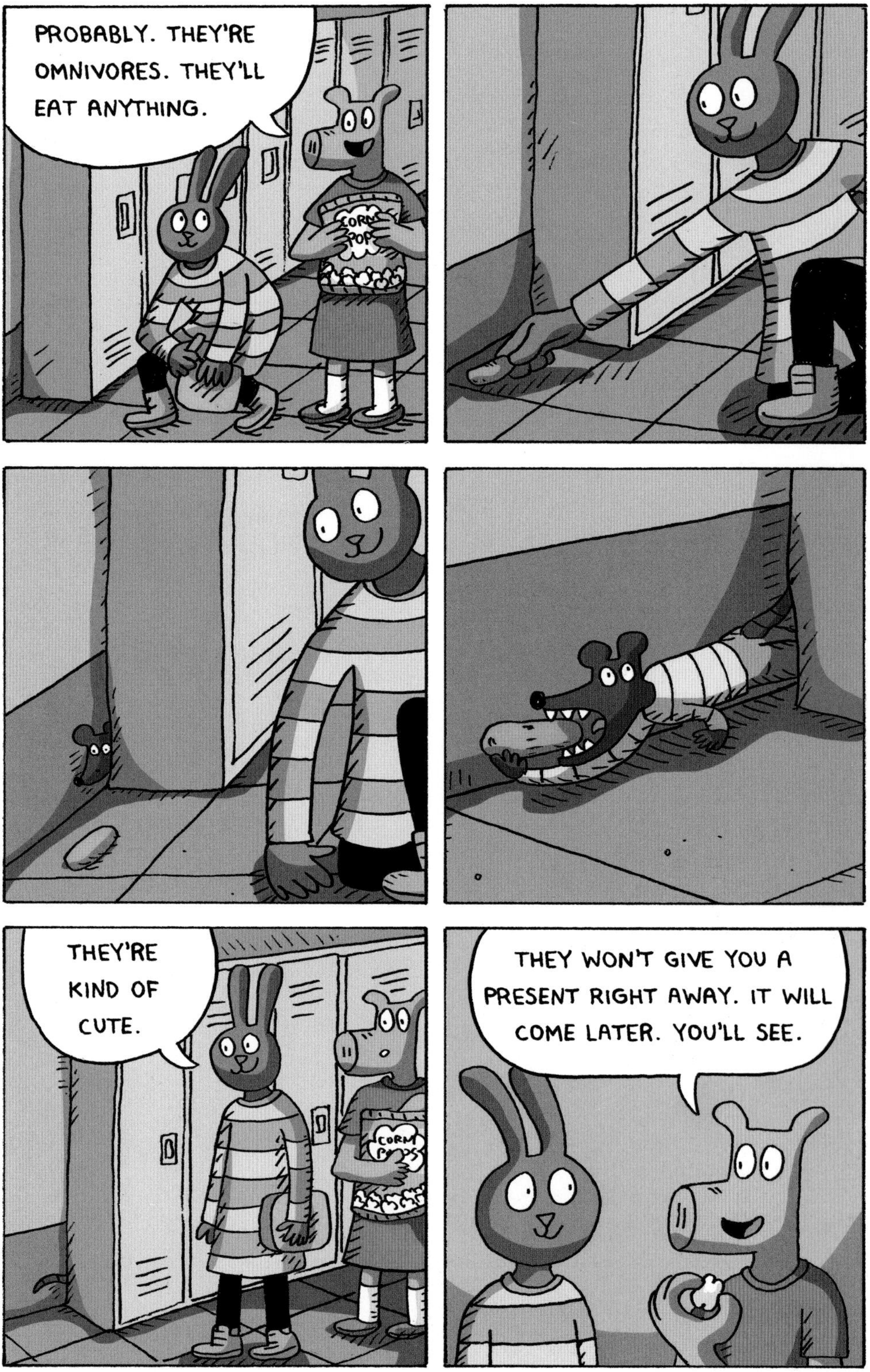
PROBABLY. THEY'RE OMNIVORES. THEY'LL EAT ANYTHING.
CORN POPS
THEY'RE KIND OF CUTE.
CORN POPS
THEY WON'T GIVE YOU A PRESENT RIGHT AWAY. IT WILL COME LATER. YOU'LL SEE.

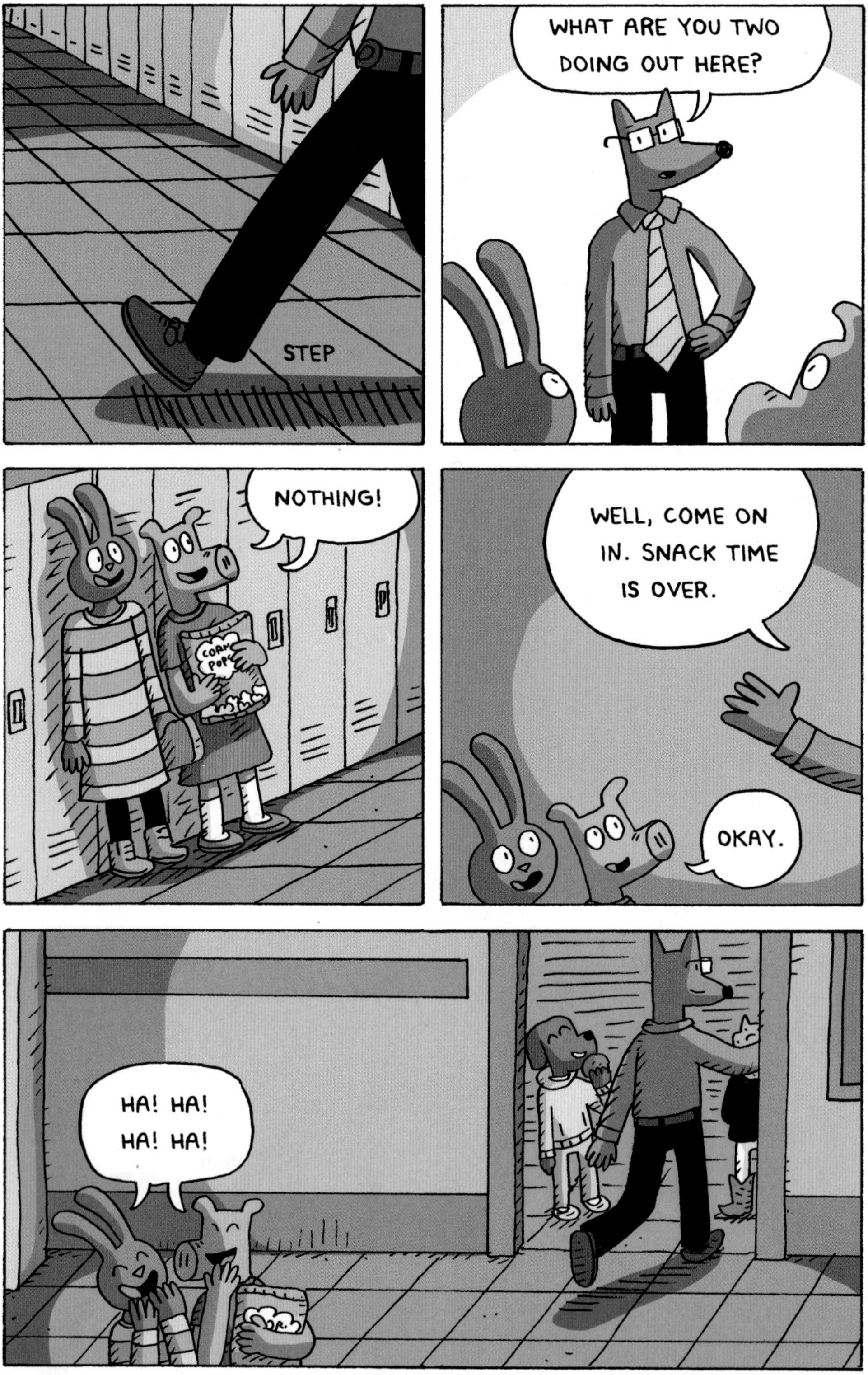
STEP
WHAT ARE YOU TWO DOING OUT HERE?
NOTHING!
WELL, COME ON IN. SNACK TIME IS OVER.
OKAY.
HA! HA! HA! HA!

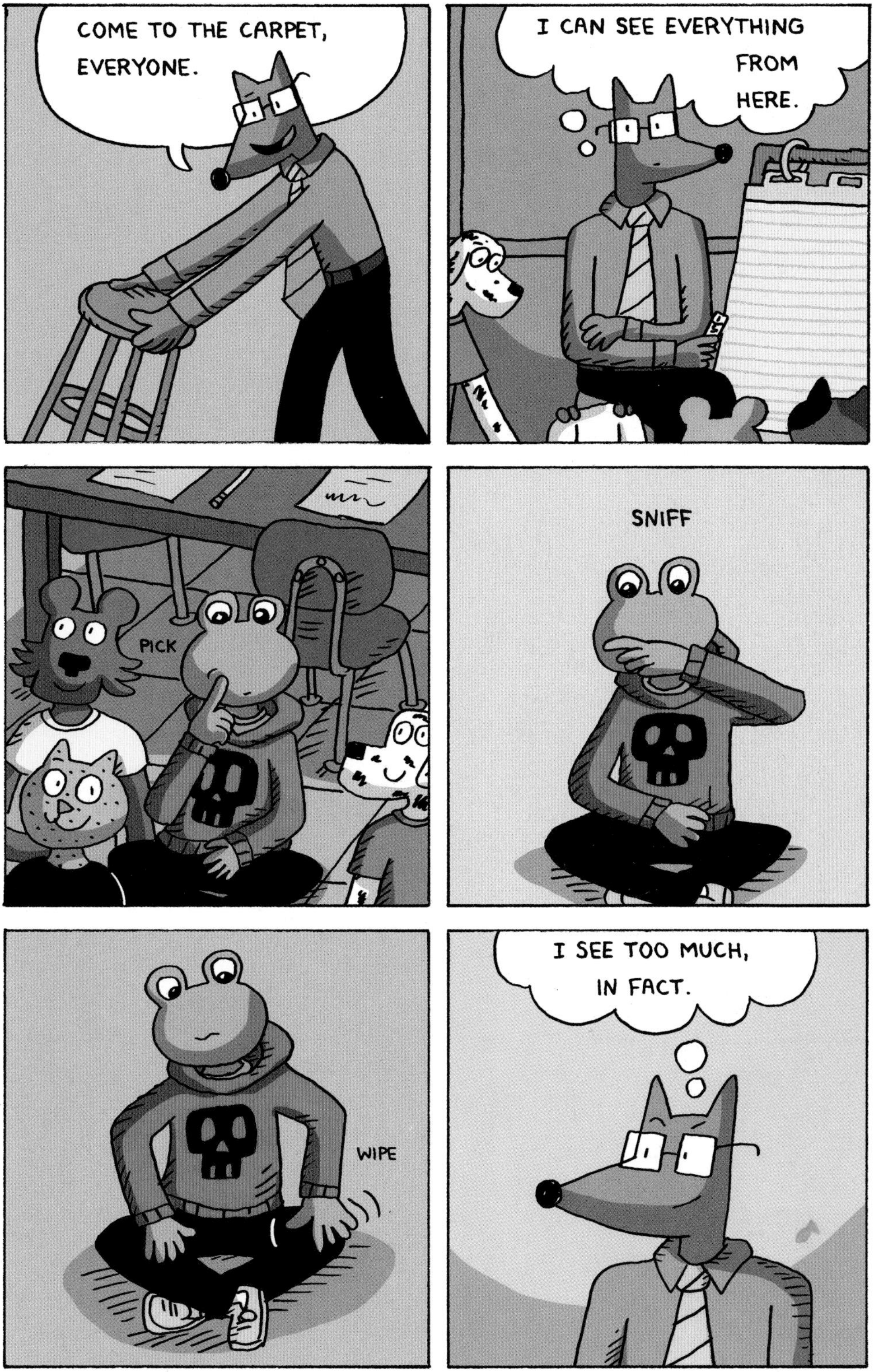
COME TO THE CARPET, EVERYONE.
I CAN SEE EVERYTHING FROM HERE.
PICK
SNIFF
WIPE
I SEE TOO MUCH, IN FACT.

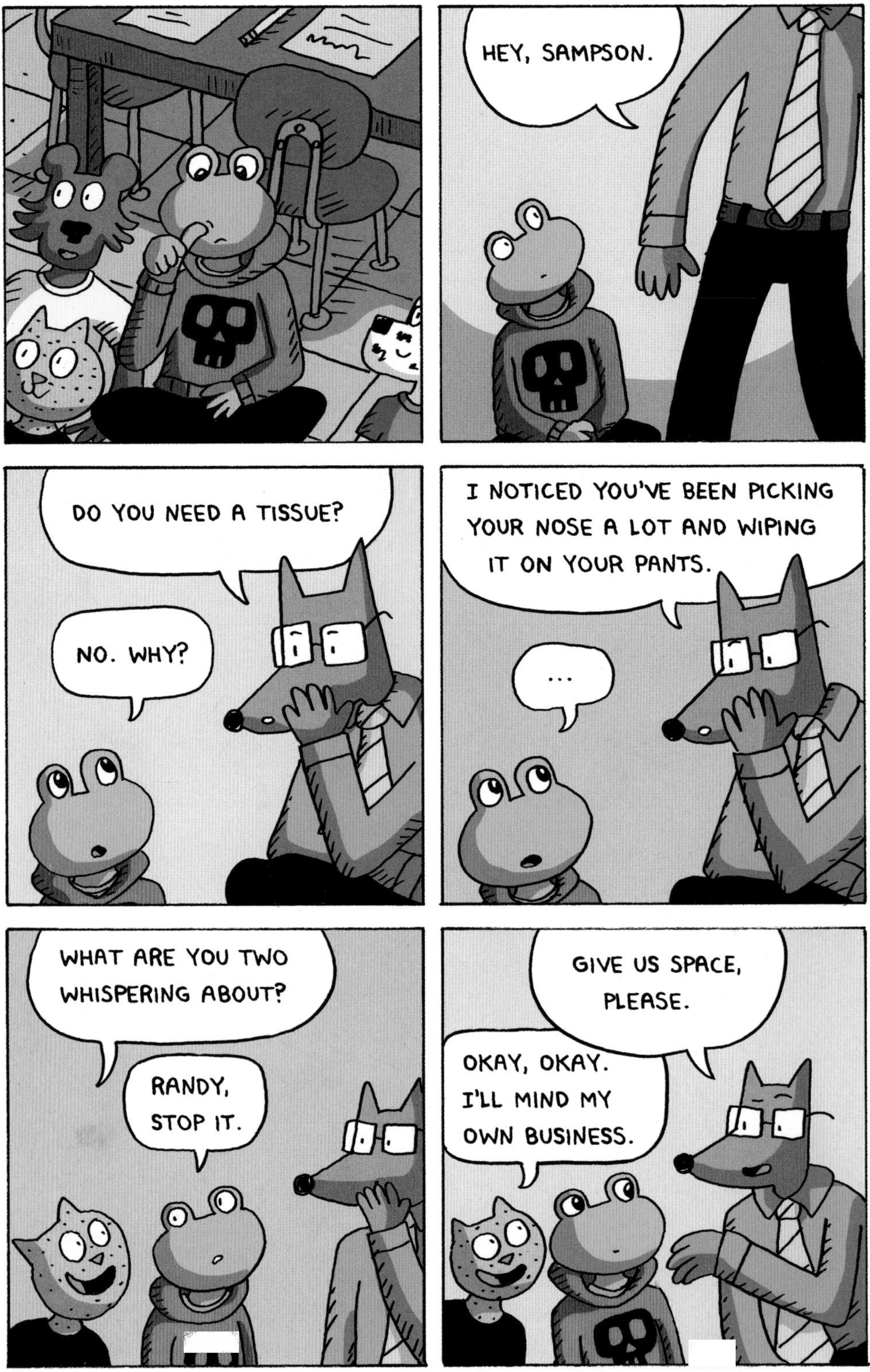
HEY, SAMPSON.
DO YOU NEED A TISSUE?
NO. WHY?
I NOTICED YOU'VE BEEN PICKING YOUR NOSE A LOT AND WIPING IT ON YOUR PANTS.
...
WHAT ARE YOU TWO WHISPERING ABOUT?
RANDY, STOP IT.
GIVE US SPACE, PLEASE.
OKAY, OKAY. I'LL MIND MY OWN BUSINESS.

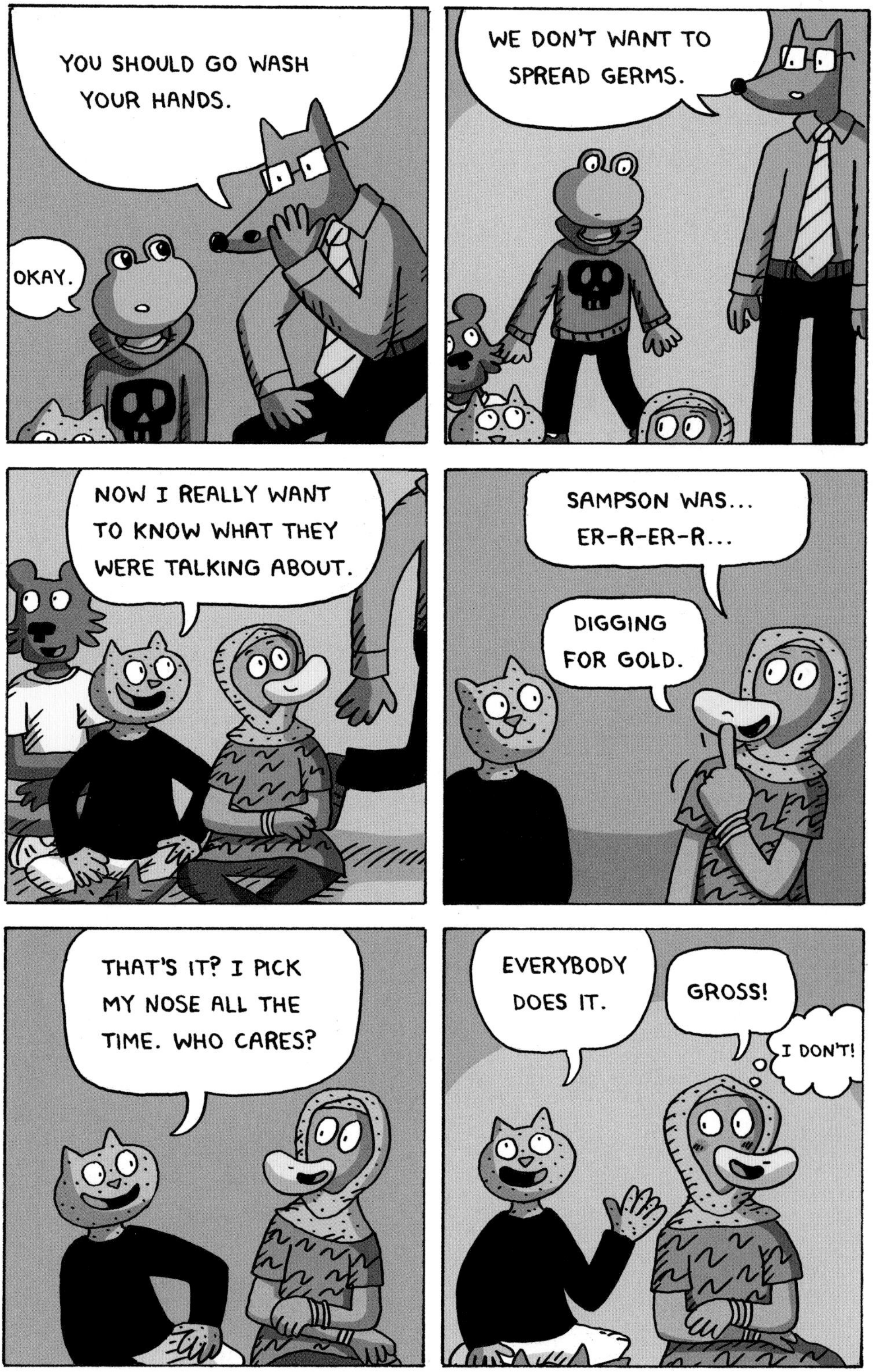
YOU SHOULD GO WASH YOUR HANDS.
OKAY.
WE DON'T WANT TO SPREAD GERMS.
NOW I REALLY WANT TO KNOW WHAT THEY WERE TALKING ABOUT.
SAMPSON WAS... ER-R-ER-R...
DIGGING FOR GOLD.
THAT'S IT? I PICK MY NOSE ALL THE TIME. WHO CARES?
EVERYBODY DOES IT.
GROSS!
I DON'T!

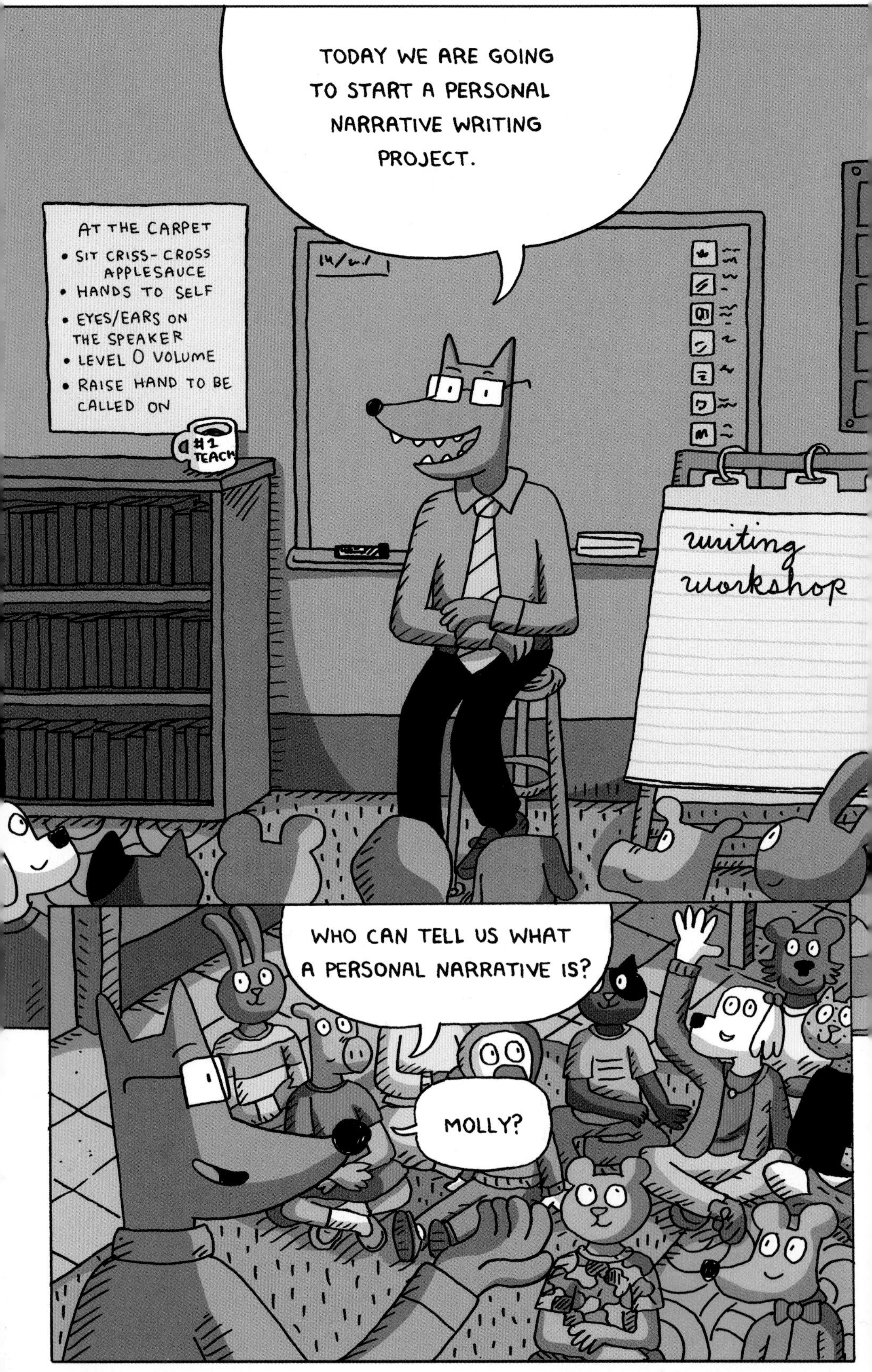

TODAY WE ARE GOING TO START A PERSONAL NARRATIVE WRITING PROJECT.
AT THE CARPET
• SIT CRISS-CROSS APPLESAUCE
• HANDS TO SELF
• EYES/EARS ON THE SPEAKER
• LEVEL 0 VOLUME
• RAISE HAND TO BE CALLED ON
#1 TEACH
writing workshop
WHO CAN TELL US WHAT A PERSONAL NARRATIVE IS?
MOLLY?

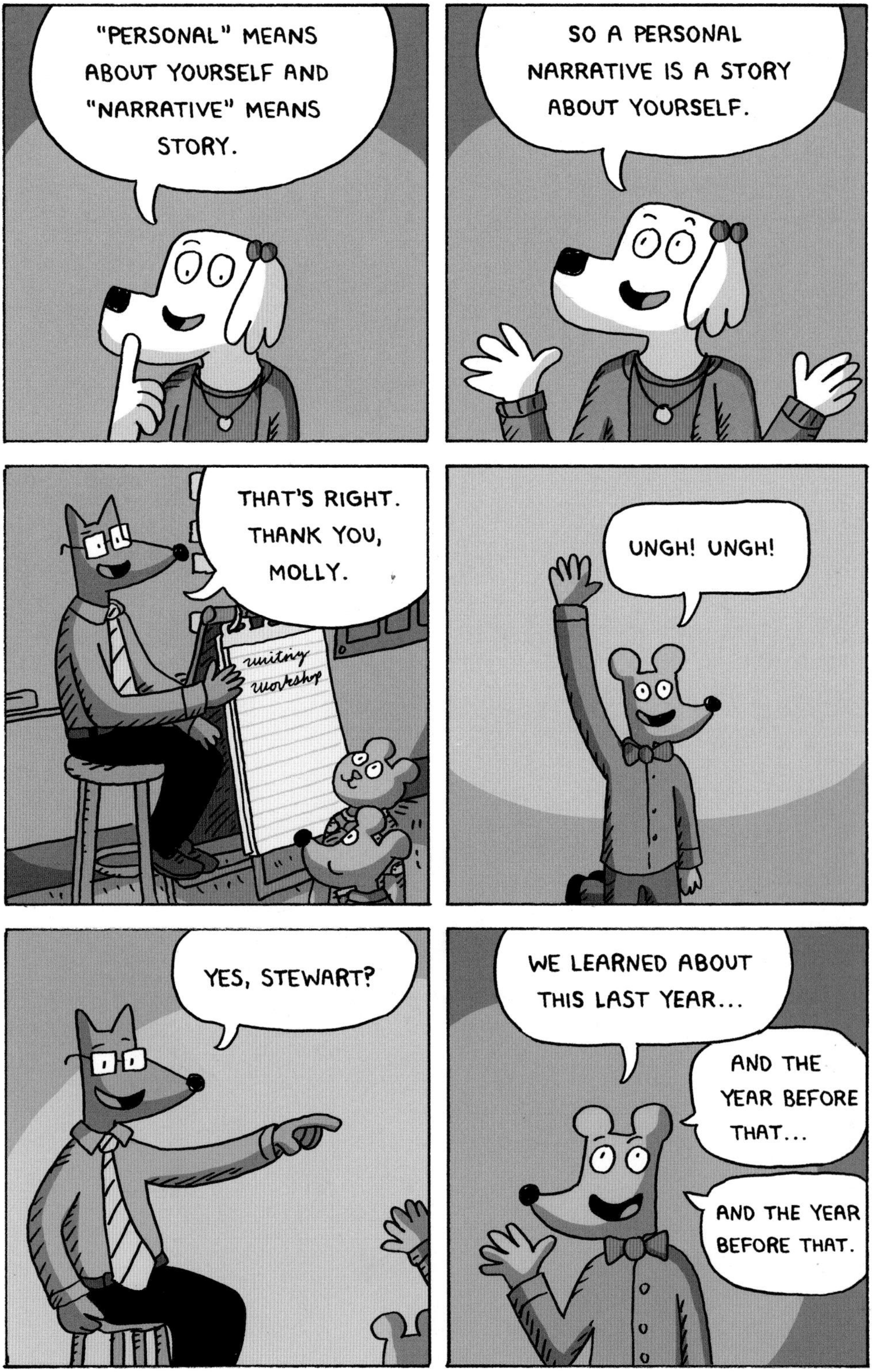
"PERSONAL" MEANS ABOUT YOURSELF AND "NARRATIVE" MEANS STORY.
SO A PERSONAL NARRATIVE IS A STORY ABOUT YOURSELF.
THAT'S RIGHT. THANK YOU, MOLLY.
writing workshop
UNGH! UNGH!
YES, STEWART?
WE LEARNED ABOUT THIS LAST YEAR...
AND THE YEAR BEFORE THAT...
AND THE YEAR BEFORE THAT.

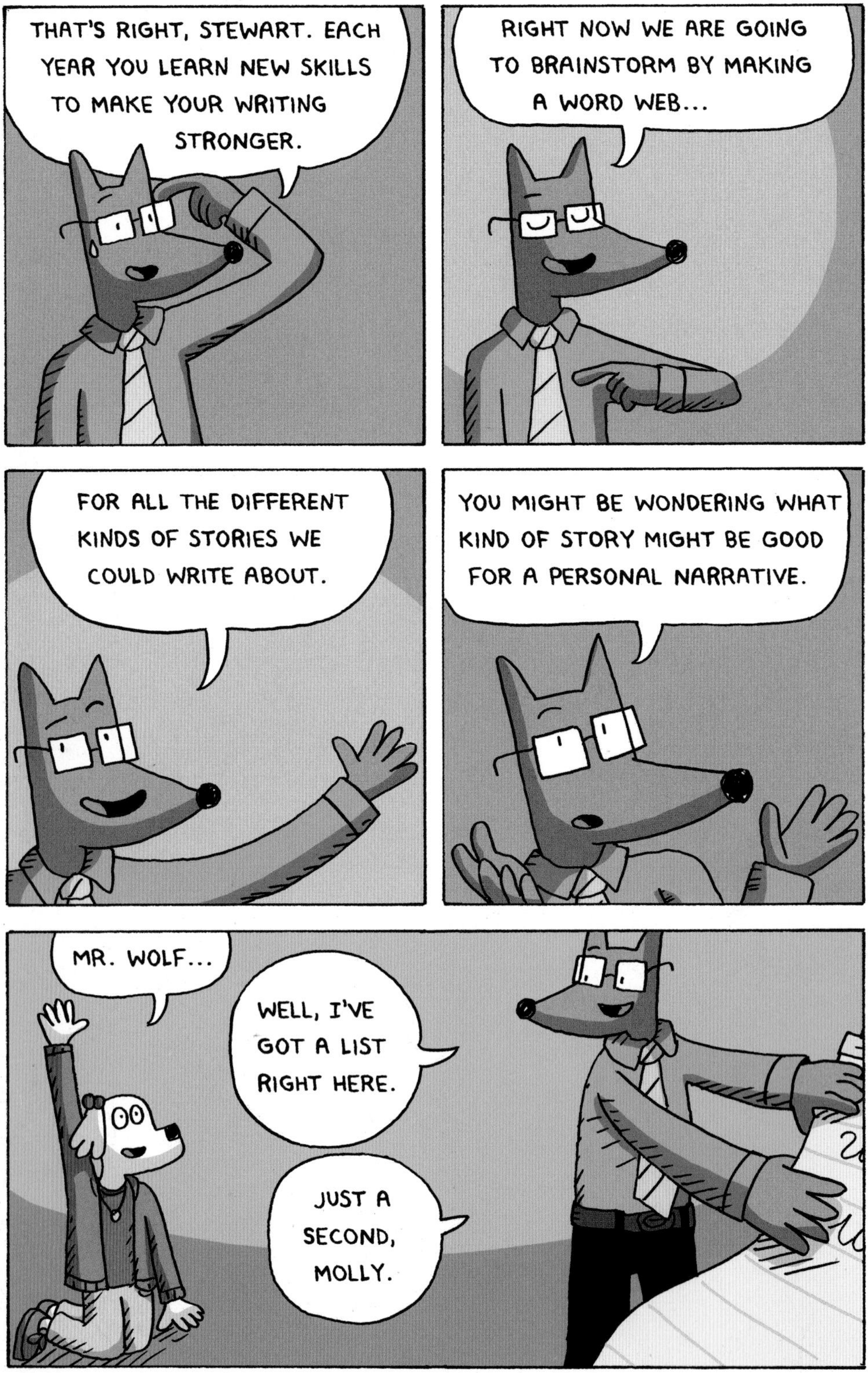
THAT'S RIGHT, STEWART. EACH YEAR YOU LEARN NEW SKILLS TO MAKE YOUR WRITING STRONGER.
RIGHT NOW WE ARE GOING TO BRAINSTORM BY MAKING A WORD WEB...
FOR ALL THE DIFFERENT KINDS OF STORIES WE COULD WRITE ABOUT.
YOU MIGHT BE WONDERING WHAT KIND OF STORY MIGHT BE GOOD FOR A PERSONAL NARRATIVE.
MR. WOLF...
WELL, I'VE GOT A LIST RIGHT HERE.
JUST A SECOND, MOLLY.

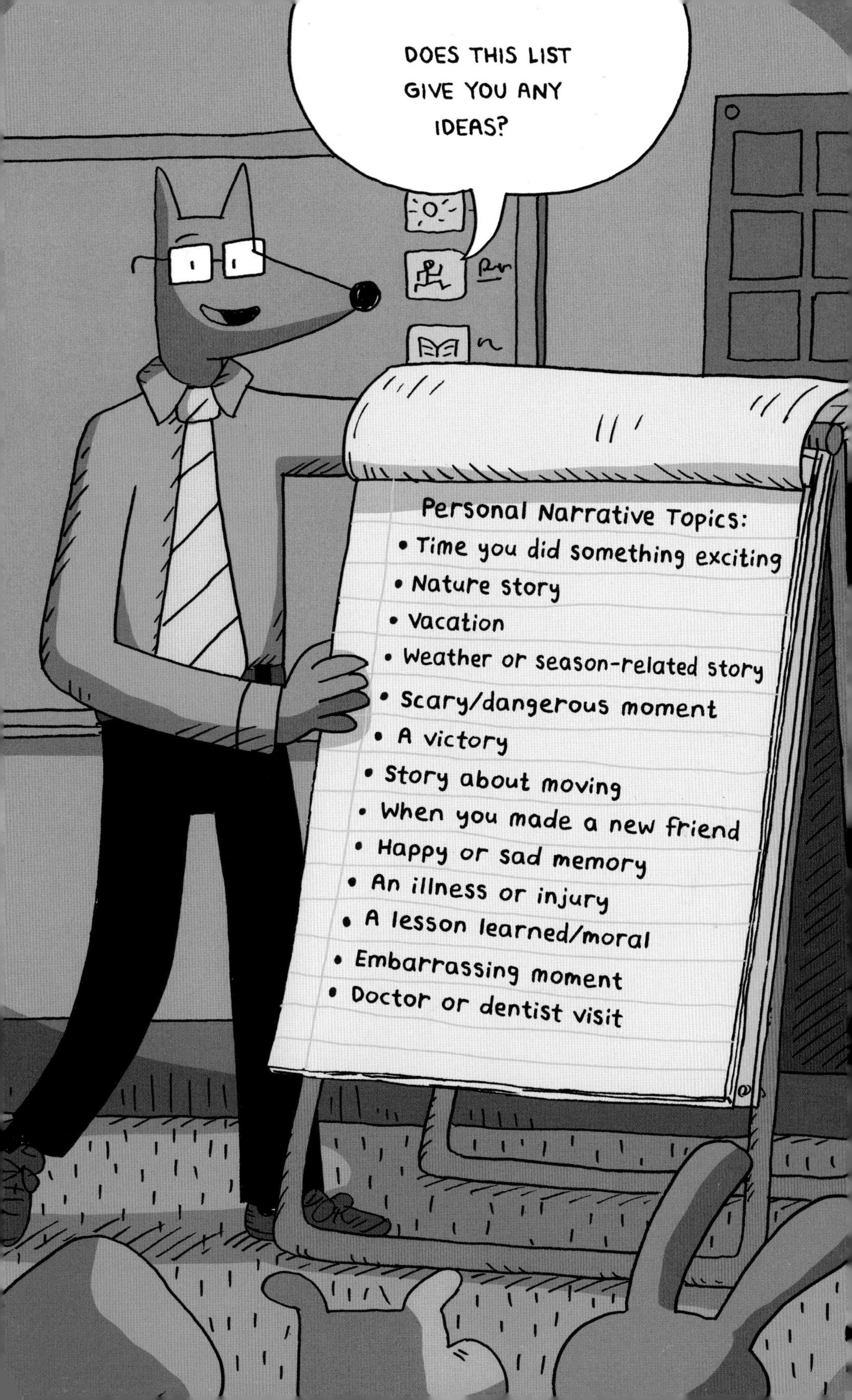
DOES THIS LIST GIVE YOU ANY IDEAS?
Personal Narrative Topics:
• Time you did something exciting
• Nature story
• Vacation
• Weather or season-related story
• Scary/dangerous moment
• A victory
• Story about moving
• When you made a new friend
• Happy or sad memory
• An illness or injury
• A lesson learned/moral
• Embarrassing moment
• Doctor or dentist visit

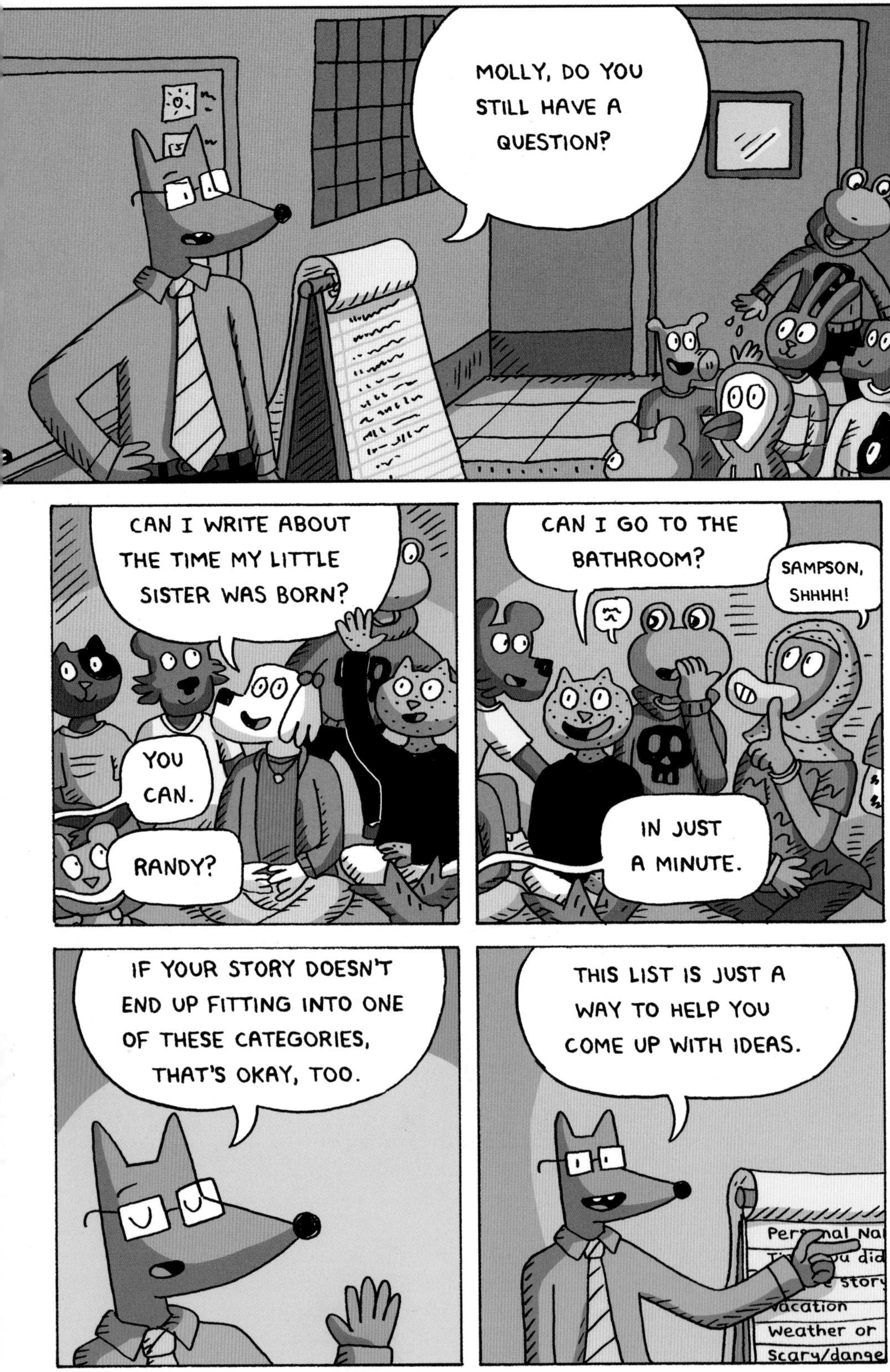
MOLLY, DO YOU STILL HAVE A QUESTION?
CAN I WRITE ABOUT THE TIME MY LITTLE SISTER WAS BORN?
YOU CAN.
RANDY?
CAN I GO TO THE BATHROOM?
SAMPSON, SHHHH!
IN JUST A MINUTE.
IF YOUR STORY DOESN'T END UP FITTING INTO ONE OF THESE CATEGORIES, THAT'S OKAY, TOO.
THIS LIST IS JUST A WAY TO HELP YOU COME UP WITH IDEAS.
vacation
Weather or

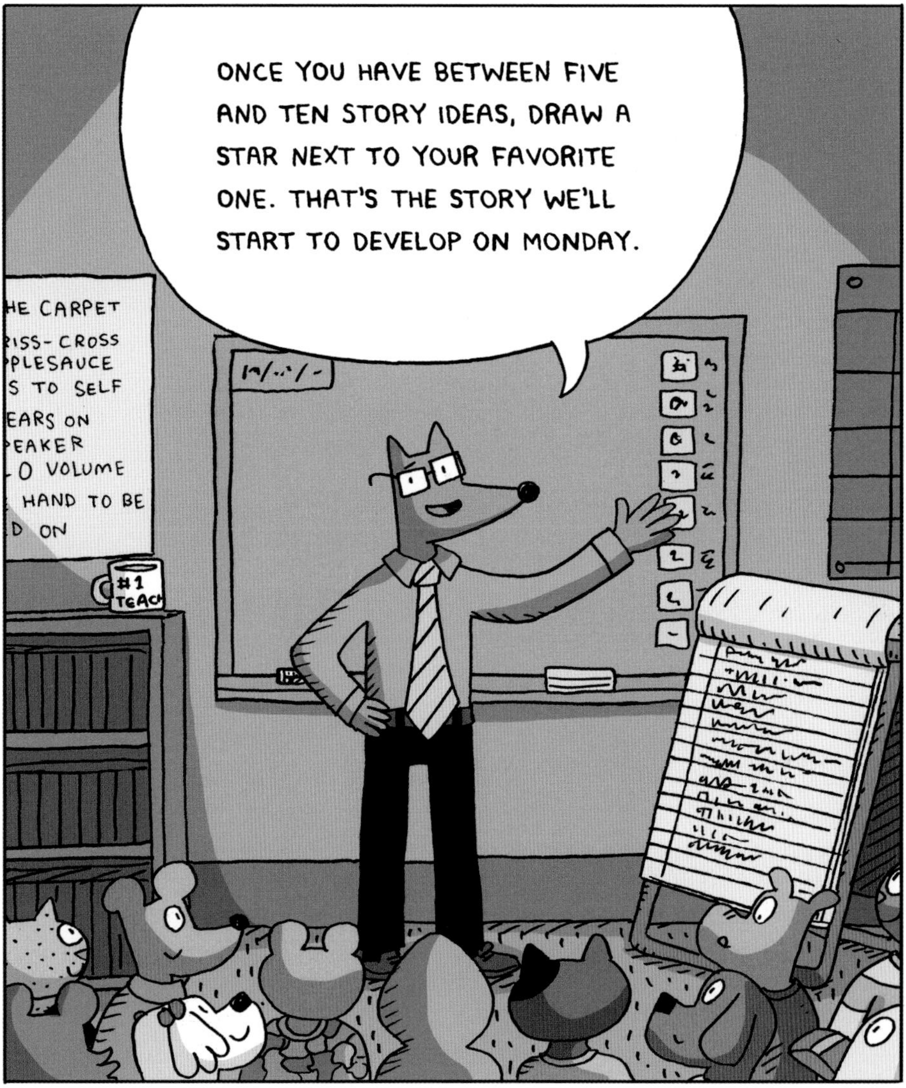
ONCE YOU HAVE BETWEEN FIVE AND TEN STORY IDEAS, DRAW A STAR NEXT TO YOUR FAVORITE ONE. THAT'S THE STORY WE'LL START TO DEVELOP ON MONDAY.

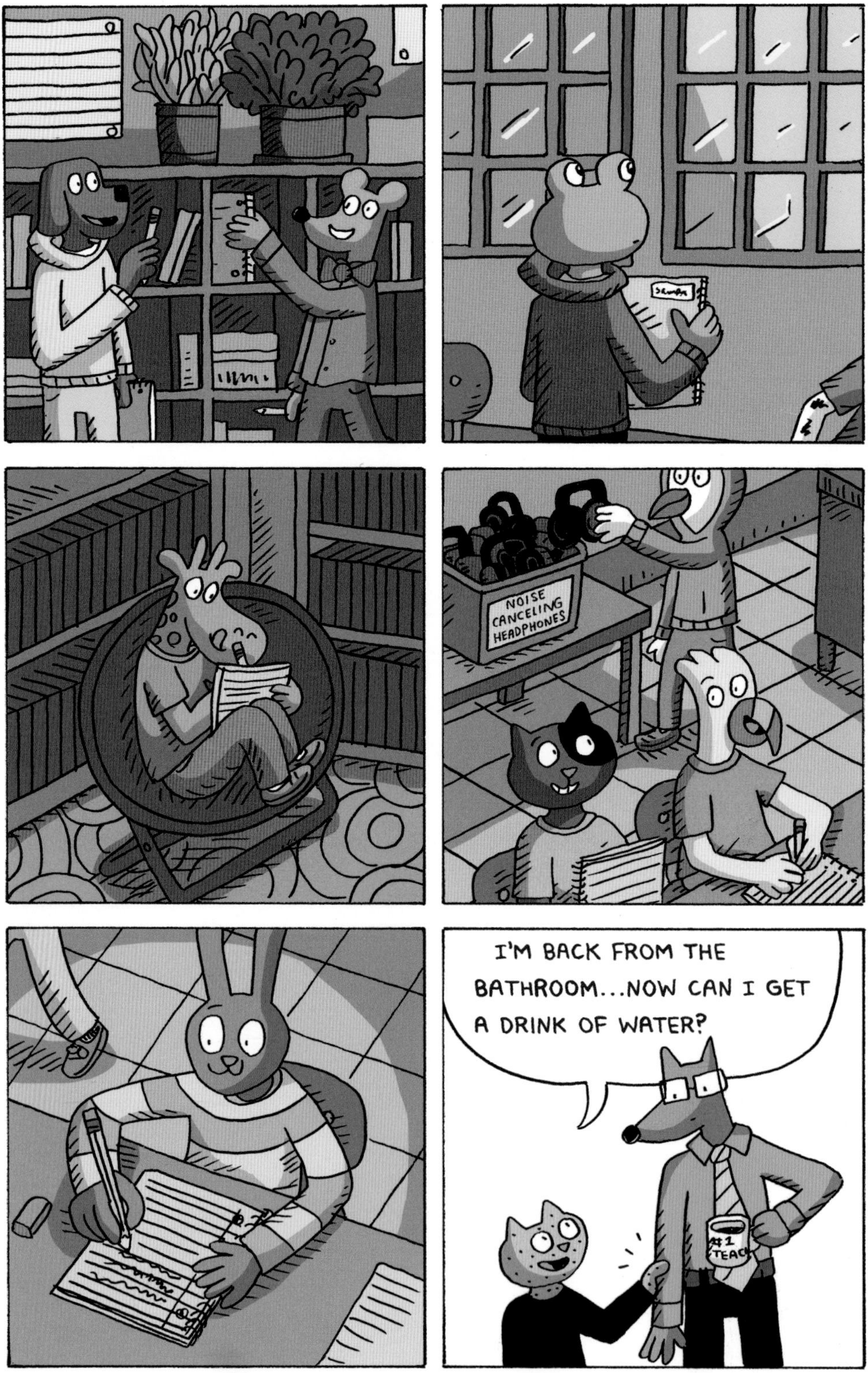
NOISE CANCELING HEADPHONES
I'M BACK FROM THE BATHROOM...NOW CAN I GET A DRINK OF WATER?
#1 TEACH

CHAPTER TWO

Writer's Block

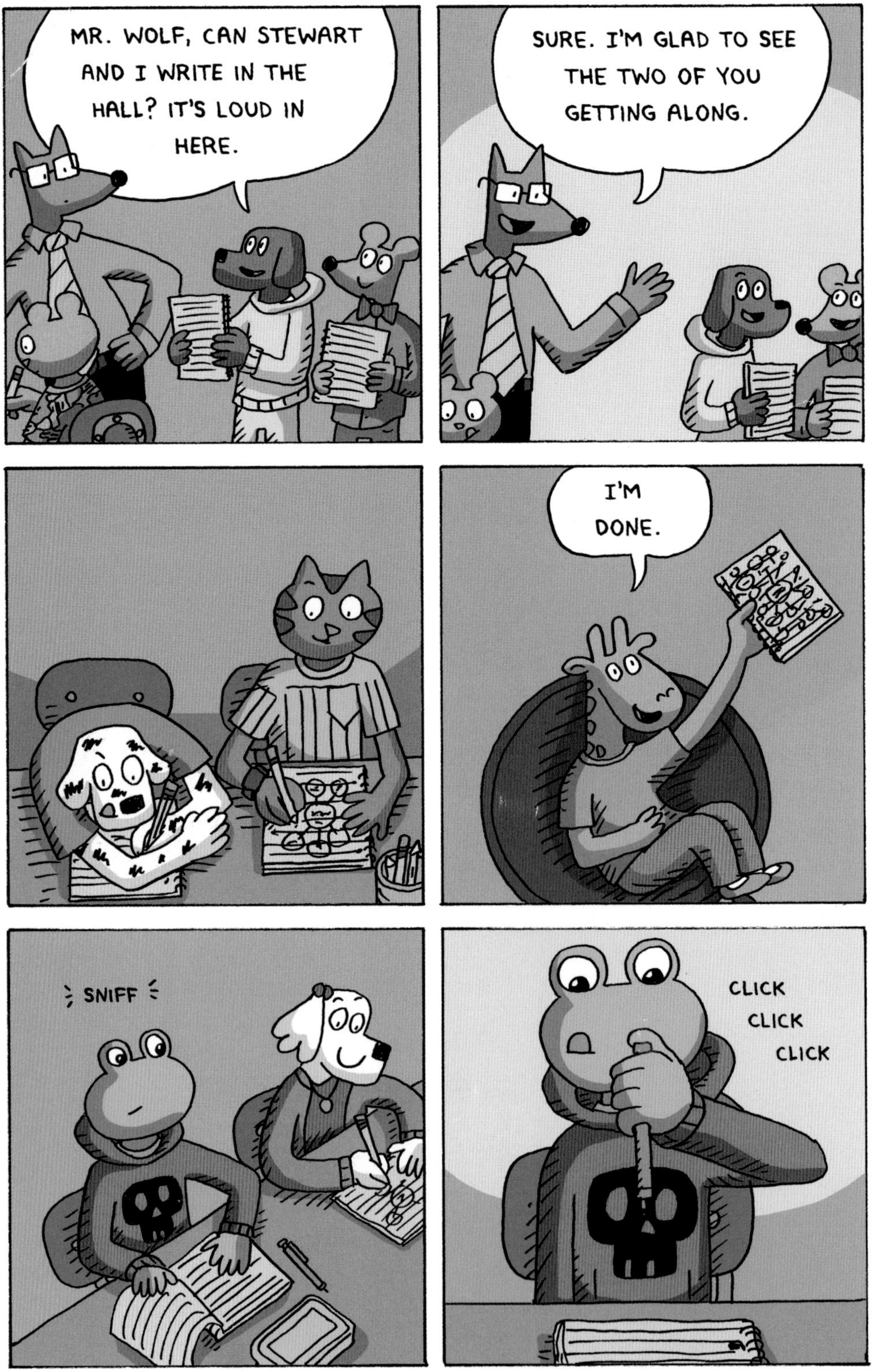
MR. WOLF, CAN STEWART AND I WRITE IN THE HALL? IT'S LOUD IN HERE.
SURE. I'M GLAD TO SEE THE TWO OF YOU GETTING ALONG.
I'M DONE.
SNIFF
CLICK
CLICK
CLICK

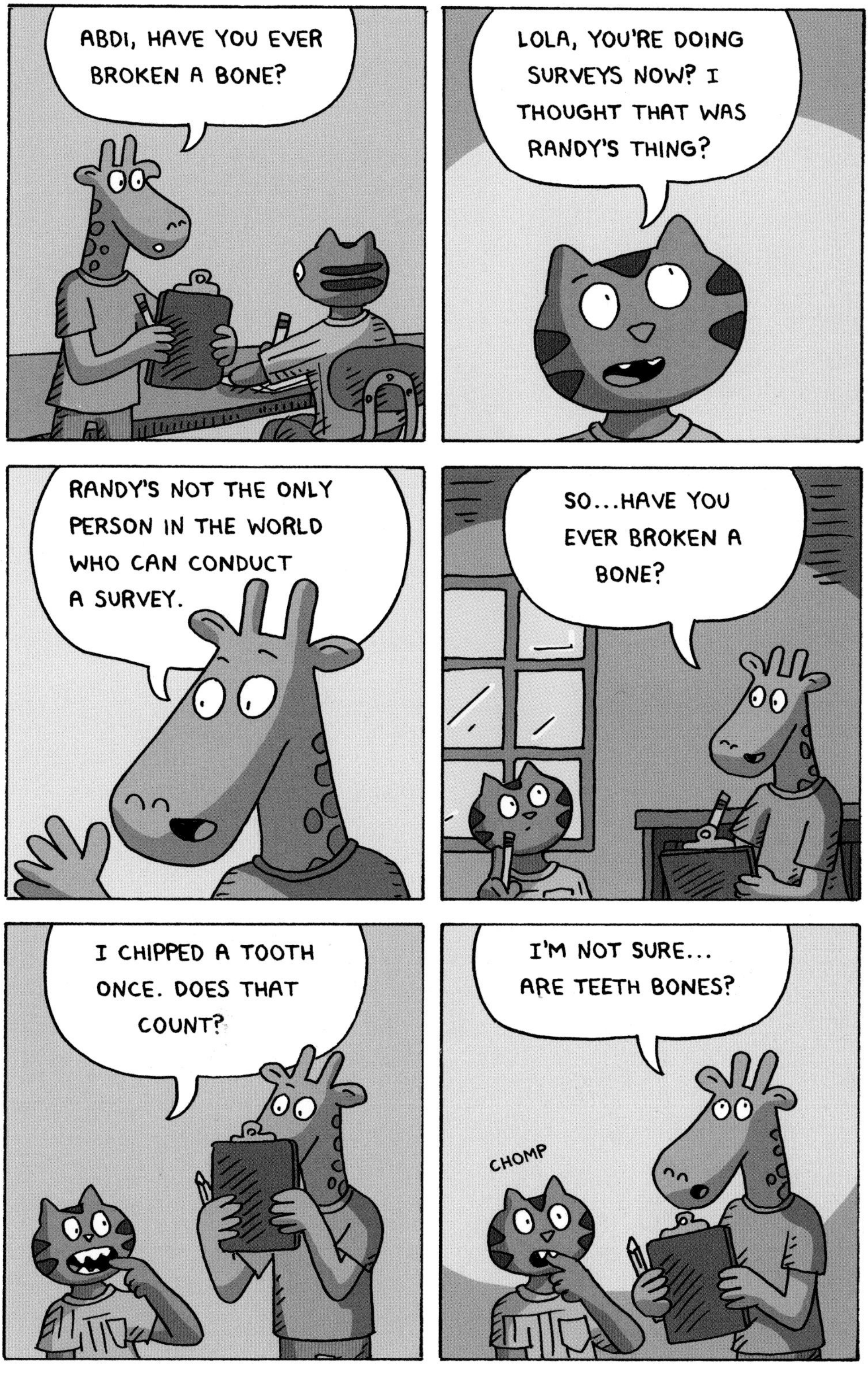
ABDI, HAVE YOU EVER BROKEN A BONE?
LOLA, YOU'RE DOING SURVEYS NOW? I THOUGHT THAT WAS RANDY'S THING?
RANDY'S NOT THE ONLY PERSON IN THE WORLD WHO CAN CONDUCT A SURVEY.
SO...HAVE YOU EVER BROKEN A BONE?
I CHIPPED A TOOTH ONCE. DOES THAT COUNT?
I'M NOT SURE... ARE TEETH BONES?
CHOMP

LET'S GO ASK MR. WOLF.
OKAY.
CLICK
CLICK
CLICK
CLICK
PUSH
CLICK
CLICK
CLICK
PULL

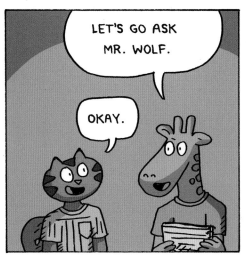

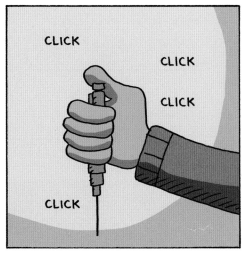

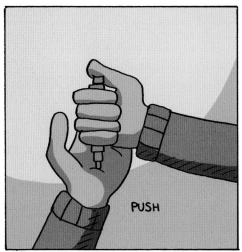

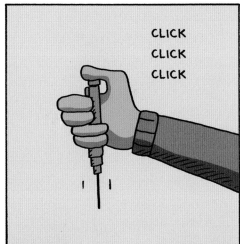

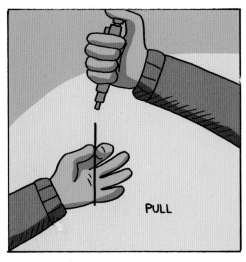

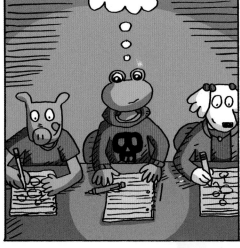

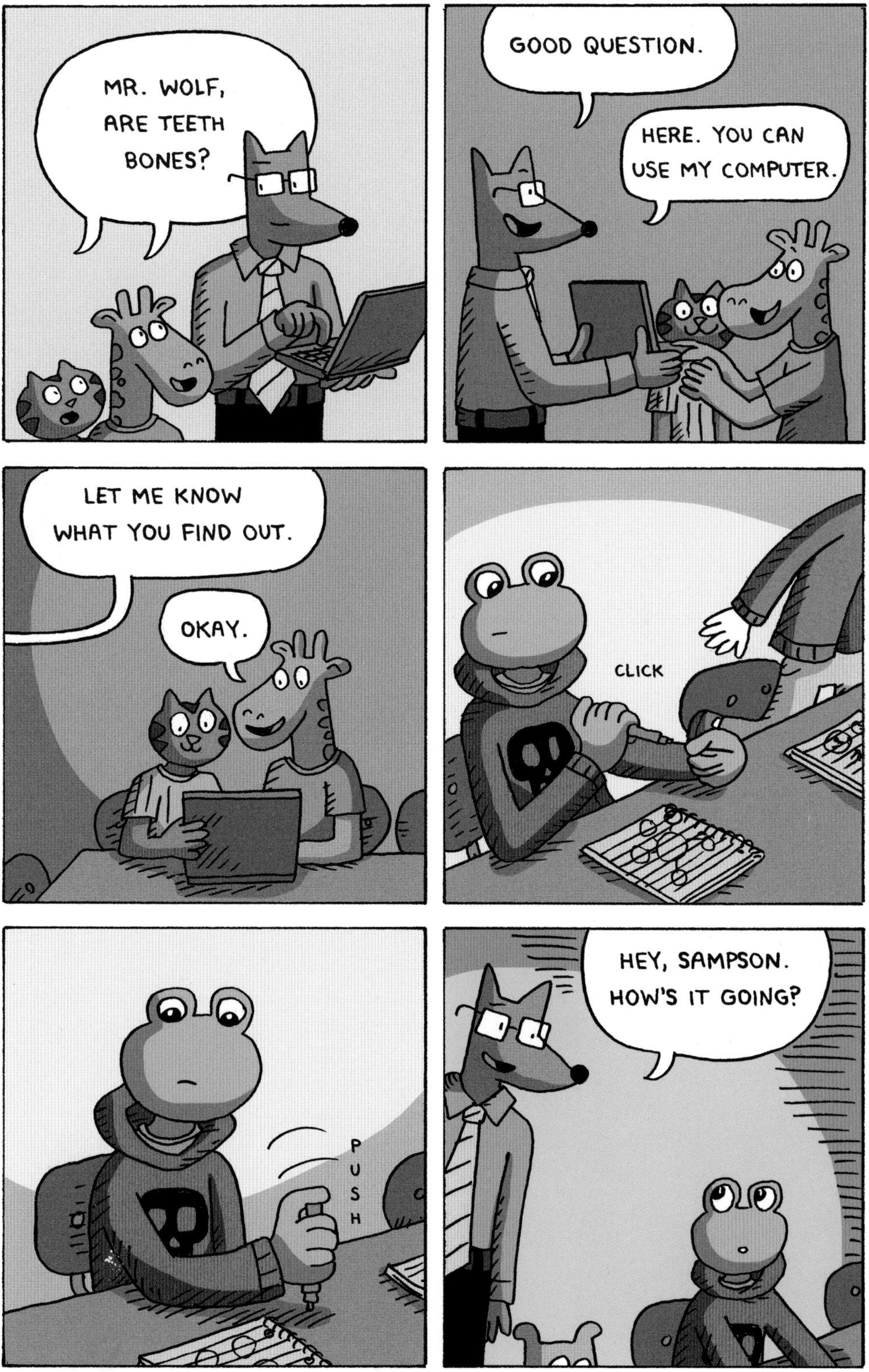
MR. WOLF, ARE TEETH BONES?
GOOD QUESTION.
HERE. YOU CAN USE MY COMPUTER.
LET ME KNOW WHAT YOU FIND OUT.
OKAY.
CLICK
PUSH
HEY, SAMPSON. HOW'S IT GOING?

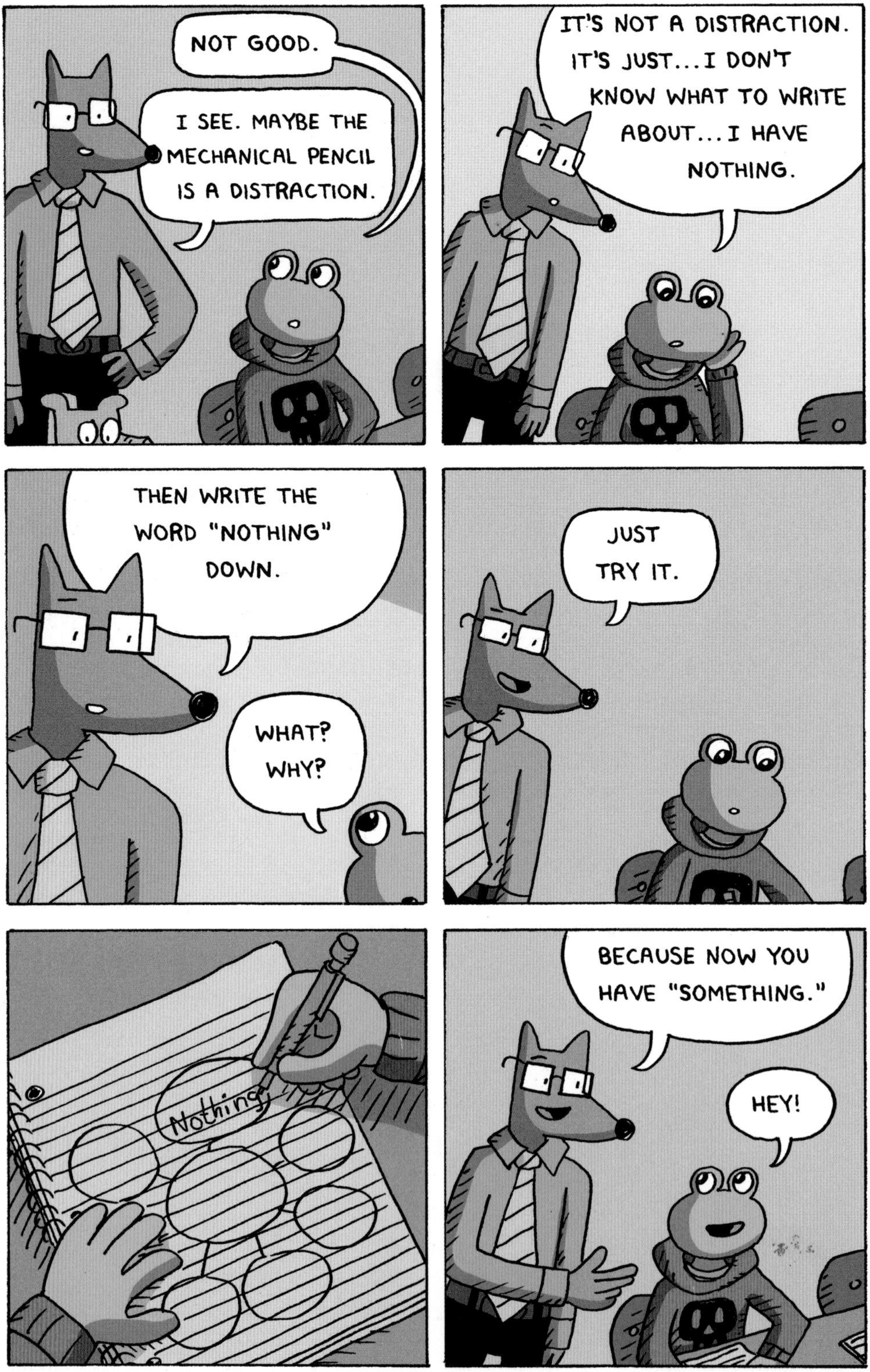

I SEE. MAYBE THE MECHANICAL PENCIL IS A DISTRACTION.
NOT GOOD.
IT'S NOT A DISTRACTION. IT'S JUST... I DON'T KNOW WHAT TO WRITE ABOUT... I HAVE NOTHING.
THEN WRITE THE WORD "NOTHING" DOWN.
WHAT? WHY?
JUST TRY IT.
Nothing
BECAUSE NOW YOU HAVE "SOMETHING."
HEY!

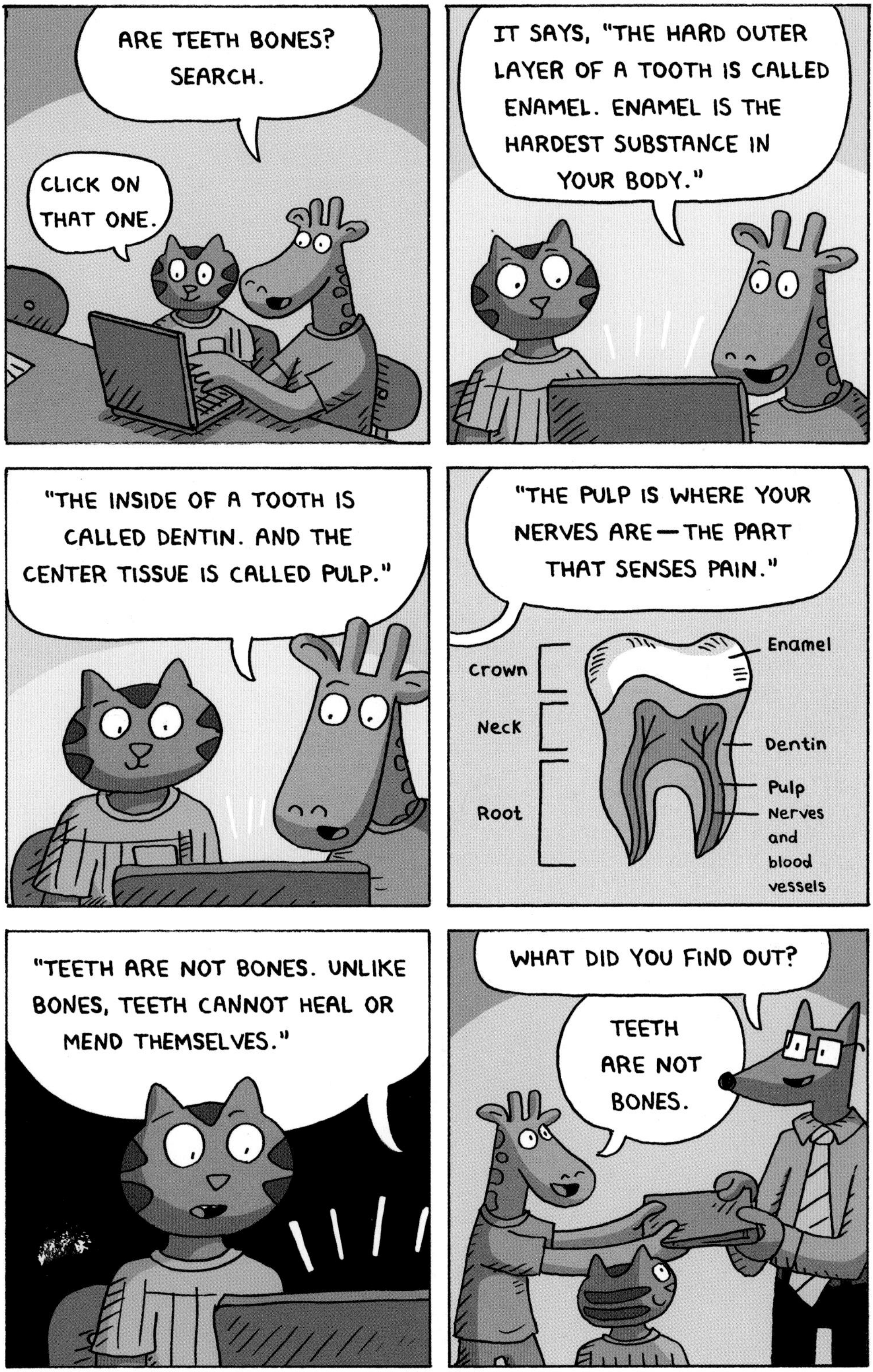
ARE TEETH BONES? SEARCH.
CLICK ON THAT ONE.
IT SAYS, "THE HARD OUTER LAYER OF A TOOTH IS CALLED ENAMEL. ENAMEL IS THE HARDEST SUBSTANCE IN YOUR BODY."
"THE INSIDE OF A TOOTH IS CALLED DENTIN. AND THE CENTER TISSUE IS CALLED PULP."
"THE PULP IS WHERE YOUR NERVES ARE—THE PART THAT SENSES PAIN."
Crown
Neck
Root
Enamel
Dentin
Pulp
Nerves and blood vessels
"TEETH ARE NOT BONES. UNLIKE BONES, TEETH CANNOT HEAL OR MEND THEMSELVES."
WHAT DID YOU FIND OUT?
TEETH ARE NOT BONES.

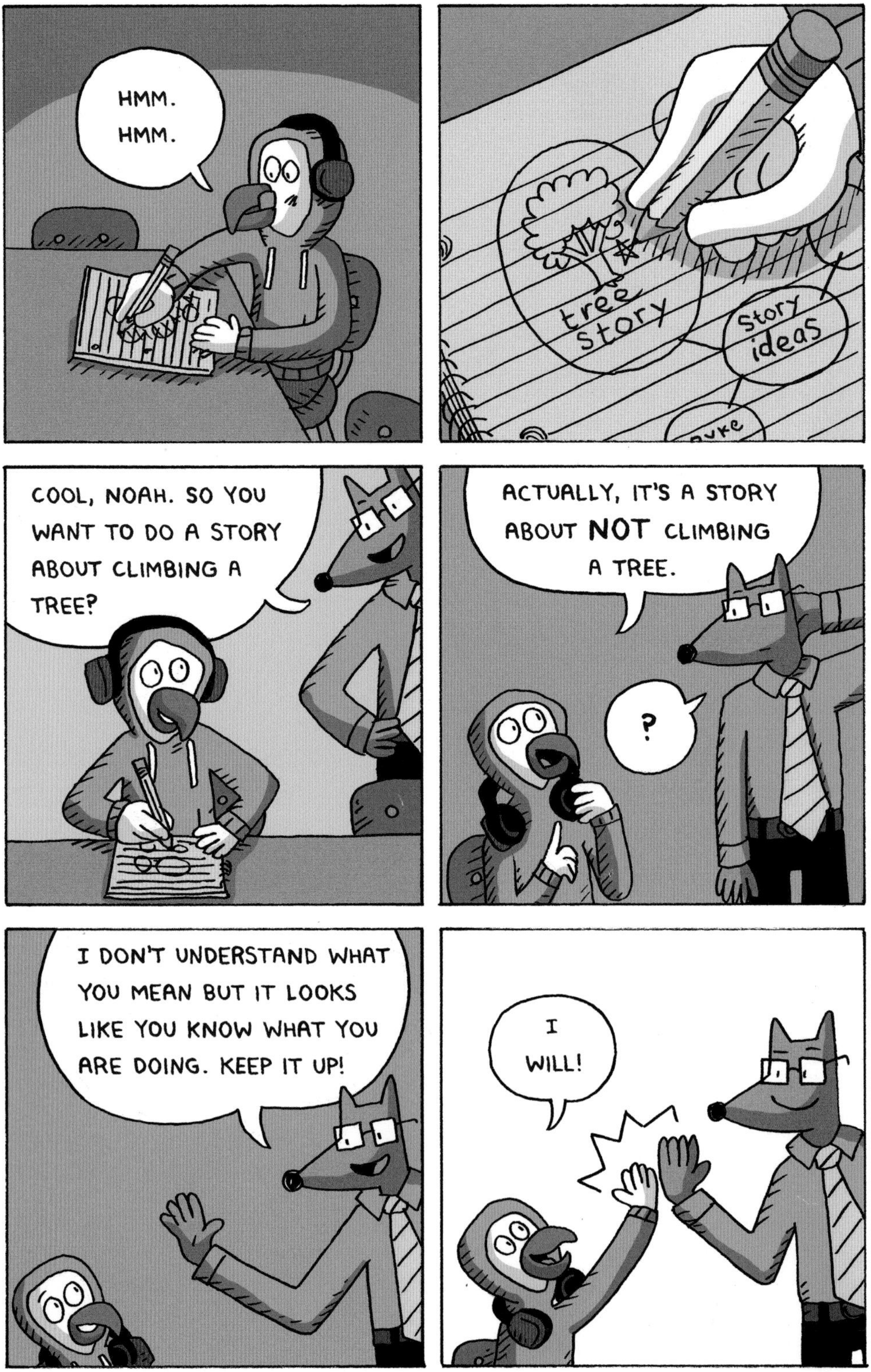
HMM.
HMM.
tree story
story ideas
COOL, NOAH. SO YOU WANT TO DO A STORY ABOUT CLIMBING A TREE?
ACTUALLY, IT'S A STORY ABOUT **NOT** CLIMBING A TREE.
?
I DON'T UNDERSTAND WHAT YOU MEAN BUT IT LOOKS LIKE YOU KNOW WHAT YOU ARE DOING. KEEP IT UP!
I WILL!

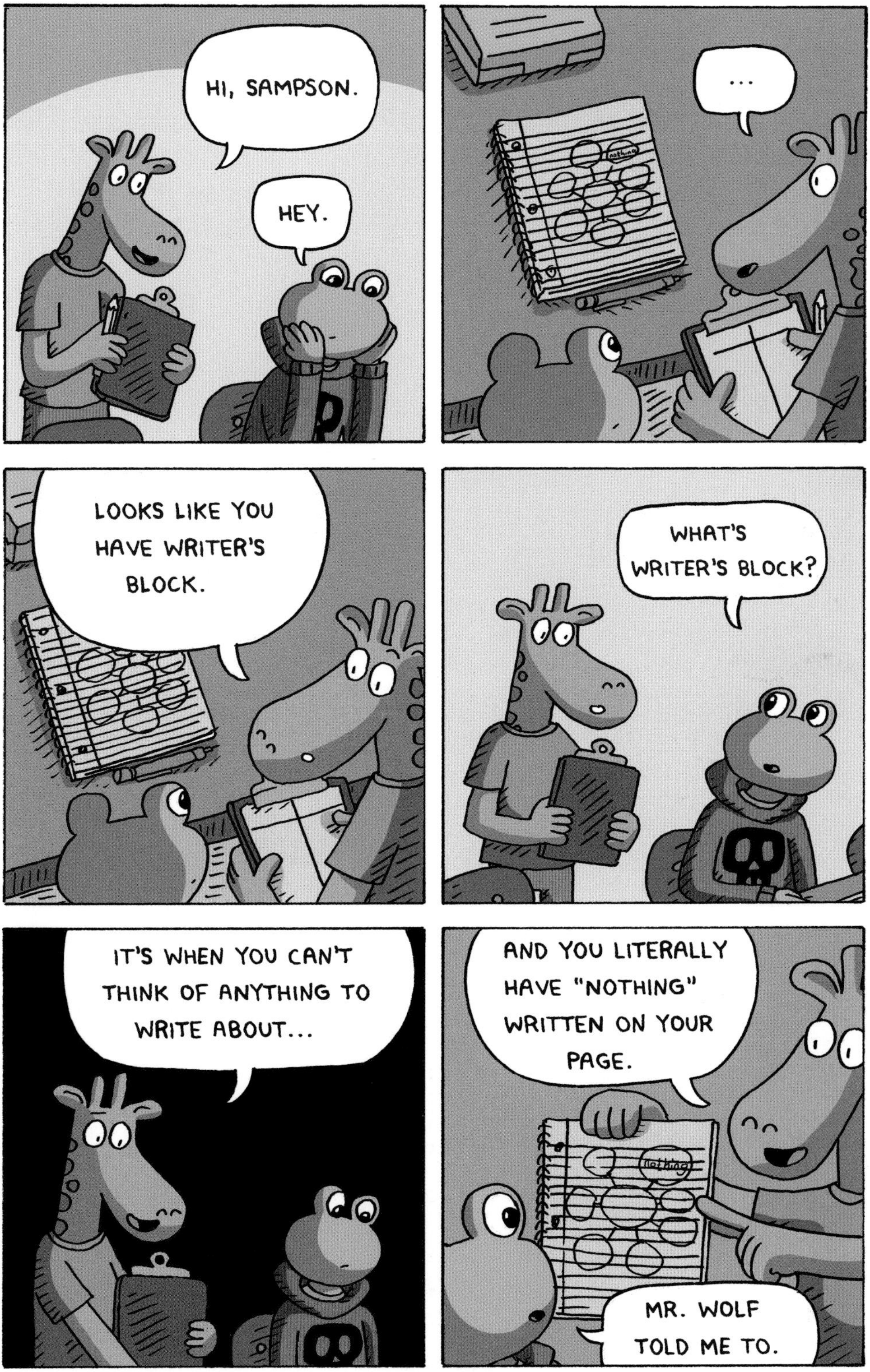
HI, SAMPSON.
HEY.
...
LOOKS LIKE YOU HAVE WRITER'S BLOCK.
WHAT'S WRITER'S BLOCK?
IT'S WHEN YOU CAN'T THINK OF ANYTHING TO WRITE ABOUT...
AND YOU LITERALLY HAVE "NOTHING" WRITTEN ON YOUR PAGE.
MR. WOLF TOLD ME TO.

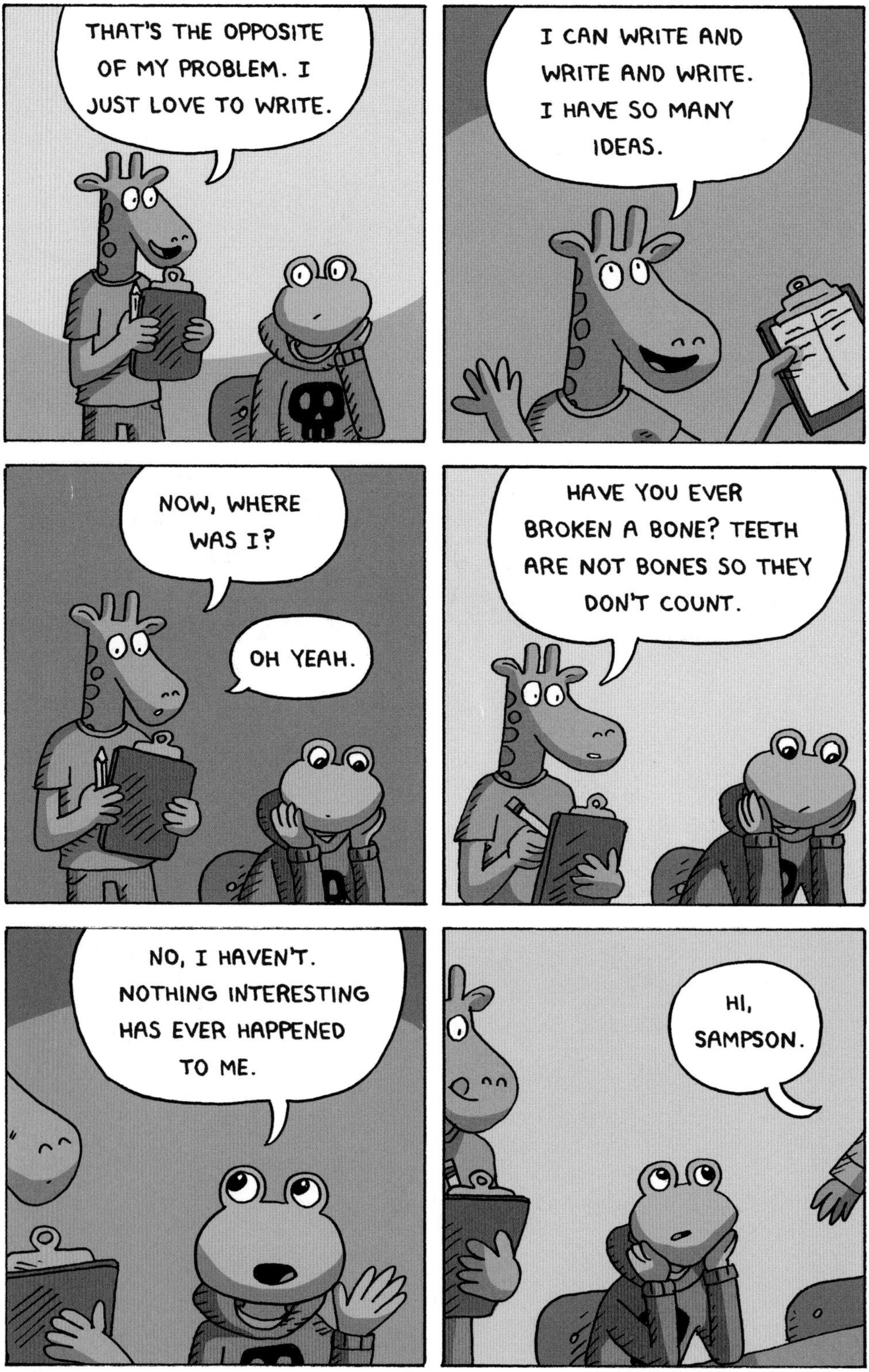
THAT'S THE OPPOSITE OF MY PROBLEM. I JUST LOVE TO WRITE.
I CAN WRITE AND WRITE AND WRITE. I HAVE SO MANY IDEAS.
NOW, WHERE WAS I?
OH YEAH.
HAVE YOU EVER BROKEN A BONE? TEETH ARE NOT BONES SO THEY DON'T COUNT.
NO, I HAVEN'T. NOTHING INTERESTING HAS EVER HAPPENED TO ME.
HI, SAMPSON.

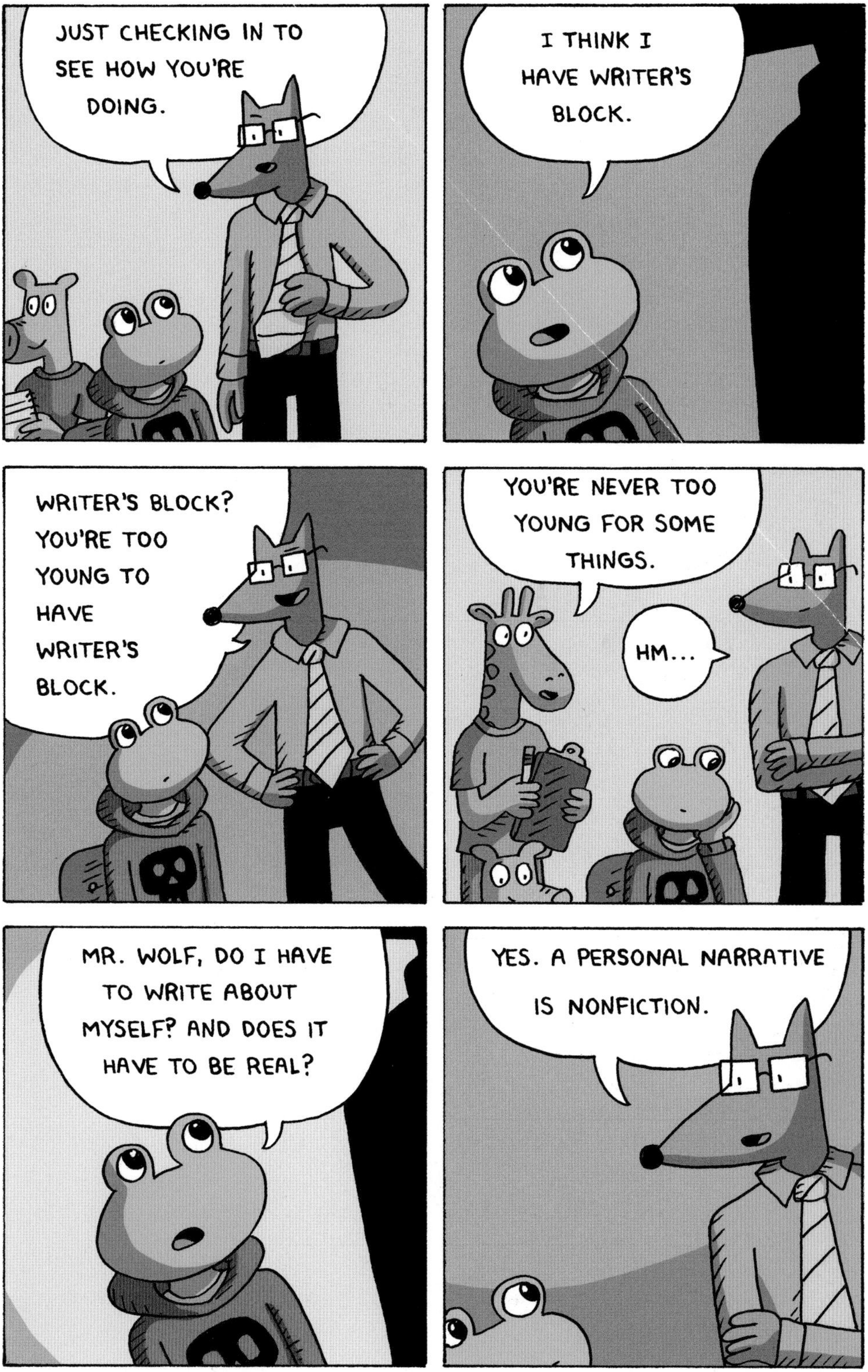
JUST CHECKING IN TO SEE HOW YOU'RE DOING.
I THINK I HAVE WRITER'S BLOCK.
WRITER'S BLOCK? YOU'RE TOO YOUNG TO HAVE WRITER'S BLOCK.
YOU'RE NEVER TOO YOUNG FOR SOME THINGS.
HM...
MR. WOLF, DO I HAVE TO WRITE ABOUT MYSELF? AND DOES IT HAVE TO BE REAL?
YES. A PERSONAL NARRATIVE IS NONFICTION.

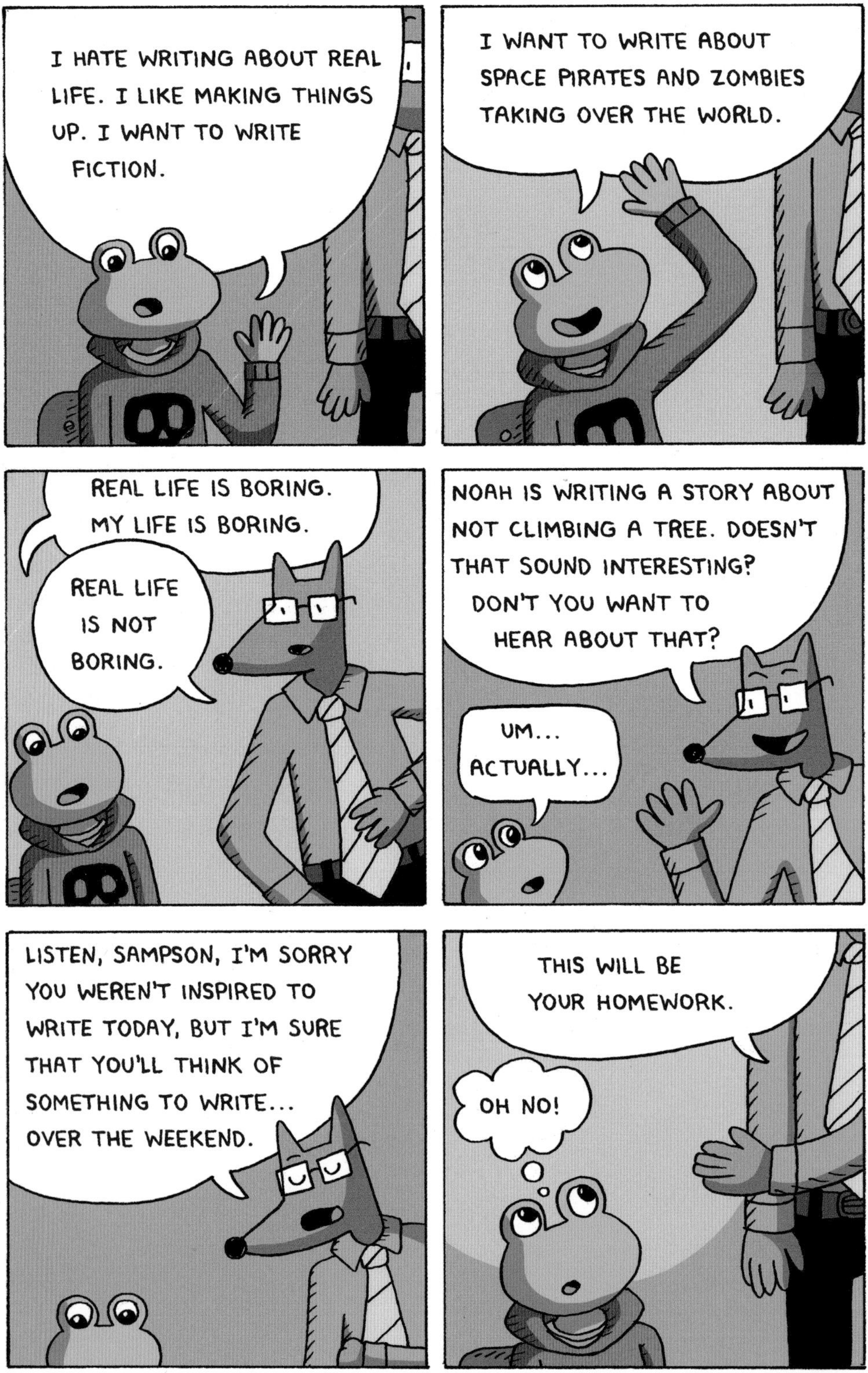
I HATE WRITING ABOUT REAL LIFE. I LIKE MAKING THINGS UP. I WANT TO WRITE FICTION.
I WANT TO WRITE ABOUT SPACE PIRATES AND ZOMBIES TAKING OVER THE WORLD.
REAL LIFE IS BORING. MY LIFE IS BORING.
REAL LIFE IS NOT BORING.
NOAH IS WRITING A STORY ABOUT NOT CLIMBING A TREE. DOESN'T THAT SOUND INTERESTING? DON'T YOU WANT TO HEAR ABOUT THAT?
UM... ACTUALLY...
LISTEN, SAMPSON, I'M SORRY YOU WEREN'T INSPIRED TO WRITE TODAY, BUT I'M SURE THAT YOU'LL THINK OF SOMETHING TO WRITE... OVER THE WEEKEND.
THIS WILL BE YOUR HOMEWORK.
OH NO!

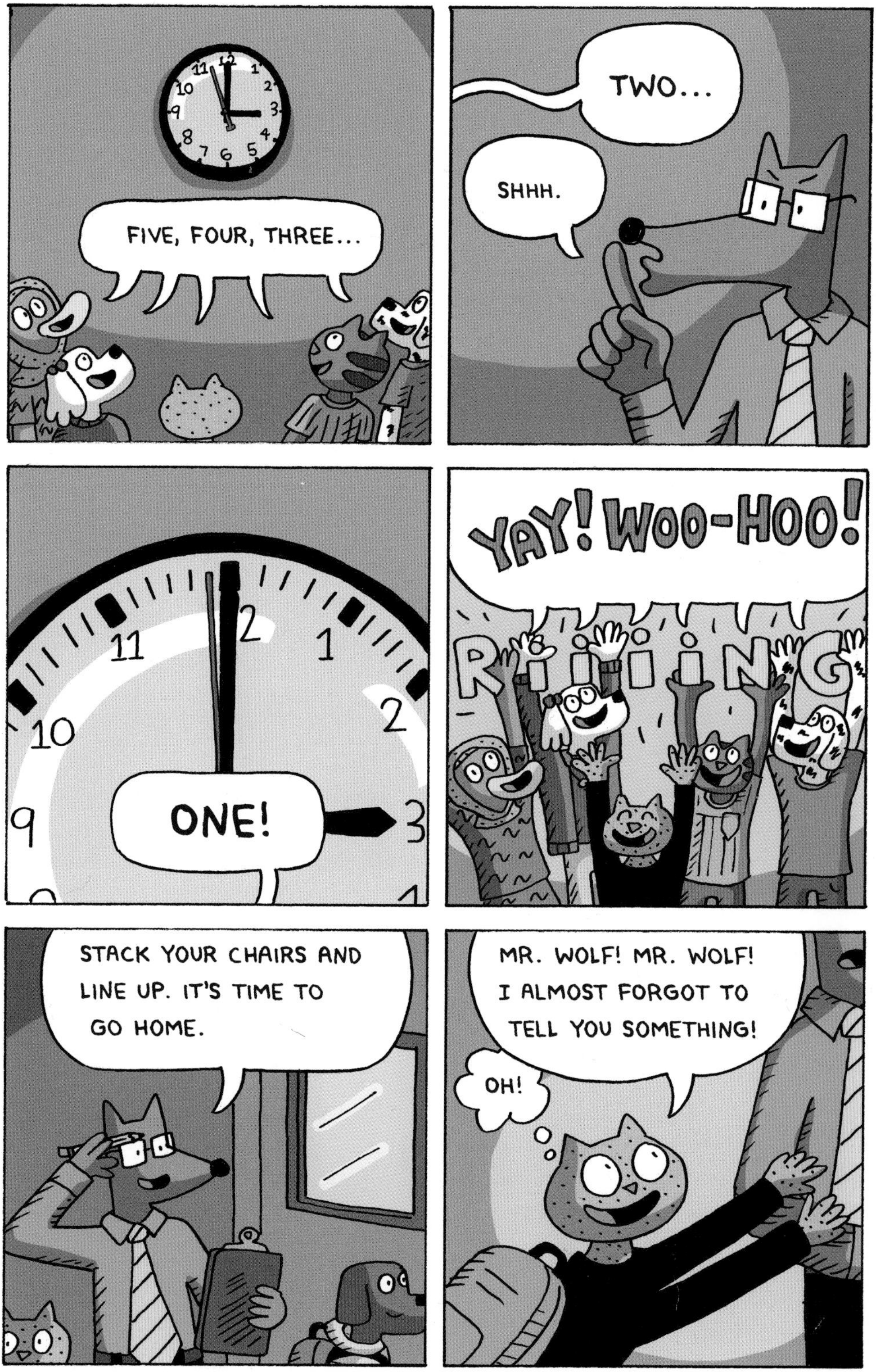
FIVE, FOUR, THREE...
TWO...
SHHH.
ONE!
YAY! WOO-HOO!
RIIIING
STACK YOUR CHAIRS AND LINE UP. IT'S TIME TO GO HOME.
MR. WOLF! MR. WOLF! I ALMOST FORGOT TO TELL YOU SOMETHING!
OH!

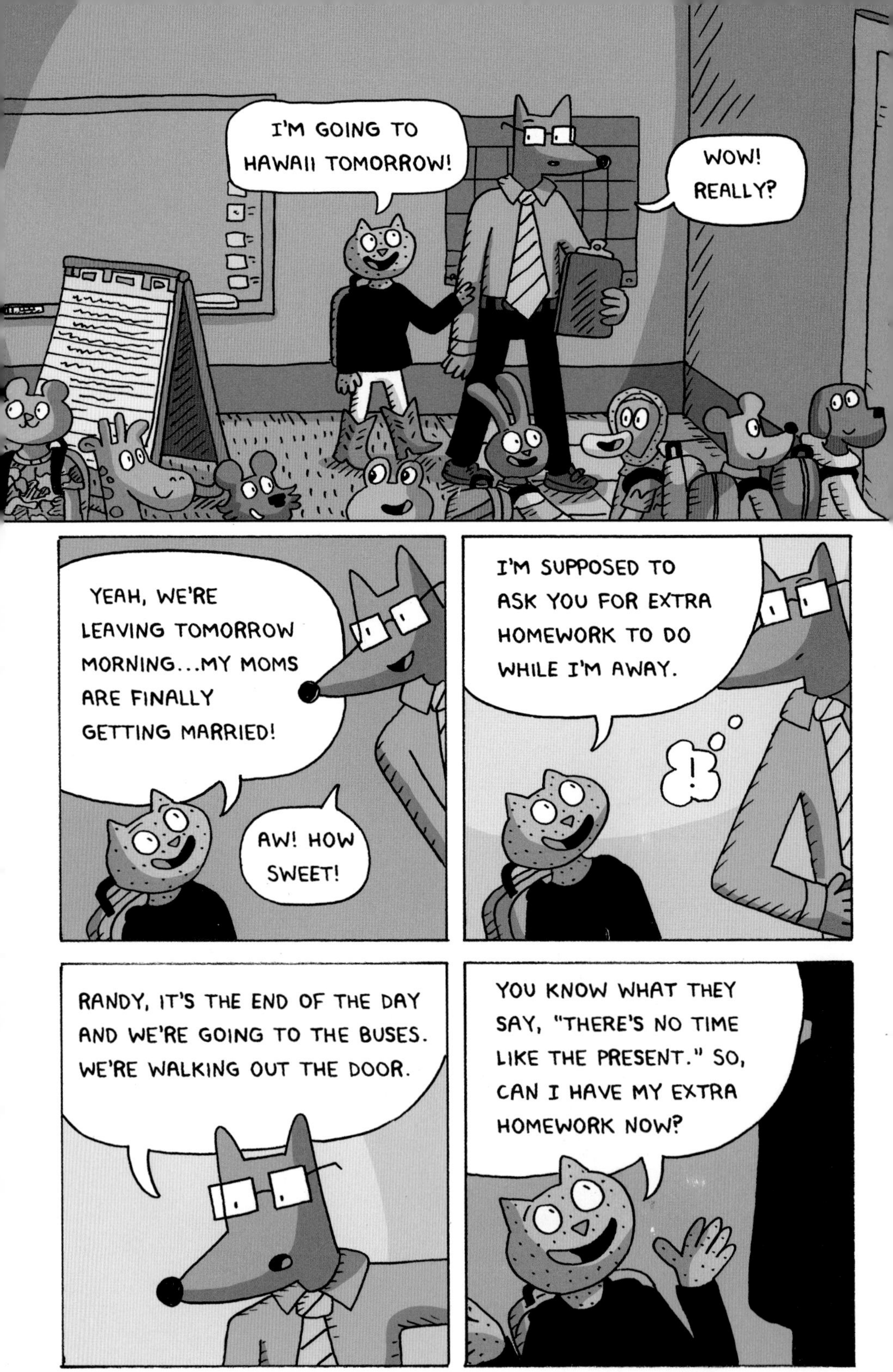
I'M GOING TO HAWAII TOMORROW!
WOW! REALLY?
YEAH, WE'RE LEAVING TOMORROW MORNING...MY MOMS ARE FINALLY GETTING MARRIED!
AW! HOW SWEET!
I'M SUPPOSED TO ASK YOU FOR EXTRA HOMEWORK TO DO WHILE I'M AWAY.
!
RANDY, IT'S THE END OF THE DAY AND WE'RE GOING TO THE BUSES. WE'RE WALKING OUT THE DOOR.
YOU KNOW WHAT THEY SAY, "THERE'S NO TIME LIKE THE PRESENT." SO, CAN I HAVE MY EXTRA HOMEWORK NOW?

CHAPTER THREE
Chicken Hill

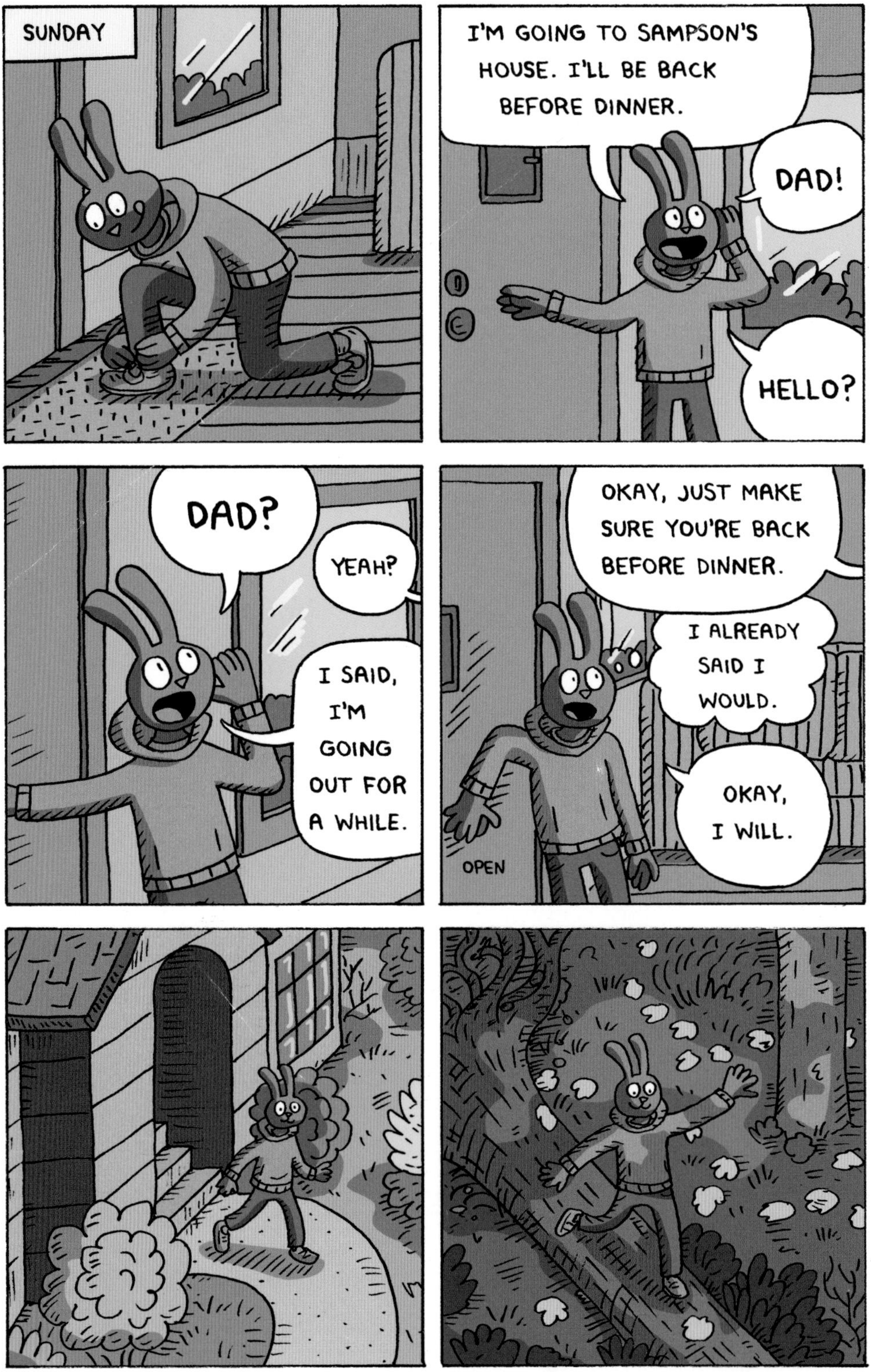
SUNDAY
I'M GOING TO SAMPSON'S HOUSE. I'LL BE BACK BEFORE DINNER.
DAD!
HELLO?
DAD?
YEAH?
I SAID, I'M GOING OUT FOR A WHILE.
OKAY, JUST MAKE SURE YOU'RE BACK BEFORE DINNER.
I ALREADY SAID I WOULD.
OKAY, I WILL.
OPEN

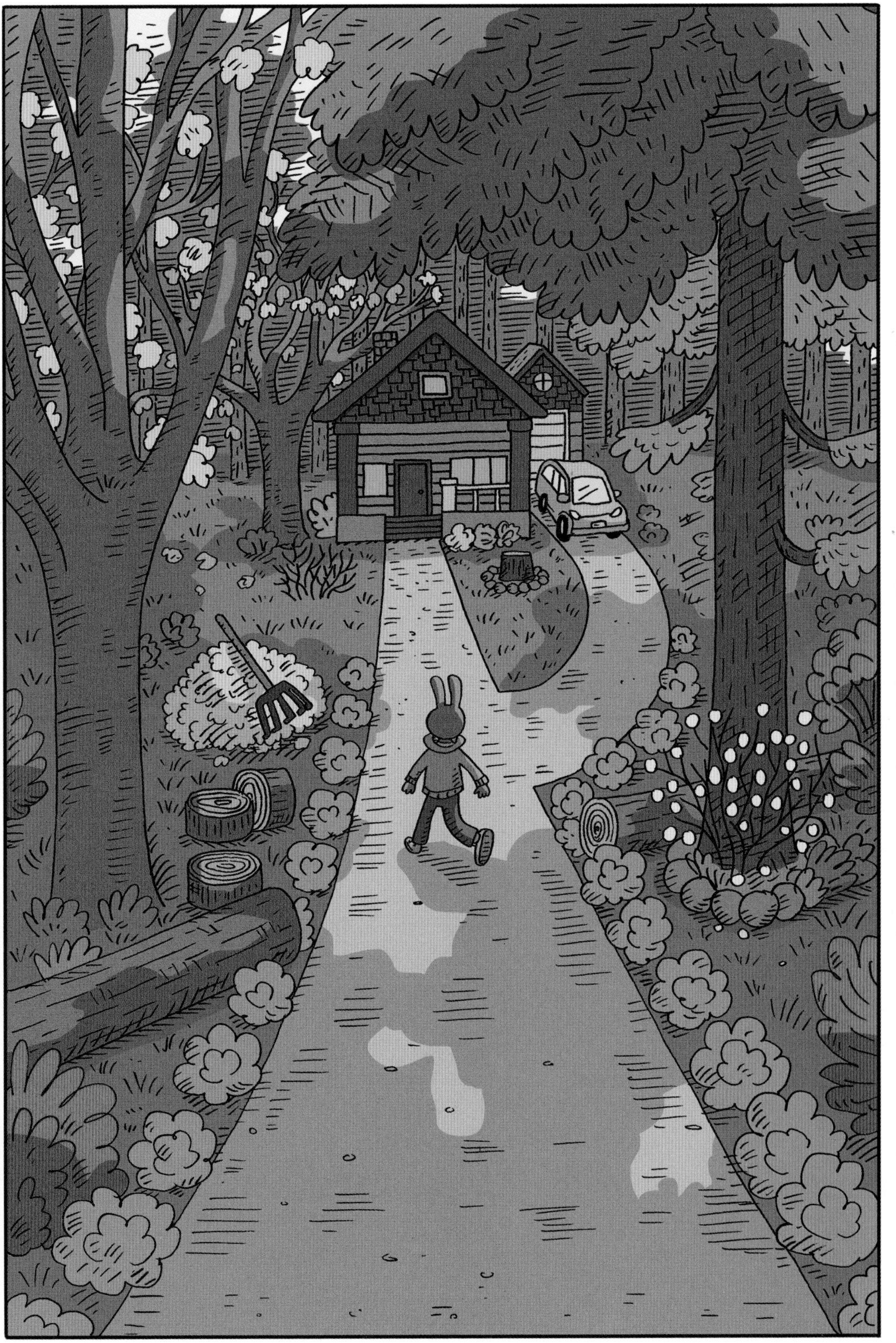

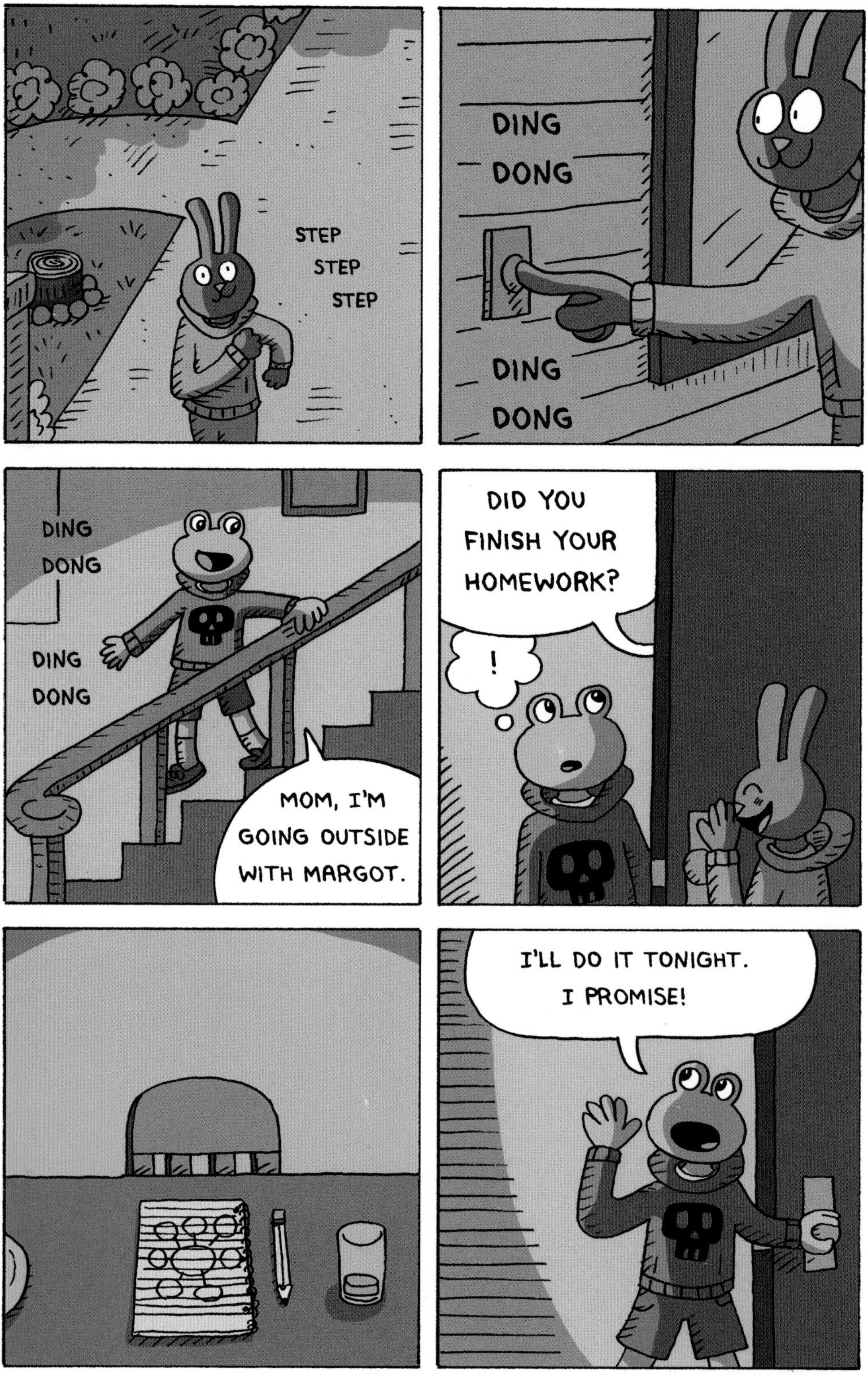
STEP
STEP
STEP
DING
DONG
DING
DONG
DING
DONG
DING
DONG
MOM, I'M GOING OUTSIDE WITH MARGOT.
DID YOU FINISH YOUR HOMEWORK?
!
I'LL DO IT TONIGHT. I PROMISE!

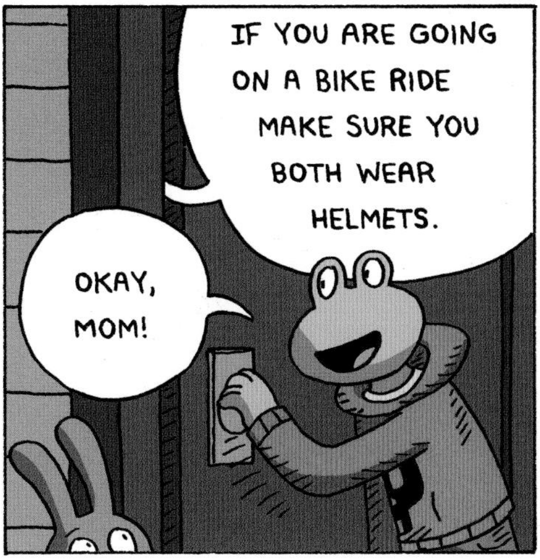
IF YOU ARE GOING ON A BIKE RIDE MAKE SURE YOU BOTH WEAR HELMETS.
OKAY, MOM!

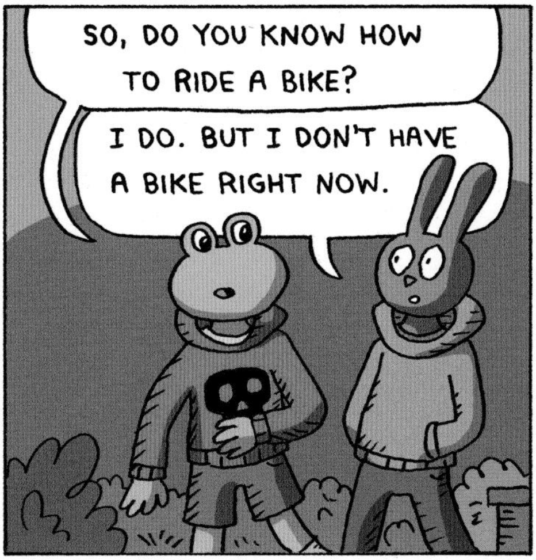
SO, DO YOU KNOW HOW TO RIDE A BIKE?
I DO. BUT I DON'T HAVE A BIKE RIGHT NOW.

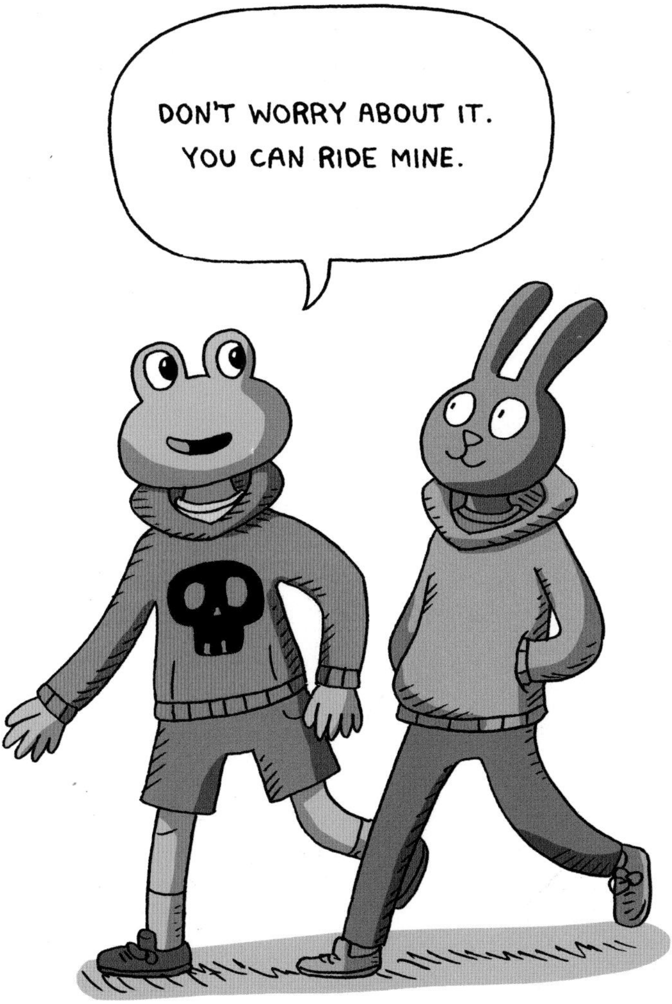
DON'T WORRY ABOUT IT. YOU CAN RIDE MINE.

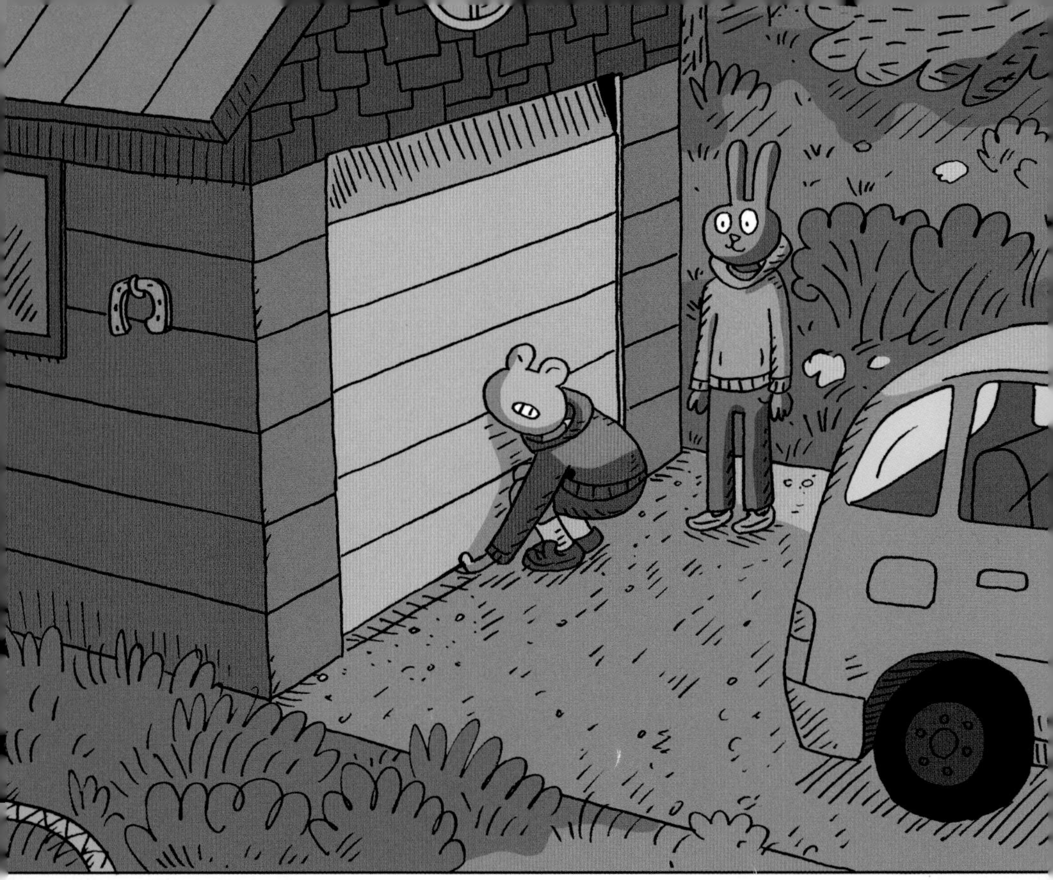

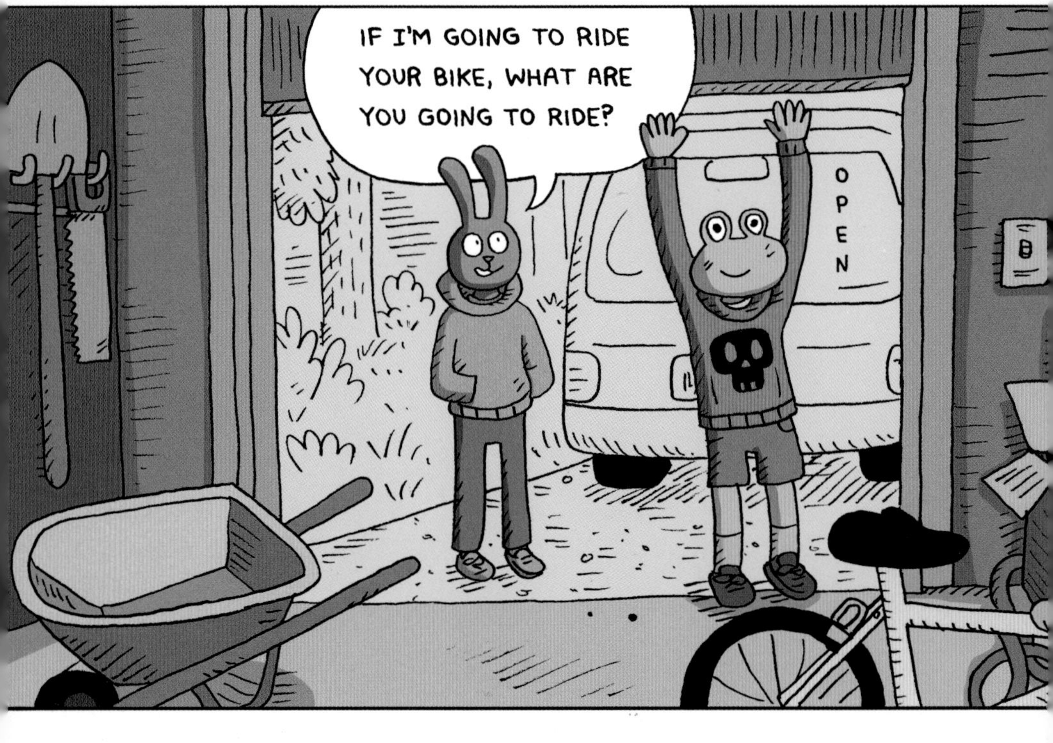
IF I'M GOING TO RIDE YOUR BIKE, WHAT ARE YOU GOING TO RIDE?
OPEN

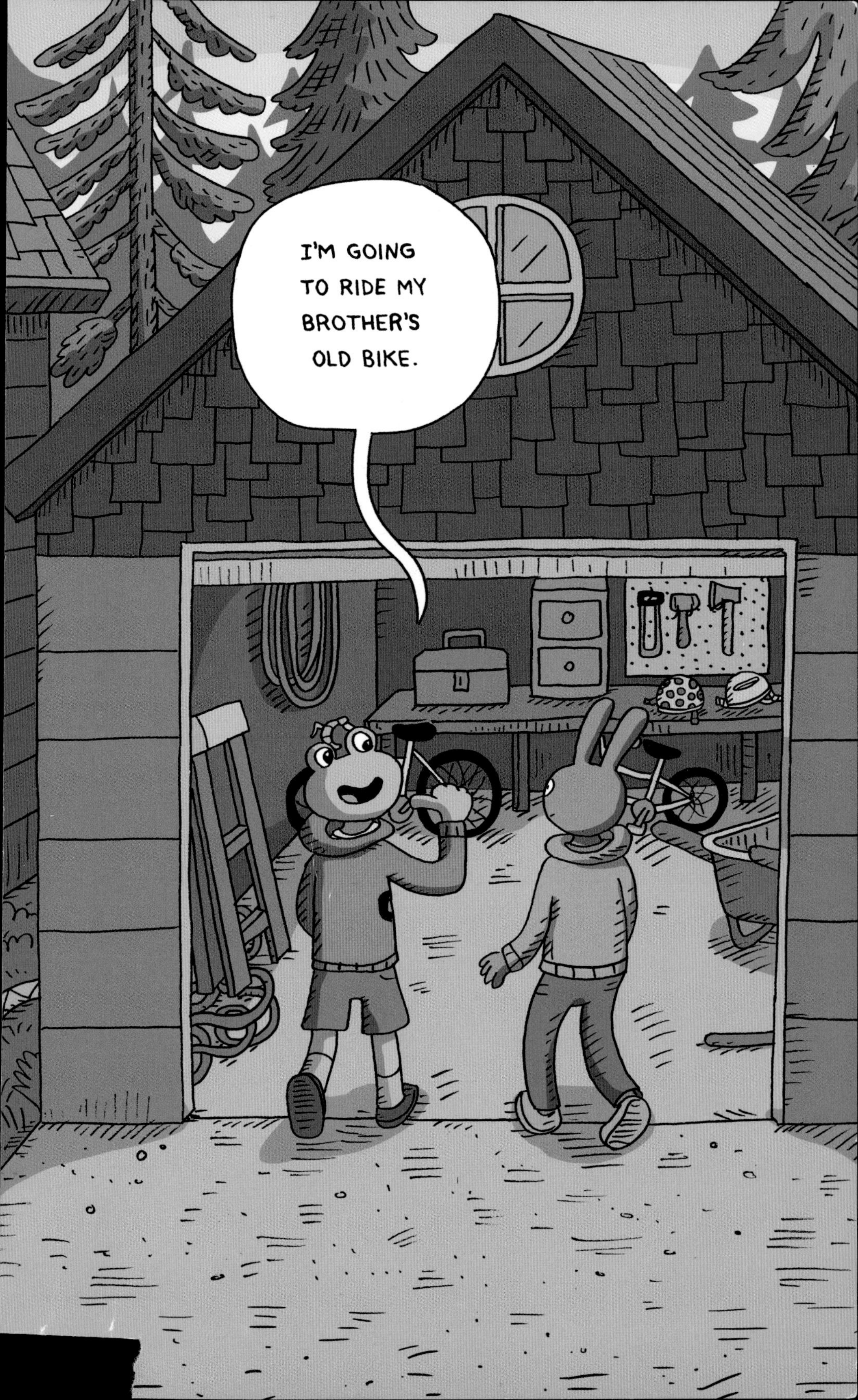
I'M GOING TO RIDE MY BROTHER'S OLD BIKE.

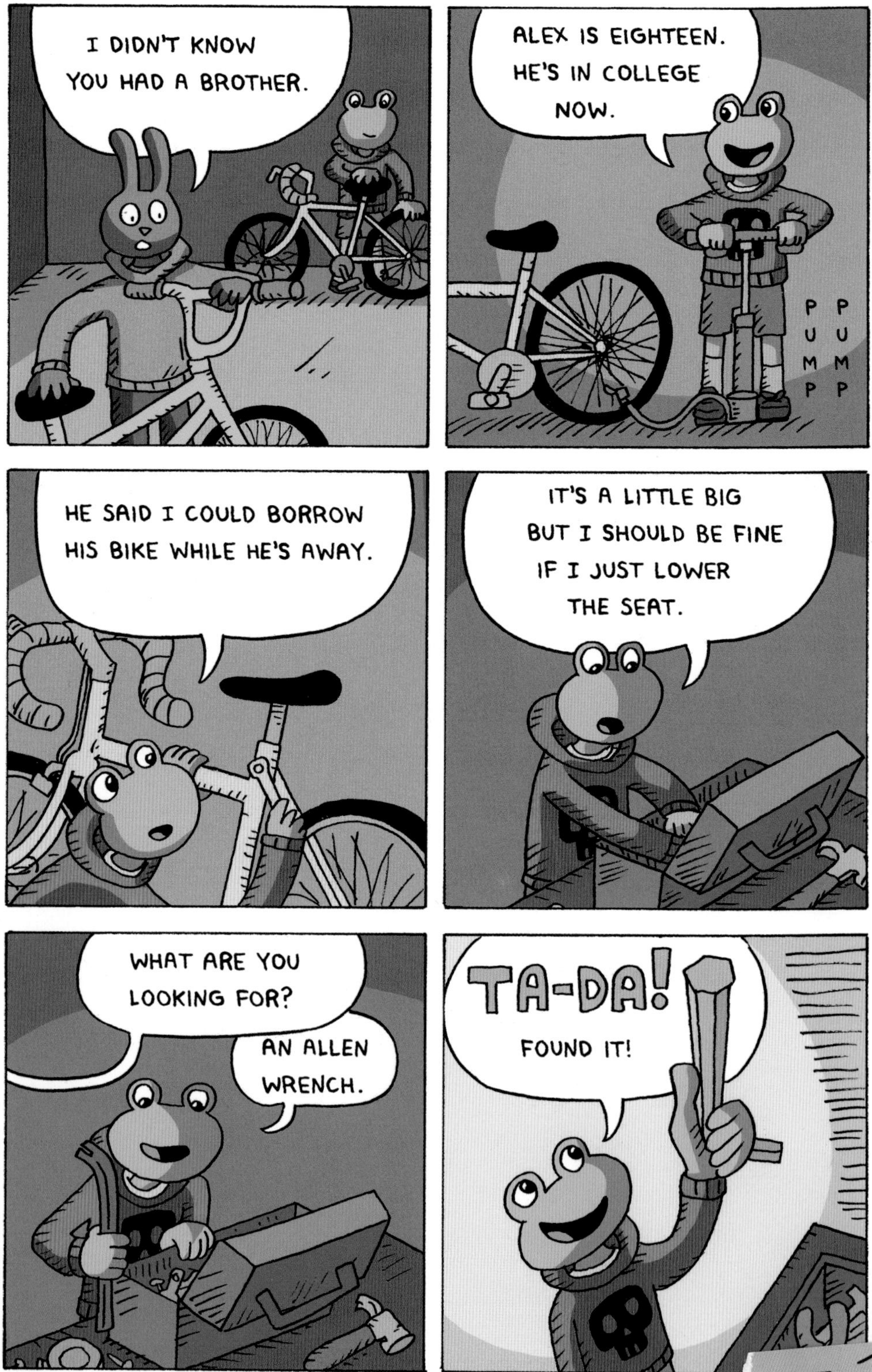
I DIDN'T KNOW YOU HAD A BROTHER.
ALEX IS EIGHTEEN. HE'S IN COLLEGE NOW.
PUMP PUMP
HE SAID I COULD BORROW HIS BIKE WHILE HE'S AWAY.
IT'S A LITTLE BIG BUT I SHOULD BE FINE IF I JUST LOWER THE SEAT.
WHAT ARE YOU LOOKING FOR?
AN ALLEN WRENCH.
TA-DA!
FOUND IT!

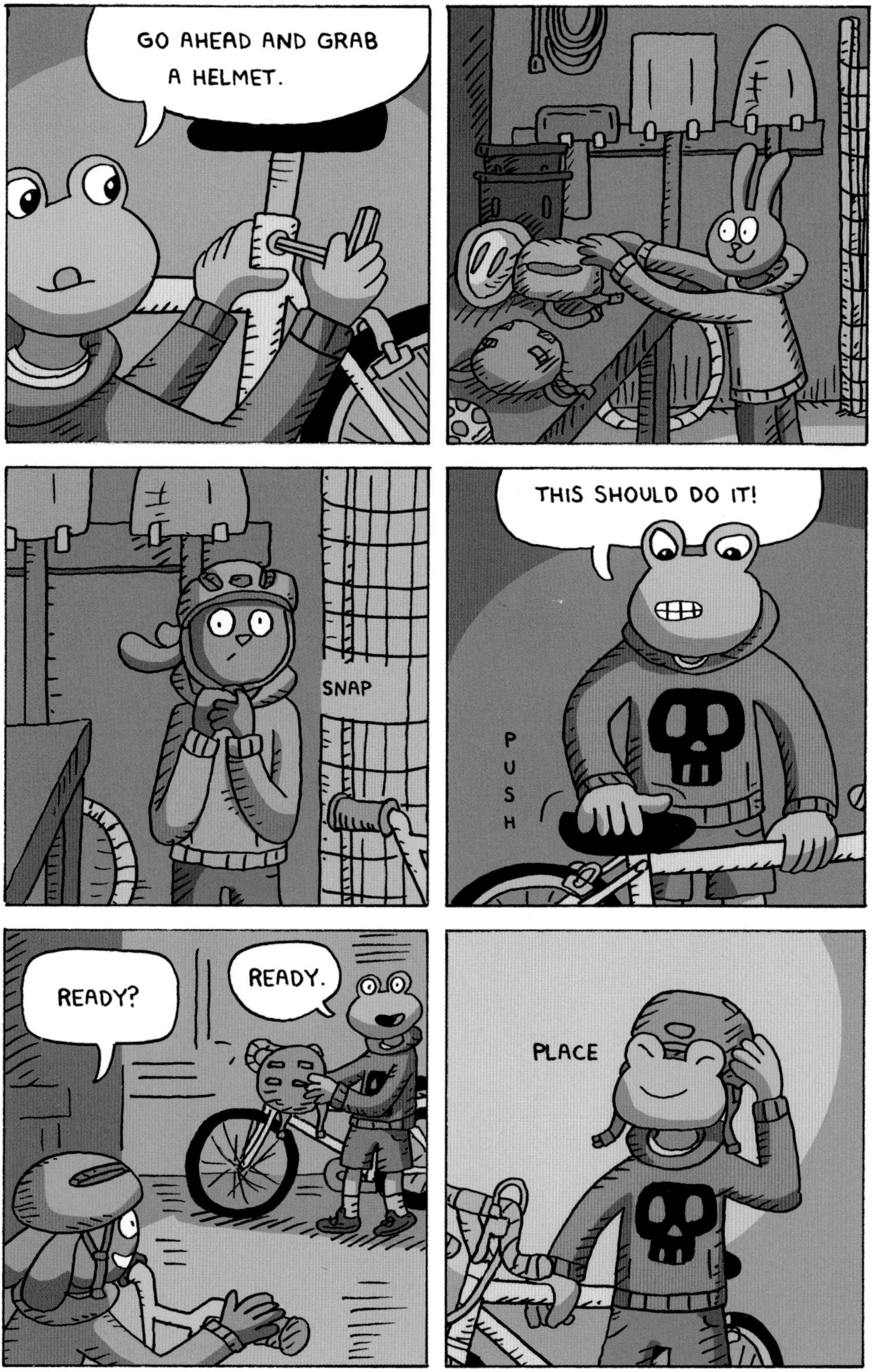
GO AHEAD AND GRAB A HELMET.
SNAP
THIS SHOULD DO IT!
PUSH
READY?
READY.
PLACE

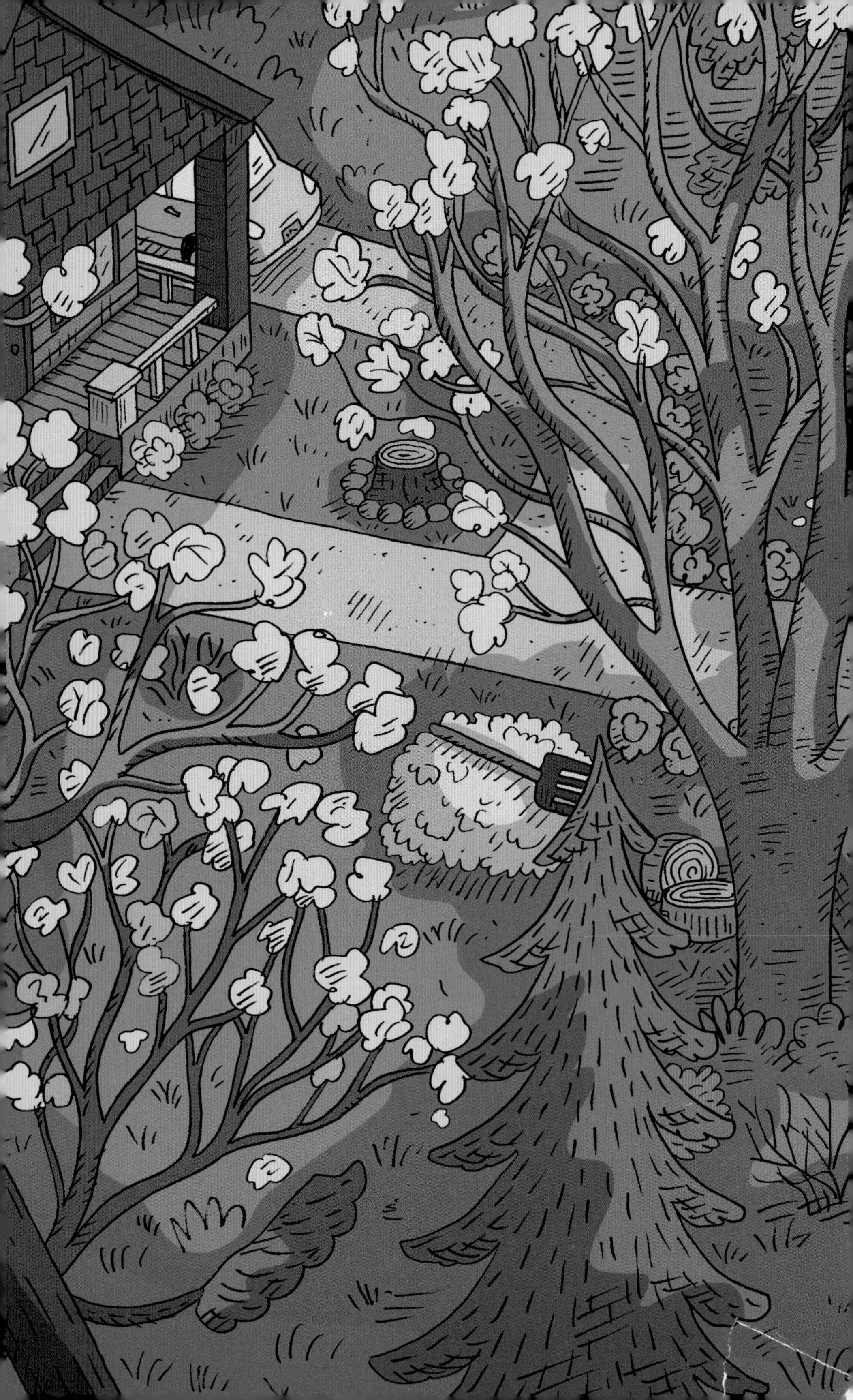

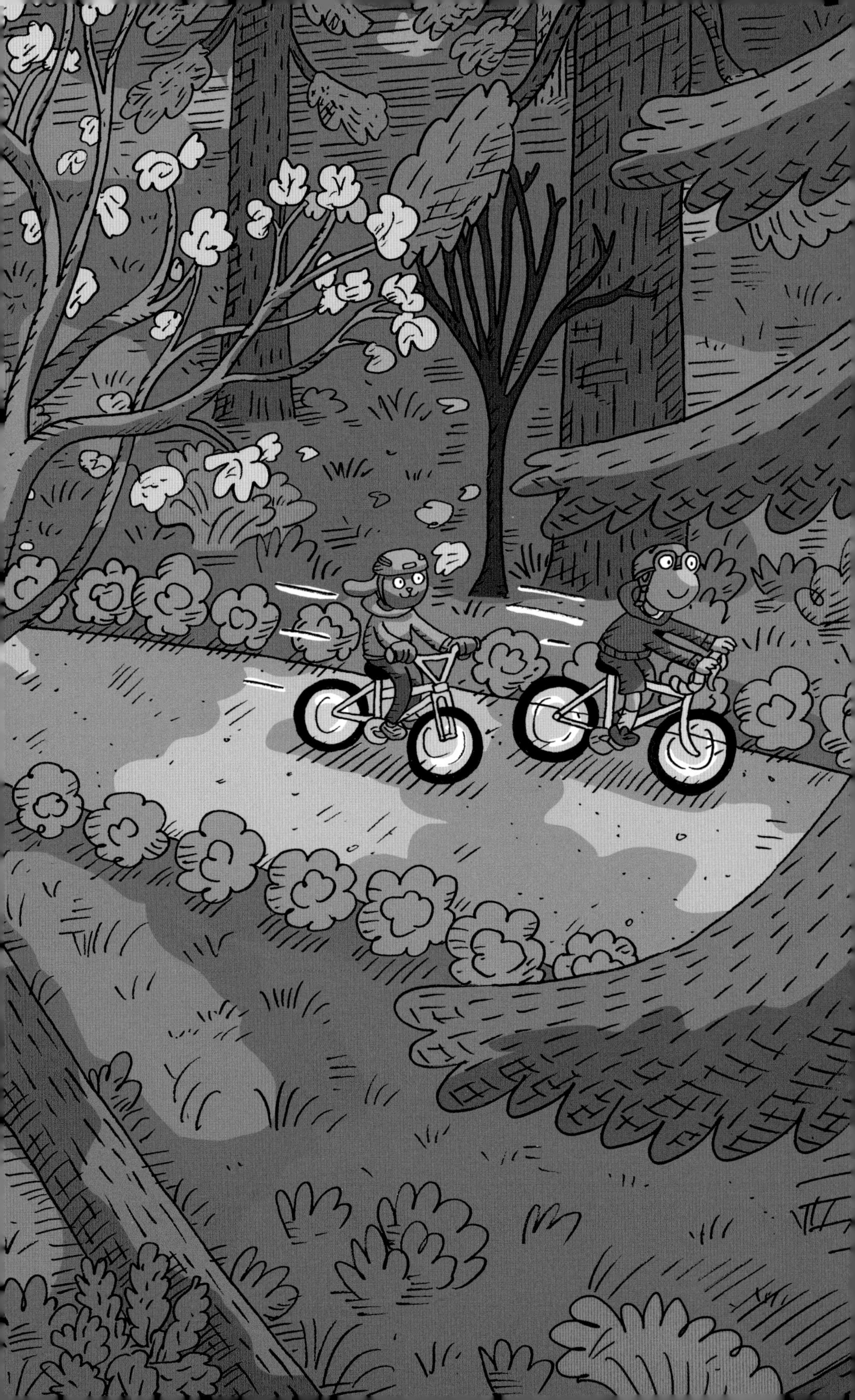

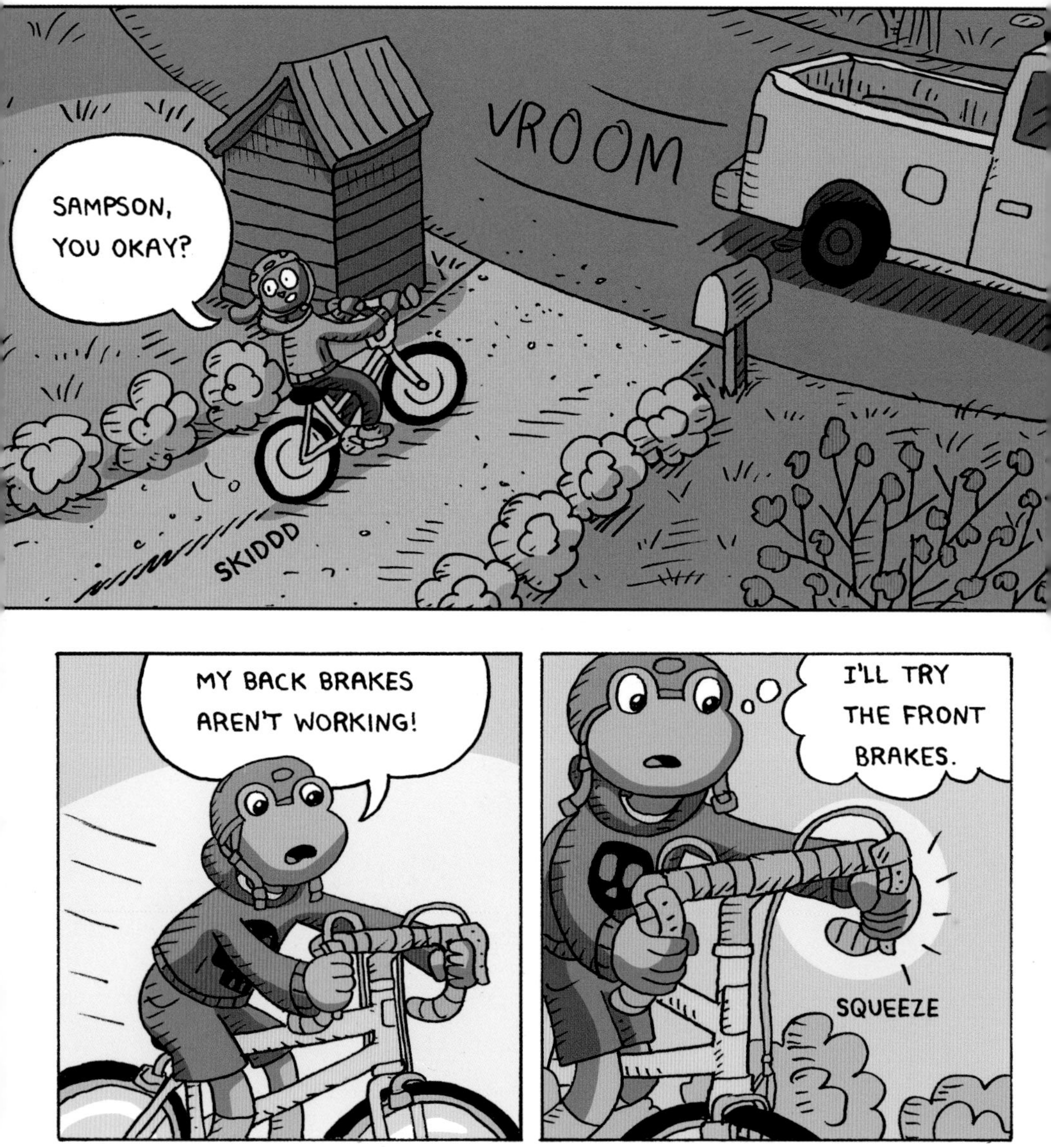
SAMPSON,
YOU OKAY?
VROOM
SKIDDD
MY BACK BRAKES
AREN'T WORKING!
I'LL TRY
THE FRONT
BRAKES.
SQUEEZE

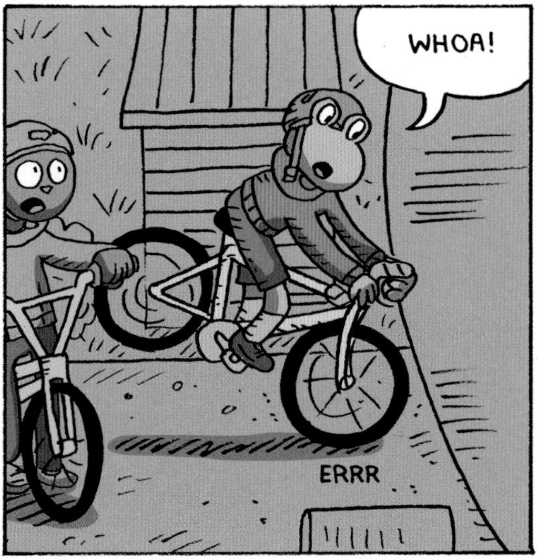
WHOA!
ERRR

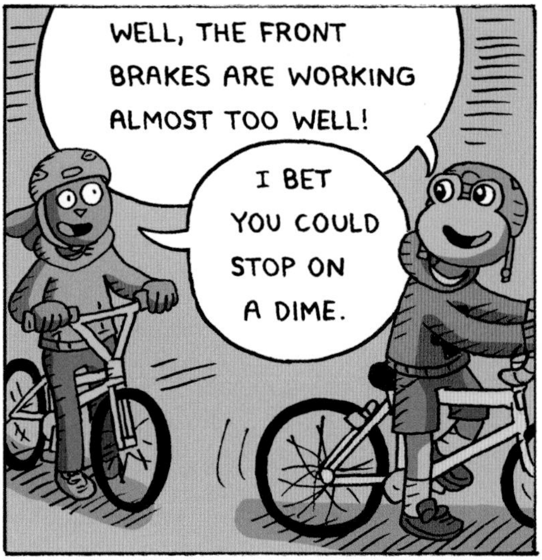
WELL, THE FRONT BRAKES ARE WORKING ALMOST TOO WELL!
I BET YOU COULD STOP ON A DIME.

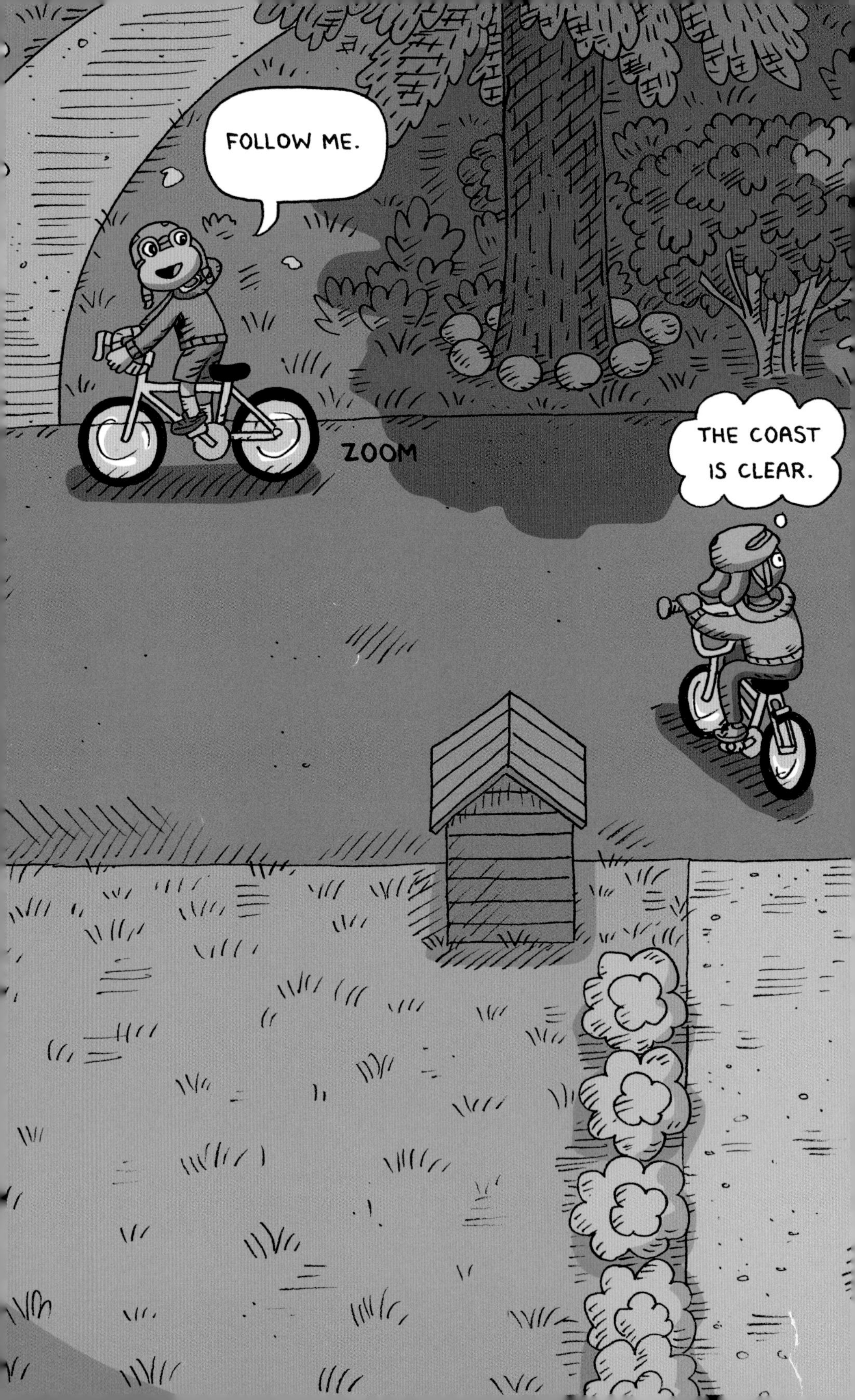
FOLLOW ME.
ZOOM
THE COAST IS CLEAR.

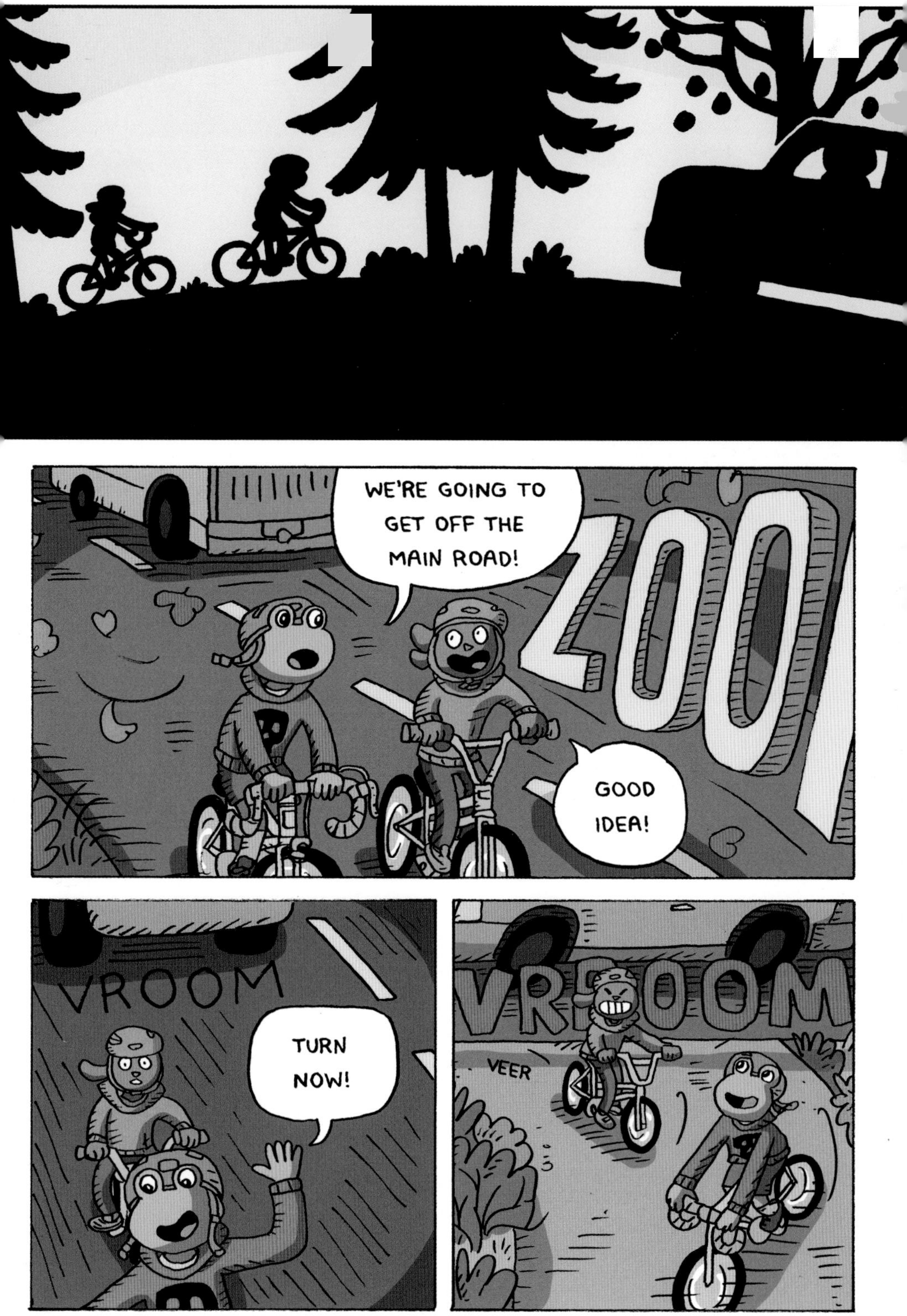
WE'RE GOING TO GET OFF THE MAIN ROAD!
ZOO
GOOD IDEA!
VROOM
TURN NOW!
VEER

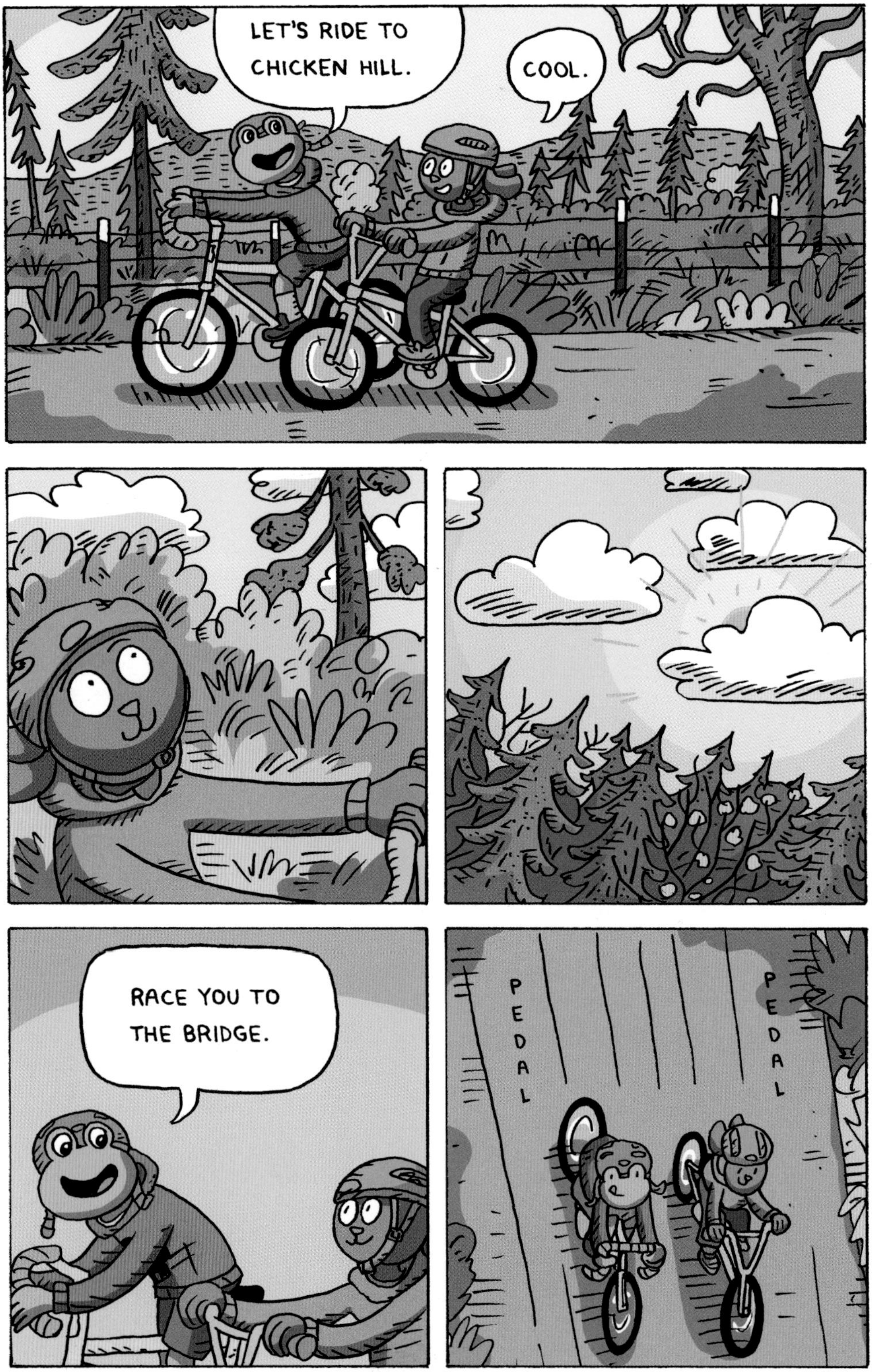
LET'S RIDE TO CHICKEN HILL.
COOL.
RACE YOU TO THE BRIDGE.
PEDAL
PEDAL

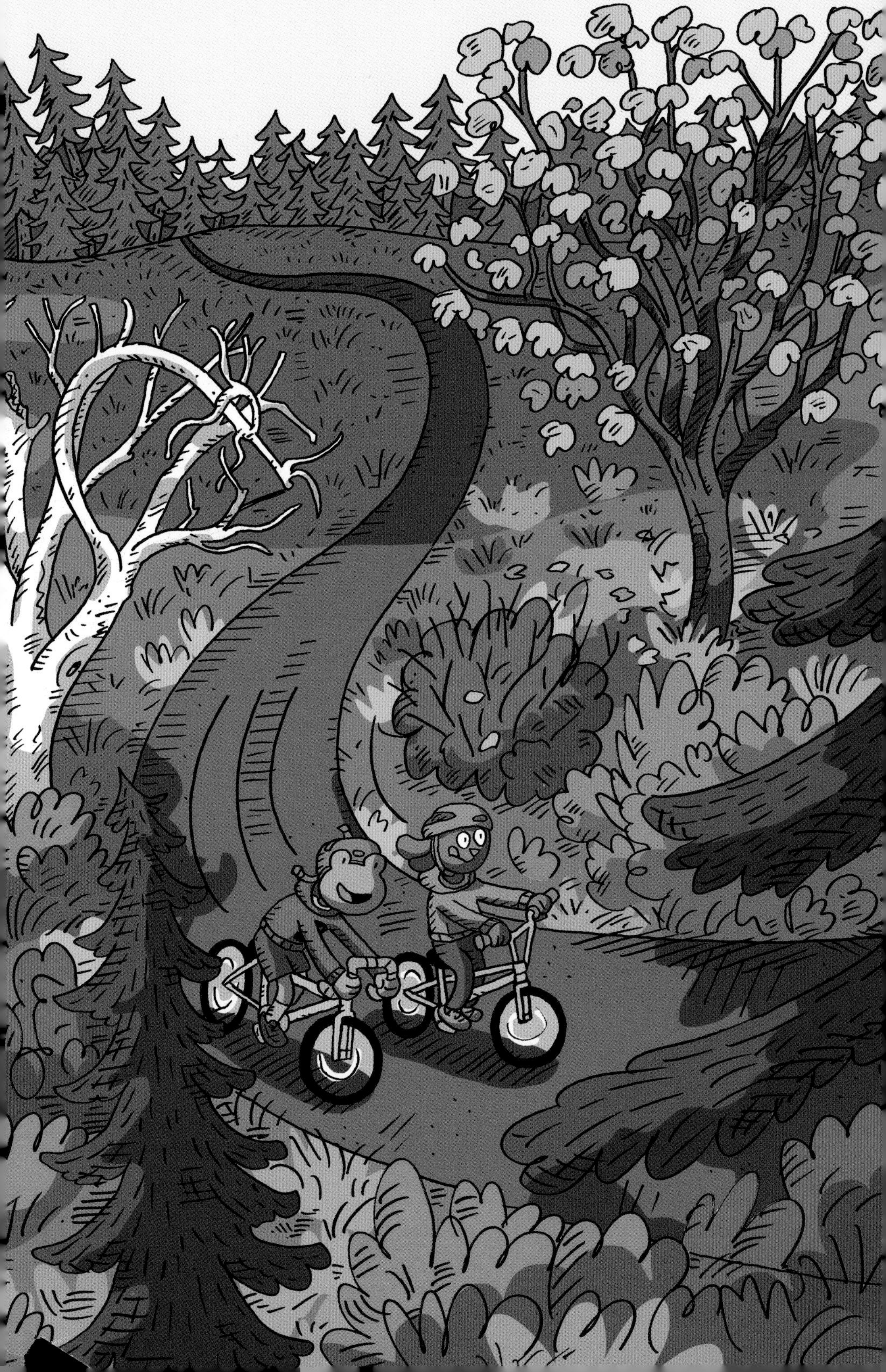

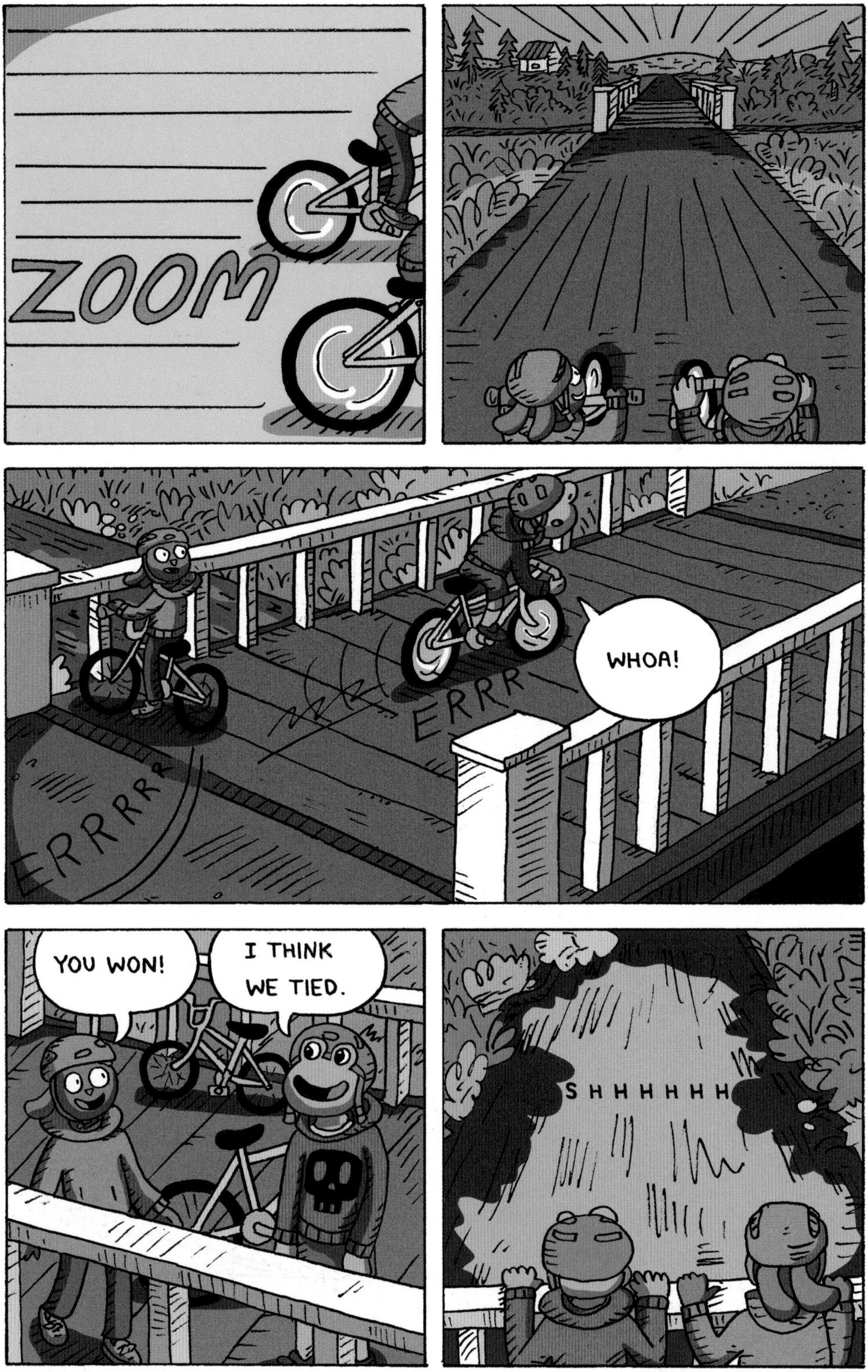
ZOOM
WHOA!
ERRR
ERRRRR
YOU WON!
I THINK WE TIED.
SHHHHHHH

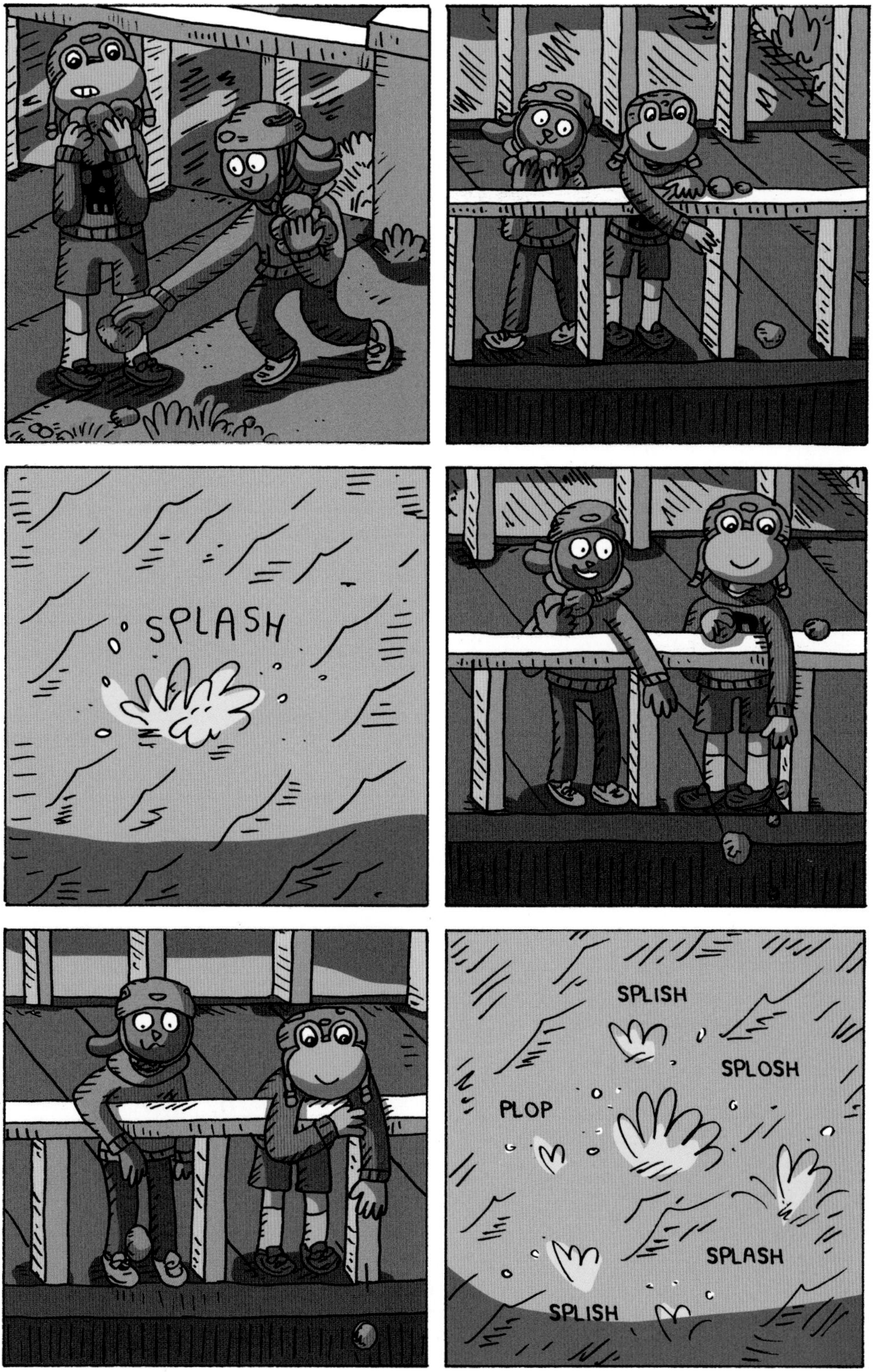
SPLASH
SPLISH
SPLOSH
PLOP
SPLASH
SPLISH

IS THAT CHICKEN HILL?... LOOKS LIKE A MOUNTAIN.

YEAH.

WHEN YOU RIDE DOWN, IT FEELS LIKE YOU'RE FLYING!

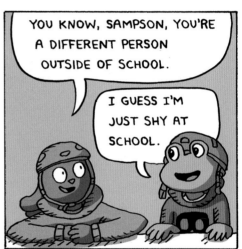

YOU KNOW, SAMPSON, YOU'RE A DIFFERENT PERSON OUTSIDE OF SCHOOL.

I GUESS I'M JUST SHY AT SCHOOL.

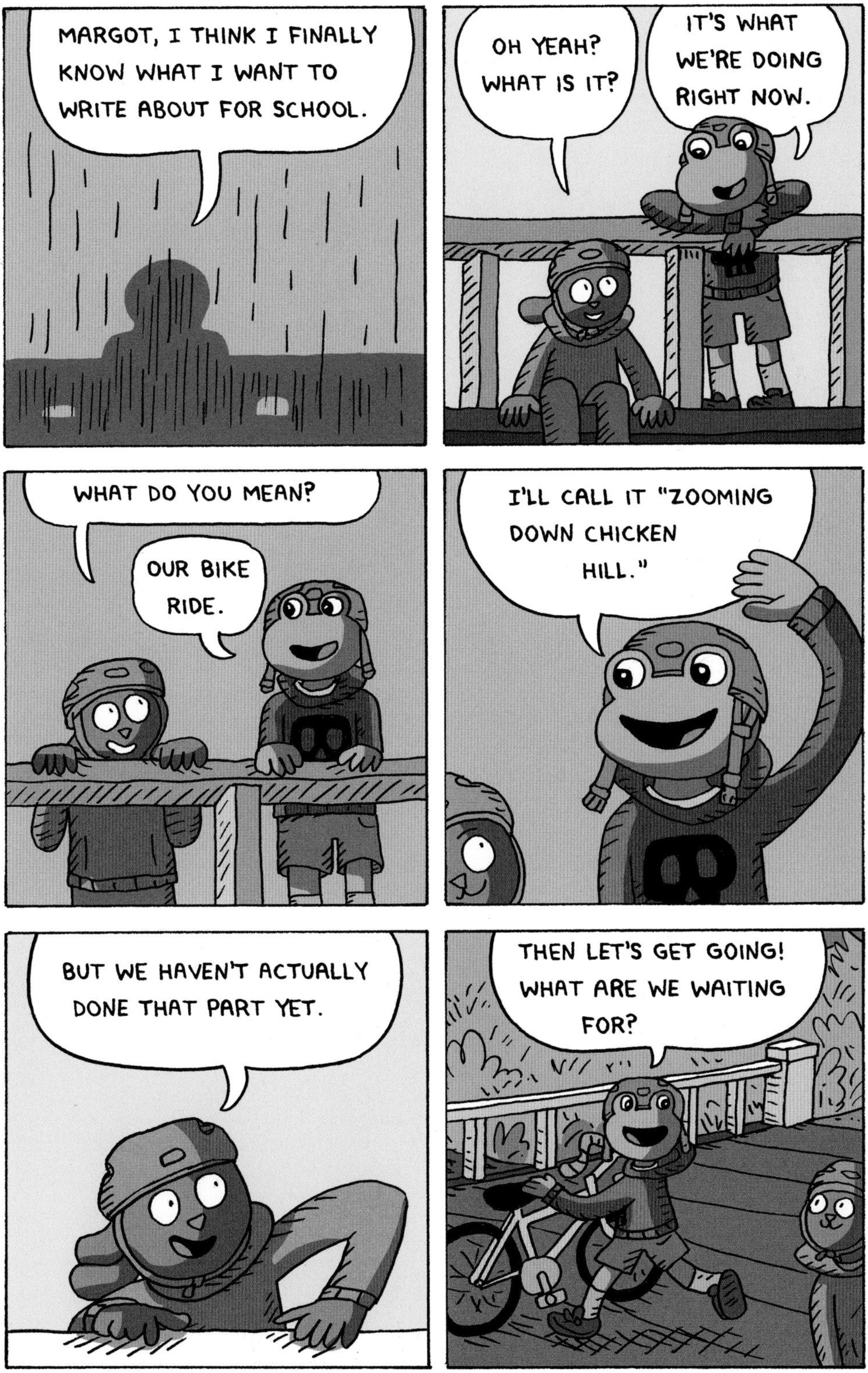
MARGOT, I THINK I FINALLY KNOW WHAT I WANT TO WRITE ABOUT FOR SCHOOL.
OH YEAH? WHAT IS IT?
IT'S WHAT WE'RE DOING RIGHT NOW.
WHAT DO YOU MEAN?
OUR BIKE RIDE.
I'LL CALL IT "ZOOMING DOWN CHICKEN HILL."
BUT WE HAVEN'T ACTUALLY DONE THAT PART YET.
THEN LET'S GET GOING! WHAT ARE WE WAITING FOR?

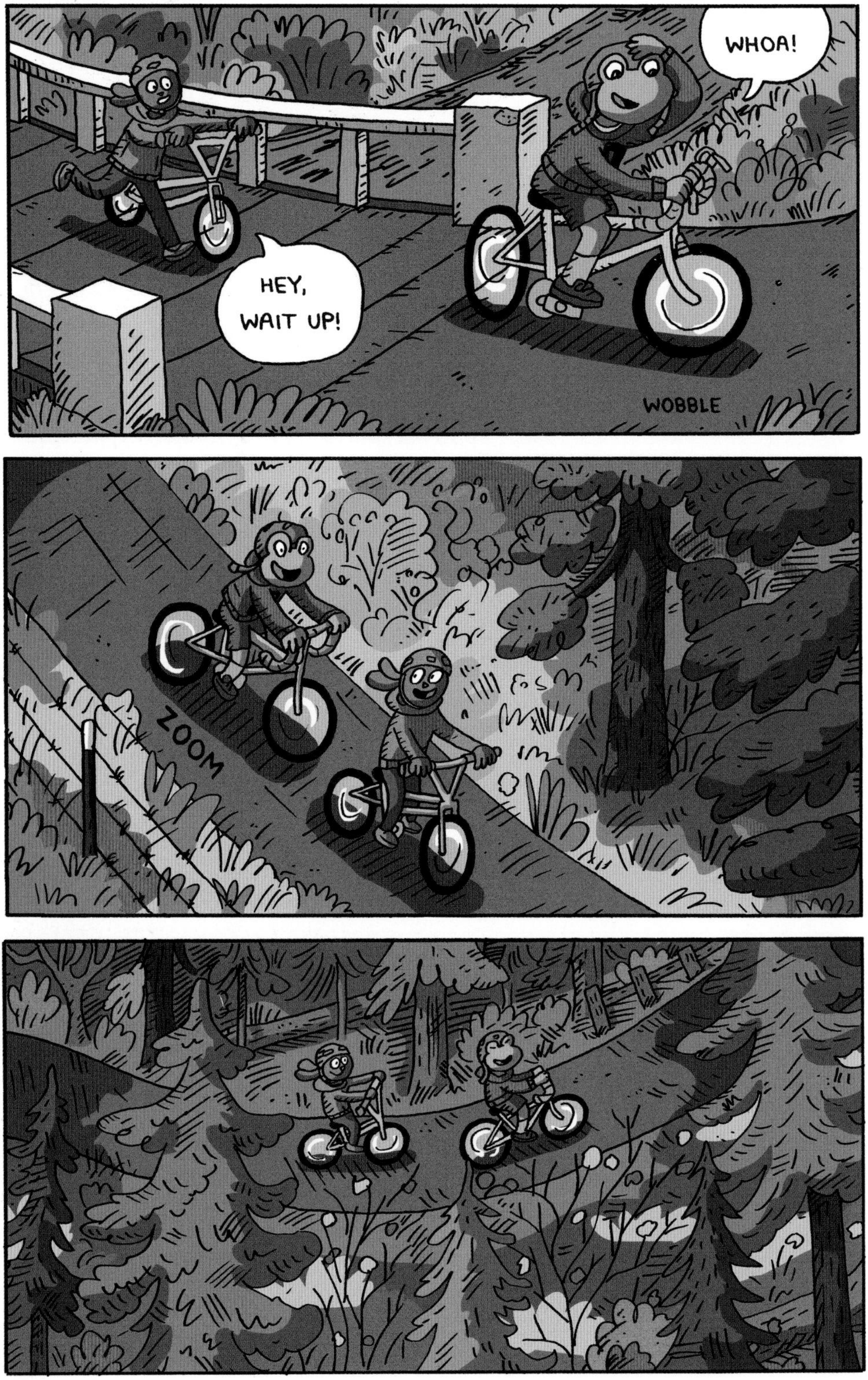
WHOA!
HEY, WAIT UP!
WOBBLE
ZOOM

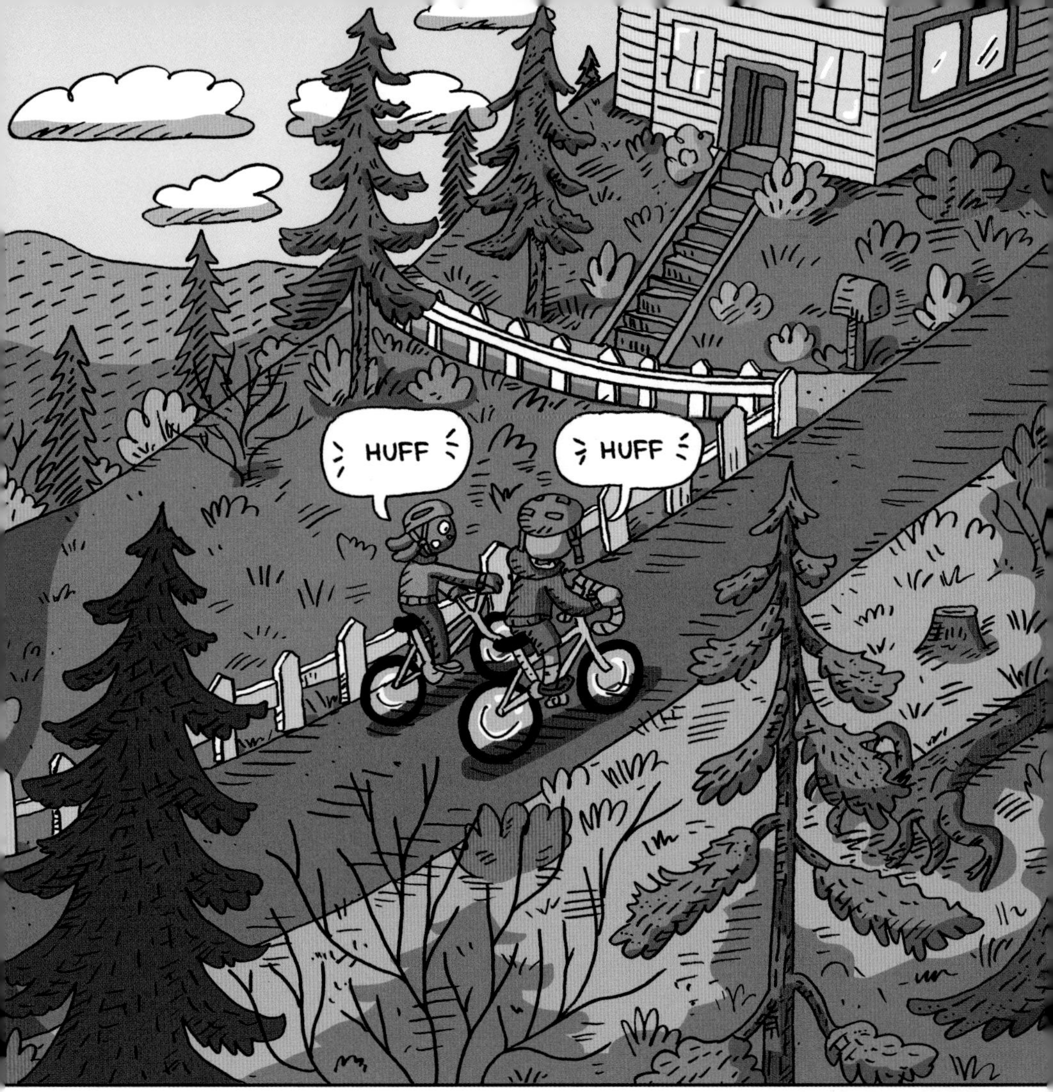
HUFF
HUFF

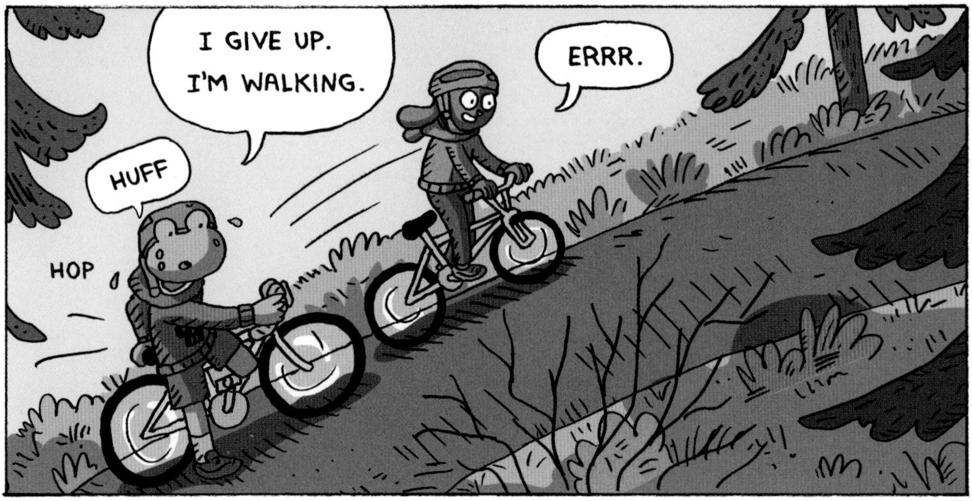
I GIVE UP. I'M WALKING.
ERRR.
HUFF
HOP

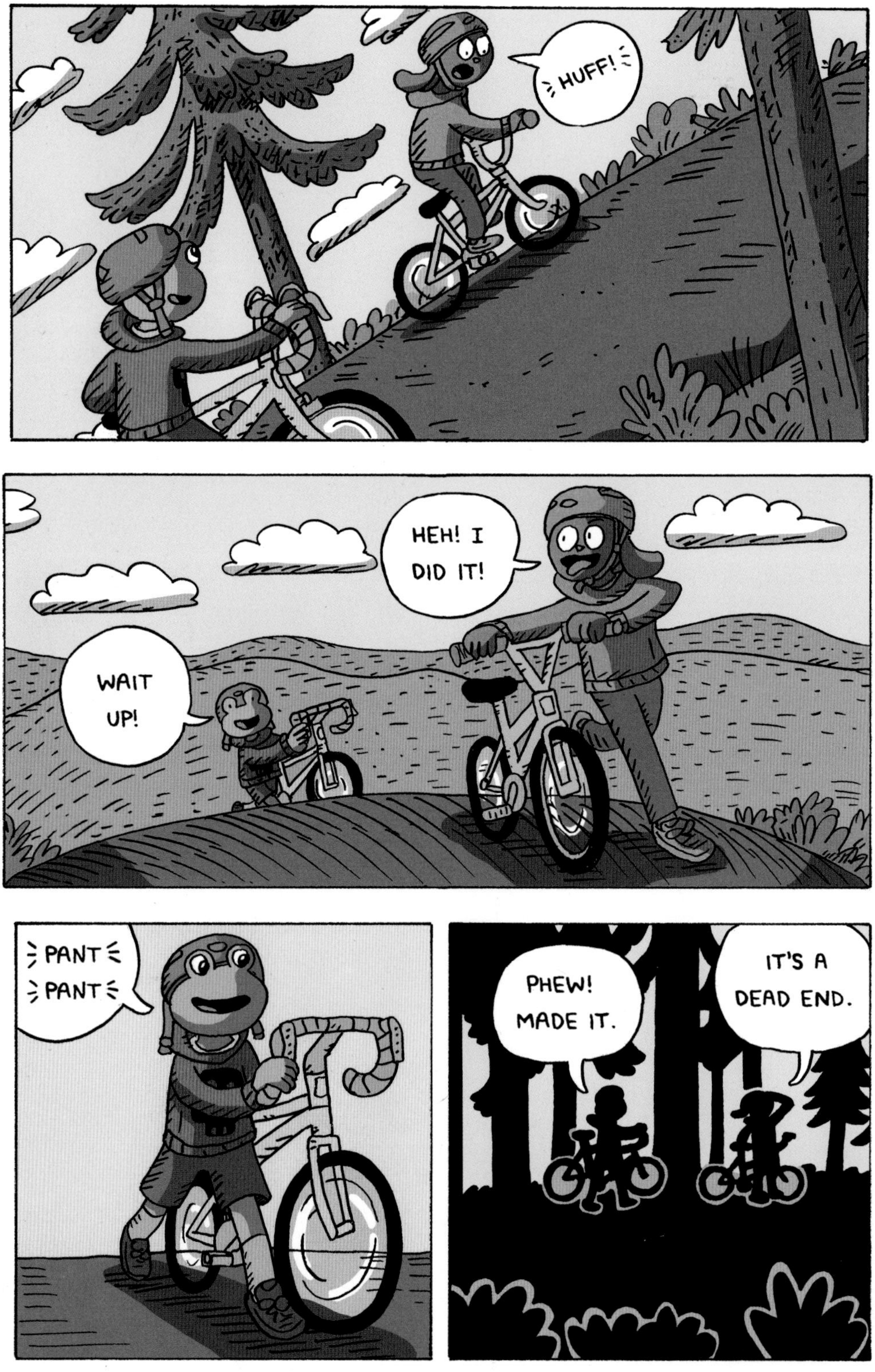
HUFF!
HEH! I DID IT!
WAIT UP!
PANT PANT
PHEW! MADE IT.
IT'S A DEAD END.

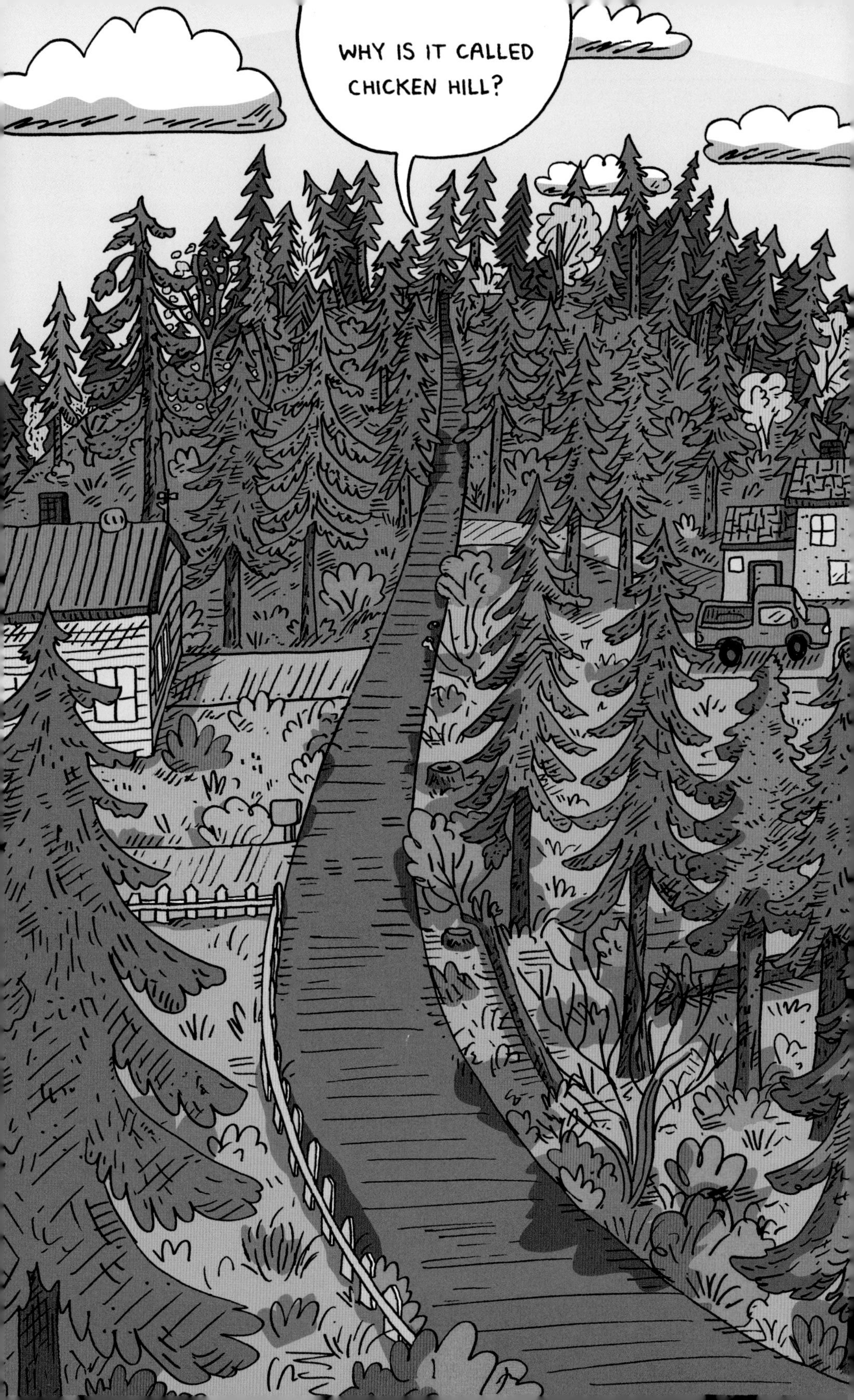
WHY IS IT CALLED CHICKEN HILL?

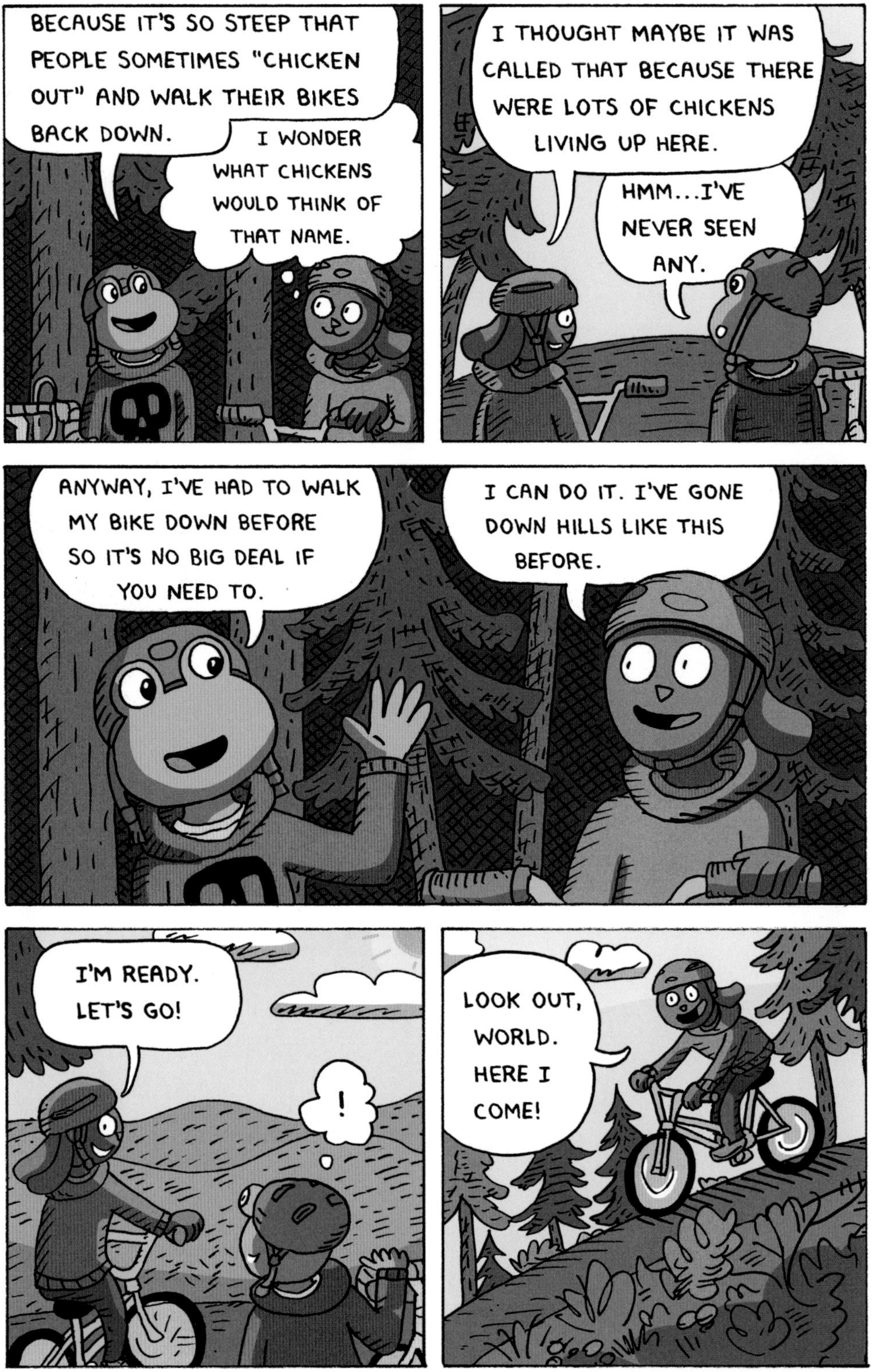
BECAUSE IT'S SO STEEP THAT PEOPLE SOMETIMES "CHICKEN OUT" AND WALK THEIR BIKES BACK DOWN.
I WONDER WHAT CHICKENS WOULD THINK OF THAT NAME.
I THOUGHT MAYBE IT WAS CALLED THAT BECAUSE THERE WERE LOTS OF CHICKENS LIVING UP HERE.
HMM...I'VE NEVER SEEN ANY.
ANYWAY, I'VE HAD TO WALK MY BIKE DOWN BEFORE SO IT'S NO BIG DEAL IF YOU NEED TO.
I CAN DO IT. I'VE GONE DOWN HILLS LIKE THIS BEFORE.
I'M READY. LET'S GO!
!
LOOK OUT, WORLD. HERE I COME!

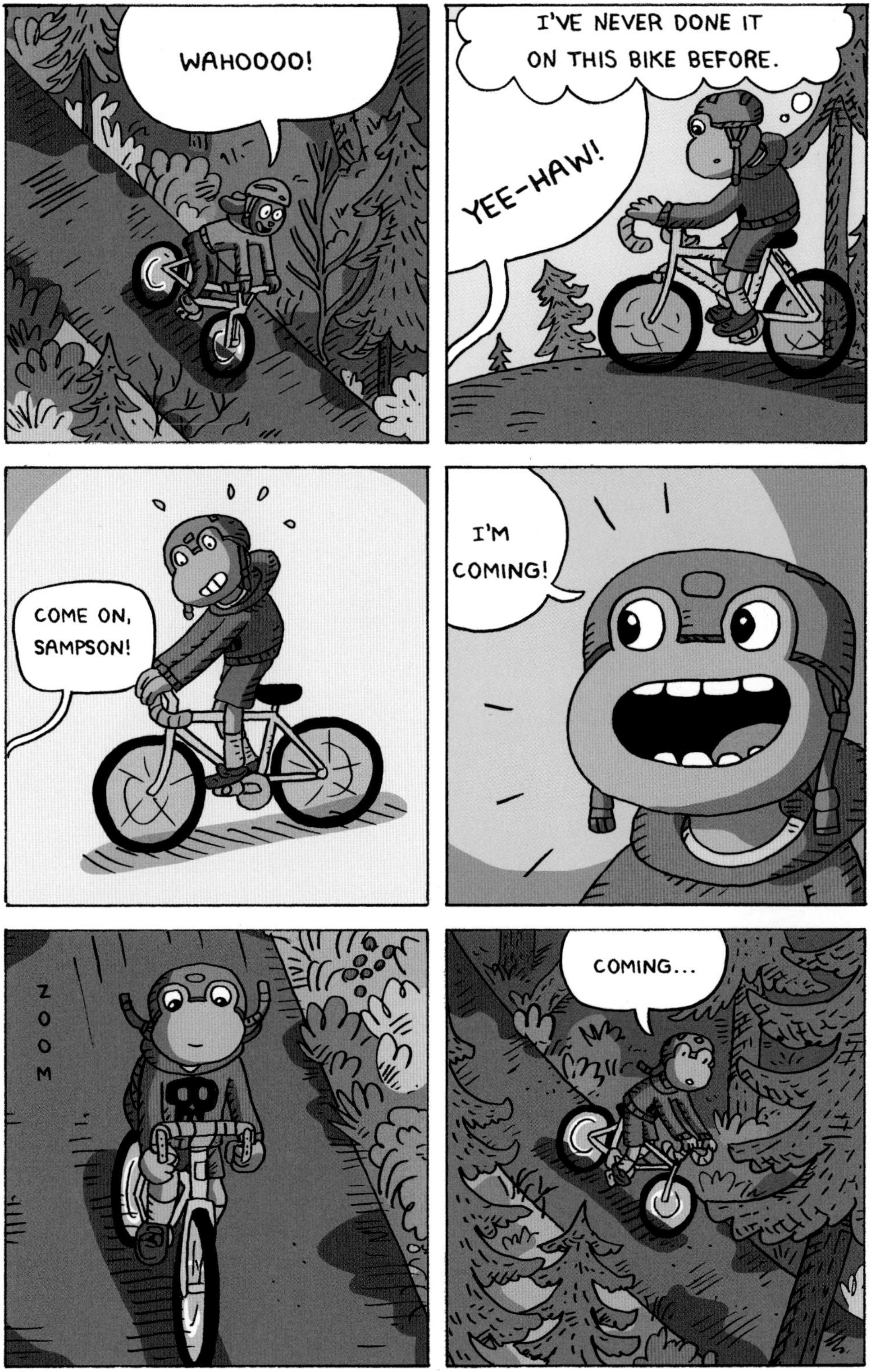
WAHOOOO!
I'VE NEVER DONE IT ON THIS BIKE BEFORE.
YEE-HAW!
COME ON, SAMPSON!
I'M COMING!
ZOOM
COMING...

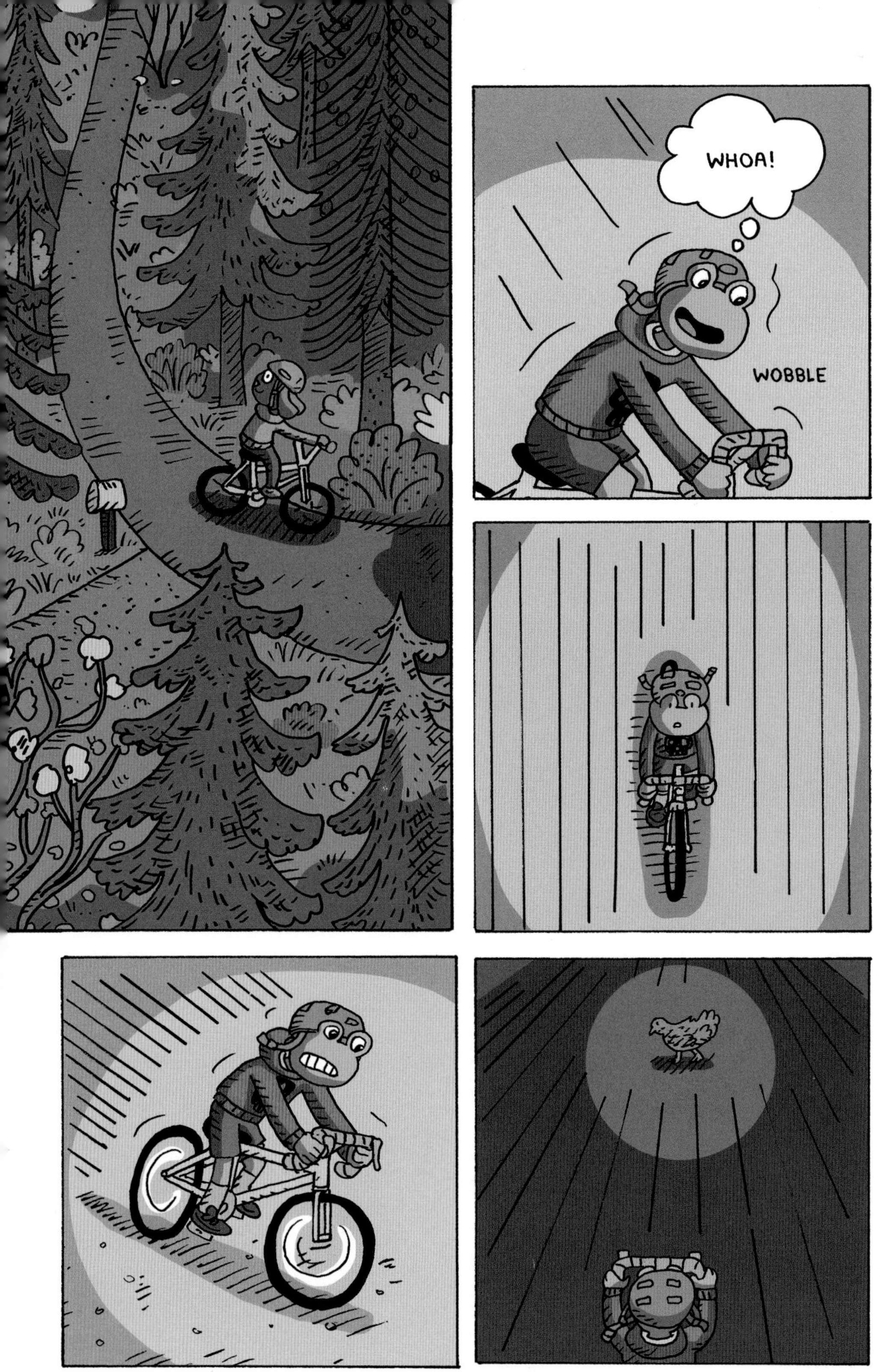
WHOA!
WOBBLE

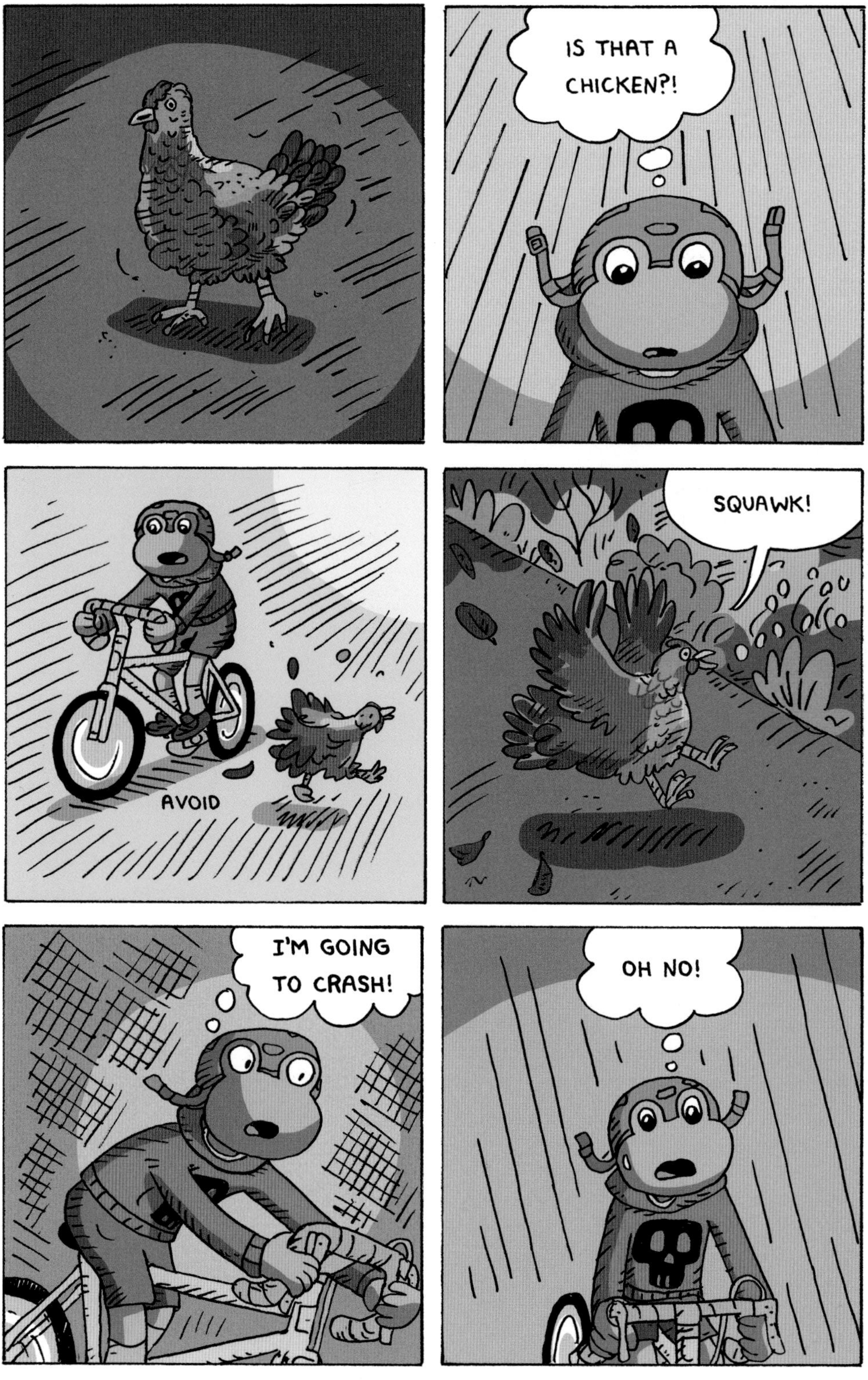
IS THAT A CHICKEN?!
AVOID
SQUAWK!
I'M GOING TO CRASH!
OH NO!

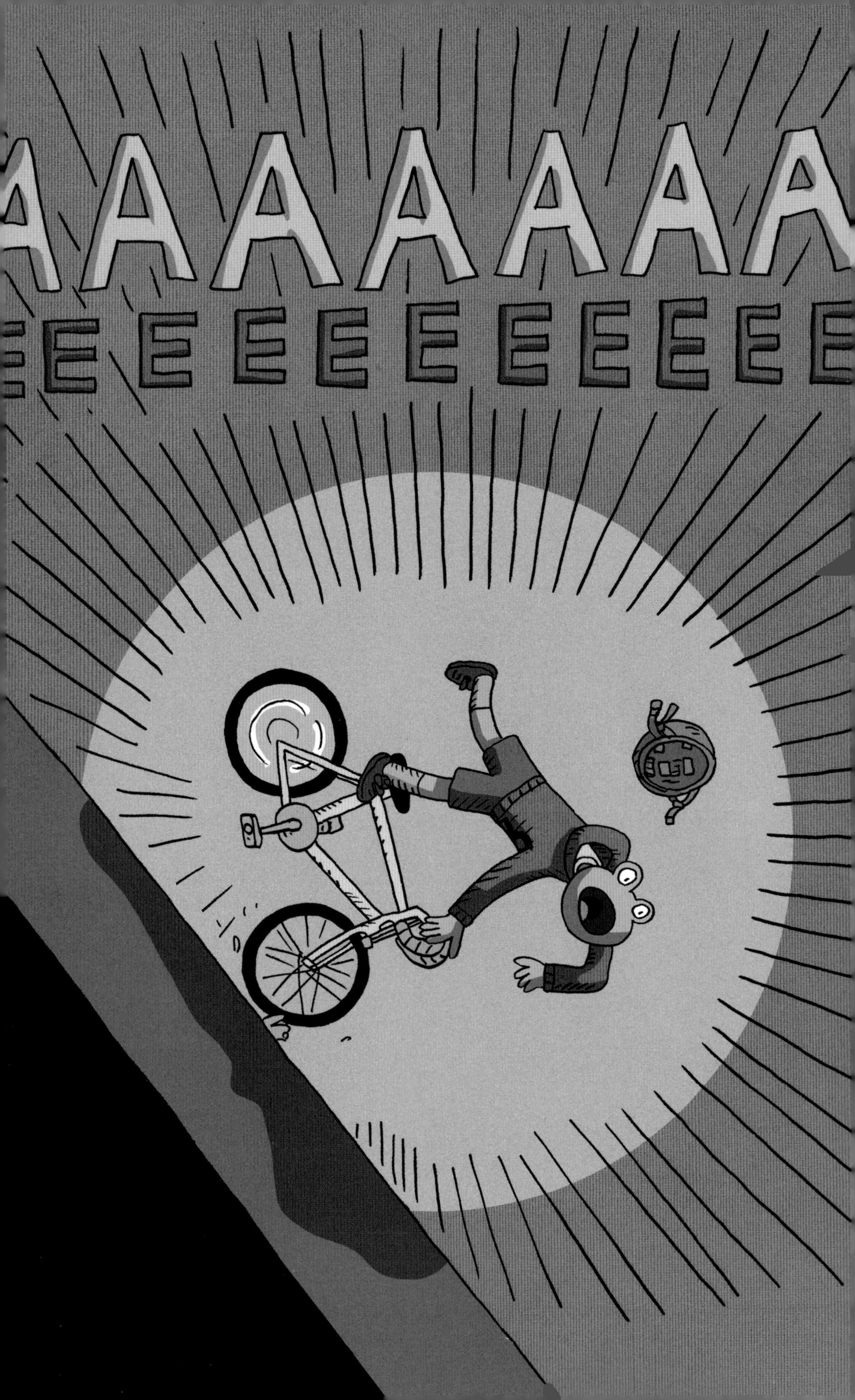
AAAAAAA
EEEEEEEEEEE

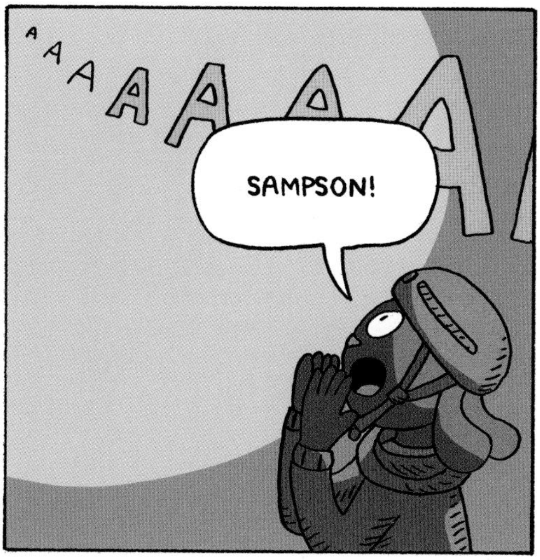
AAAAAAAA
SAMPSON!

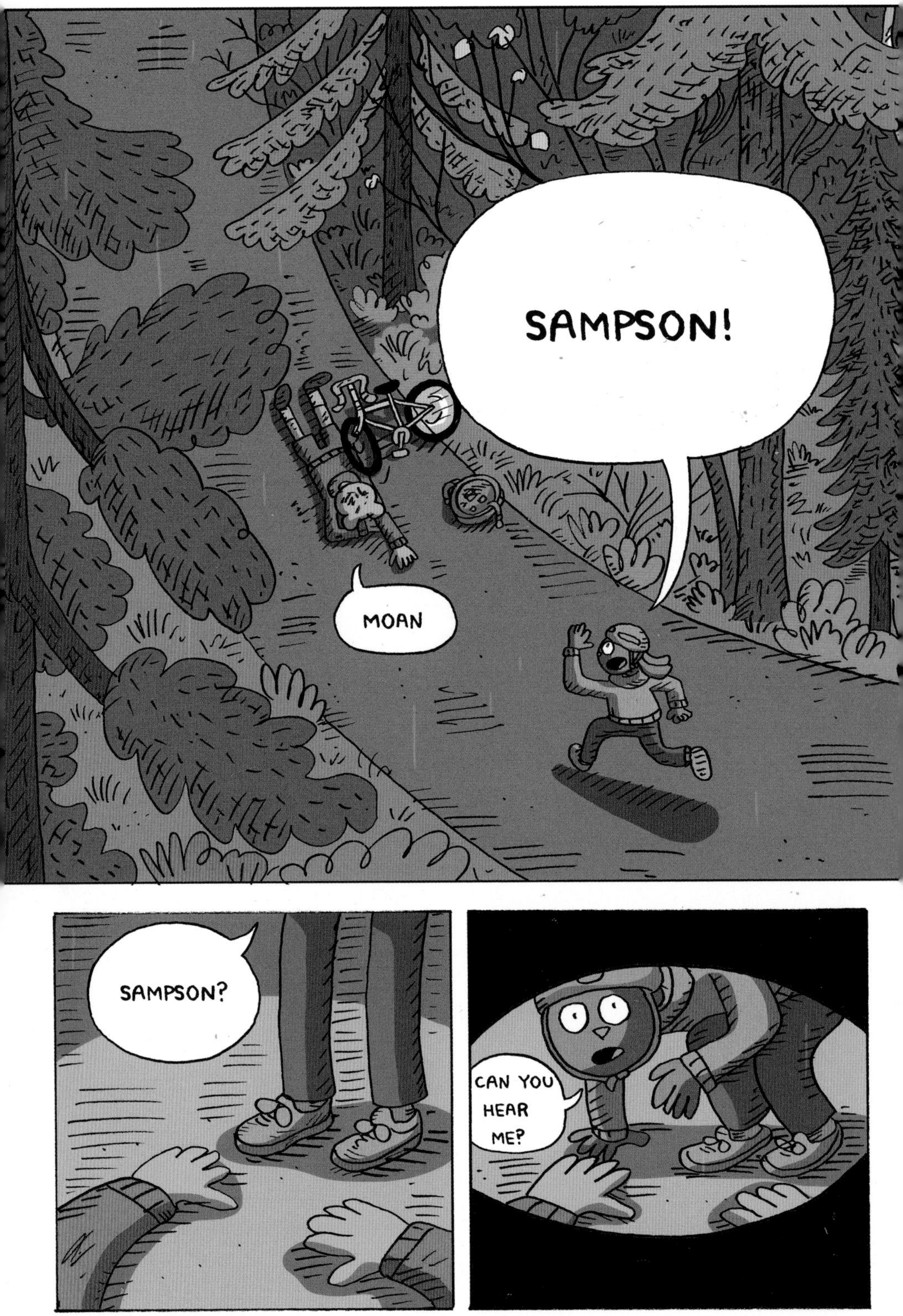
SAMPSON!
MOAN
SAMPSON?
CAN YOU HEAR ME?

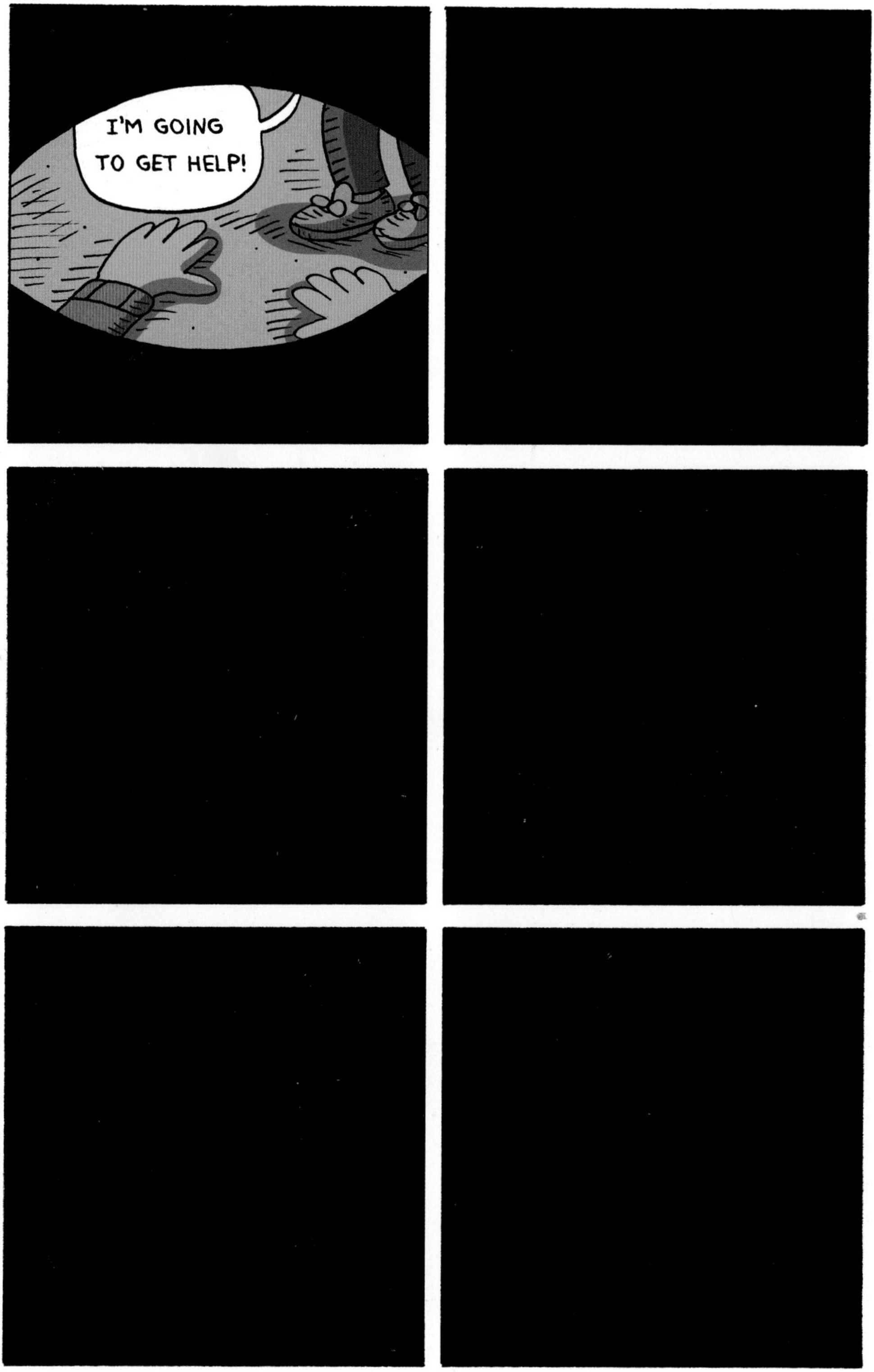
I'M GOING TO GET HELP!

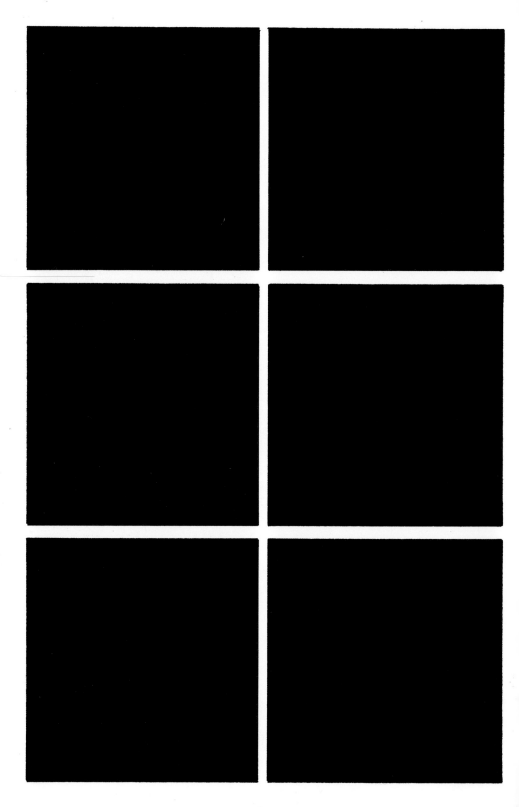

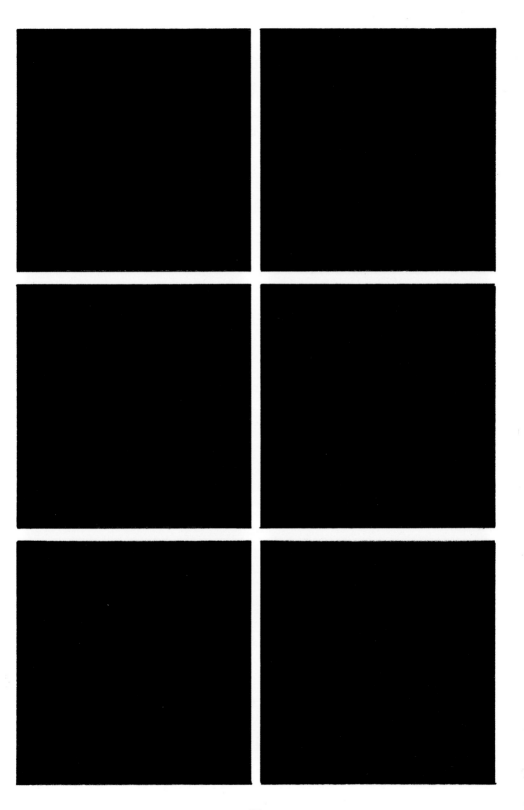

I THINK HE'S STARTING TO WAKE UP.

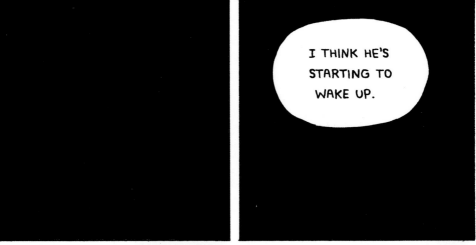

I THINK YOU'RE RIGHT ABOUT THAT.

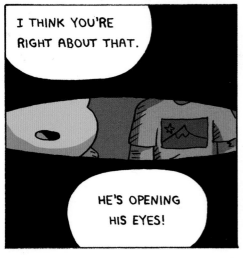

HE'S OPENING HIS EYES!

HI, SAMMY. WELCOME BACK! HOW ARE YOU FEELING?

CHAPTER FOUR
Thank Your Lucky Stars

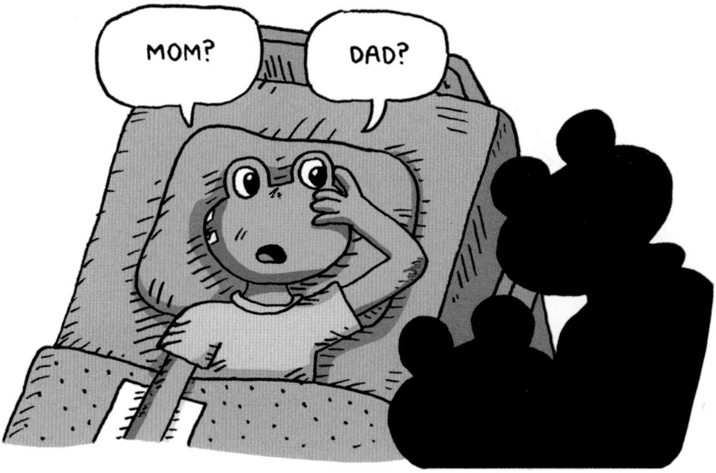
MOM?
DAD?

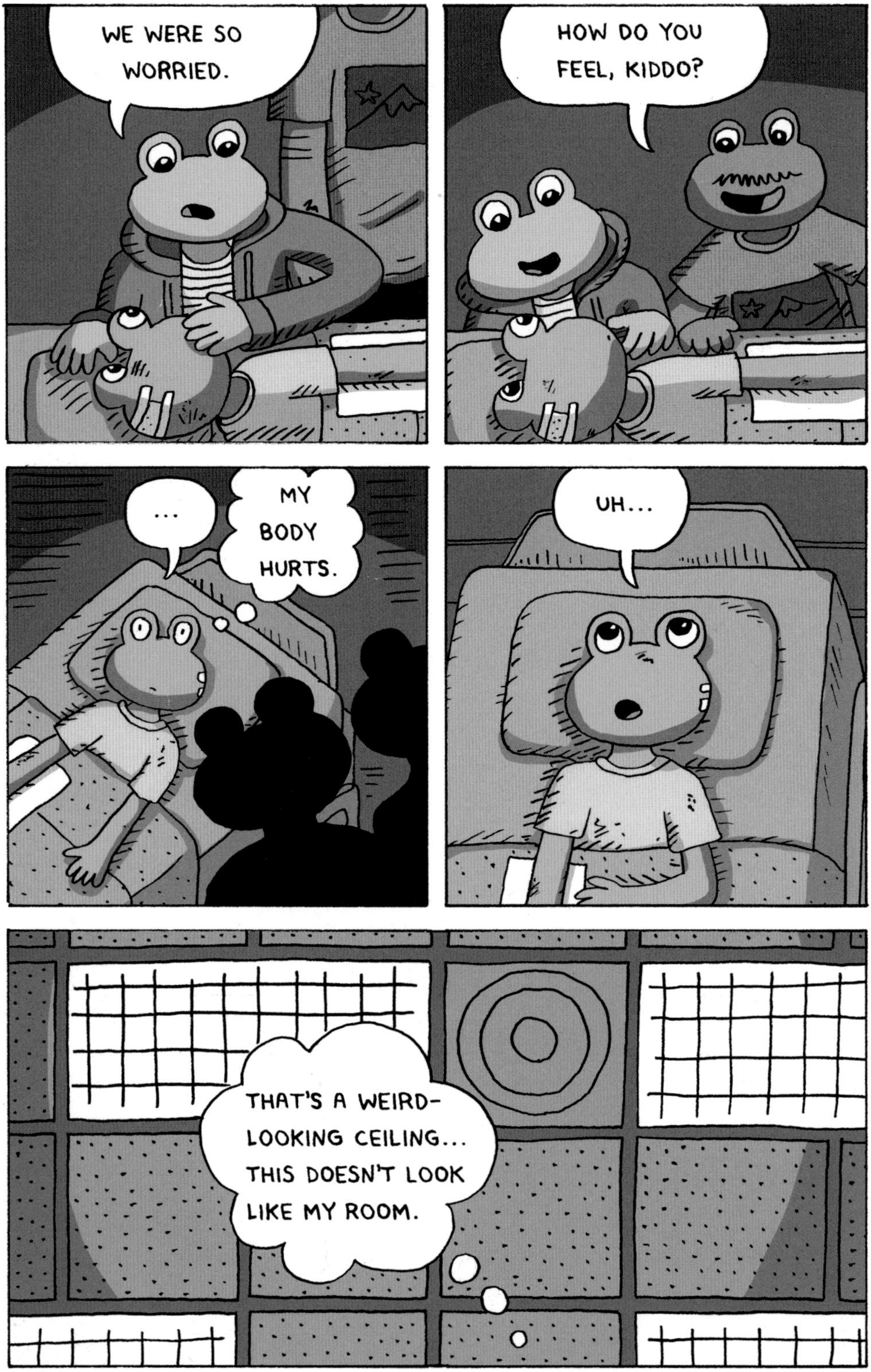
WE WERE SO WORRIED.
HOW DO YOU FEEL, KIDDO?
...
MY BODY HURTS.
UH...
THAT'S A WEIRD-LOOKING CEILING... THIS DOESN'T LOOK LIKE MY ROOM.

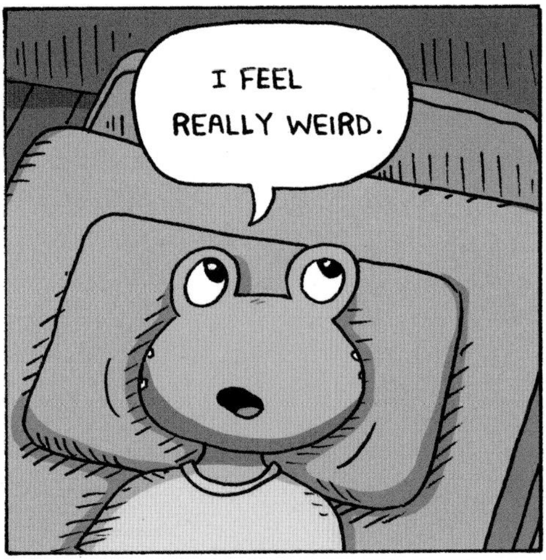
I FEEL
REALLY WEIRD.

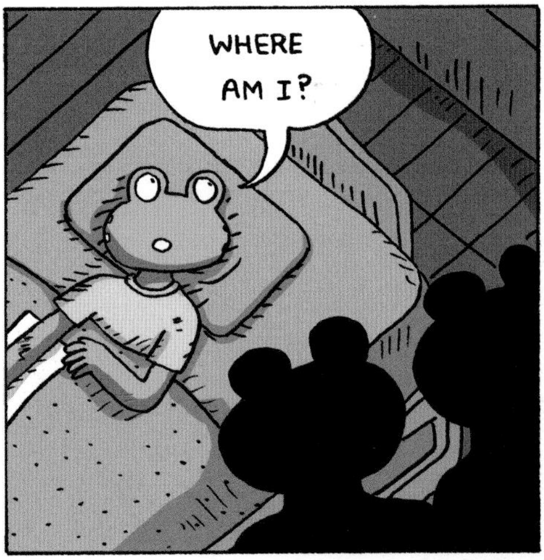
WHERE
AM I?

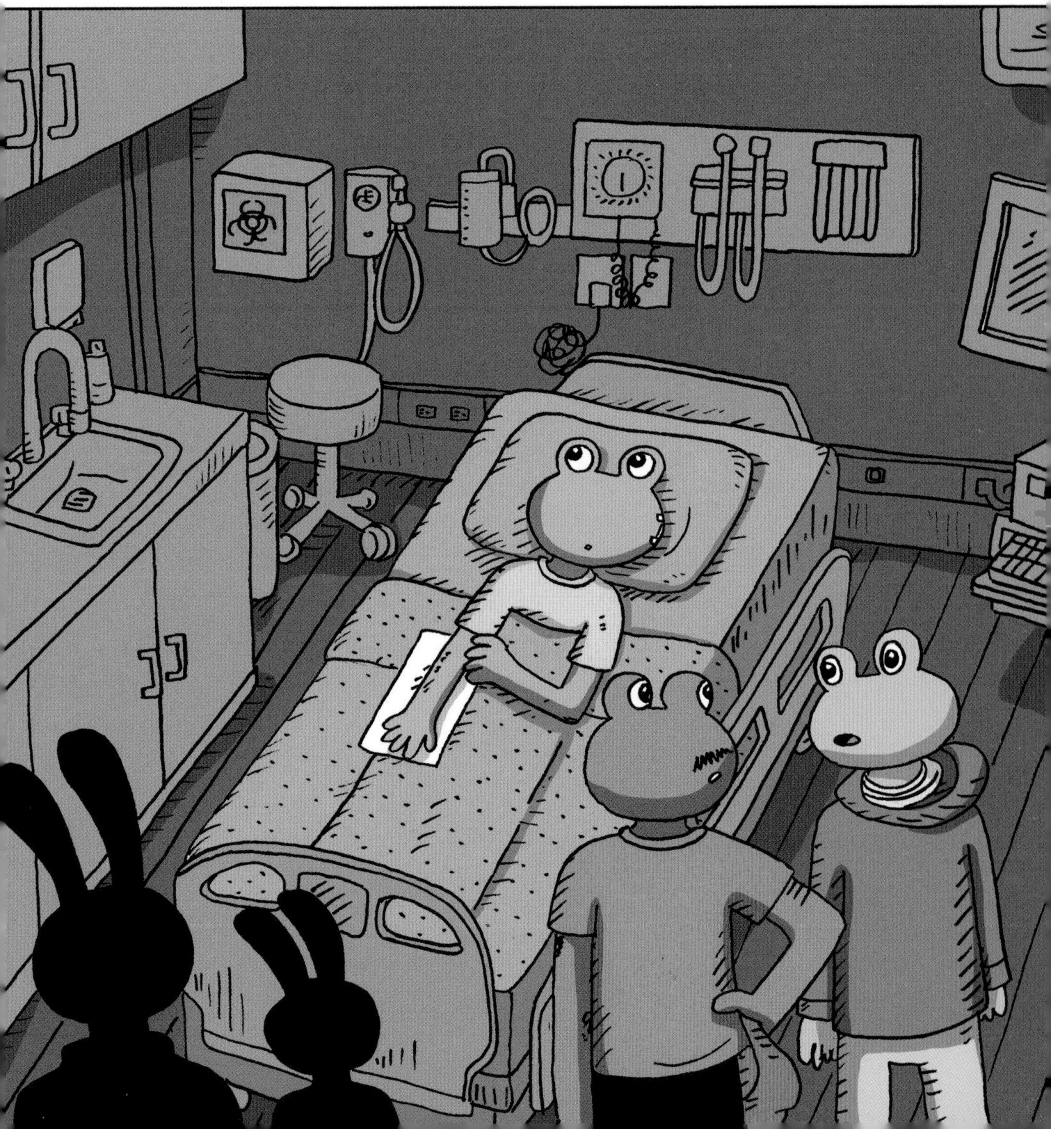

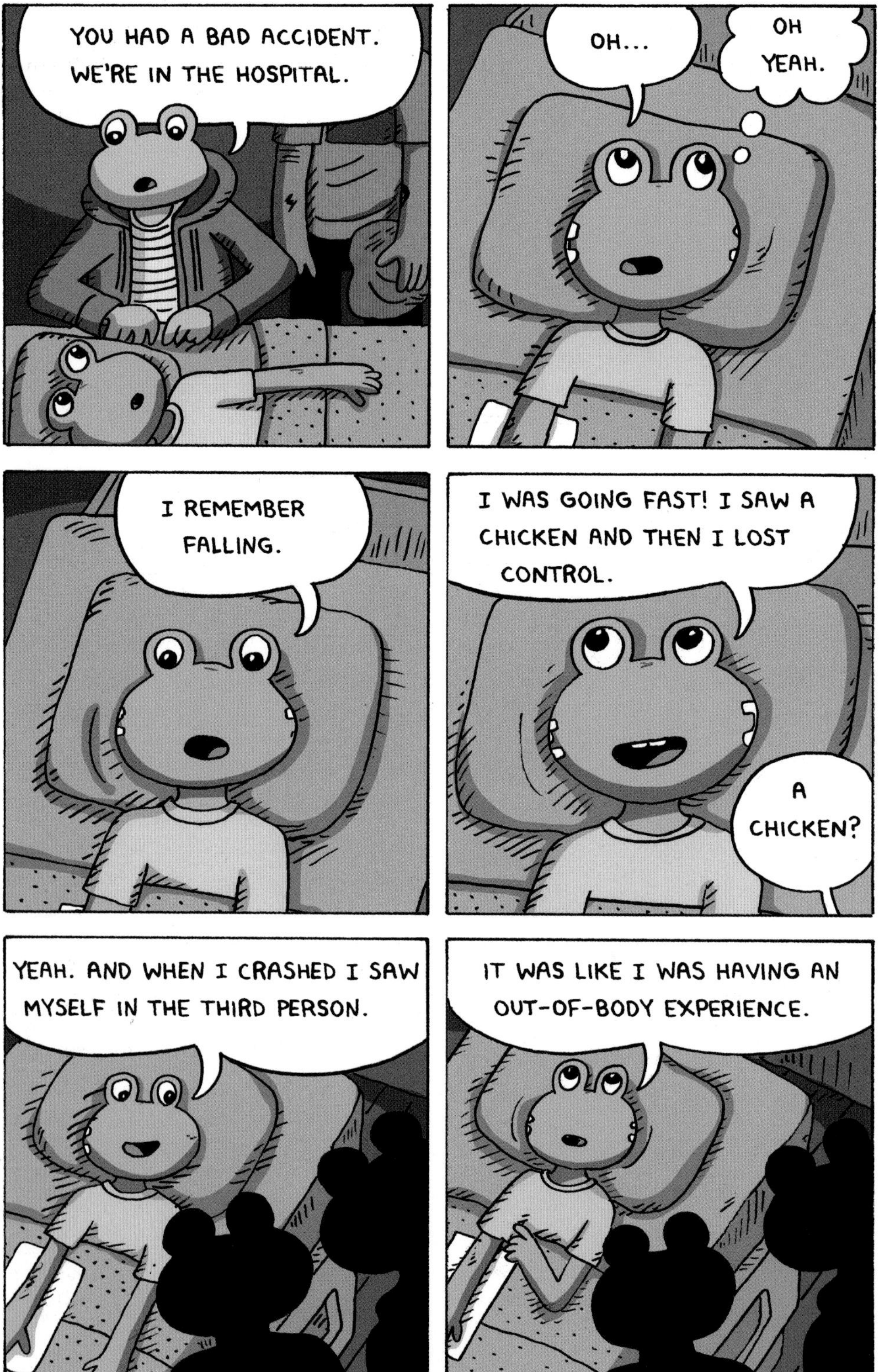
YOU HAD A BAD ACCIDENT. WE'RE IN THE HOSPITAL.
OH...
OH YEAH.
I REMEMBER FALLING.
I WAS GOING FAST! I SAW A CHICKEN AND THEN I LOST CONTROL.
A CHICKEN?
YEAH. AND WHEN I CRASHED I SAW MYSELF IN THE THIRD PERSON.
IT WAS LIKE I WAS HAVING AN OUT-OF-BODY EXPERIENCE.

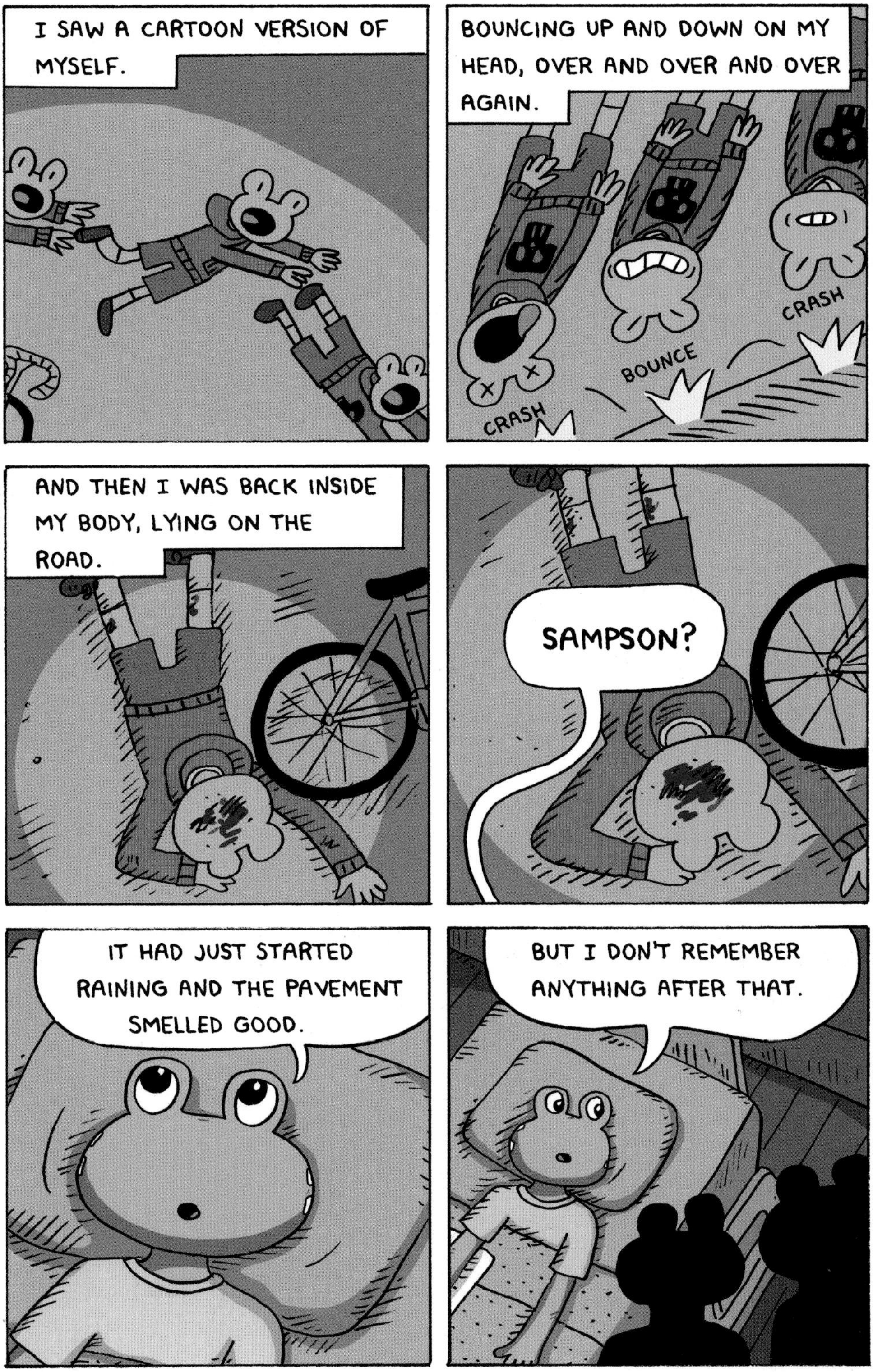
I SAW A CARTOON VERSION OF MYSELF.
BOUNCING UP AND DOWN ON MY HEAD, OVER AND OVER AND OVER AGAIN.
CRASH
BOUNCE
CRASH
AND THEN I WAS BACK INSIDE MY BODY, LYING ON THE ROAD.
SAMPSON?
IT HAD JUST STARTED RAINING AND THE PAVEMENT SMELLED GOOD.
BUT I DON'T REMEMBER ANYTHING AFTER THAT.

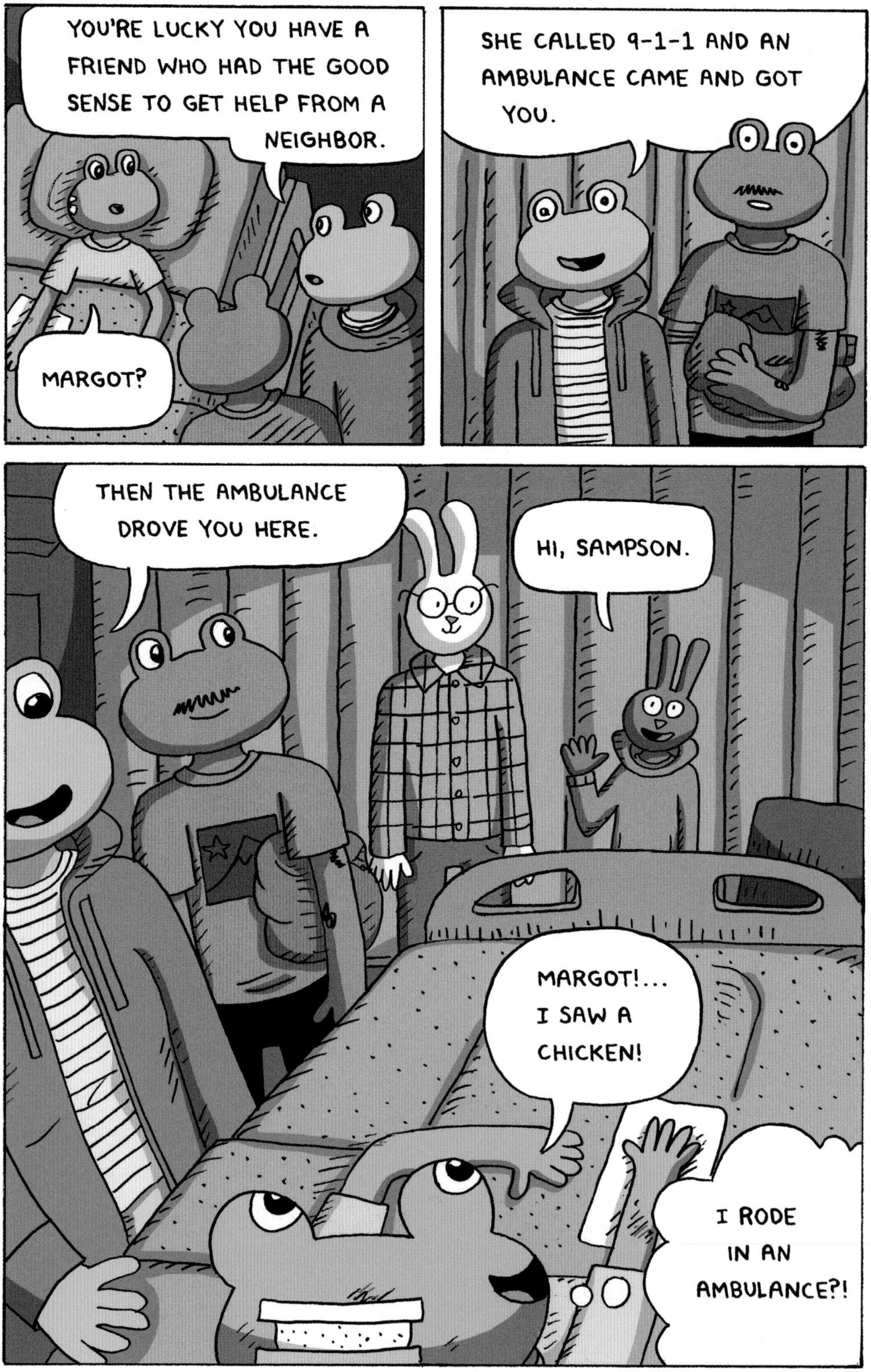
YOU'RE LUCKY YOU HAVE A FRIEND WHO HAD THE GOOD SENSE TO GET HELP FROM A NEIGHBOR.
MARGOT?
SHE CALLED 9-1-1 AND AN AMBULANCE CAME AND GOT YOU.
THEN THE AMBULANCE DROVE YOU HERE.
HI, SAMPSON.
MARGOT!... I SAW A CHICKEN!
I RODE IN AN AMBULANCE?!

YOU'VE BEEN ASLEEP FOR NEARLY AN HOUR.

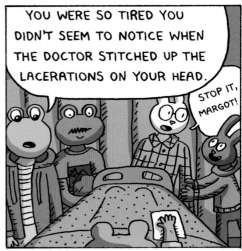

YOU WERE SO TIRED YOU DIDN'T SEEM TO NOTICE WHEN THE DOCTOR STITCHED UP THE LACERATIONS ON YOUR HEAD.

STOP IT, MARGOT!

YOU DIDN'T EVEN WAKE UP WHEN SHE SET YOUR ARM. YOU JUST CRIED OUT A LITTLE.

STOP.

SET MY ARM? YOU MEAN I BROKE MY ARM?!

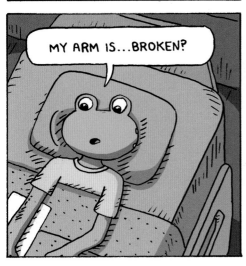

MY ARM IS...BROKEN?

WUH-HUH-HUH!

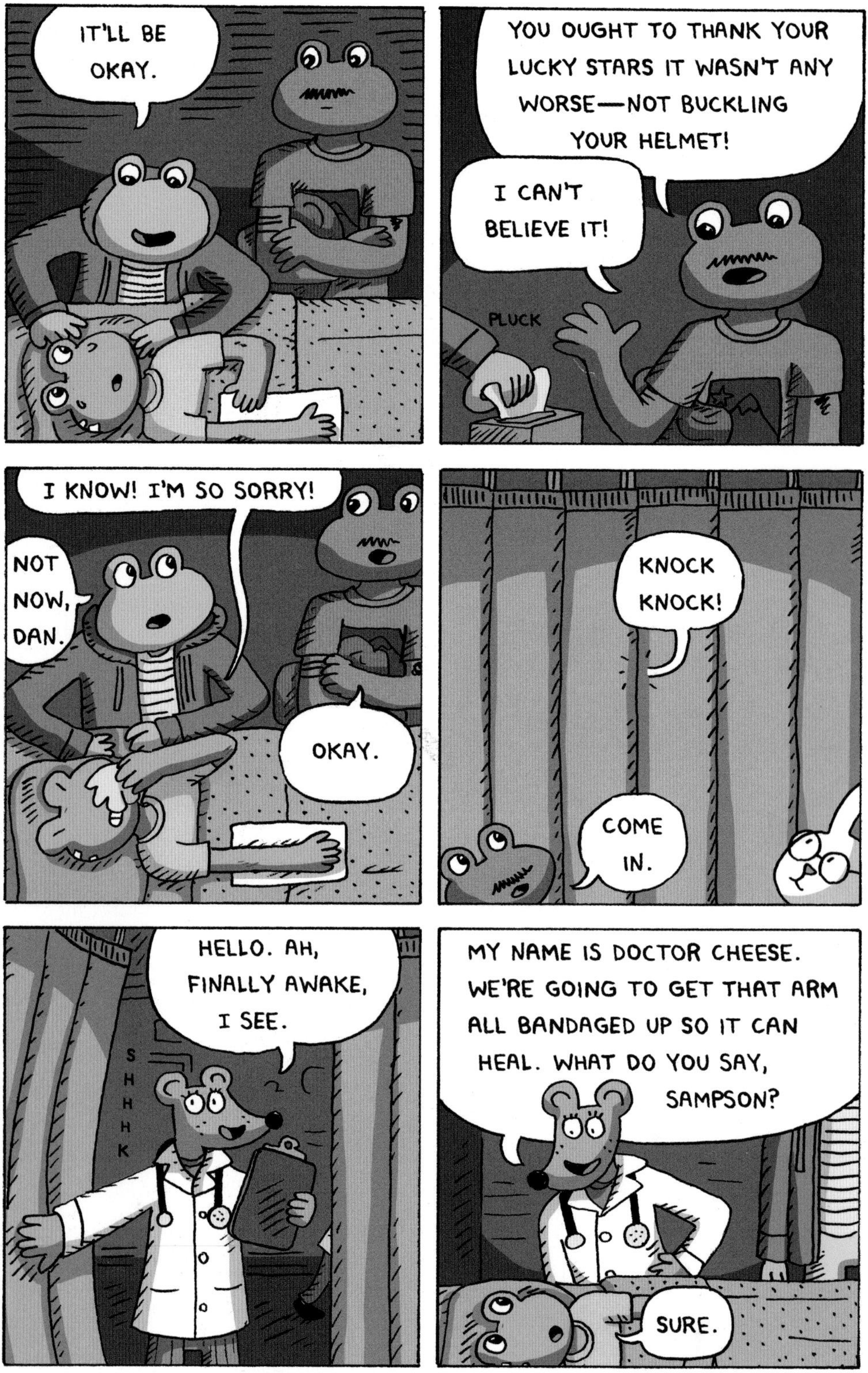
IT'LL BE OKAY.
YOU OUGHT TO THANK YOUR LUCKY STARS IT WASN'T ANY WORSE—NOT BUCKLING YOUR HELMET!
I CAN'T BELIEVE IT!
PLUCK
I KNOW! I'M SO SORRY!
NOT NOW, DAN.
OKAY.
KNOCK KNOCK!
COME IN.
HELLO. AH, FINALLY AWAKE, I SEE.
SHHHK
MY NAME IS DOCTOR CHEESE. WE'RE GOING TO GET THAT ARM ALL BANDAGED UP SO IT CAN HEAL. WHAT DO YOU SAY, SAMPSON?
SURE.

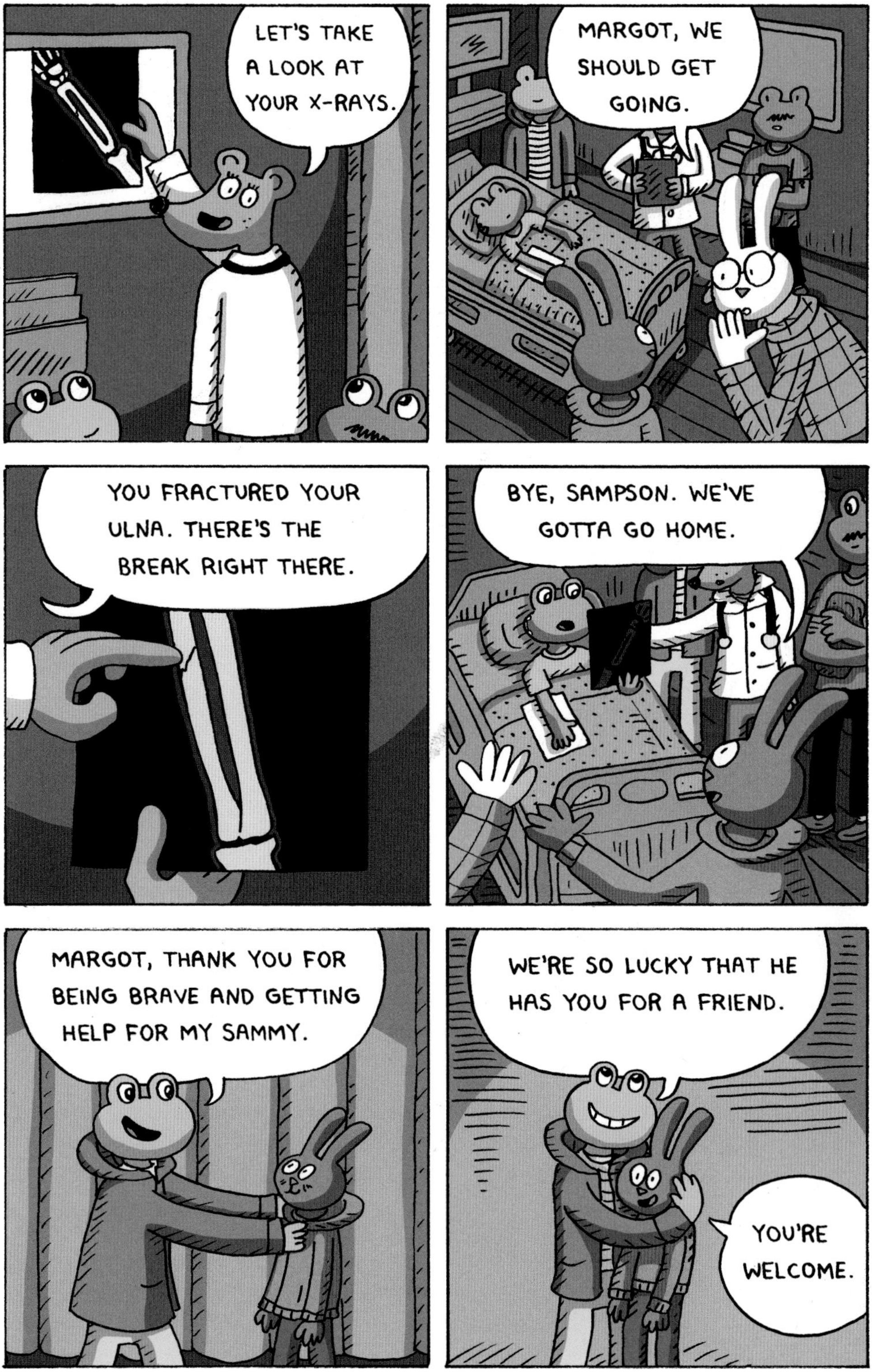
LET'S TAKE A LOOK AT YOUR X-RAYS.
MARGOT, WE SHOULD GET GOING.
YOU FRACTURED YOUR ULNA. THERE'S THE BREAK RIGHT THERE.
BYE, SAMPSON. WE'VE GOTTA GO HOME.
MARGOT, THANK YOU FOR BEING BRAVE AND GETTING HELP FOR MY SAMMY.
WE'RE SO LUCKY THAT HE HAS YOU FOR A FRIEND.
YOU'RE WELCOME.

I NEED YOU TO HOLD YOUR ARM UP FOR ME.
!
SO...
I HEARD THAT...
PULL
YOU DIDN'T BUCKLE YOUR HELMET.
WRAP
...
WRAP
WRAP
SNIP

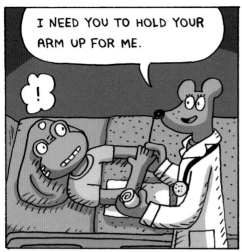

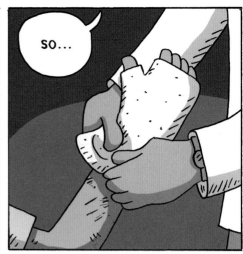

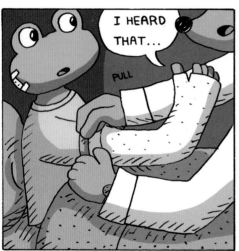

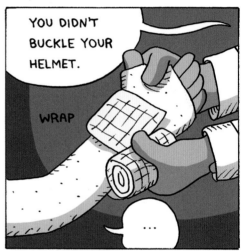

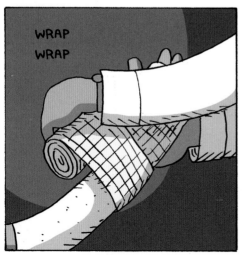

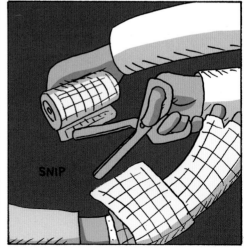

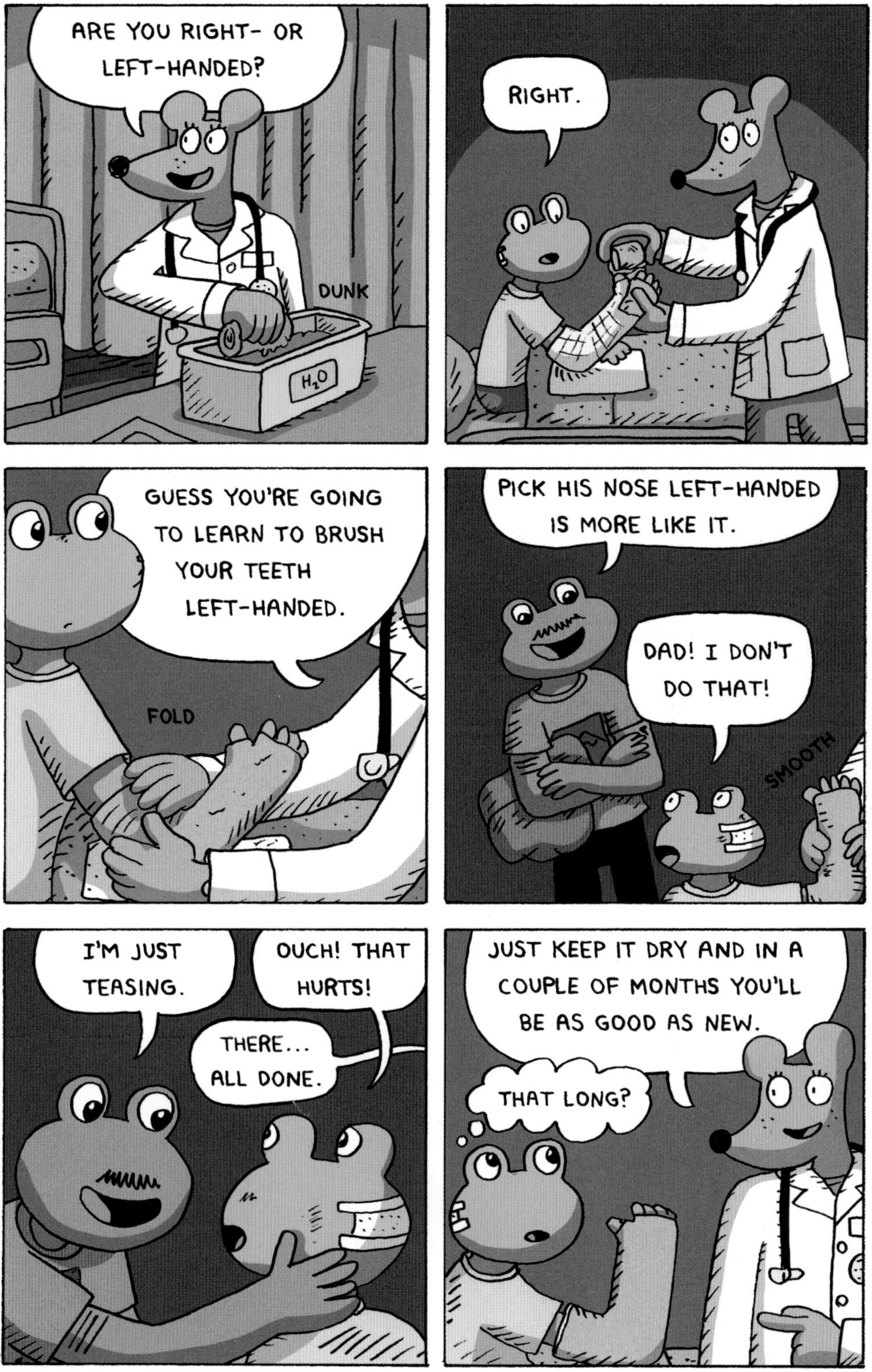
ARE YOU RIGHT- OR LEFT-HANDED?
DUNK
H2O
RIGHT.
GUESS YOU'RE GOING TO LEARN TO BRUSH YOUR TEETH LEFT-HANDED.
FOLD
PICK HIS NOSE LEFT-HANDED IS MORE LIKE IT.
DAD! I DON'T DO THAT!
SMOOTH
I'M JUST TEASING.
OUCH! THAT HURTS!
THERE... ALL DONE.
JUST KEEP IT DRY AND IN A COUPLE OF MONTHS YOU'LL BE AS GOOD AS NEW.
THAT LONG?

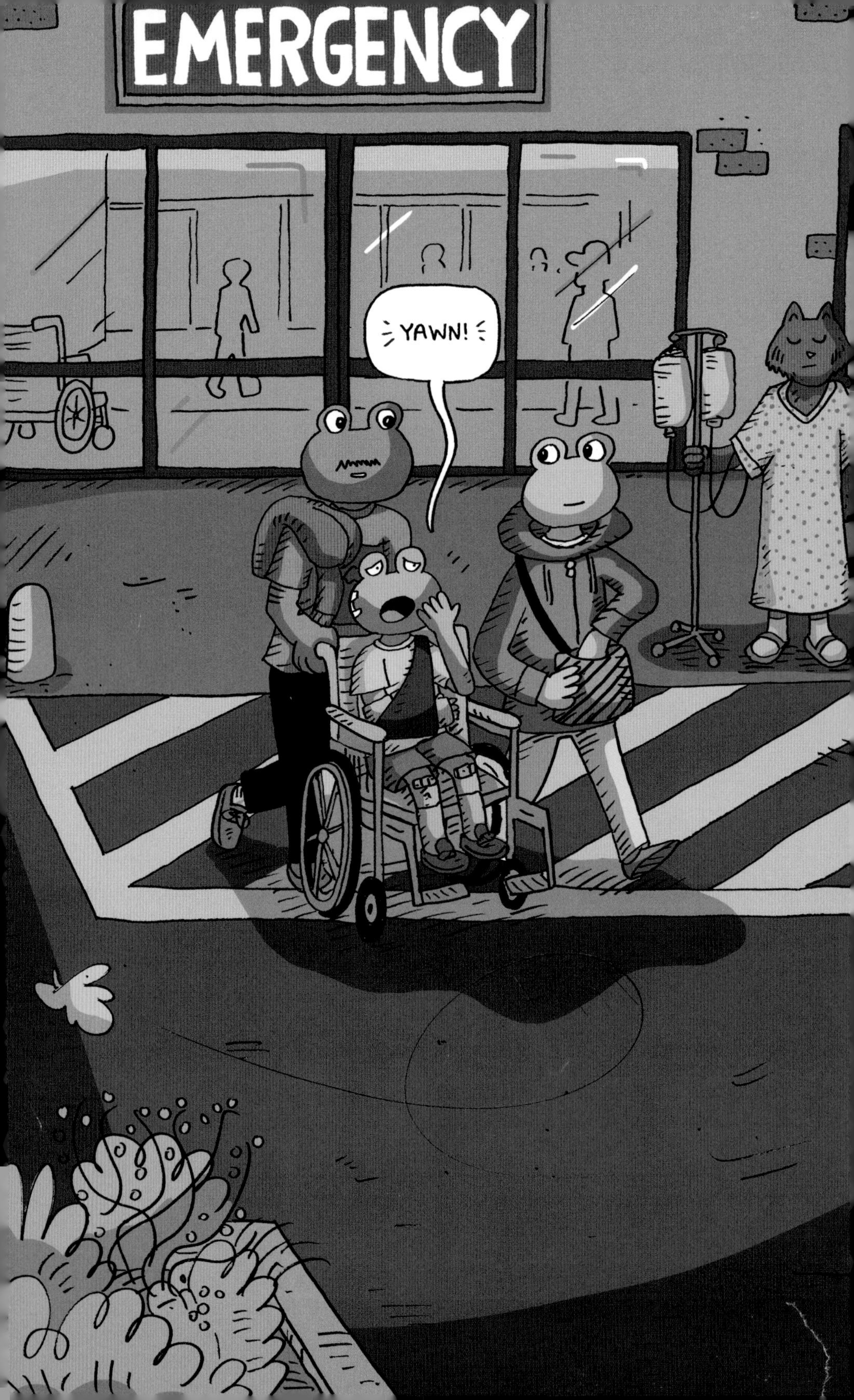
EMERGENCY
YAWN!

CHAPTER FIVE

The Day After

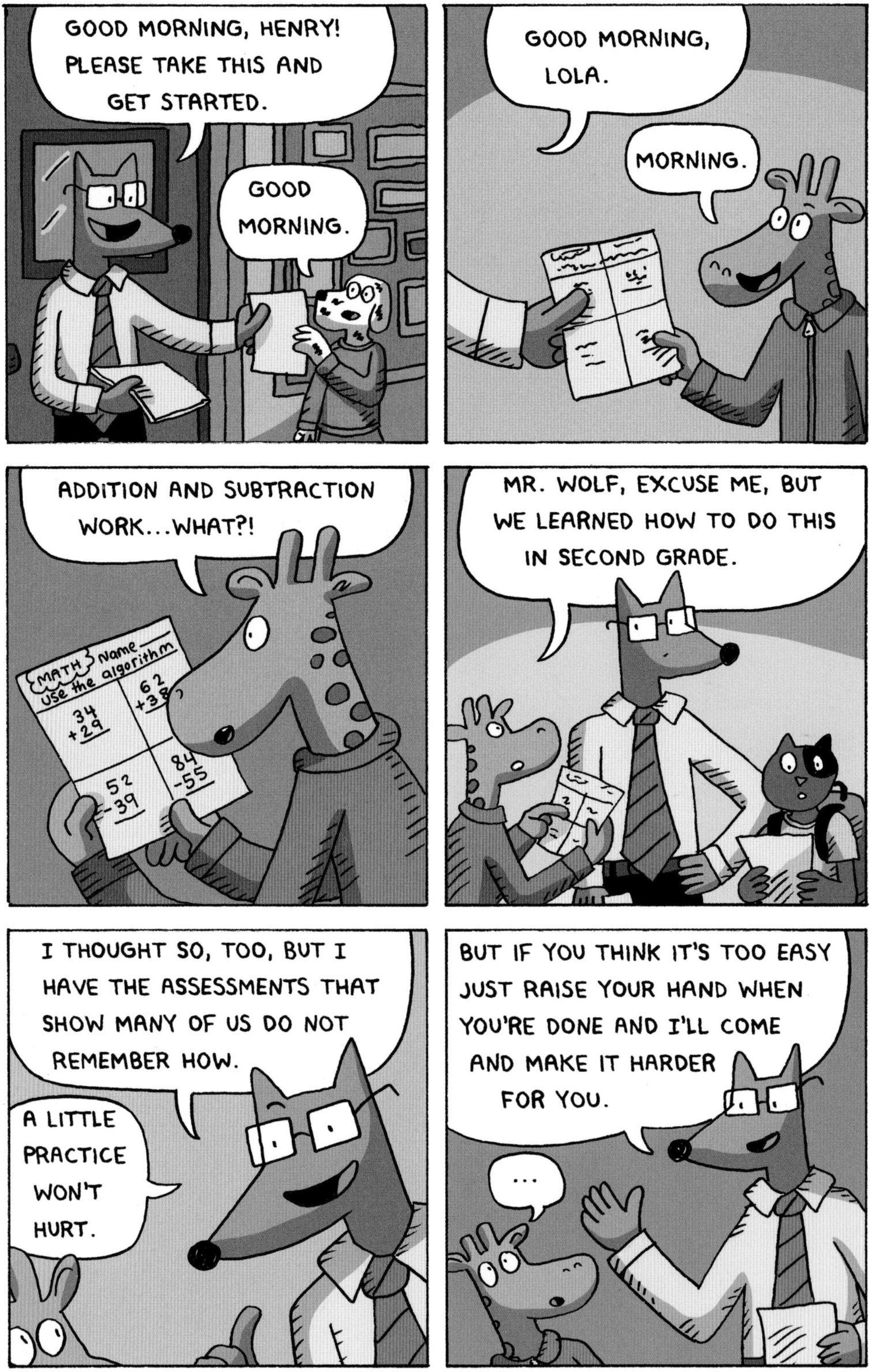
GOOD MORNING, HENRY! PLEASE TAKE THIS AND GET STARTED.
GOOD MORNING.
GOOD MORNING, LOLA.
MORNING.
ADDITION AND SUBTRACTION WORK...WHAT?!
MATH Name
Use the algorithm
34 +29
62 +38
52 -39
84 -55
MR. WOLF, EXCUSE ME, BUT WE LEARNED HOW TO DO THIS IN SECOND GRADE.
I THOUGHT SO, TOO, BUT I HAVE THE ASSESSMENTS THAT SHOW MANY OF US DO NOT REMEMBER HOW.
A LITTLE PRACTICE WON'T HURT.
BUT IF YOU THINK IT'S TOO EASY JUST RAISE YOUR HAND WHEN YOU'RE DONE AND I'LL COME AND MAKE IT HARDER FOR YOU.
...

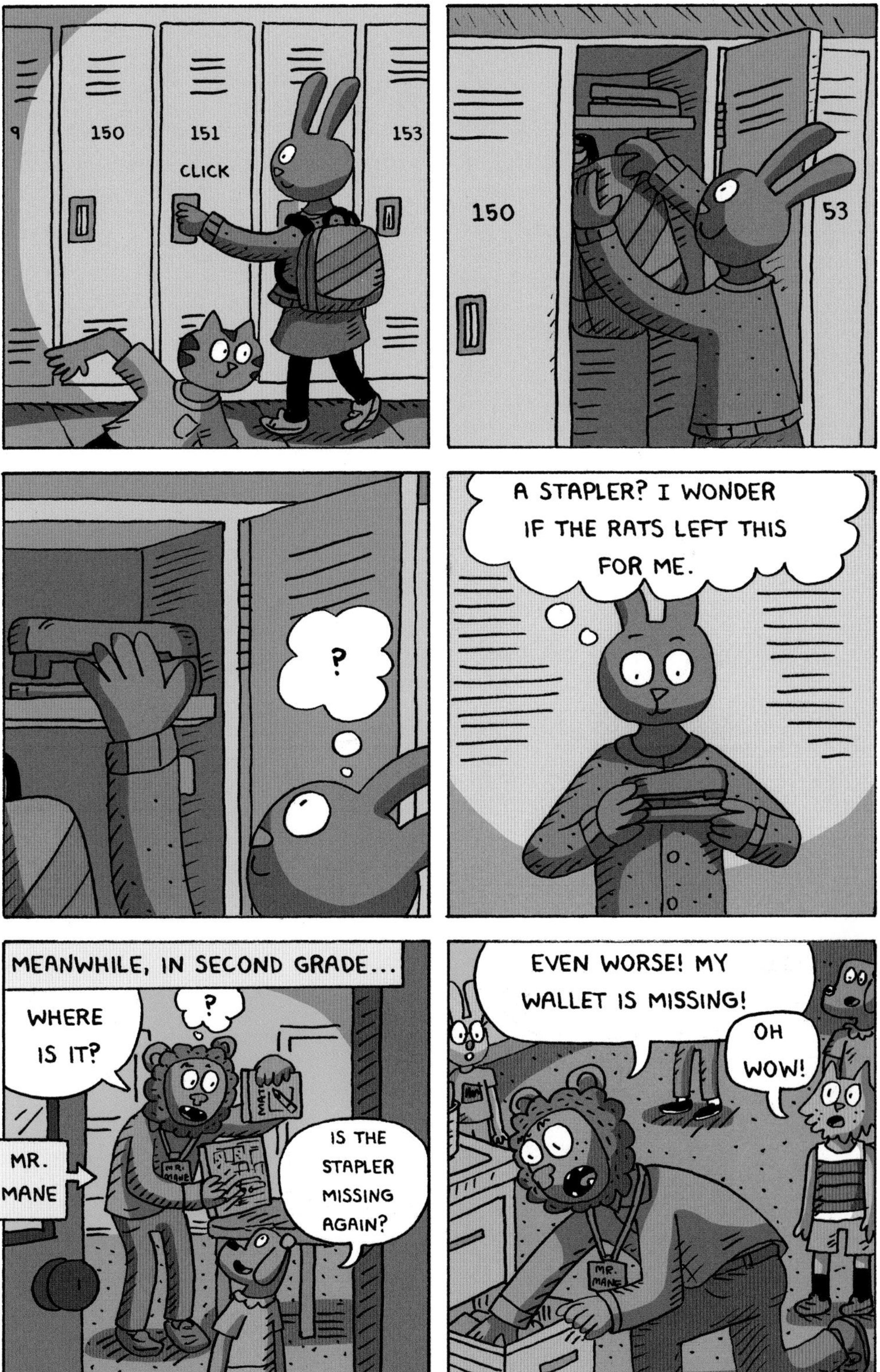
150
151
153
CLICK
150
53
?
A STAPLER? I WONDER IF THE RATS LEFT THIS FOR ME.
MEANWHILE, IN SECOND GRADE...
WHERE IS IT?
?
MR. MANE
IS THE STAPLER MISSING AGAIN?
EVEN WORSE! MY WALLET IS MISSING!
OH WOW!

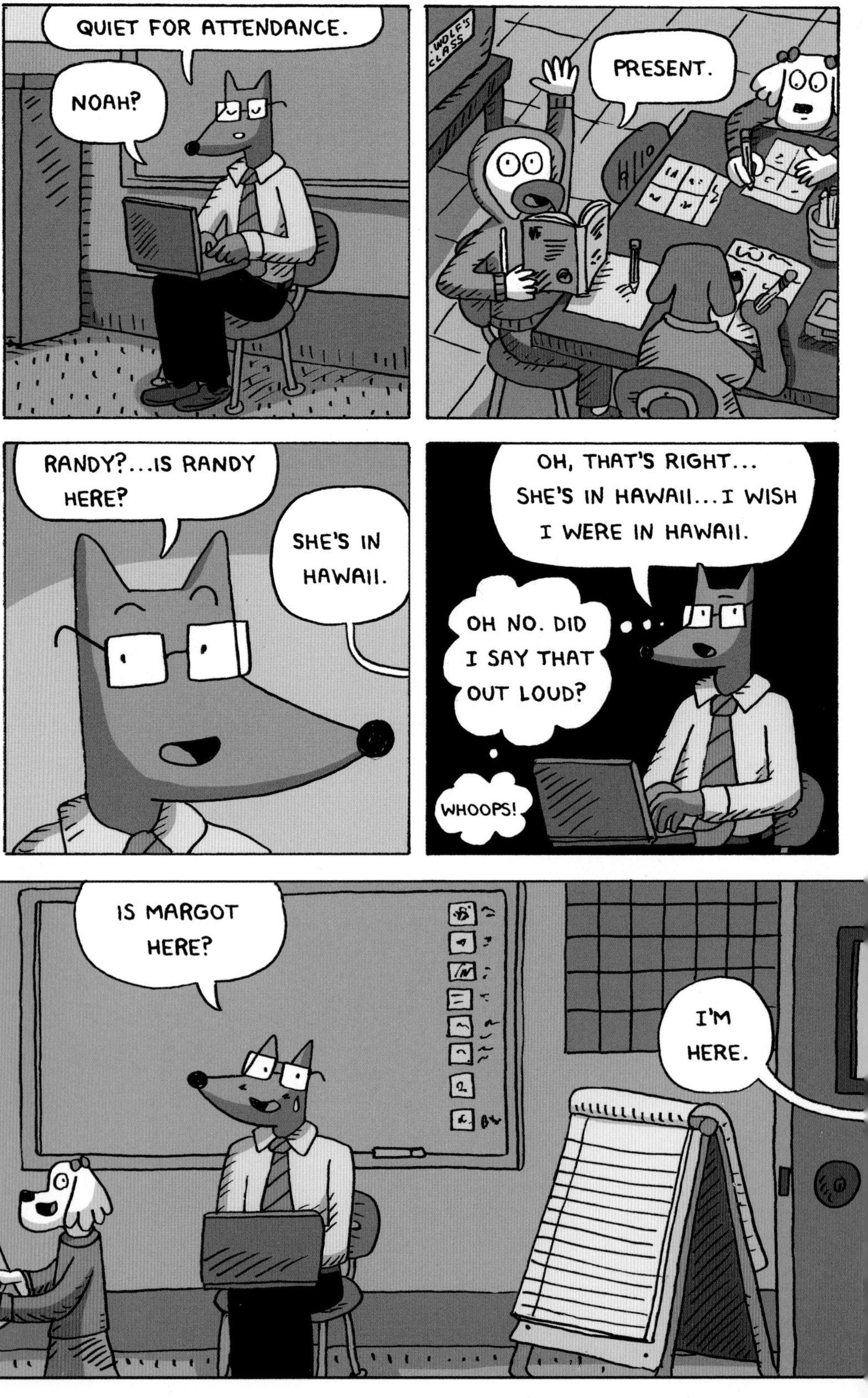
QUIET FOR ATTENDANCE.
NOAH?
WOLF'S CLASS
PRESENT.
RANDY?...IS RANDY HERE?
SHE'S IN HAWAII.
OH, THAT'S RIGHT... SHE'S IN HAWAII...I WISH I WERE IN HAWAII.
OH NO. DID I SAY THAT OUT LOUD?
WHOOPS!
IS MARGOT HERE?
I'M HERE.

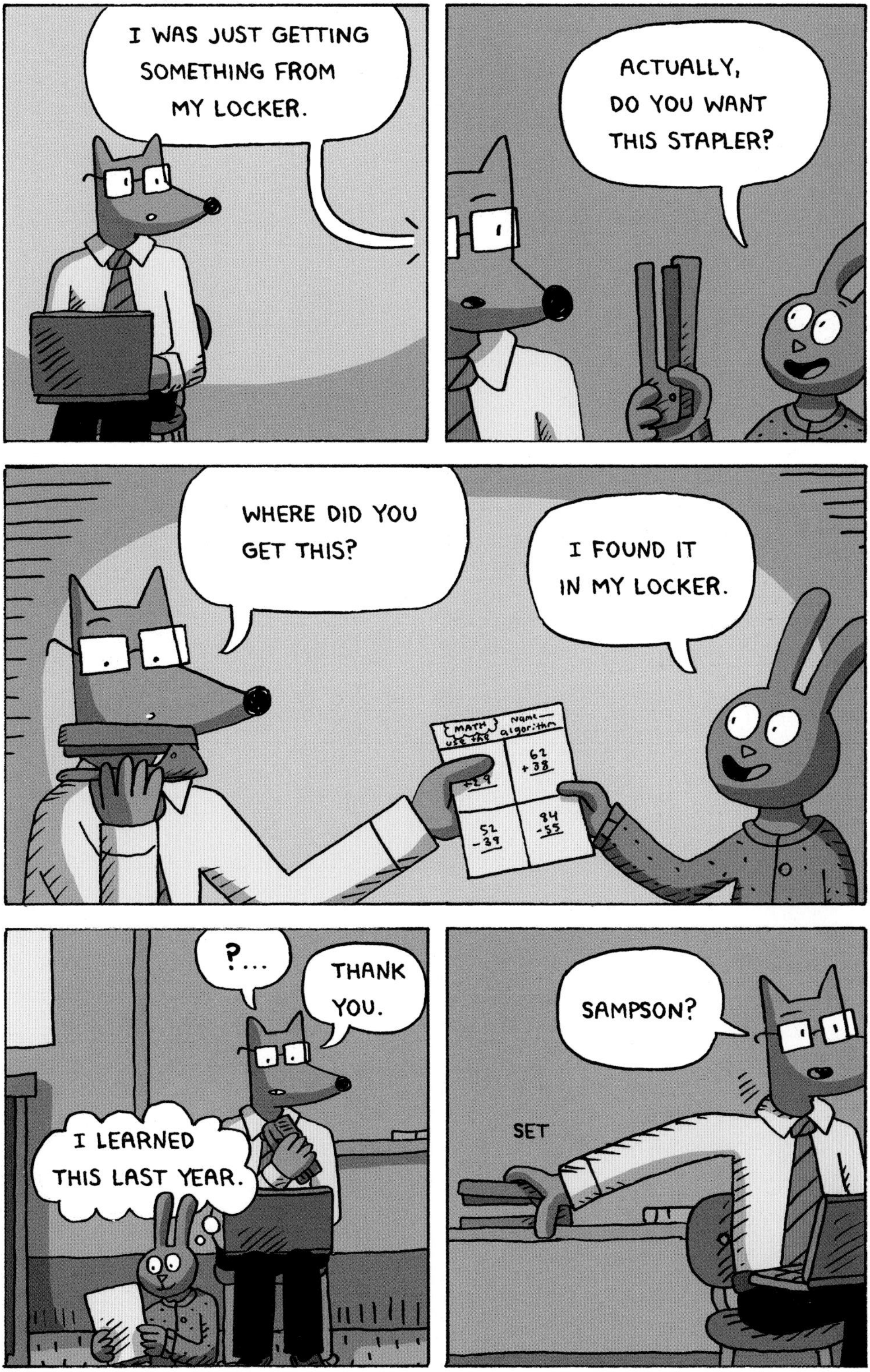
I WAS JUST GETTING SOMETHING FROM MY LOCKER.
ACTUALLY, DO YOU WANT THIS STAPLER?
WHERE DID YOU GET THIS?
I FOUND IT IN MY LOCKER.
MATH
?...
THANK YOU.
I LEARNED THIS LAST YEAR.
SAMPSON?
SET

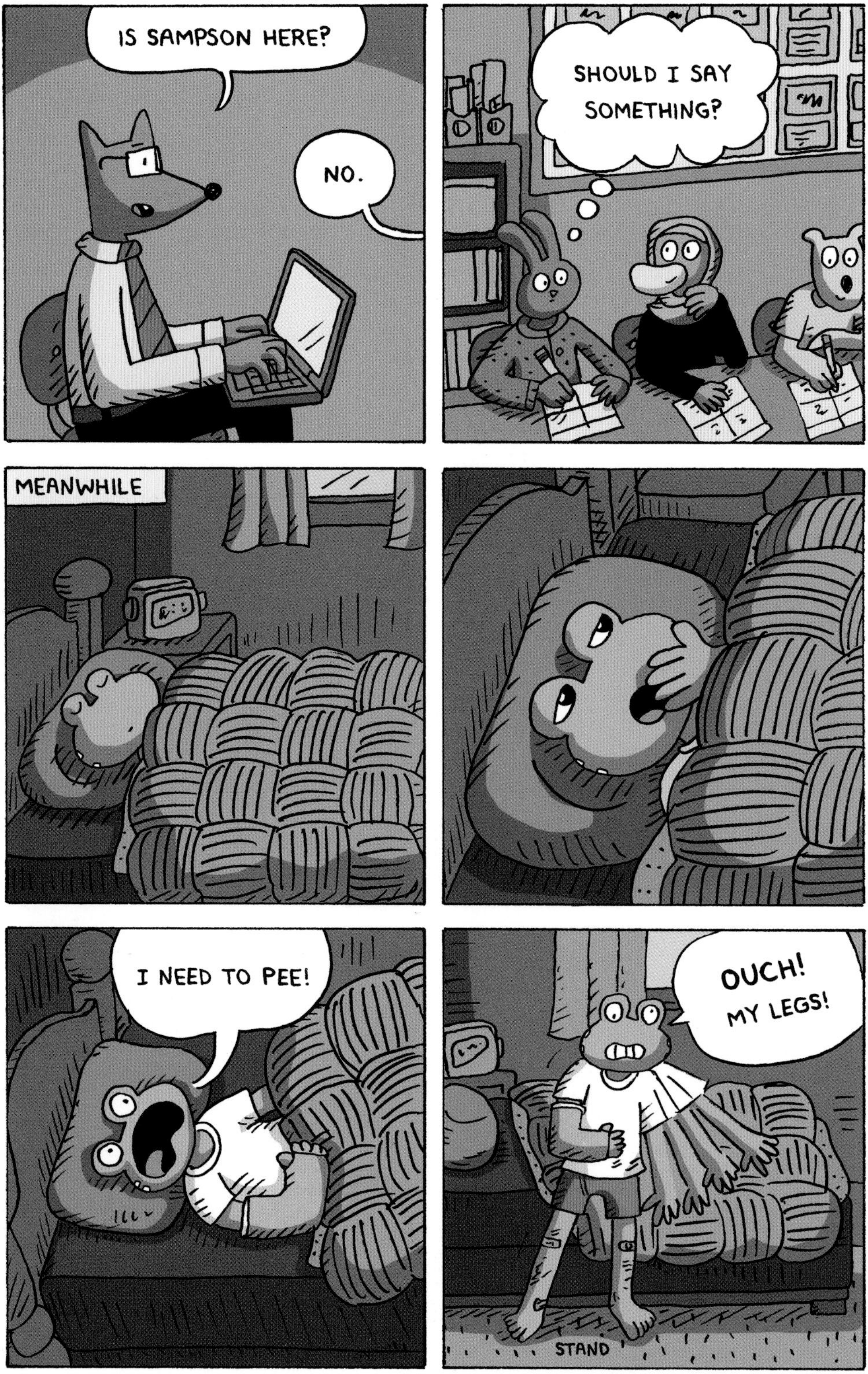
IS SAMPSON HERE?
NO.
SHOULD I SAY SOMETHING?
MEANWHILE
I NEED TO PEE!
OUCH! MY LEGS!
STAND

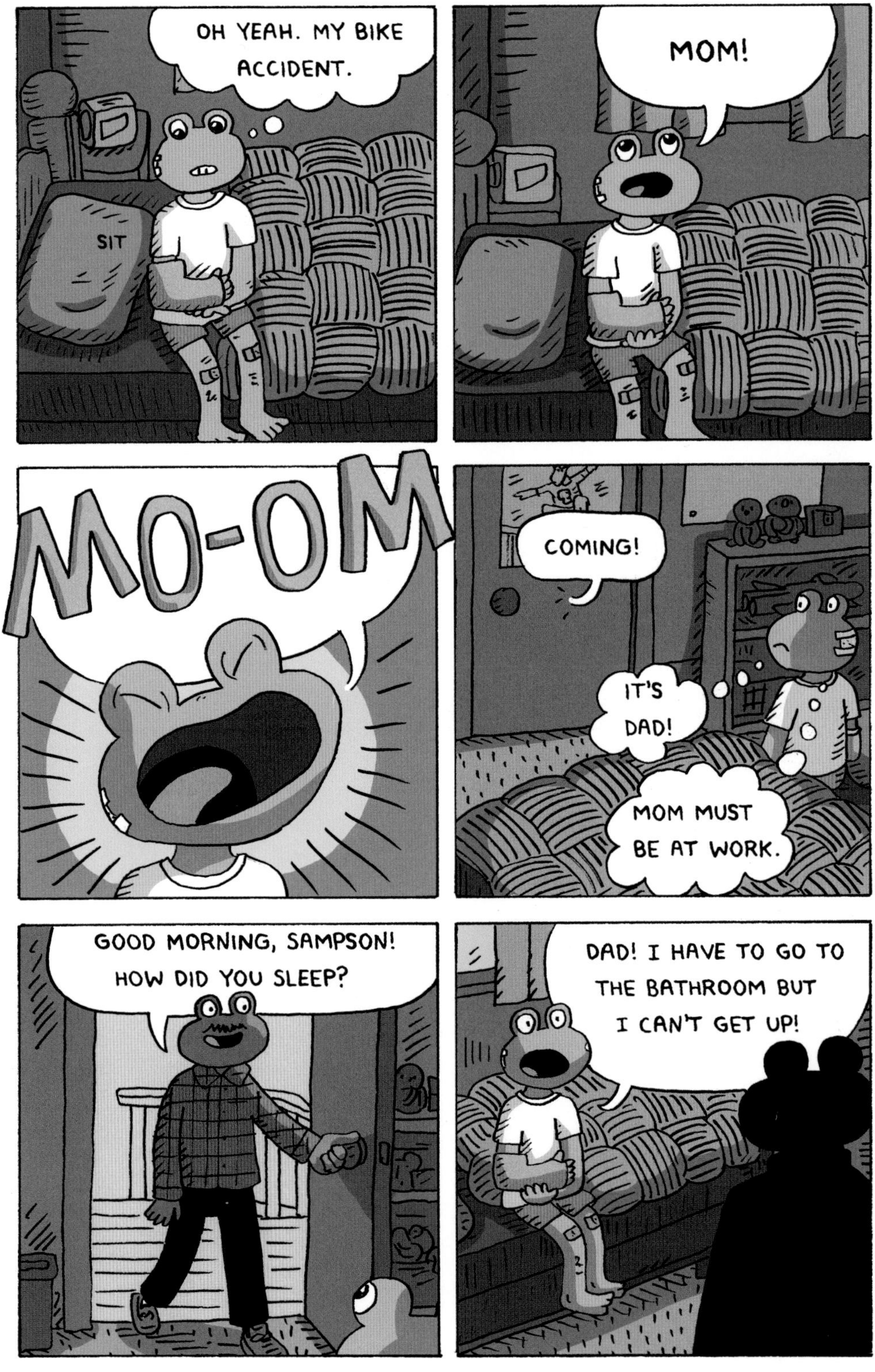
OH YEAH. MY BIKE ACCIDENT.
SIT
MOM!
MO-OM
COMING!
IT'S DAD!
MOM MUST BE AT WORK.
GOOD MORNING, SAMPSON! HOW DID YOU SLEEP?
DAD! I HAVE TO GO TO THE BATHROOM BUT I CAN'T GET UP!

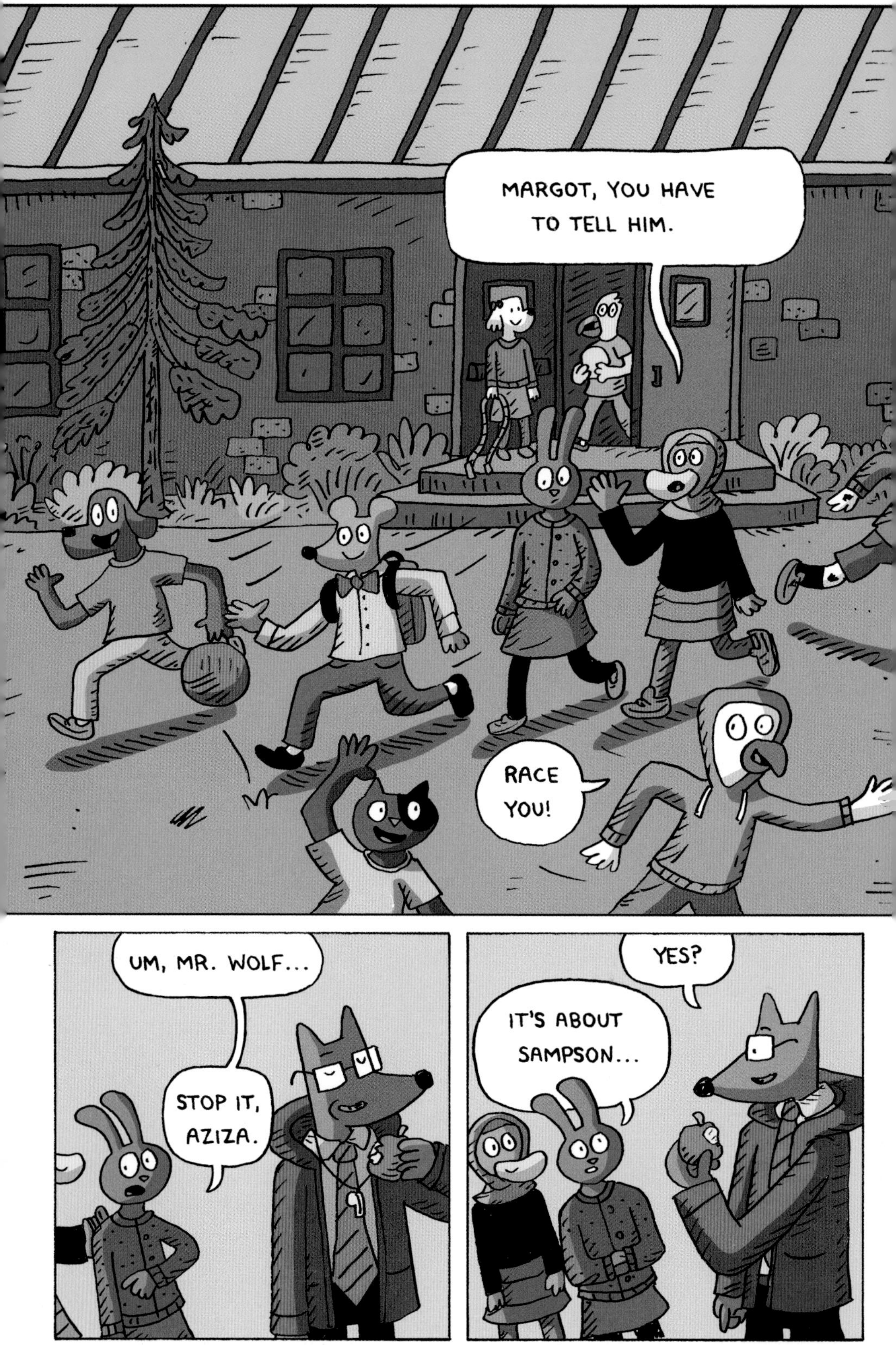
MARGOT, YOU HAVE TO TELL HIM.
RACE YOU!
UM, MR. WOLF...
STOP IT, AZIZA.
YES?
IT'S ABOUT SAMPSON...

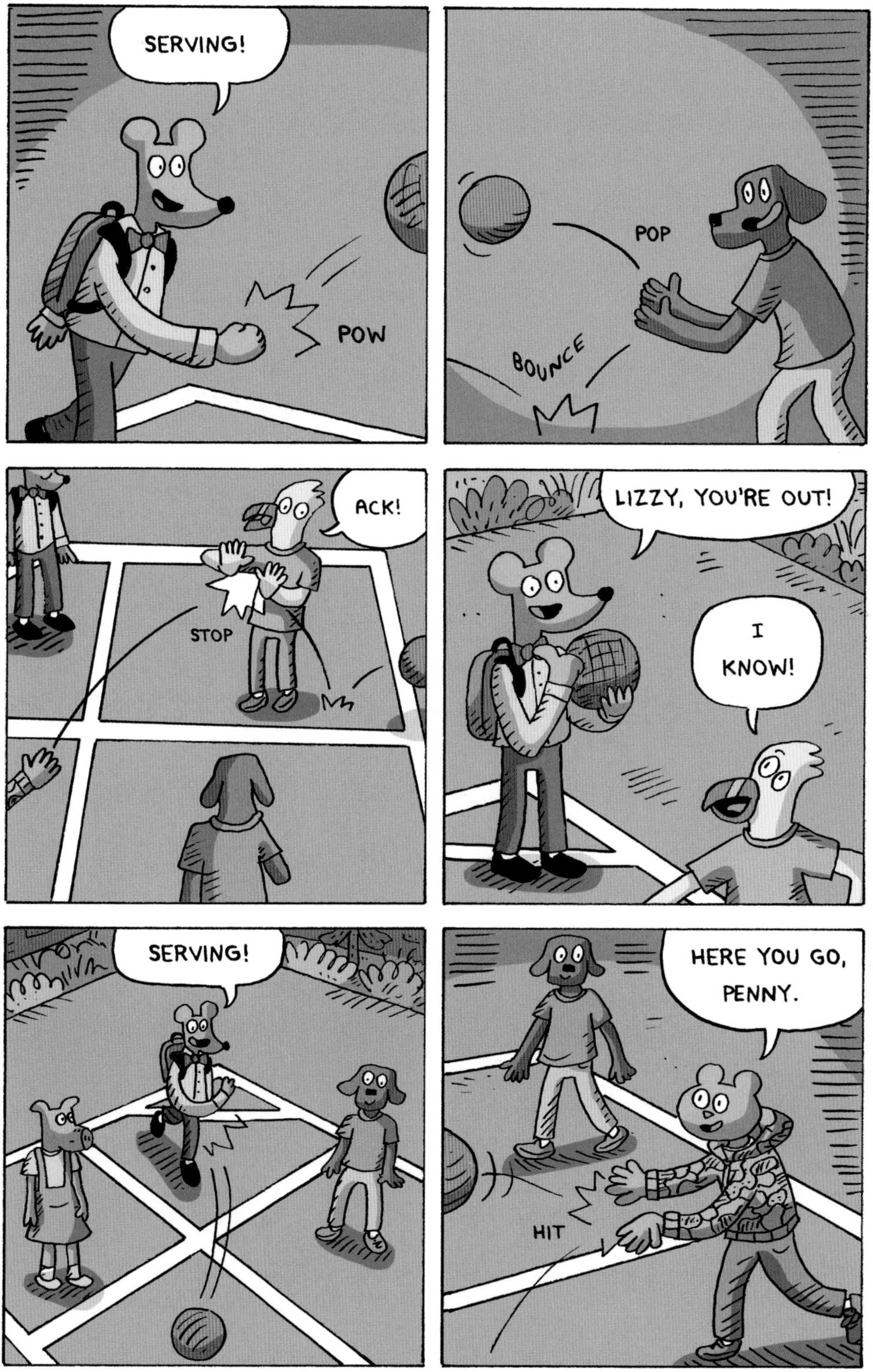
SERVING!
POW
POP
BOUNCE
ACK!
STOP
LIZZY, YOU'RE OUT!
I KNOW!
SERVING!
HERE YOU GO, PENNY.
HIT

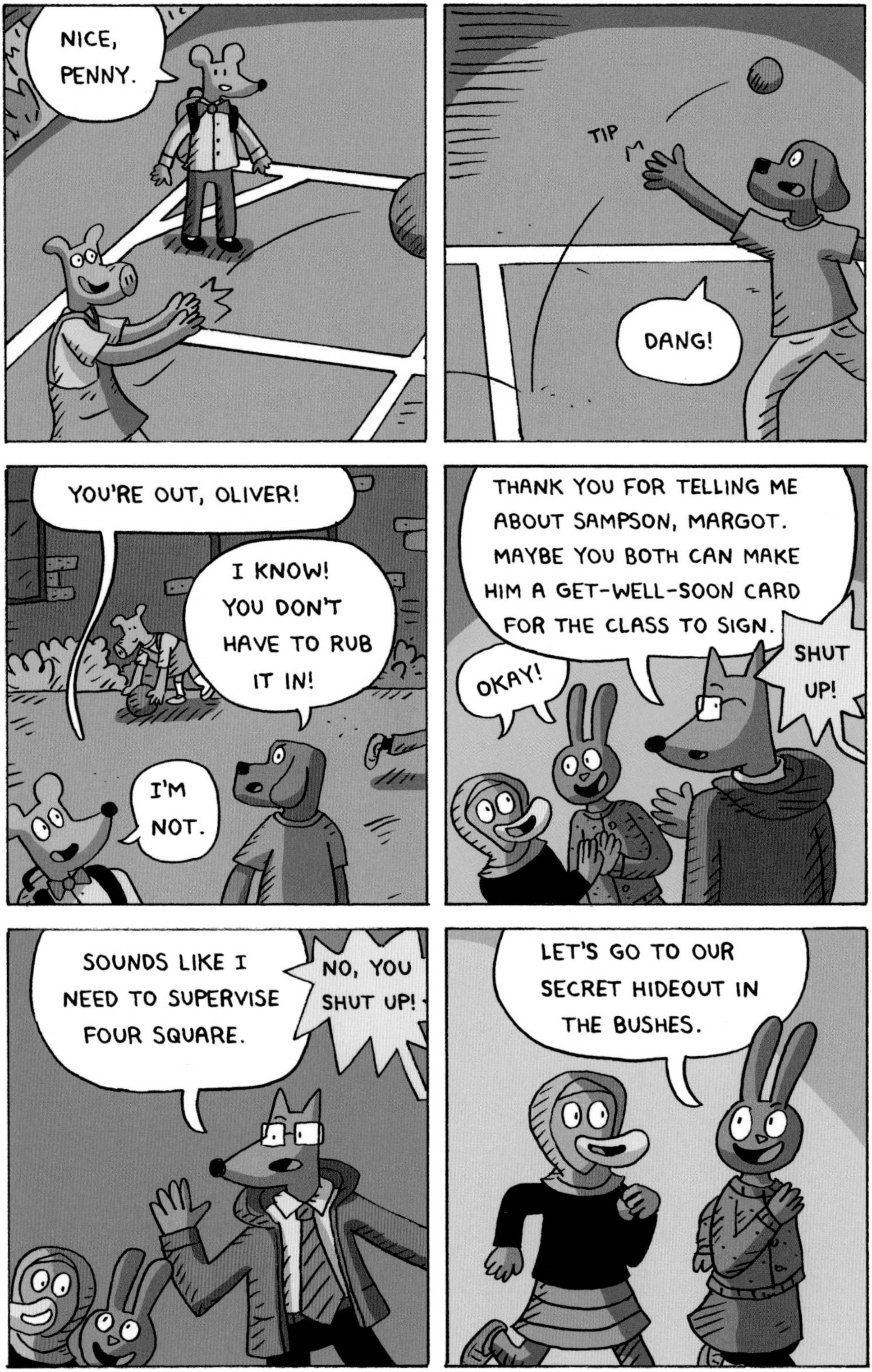
NICE, PENNY.
TIP
DANG!
YOU'RE OUT, OLIVER!
I KNOW! YOU DON'T HAVE TO RUB IT IN!
I'M NOT.
THANK YOU FOR TELLING ME ABOUT SAMPSON, MARGOT. MAYBE YOU BOTH CAN MAKE HIM A GET-WELL-SOON CARD FOR THE CLASS TO SIGN.
SHUT UP!
OKAY!
SOUNDS LIKE I NEED TO SUPERVISE FOUR SQUARE.
NO, YOU SHUT UP!
LET'S GO TO OUR SECRET HIDEOUT IN THE BUSHES.

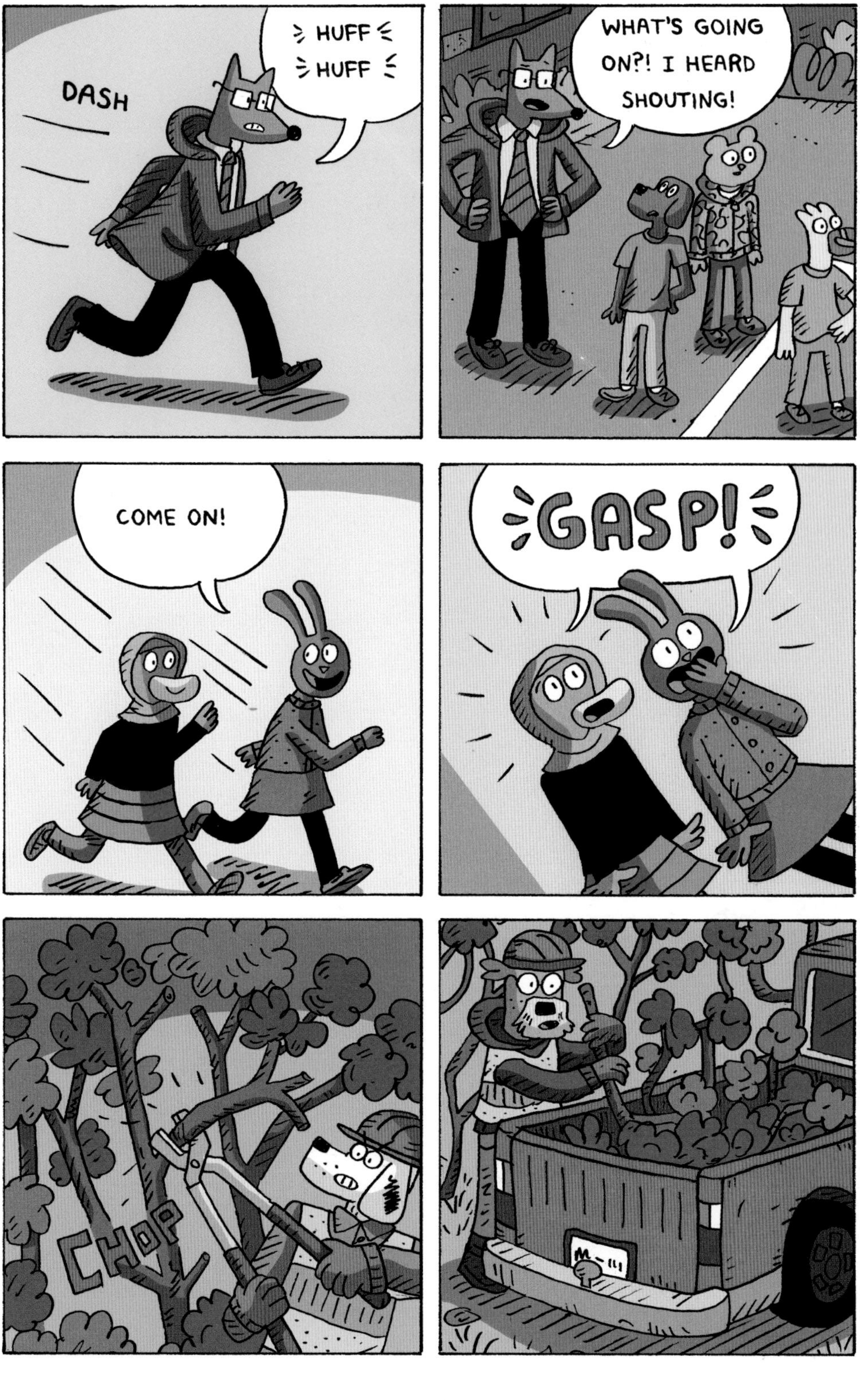
DASH
HUFF
HUFF
WHAT'S GOING ON?! I HEARD SHOUTING!
COME ON!
GASP!
CHOP
M-111

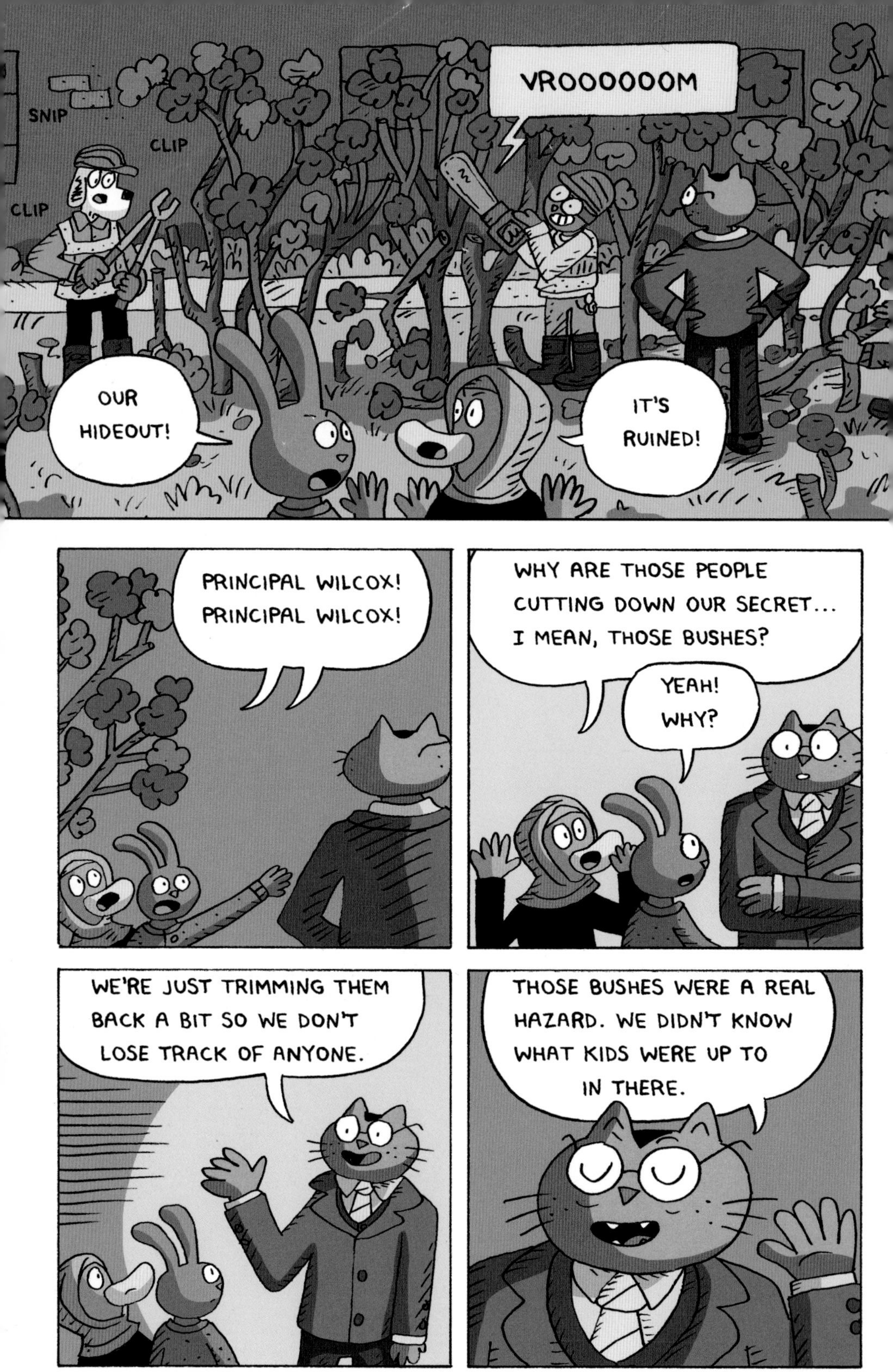
SNIP
CLIP
CLIP
VROOOOOOM
OUR HIDEOUT!
IT'S RUINED!
PRINCIPAL WILCOX! PRINCIPAL WILCOX!
WHY ARE THOSE PEOPLE CUTTING DOWN OUR SECRET... I MEAN, THOSE BUSHES?
YEAH! WHY?
WE'RE JUST TRIMMING THEM BACK A BIT SO WE DON'T LOSE TRACK OF ANYONE.
THOSE BUSHES WERE A REAL HAZARD. WE DIDN'T KNOW WHAT KIDS WERE UP TO IN THERE.

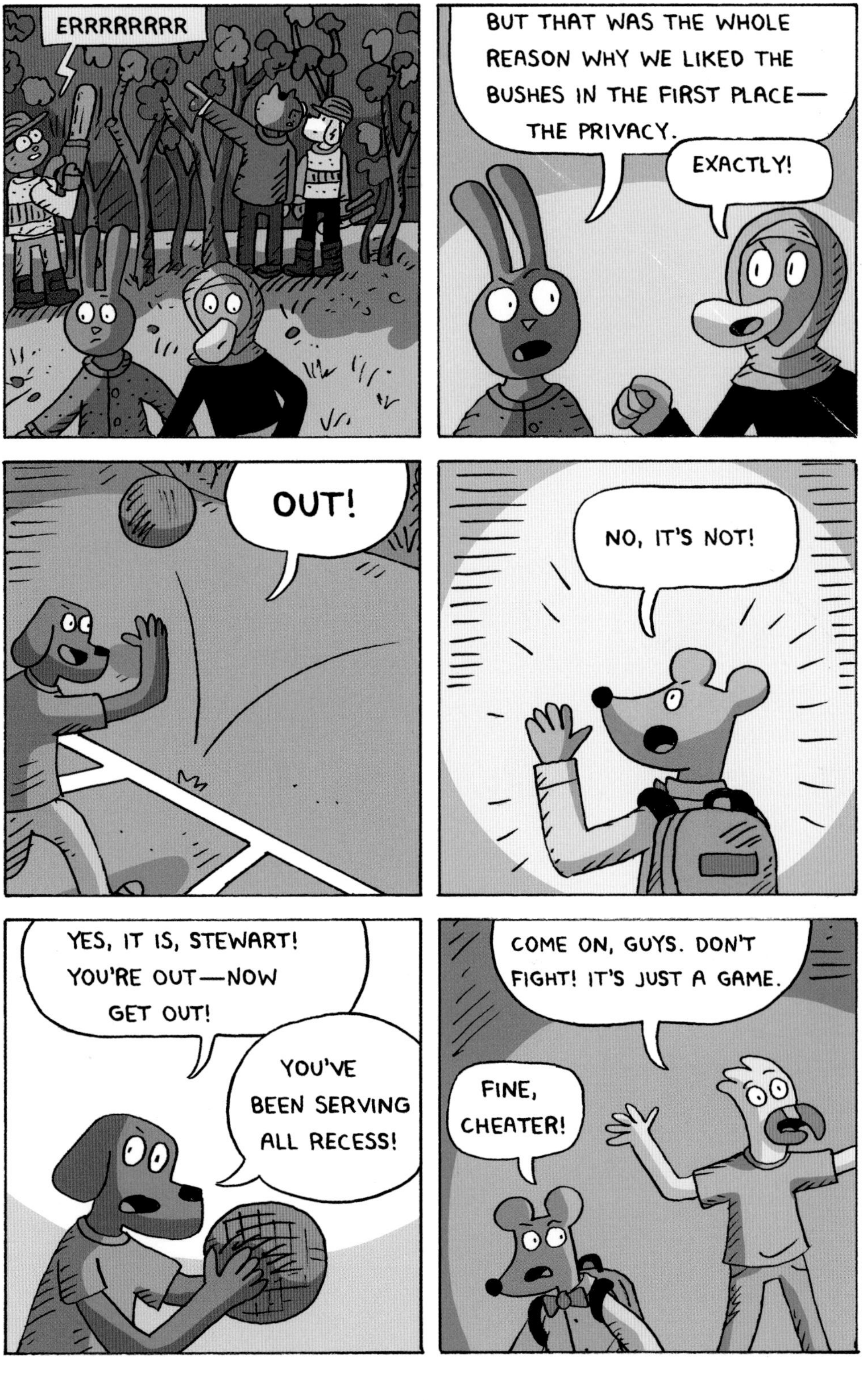
ERRRRRRRR
BUT THAT WAS THE WHOLE REASON WHY WE LIKED THE BUSHES IN THE FIRST PLACE— THE PRIVACY.
EXACTLY!
OUT!
NO, IT'S NOT!
YES, IT IS, STEWART! YOU'RE OUT—NOW GET OUT!
YOU'VE BEEN SERVING ALL RECESS!
COME ON, GUYS. DON'T FIGHT! IT'S JUST A GAME.
FINE, CHEATER!

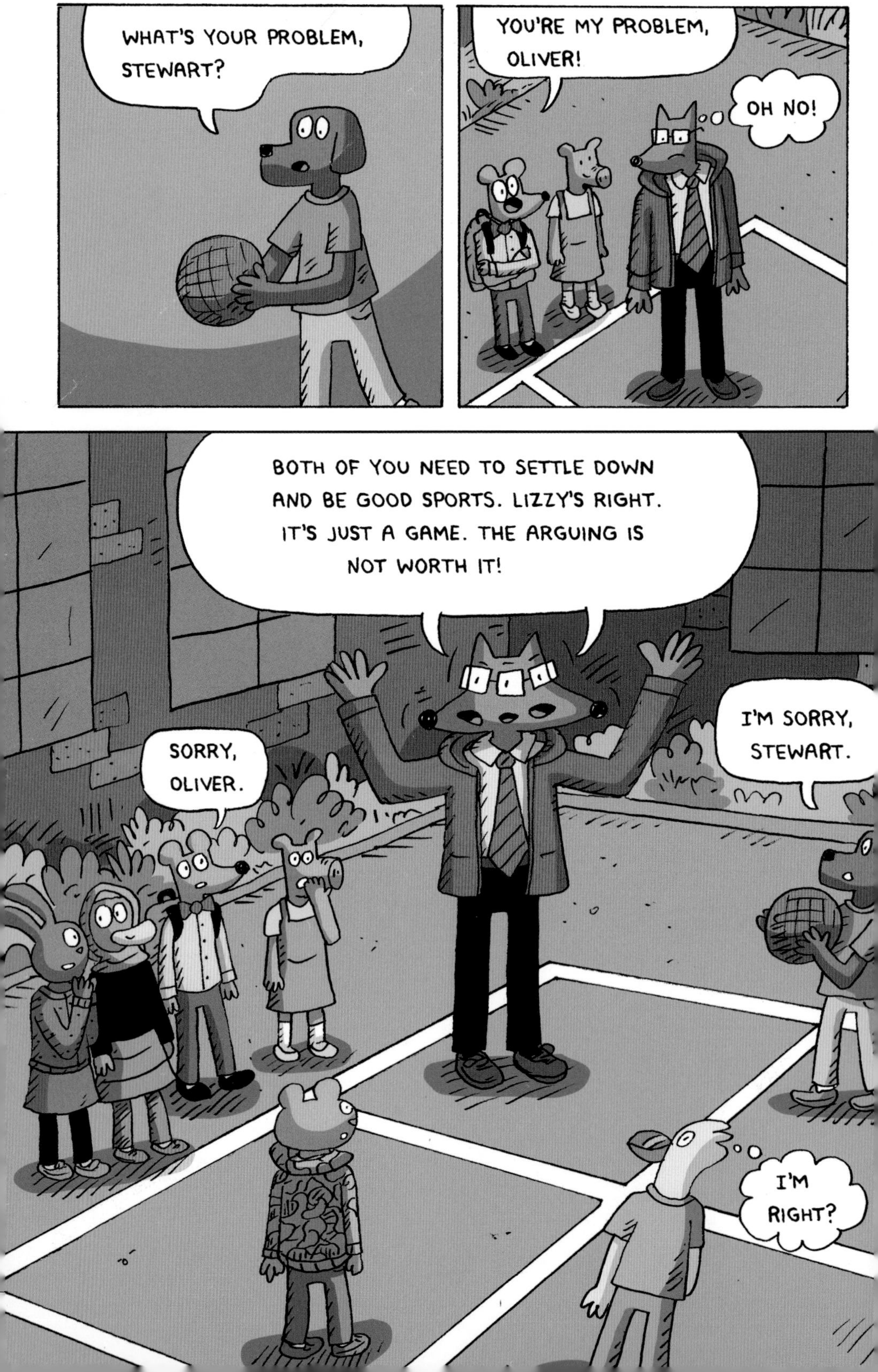
WHAT'S YOUR PROBLEM, STEWART?
YOU'RE MY PROBLEM, OLIVER!
OH NO!
BOTH OF YOU NEED TO SETTLE DOWN AND BE GOOD SPORTS. LIZZY'S RIGHT. IT'S JUST A GAME. THE ARGUING IS NOT WORTH IT!
SORRY, OLIVER.
I'M SORRY, STEWART.
I'M RIGHT?

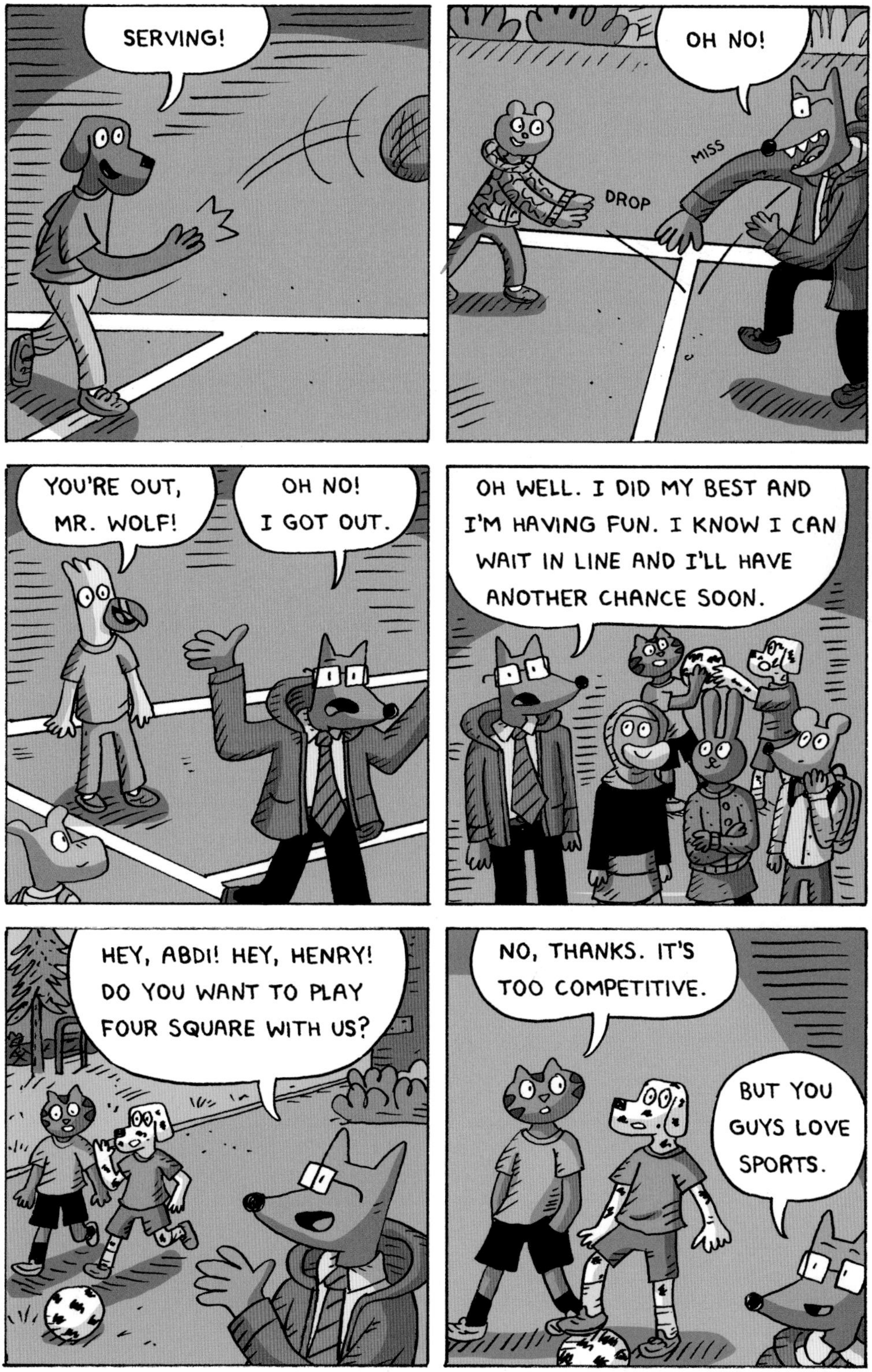
SERVING!
OH NO!
MISS
DROP
YOU'RE OUT, MR. WOLF!
OH NO! I GOT OUT.
OH WELL. I DID MY BEST AND I'M HAVING FUN. I KNOW I CAN WAIT IN LINE AND I'LL HAVE ANOTHER CHANCE SOON.
HEY, ABDI! HEY, HENRY! DO YOU WANT TO PLAY FOUR SQUARE WITH US?
NO, THANKS. IT'S TOO COMPETITIVE.
BUT YOU GUYS LOVE SPORTS.

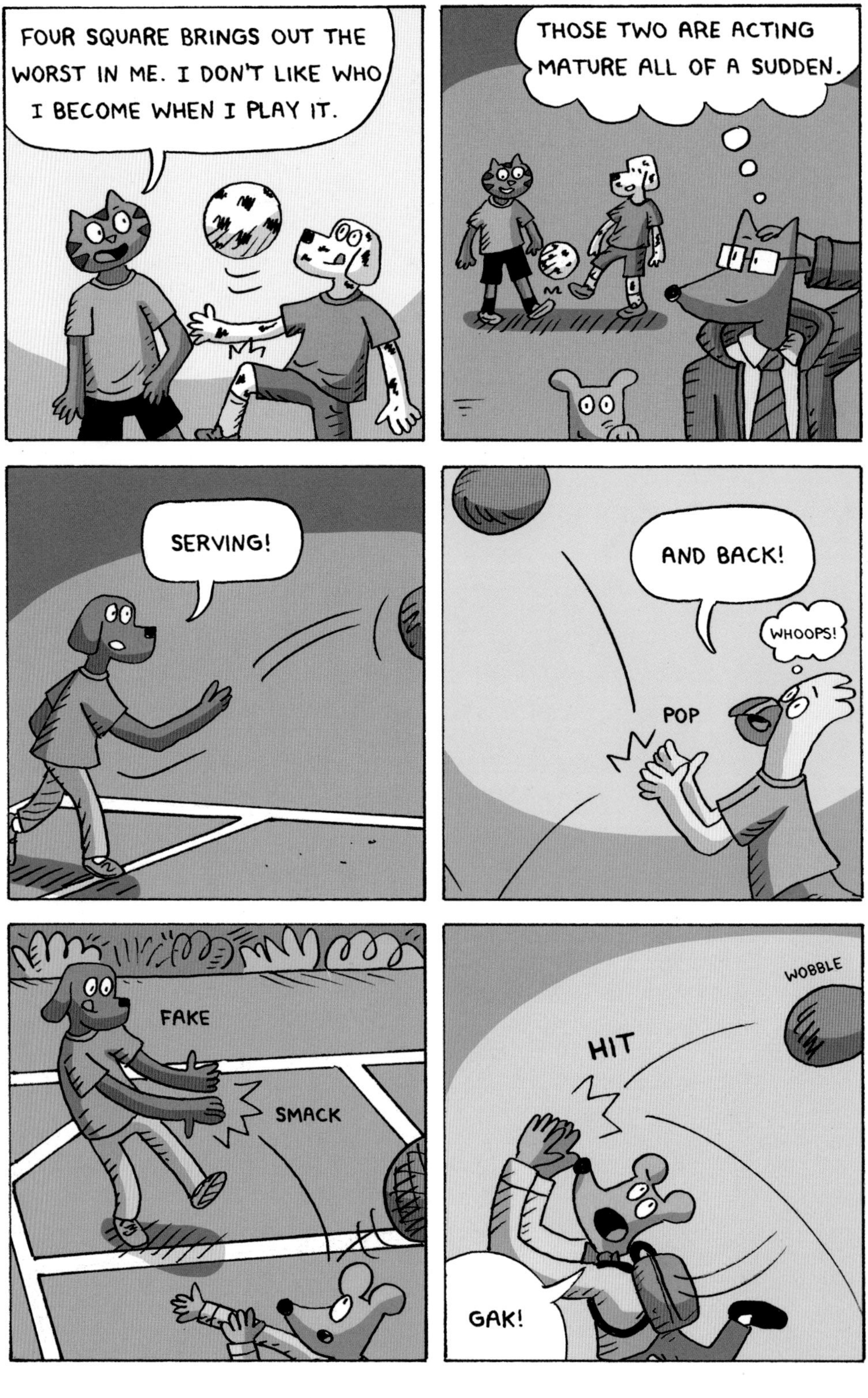
FOUR SQUARE BRINGS OUT THE WORST IN ME. I DON'T LIKE WHO I BECOME WHEN I PLAY IT.
THOSE TWO ARE ACTING MATURE ALL OF A SUDDEN.
SERVING!
AND BACK!
WHOOPS!
POP
FAKE
SMACK
WOBBLE
HIT
GAK!

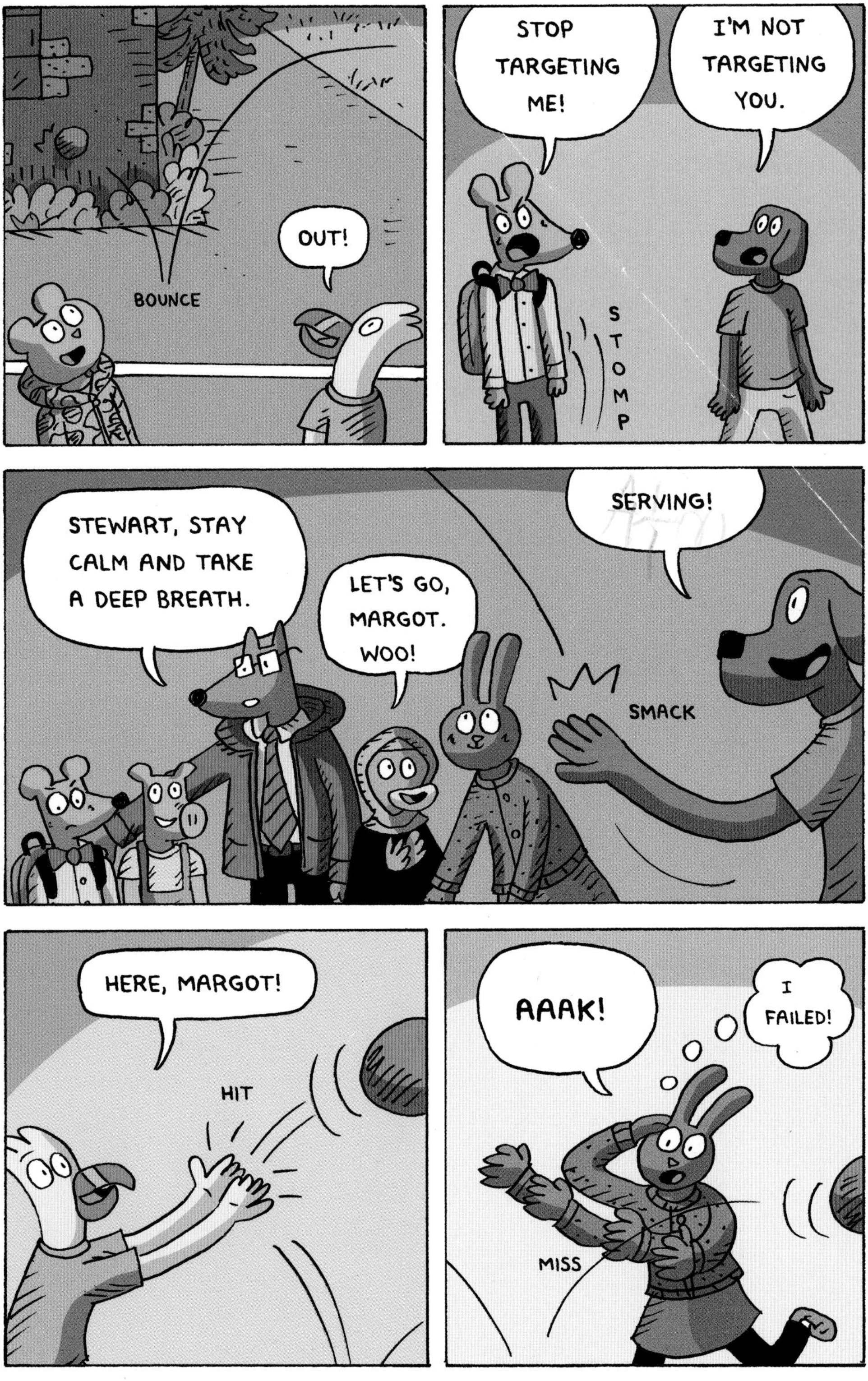
BOUNCE
OUT!
STOP TARGETING ME!
I'M NOT TARGETING YOU.
STOMP
STEWART, STAY CALM AND TAKE A DEEP BREATH.
LET'S GO, MARGOT. WOO!
SERVING!
SMACK
HERE, MARGOT!
HIT
AAAK!
I FAILED!
MISS

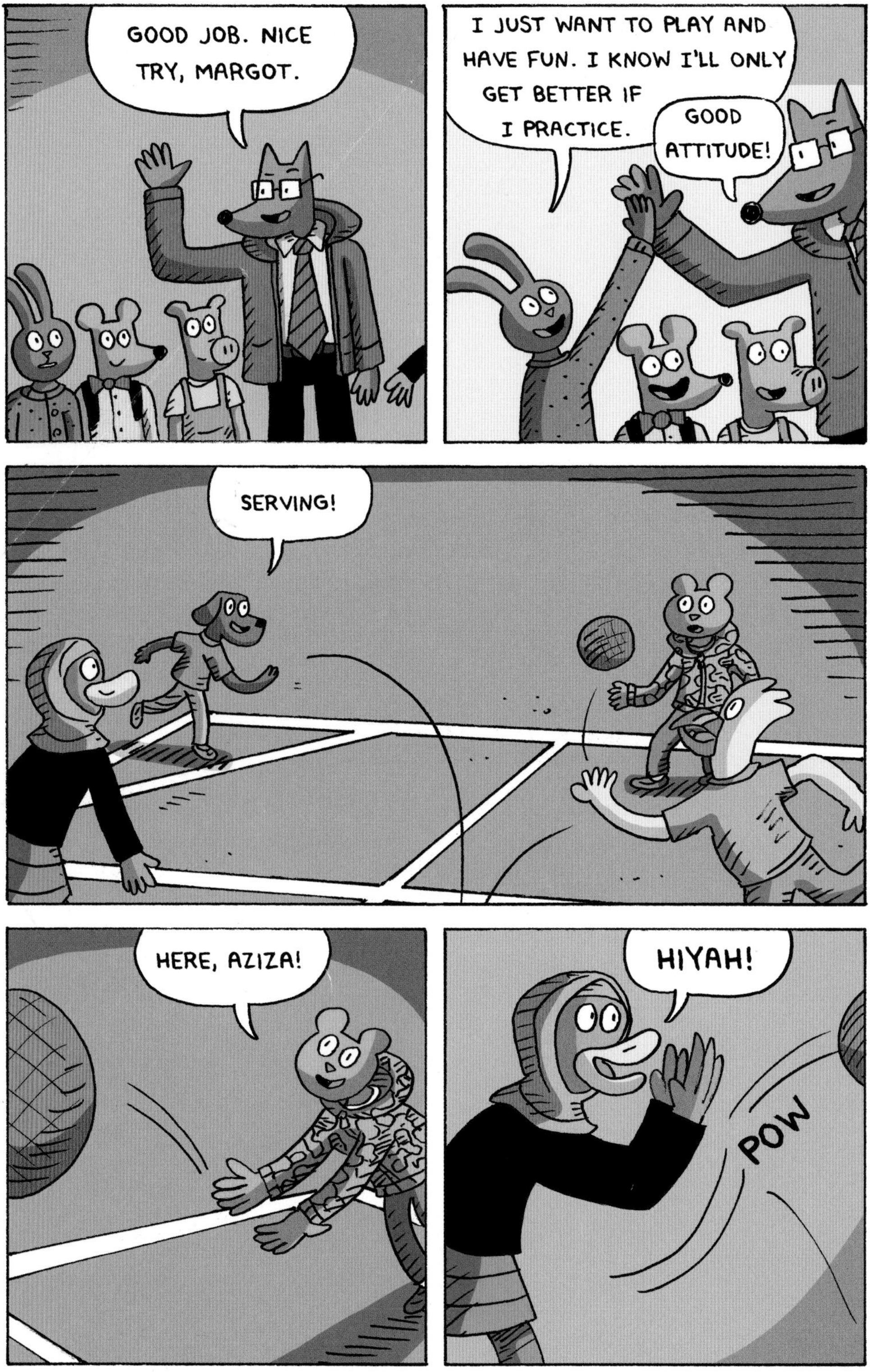

GOOD JOB. NICE TRY, MARGOT.
I JUST WANT TO PLAY AND HAVE FUN. I KNOW I'LL ONLY GET BETTER IF I PRACTICE.
GOOD ATTITUDE!
SERVING!
HERE, AZIZA!
HIYAH!
POW

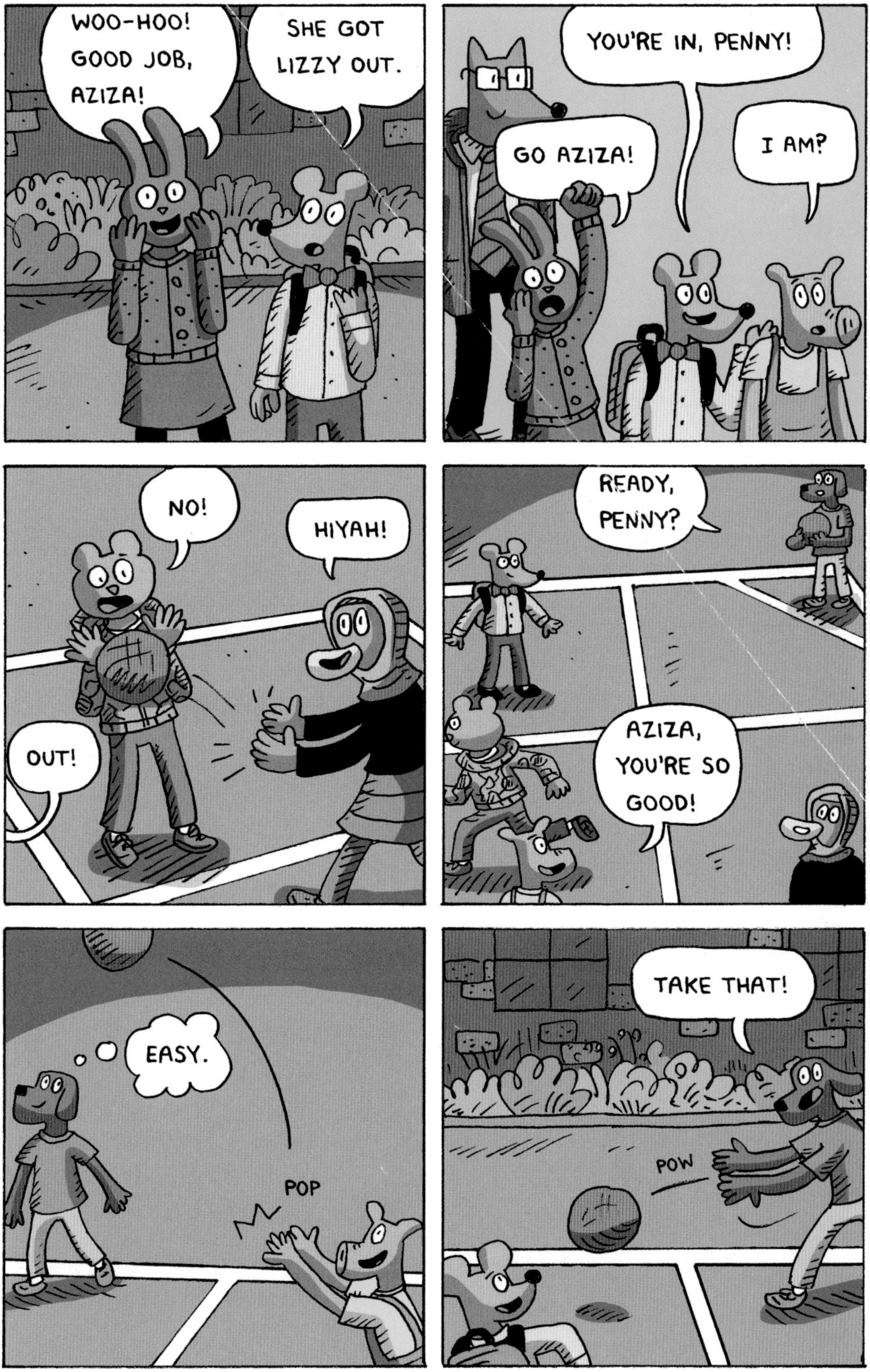
WOO-HOO! GOOD JOB, AZIZA!
SHE GOT LIZZY OUT.
YOU'RE IN, PENNY!
GO AZIZA!
I AM?
NO!
HIYAH!
OUT!
READY, PENNY?
AZIZA, YOU'RE SO GOOD!
EASY.
POP
TAKE THAT!
POW

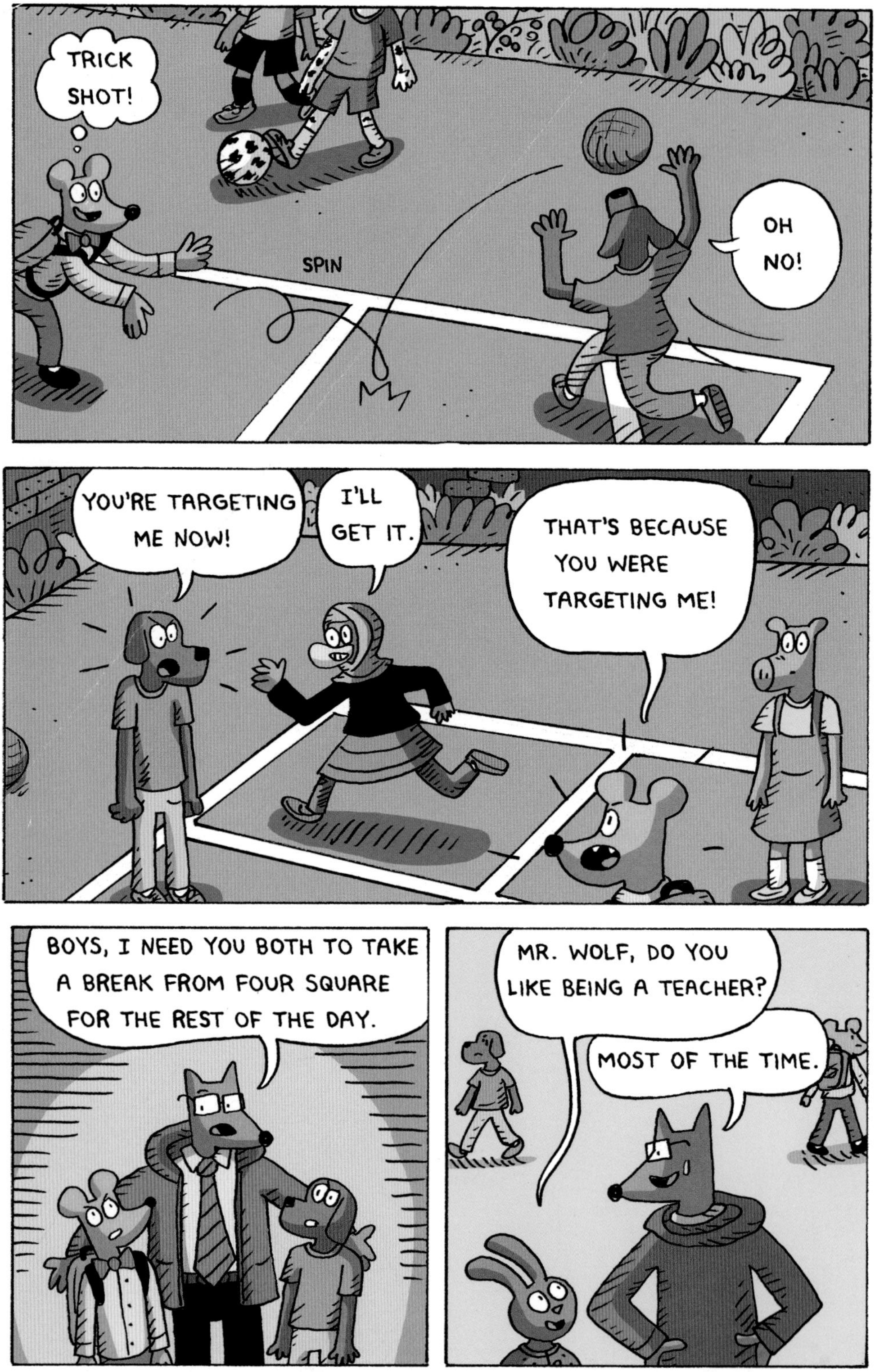
TRICK SHOT!
SPIN
OH NO!
YOU'RE TARGETING ME NOW!
I'LL GET IT.
THAT'S BECAUSE YOU WERE TARGETING ME!
BOYS, I NEED YOU BOTH TO TAKE A BREAK FROM FOUR SQUARE FOR THE REST OF THE DAY.
MR. WOLF, DO YOU LIKE BEING A TEACHER?
MOST OF THE TIME.

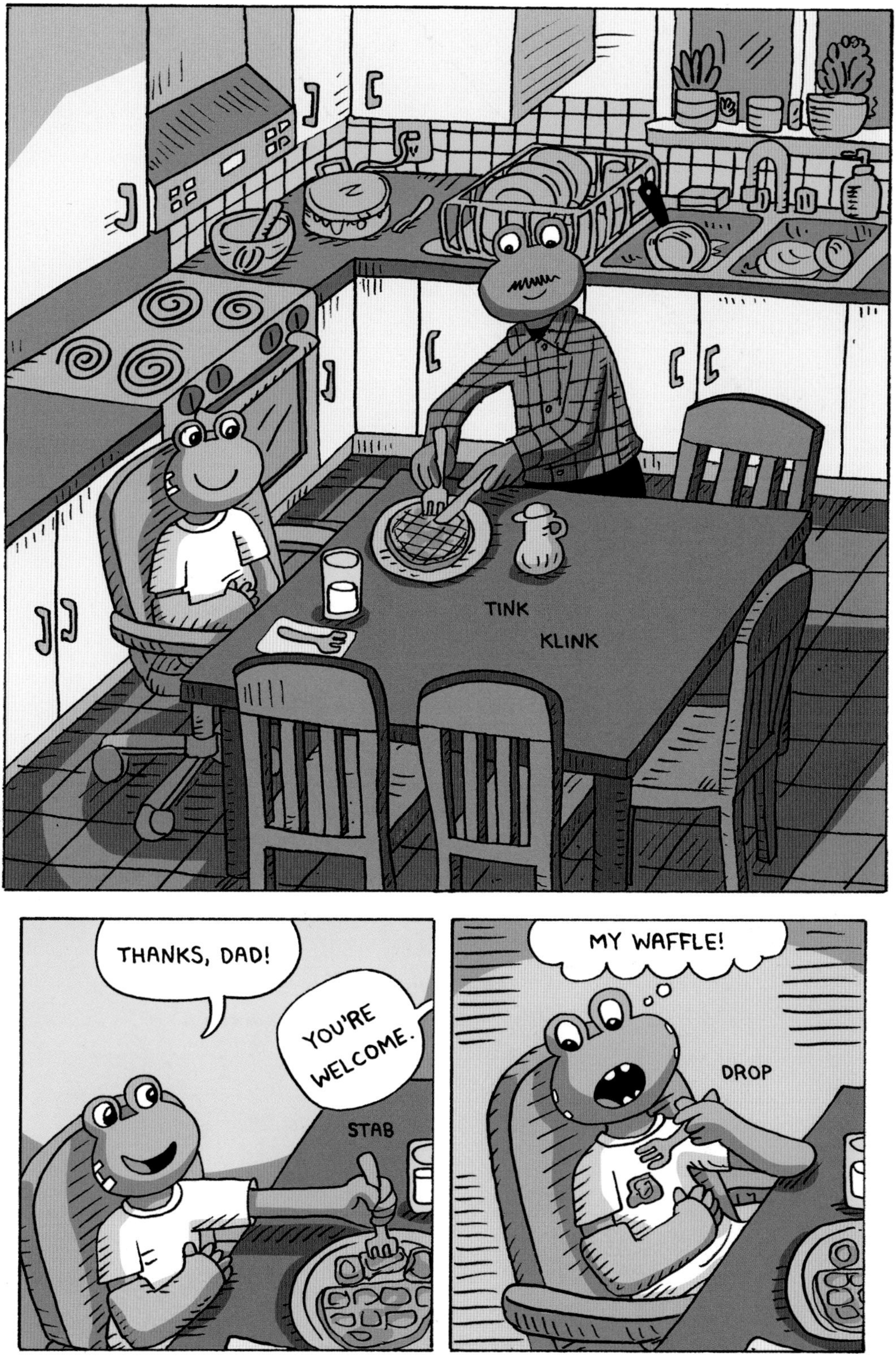
TINK
KLINK
THANKS, DAD!
YOU'RE WELCOME.
STAB
MY WAFFLE!
DROP

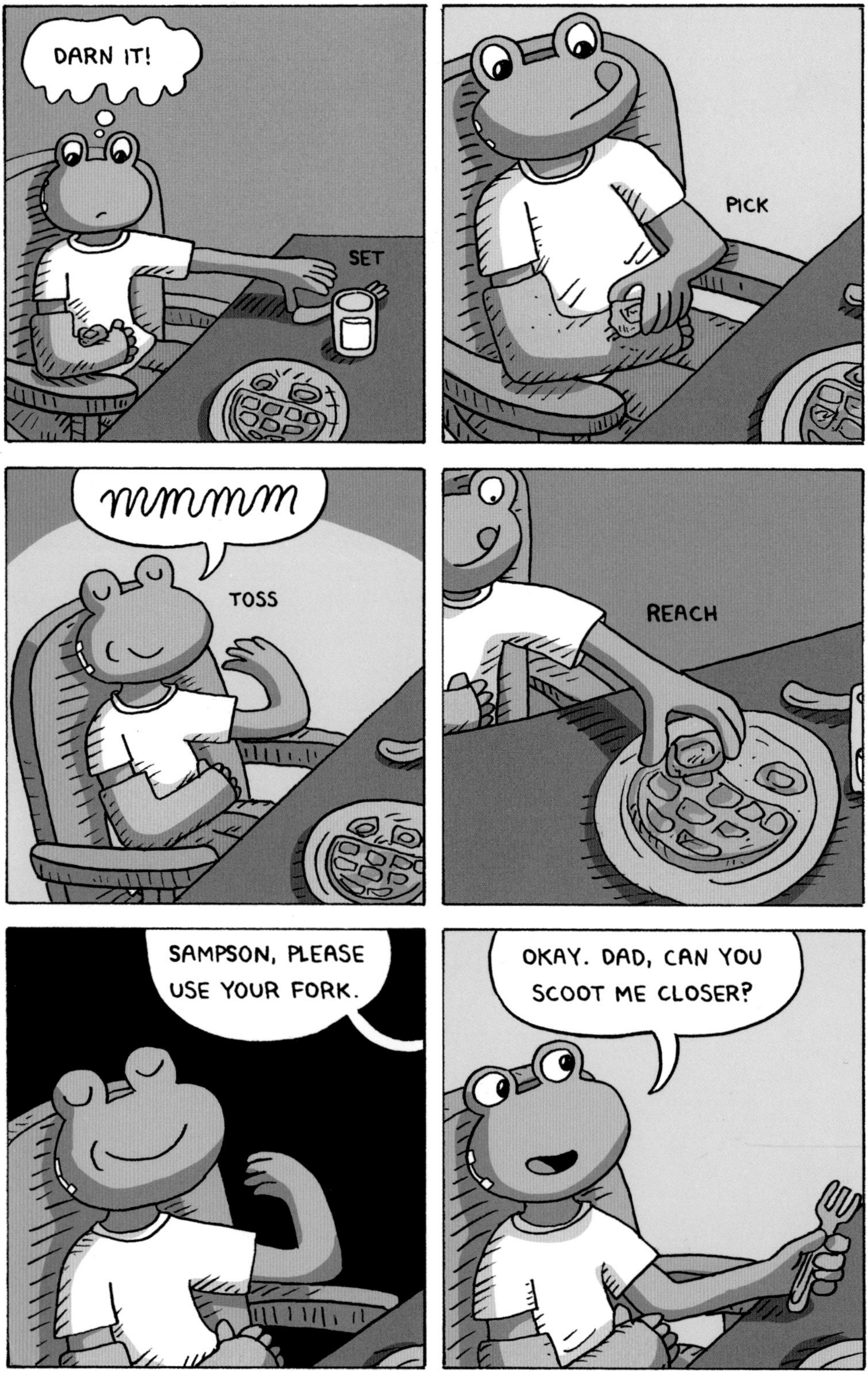
DARN IT!
SET
PICK
mmmmm
TOSS
REACH
SAMPSON, PLEASE USE YOUR FORK.
OKAY. DAD, CAN YOU SCOOT ME CLOSER?

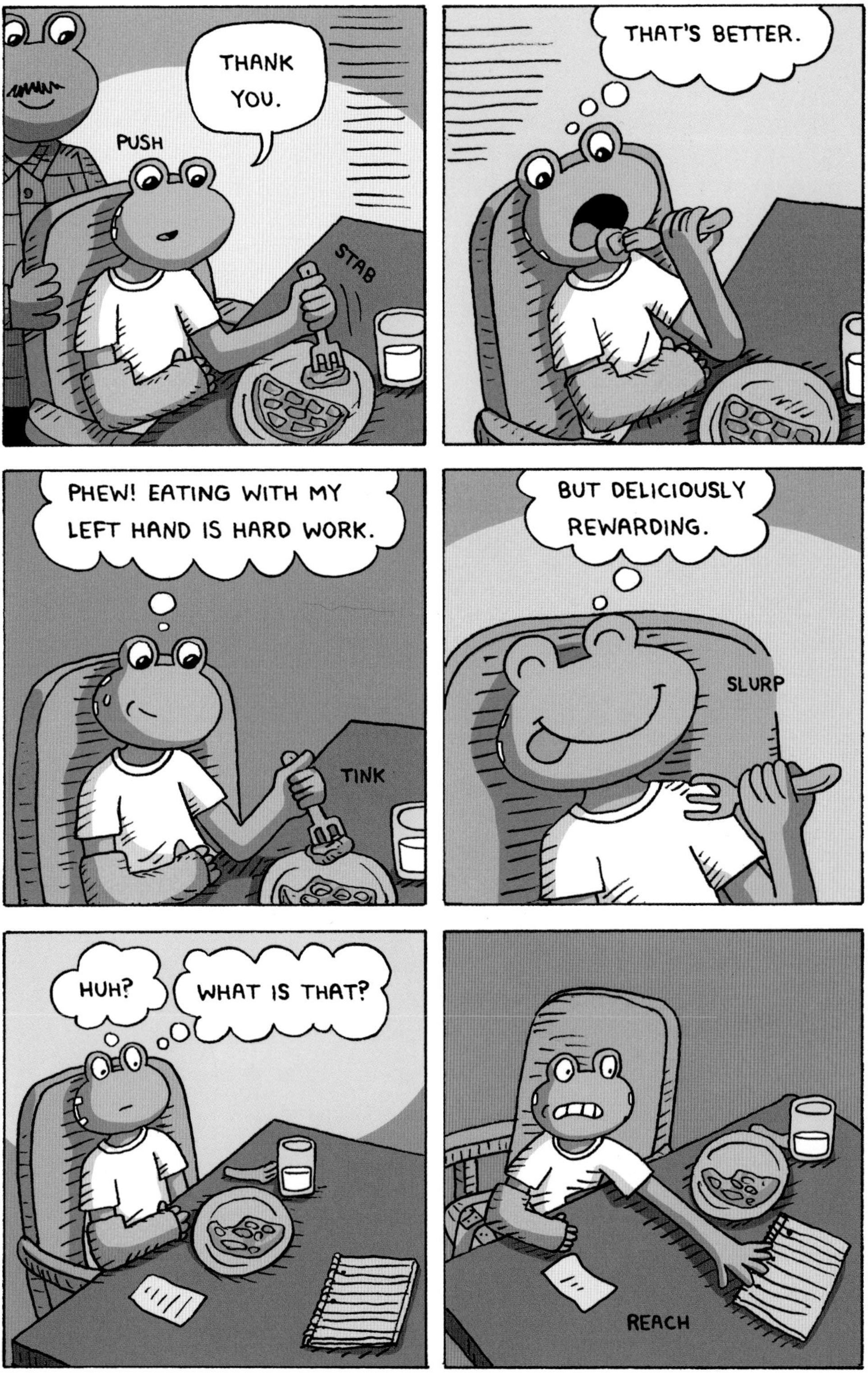
THANK YOU.
PUSH
STAB
THAT'S BETTER.
PHEW! EATING WITH MY LEFT HAND IS HARD WORK.
TINK
BUT DELICIOUSLY REWARDING.
SLURP
HUH?
WHAT IS THAT?
REACH

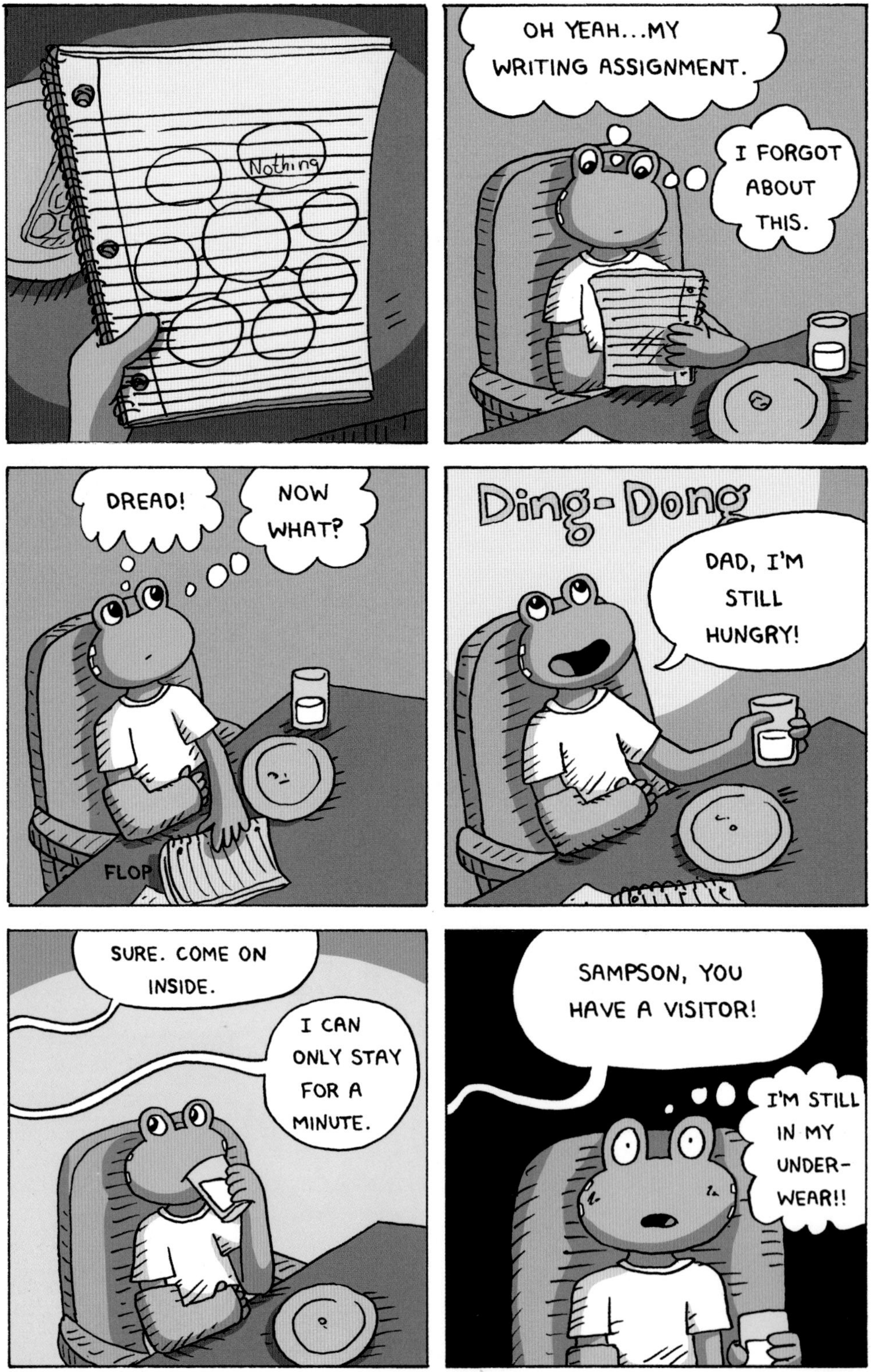
Nothing
OH YEAH...MY WRITING ASSIGNMENT.
I FORGOT ABOUT THIS.
DREAD!
NOW WHAT?
FLOP
Ding-Dong
DAD, I'M STILL HUNGRY!
SURE. COME ON INSIDE.
I CAN ONLY STAY FOR A MINUTE.
SAMPSON, YOU HAVE A VISITOR!
I'M STILL IN MY UNDER-WEAR!!

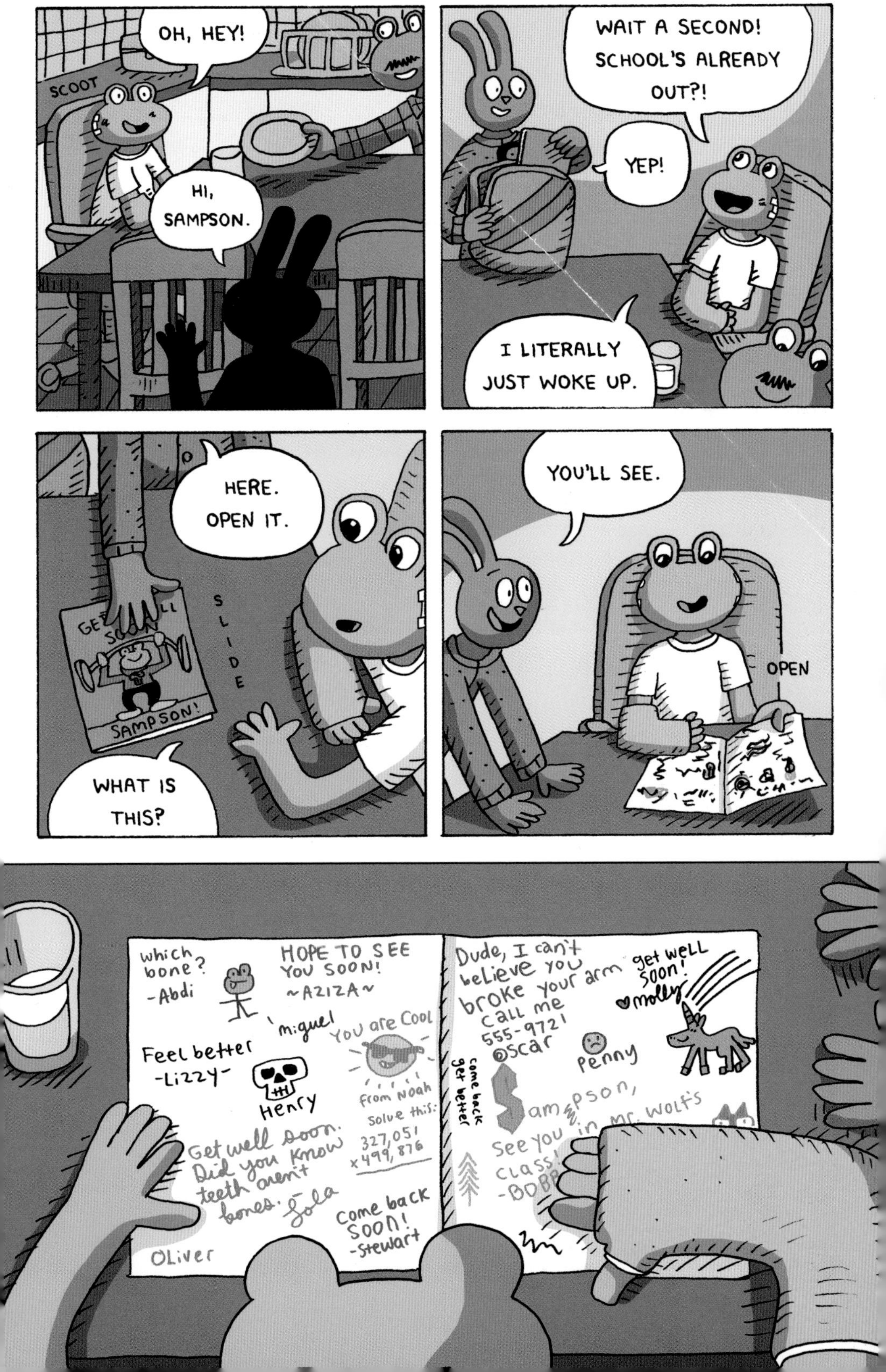
OH, HEY!
SCOOT
HI, SAMPSON.
WAIT A SECOND! SCHOOL'S ALREADY OUT?!
YEP!
I LITERALLY JUST WOKE UP.
HERE. OPEN IT.
SAMPSON!
SLIDE
WHAT IS THIS?
YOU'LL SEE.
OPEN
which bone? -Abdi
HOPE TO SEE YOU SOON! ~AZIZA~
miguel
You are Cool
Feel better -Lizzy-
Henry
From Noah
Solve this: 327,051 x499,876
Get well soon. Did you know teeth aren't bones. Lola
Come back soon! -Stewart
Oliver
Dude, I can't believe you broke your arm call me 555-9721 Oscar
get well soon! molly
penny
come back get better
Sampson, See you in Mr. Wolf's class! -BOBB

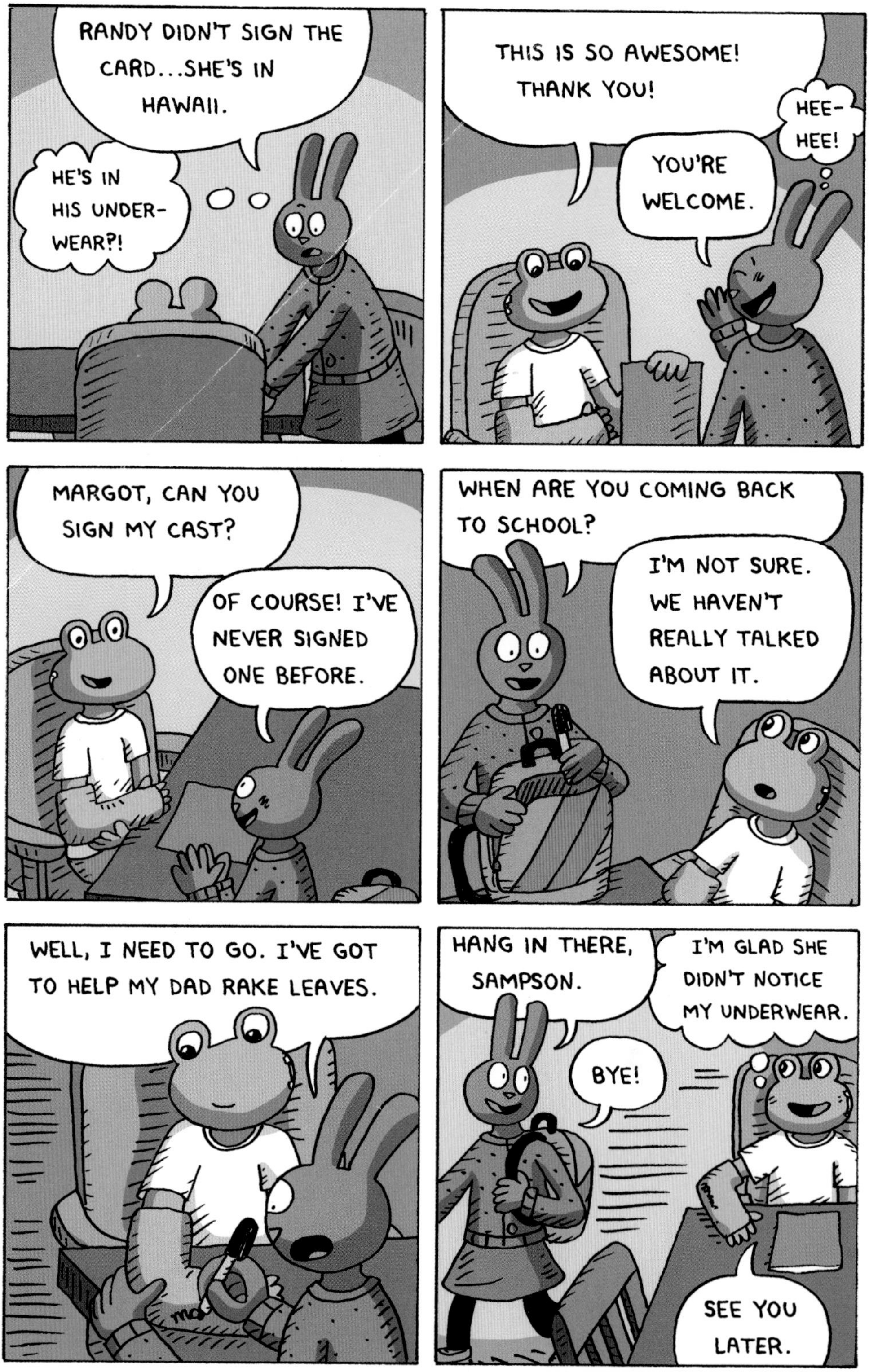
RANDY DIDN'T SIGN THE CARD...SHE'S IN HAWAII.
HE'S IN HIS UNDER-WEAR?!
THIS IS SO AWESOME! THANK YOU!
YOU'RE WELCOME.
HEE-HEE!
MARGOT, CAN YOU SIGN MY CAST?
OF COURSE! I'VE NEVER SIGNED ONE BEFORE.
WHEN ARE YOU COMING BACK TO SCHOOL?
I'M NOT SURE. WE HAVEN'T REALLY TALKED ABOUT IT.
WELL, I NEED TO GO. I'VE GOT TO HELP MY DAD RAKE LEAVES.
HANG IN THERE, SAMPSON.
I'M GLAD SHE DIDN'T NOTICE MY UNDERWEAR.
BYE!
SEE YOU LATER.

CHAPTER SIX
Noah's Tree Story

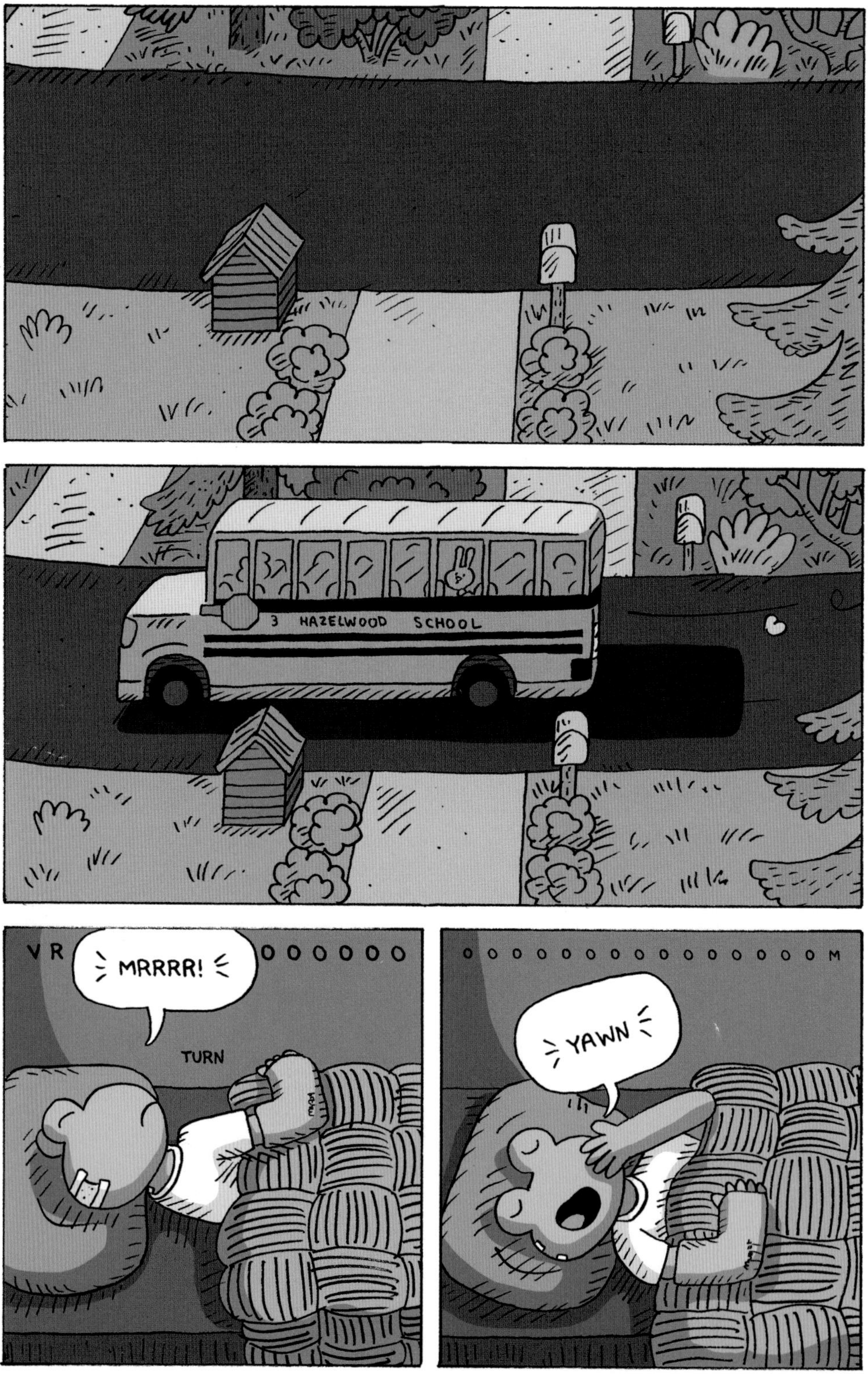
3 HAZELWOOD SCHOOL
VR
MRRRR!
OOOOOO
TURN
OOOOOOOOOOOOOOOM
YAWN

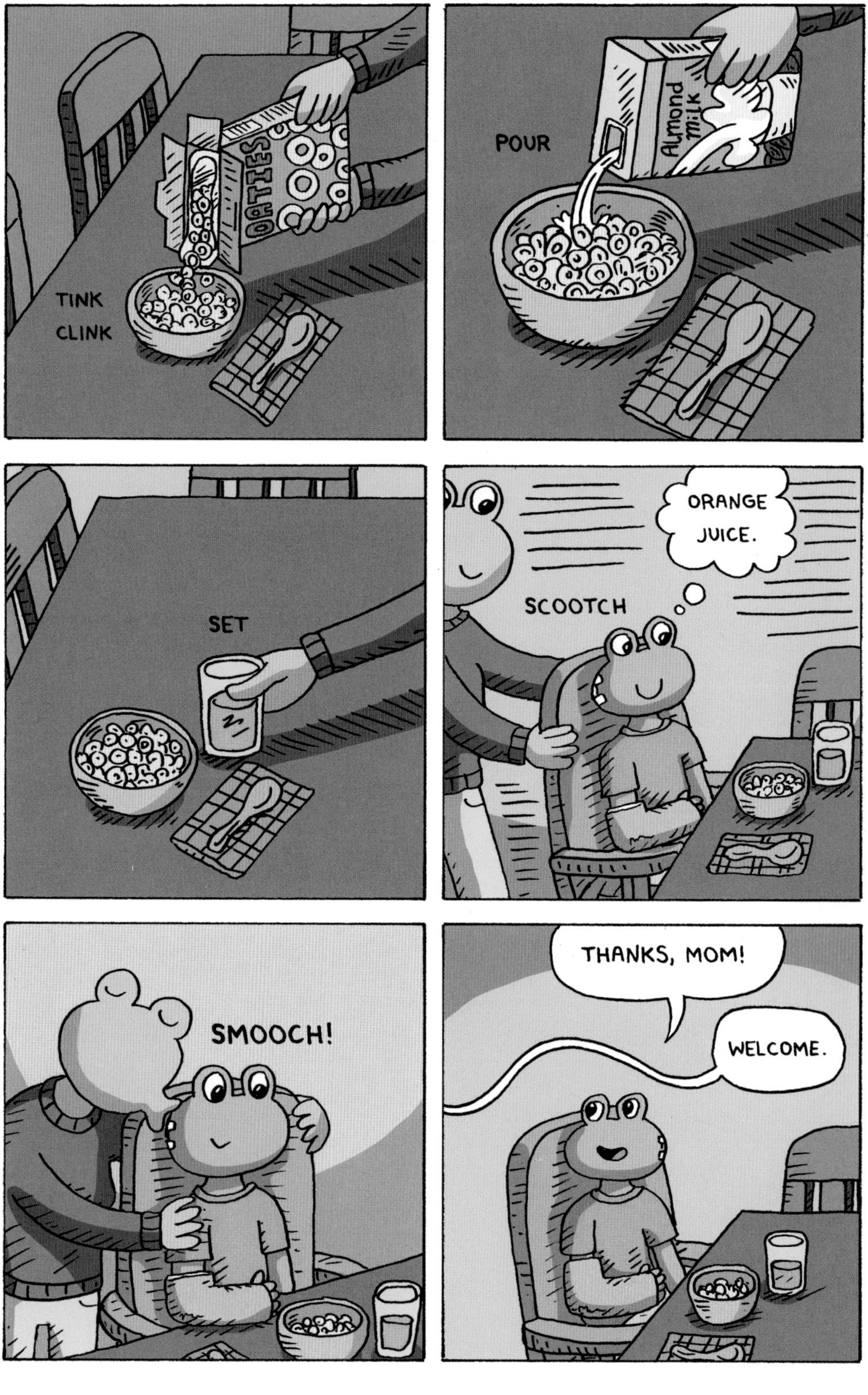
OATIES
TINK
CLINK
Almond milk
POUR
SET
ORANGE JUICE.
SCOOTCH
SMOOCH!
THANKS, MOM!
WELCOME.

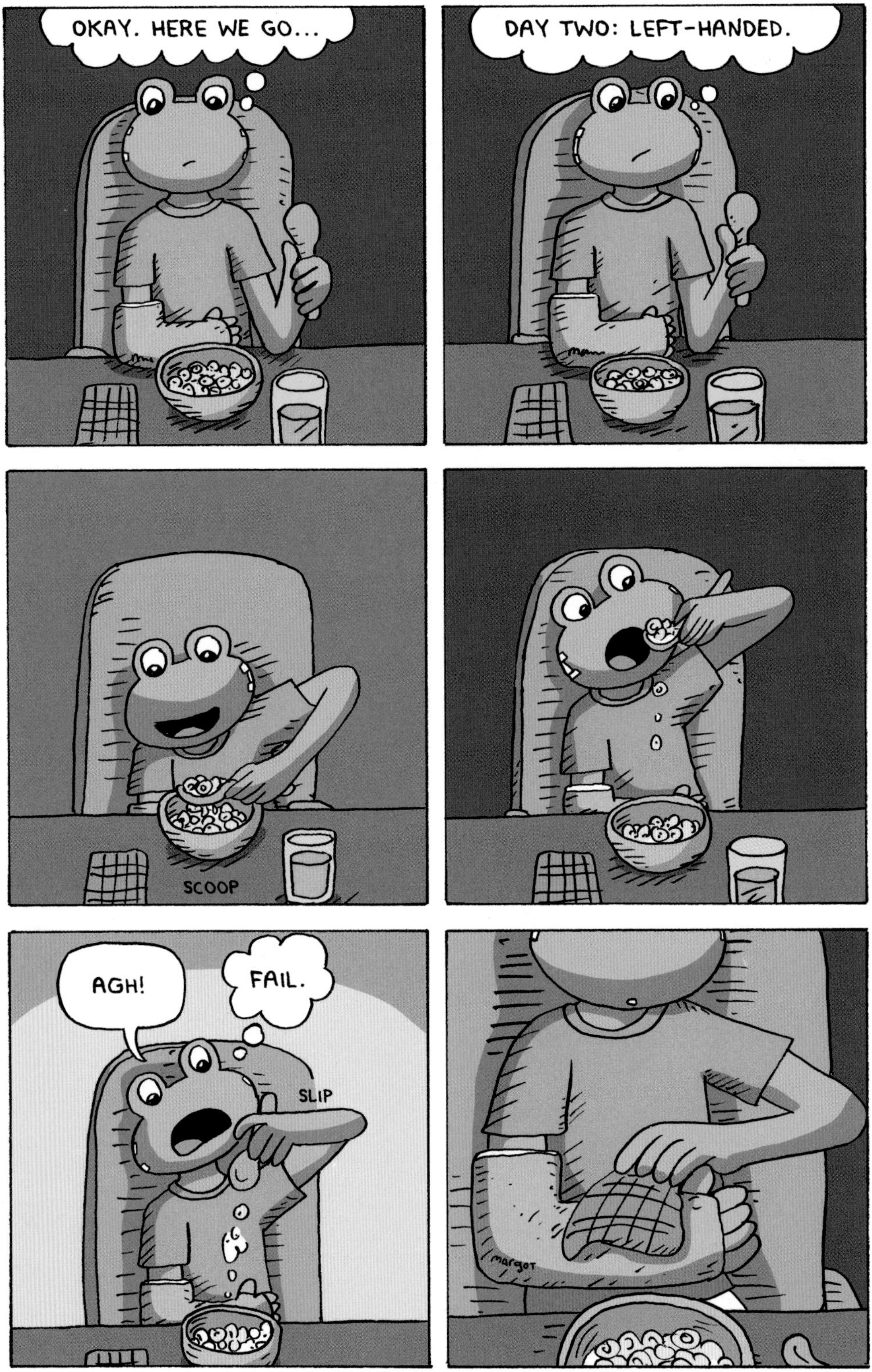
OKAY. HERE WE GO...
DAY TWO: LEFT-HANDED.
SCOOP
AGH!
FAIL.
SLIP
margot

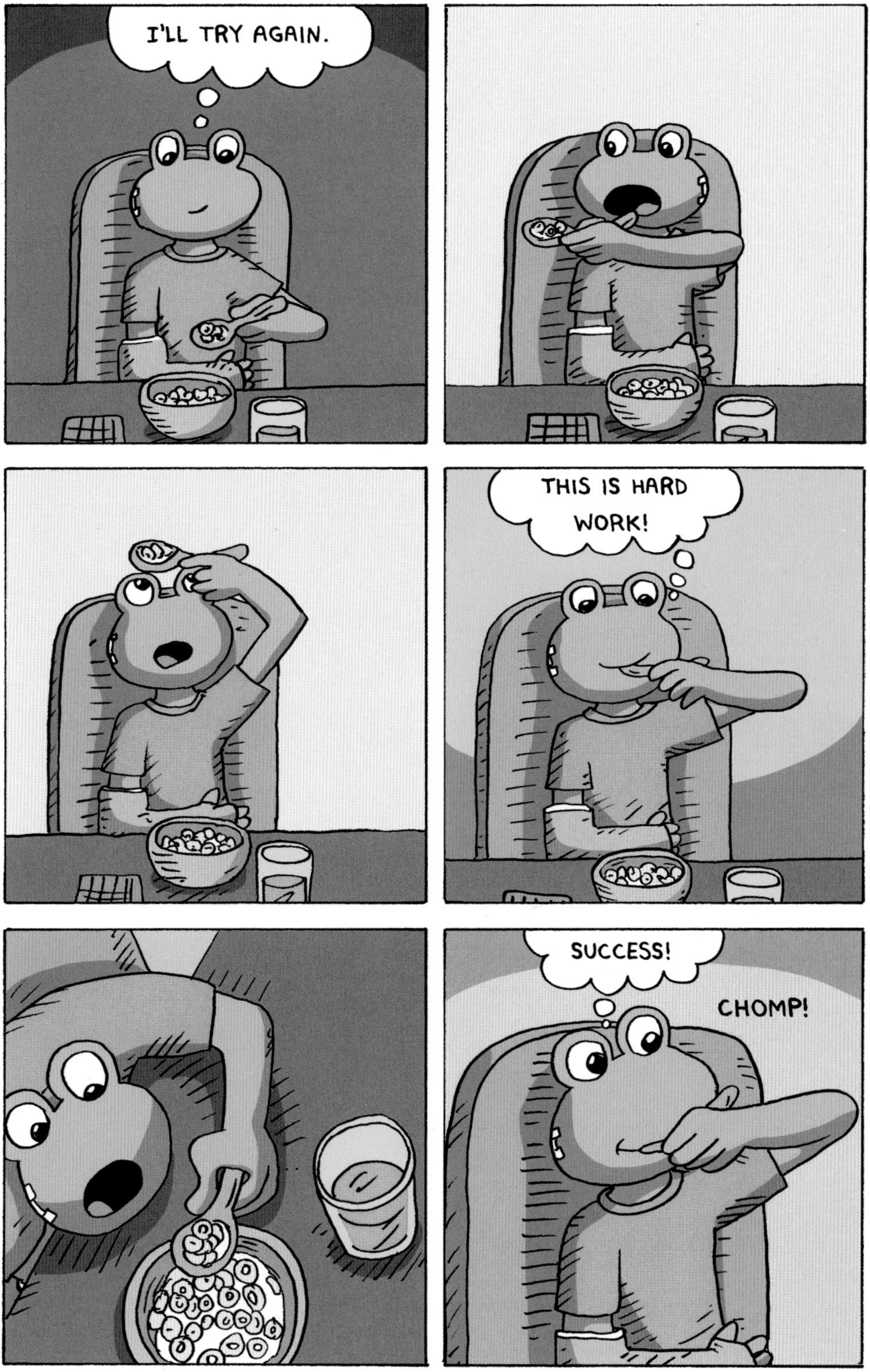
I'LL TRY AGAIN.
THIS IS HARD WORK!
SUCCESS!
CHOMP!

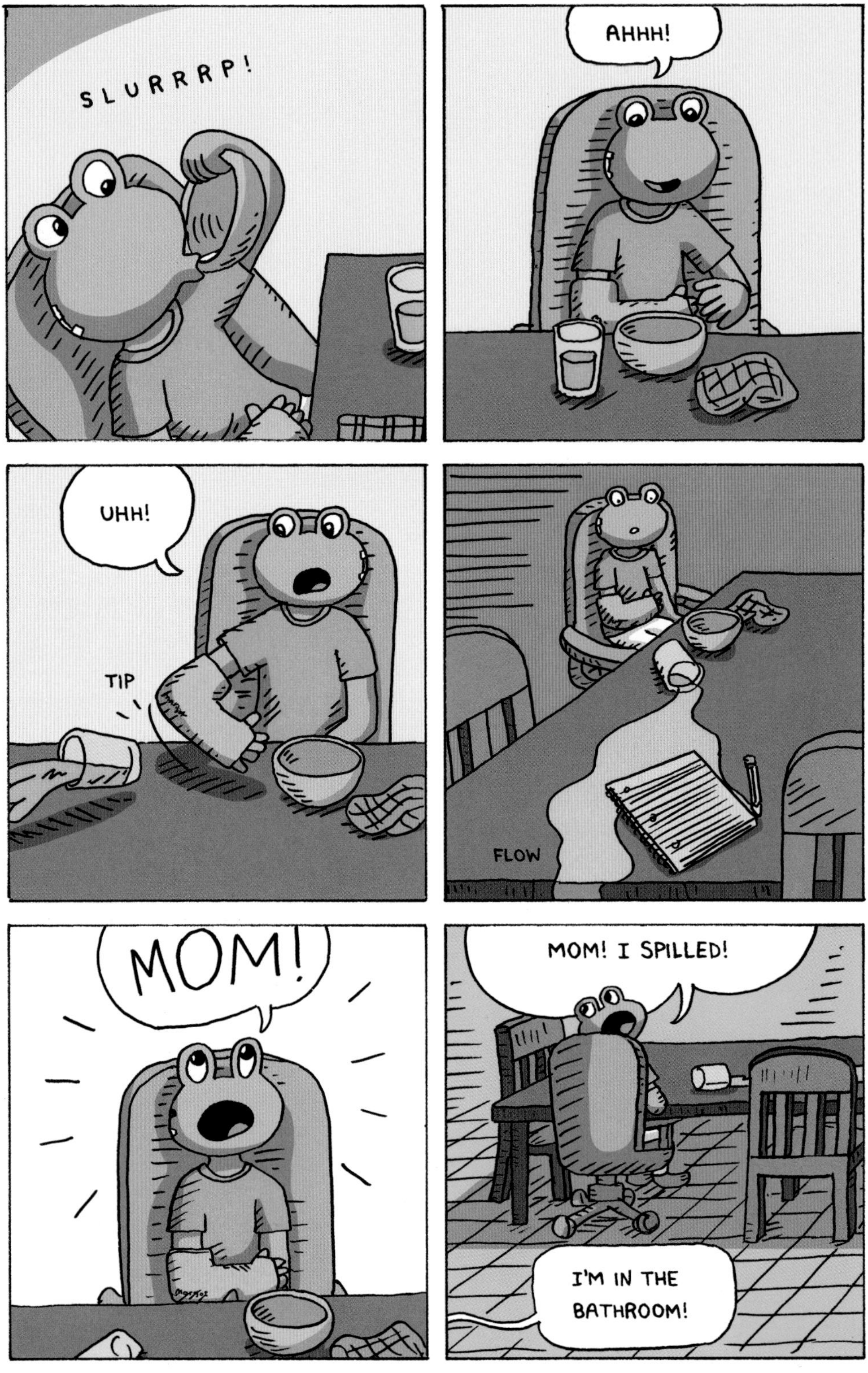
SLURRRP!
AHHH!
UHH!
TIP
FLOW
MOM!
MOM! I SPILLED!
I'M IN THE BATHROOM!

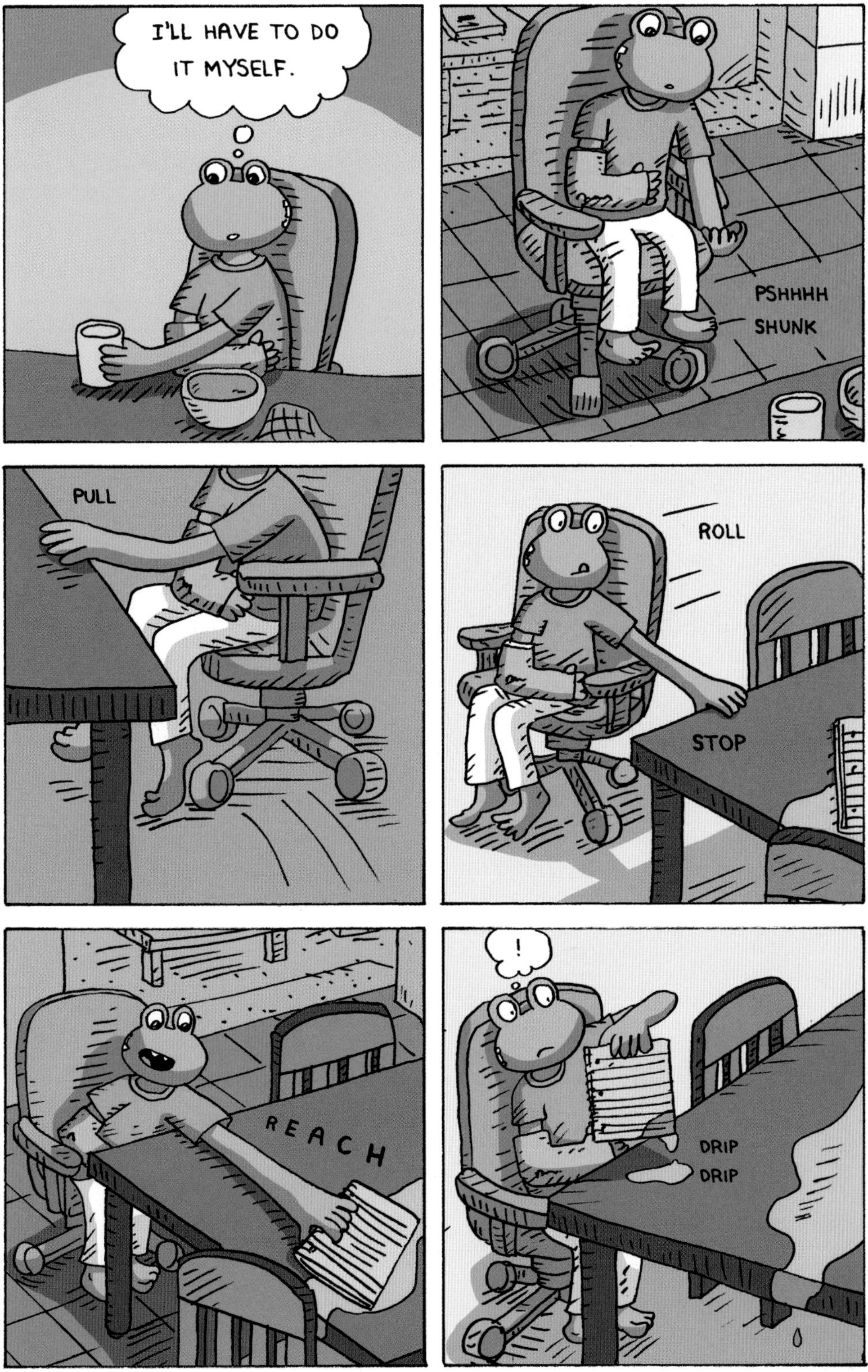
I'LL HAVE TO DO IT MYSELF.
PSHHHH
SHUNK
PULL
ROLL
STOP
REACH
!
DRIP
DRIP

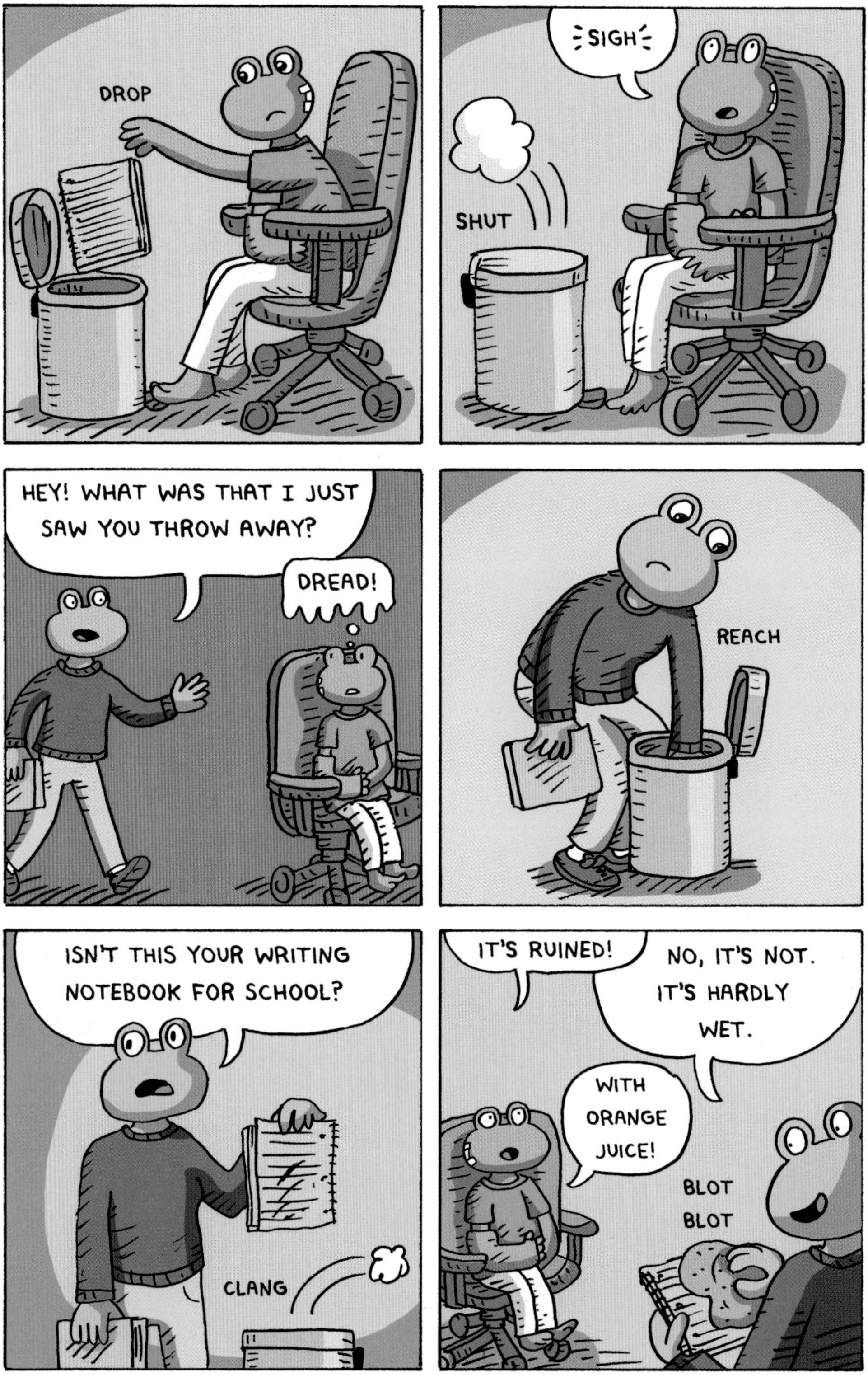
DROP
SIGH
SHUT
HEY! WHAT WAS THAT I JUST SAW YOU THROW AWAY?
DREAD!
REACH
ISN'T THIS YOUR WRITING NOTEBOOK FOR SCHOOL?
CLANG
IT'S RUINED!
NO, IT'S NOT. IT'S HARDLY WET.
WITH ORANGE JUICE!
BLOT
BLOT

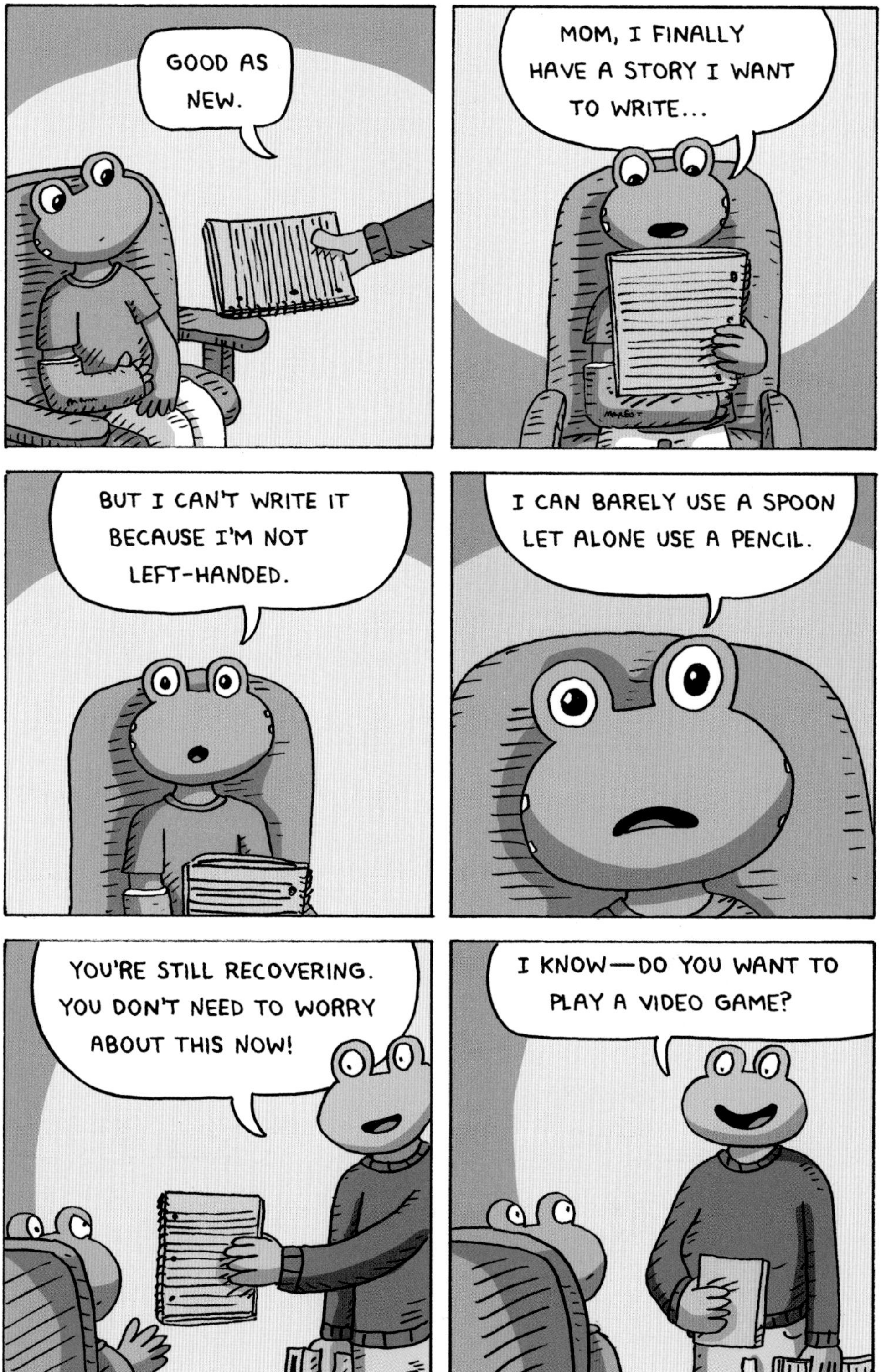
GOOD AS NEW.
MOM, I FINALLY HAVE A STORY I WANT TO WRITE...
BUT I CAN'T WRITE IT BECAUSE I'M NOT LEFT-HANDED.
I CAN BARELY USE A SPOON LET ALONE USE A PENCIL.
YOU'RE STILL RECOVERING. YOU DON'T NEED TO WORRY ABOUT THIS NOW!
I KNOW—DO YOU WANT TO PLAY A VIDEO GAME?

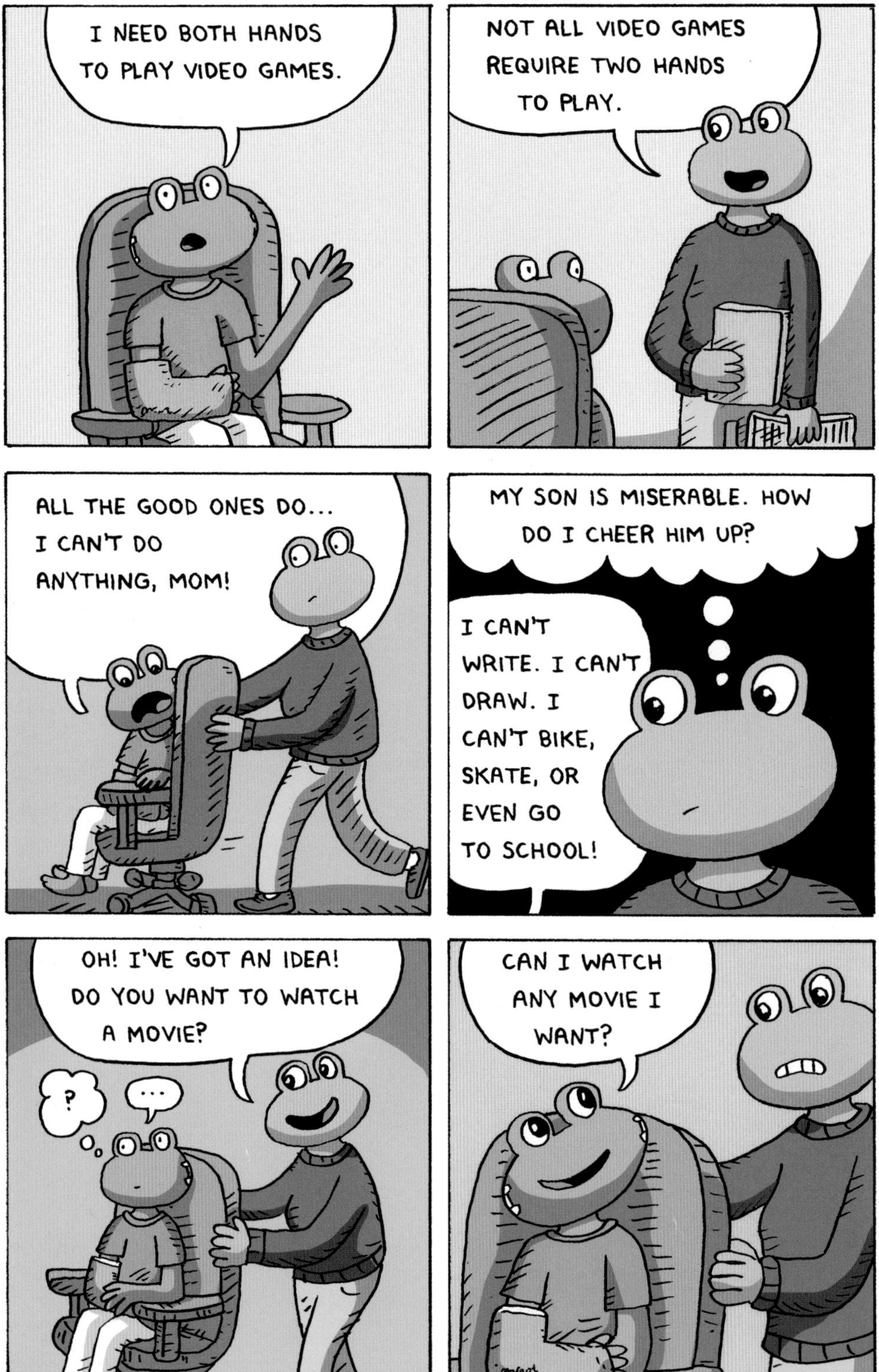
I NEED BOTH HANDS TO PLAY VIDEO GAMES.
NOT ALL VIDEO GAMES REQUIRE TWO HANDS TO PLAY.
ALL THE GOOD ONES DO... I CAN'T DO ANYTHING, MOM!
MY SON IS MISERABLE. HOW DO I CHEER HIM UP?
I CAN'T WRITE. I CAN'T DRAW. I CAN'T BIKE, SKATE, OR EVEN GO TO SCHOOL!
OH! I'VE GOT AN IDEA! DO YOU WANT TO WATCH A MOVIE?
?
...
CAN I WATCH ANY MOVIE I WANT?
margot

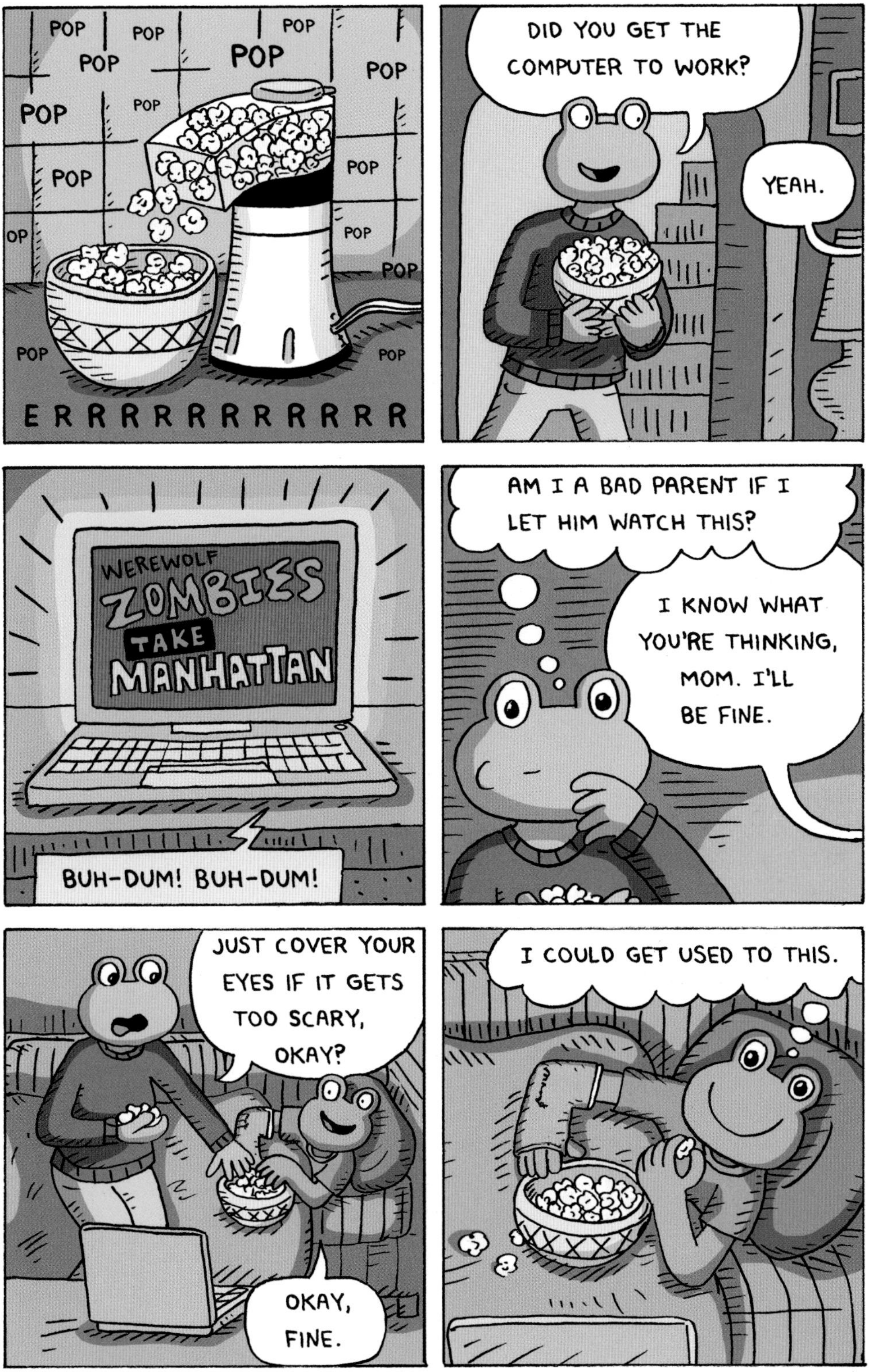
POP POP POP POP POP
POP POP POP POP POP POP
OP POP POP POP
ERRRRRRRRRRR
DID YOU GET THE COMPUTER TO WORK?
YEAH.
WEREWOLF ZOMBIES TAKE MANHATTAN
BUH-DUM! BUH-DUM!
AM I A BAD PARENT IF I LET HIM WATCH THIS?
I KNOW WHAT YOU'RE THINKING, MOM. I'LL BE FINE.
JUST COVER YOUR EYES IF IT GETS TOO SCARY, OKAY?
OKAY, FINE.
I COULD GET USED TO THIS.

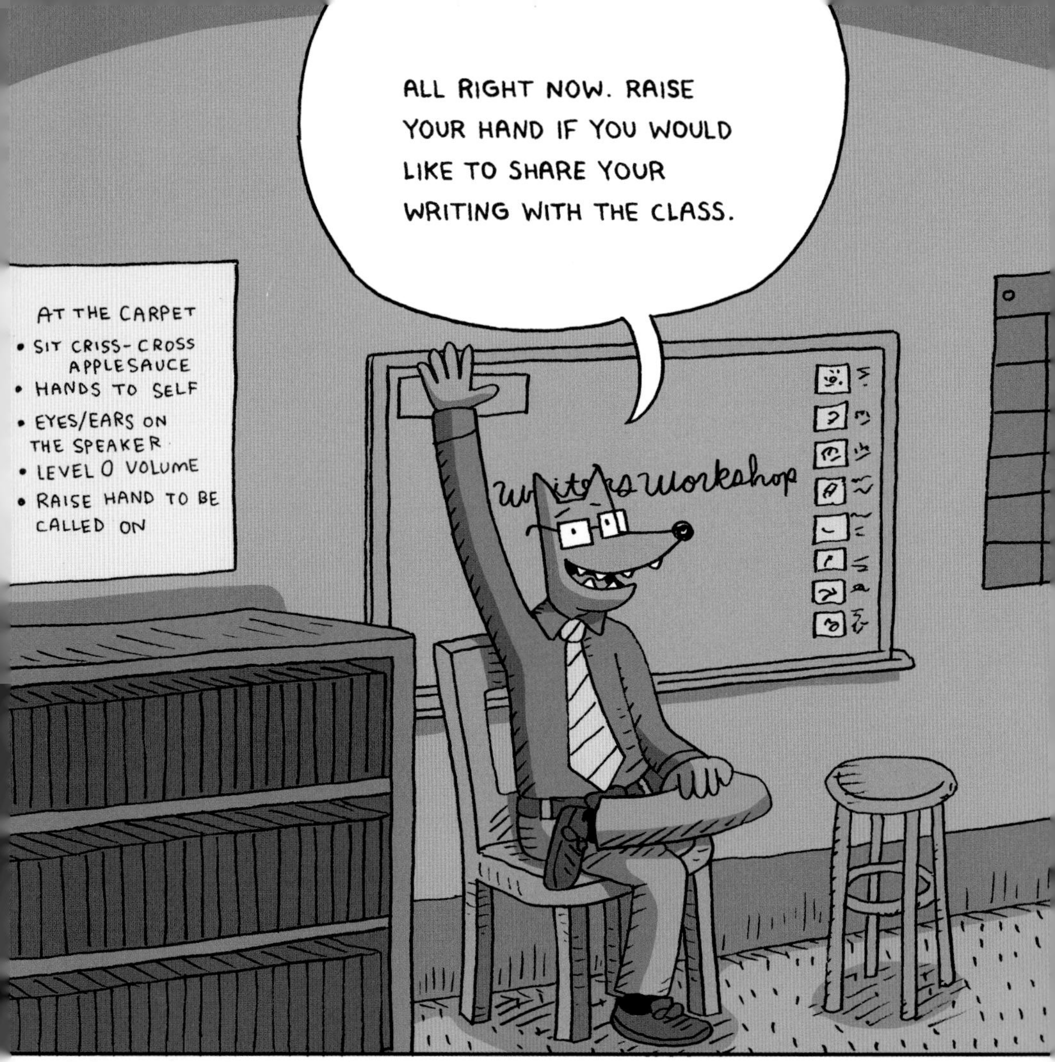
ALL RIGHT NOW. RAISE YOUR HAND IF YOU WOULD LIKE TO SHARE YOUR WRITING WITH THE CLASS.
AT THE CARPET
• SIT CRISS-CROSS APPLESAUCE
• HANDS TO SELF
• EYES/EARS ON THE SPEAKER
• LEVEL 0 VOLUME
• RAISE HAND TO BE CALLED ON
Writers Workshop

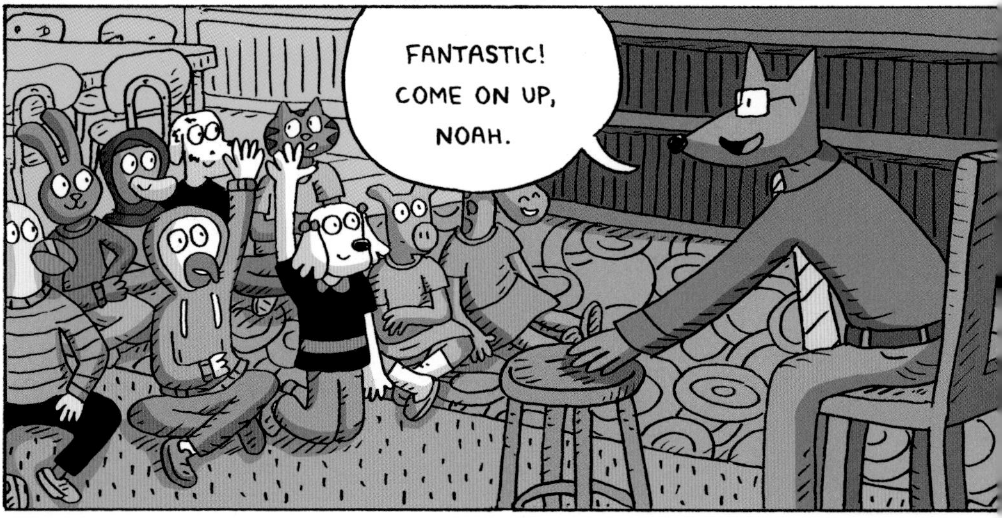
FANTASTIC! COME ON UP, NOAH.

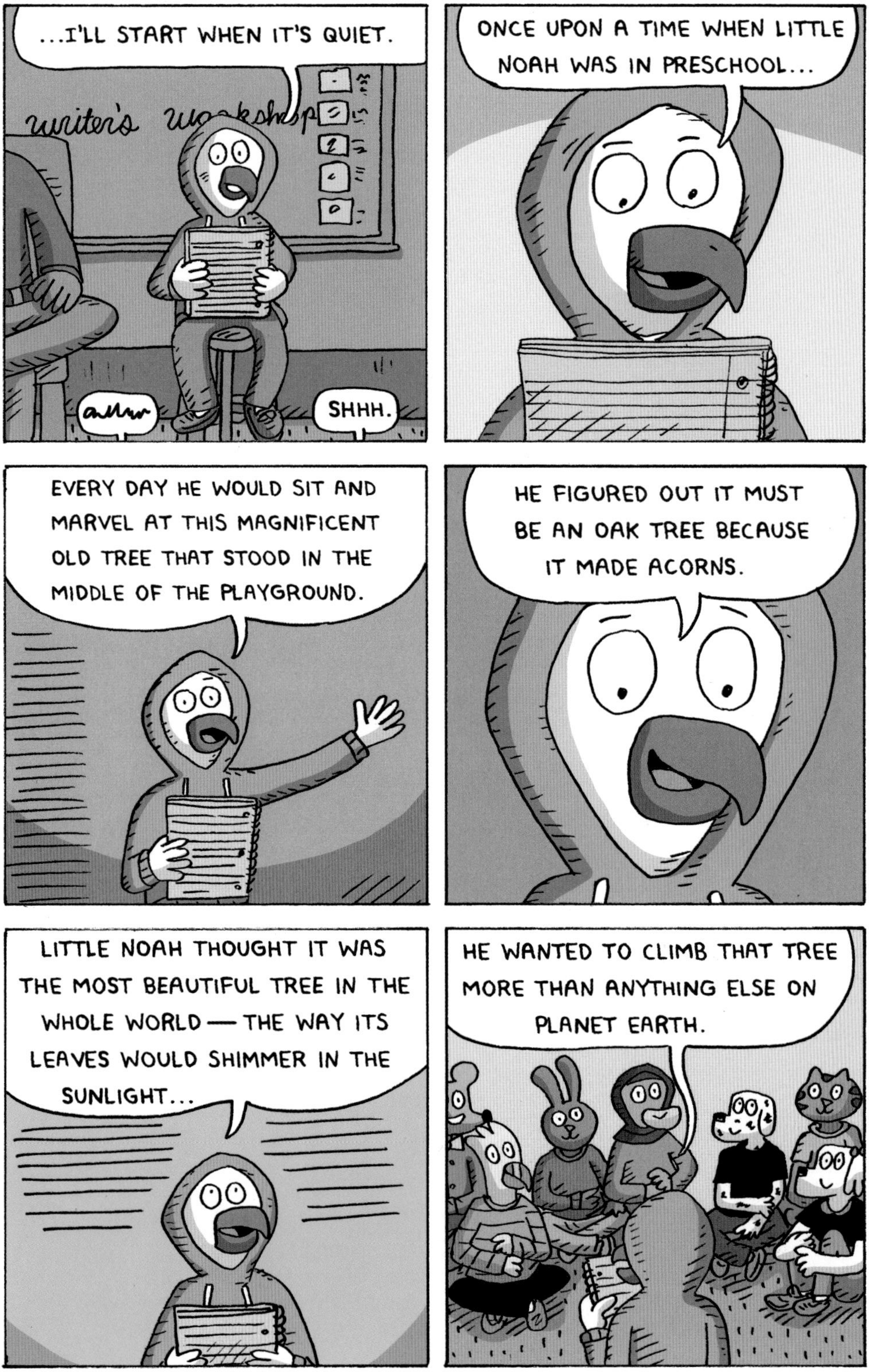
...I'LL START WHEN IT'S QUIET.
writer's workshop
SHHH.
ONCE UPON A TIME WHEN LITTLE NOAH WAS IN PRESCHOOL...
EVERY DAY HE WOULD SIT AND MARVEL AT THIS MAGNIFICENT OLD TREE THAT STOOD IN THE MIDDLE OF THE PLAYGROUND.
HE FIGURED OUT IT MUST BE AN OAK TREE BECAUSE IT MADE ACORNS.
LITTLE NOAH THOUGHT IT WAS THE MOST BEAUTIFUL TREE IN THE WHOLE WORLD — THE WAY ITS LEAVES WOULD SHIMMER IN THE SUNLIGHT...
HE WANTED TO CLIMB THAT TREE MORE THAN ANYTHING ELSE ON PLANET EARTH.

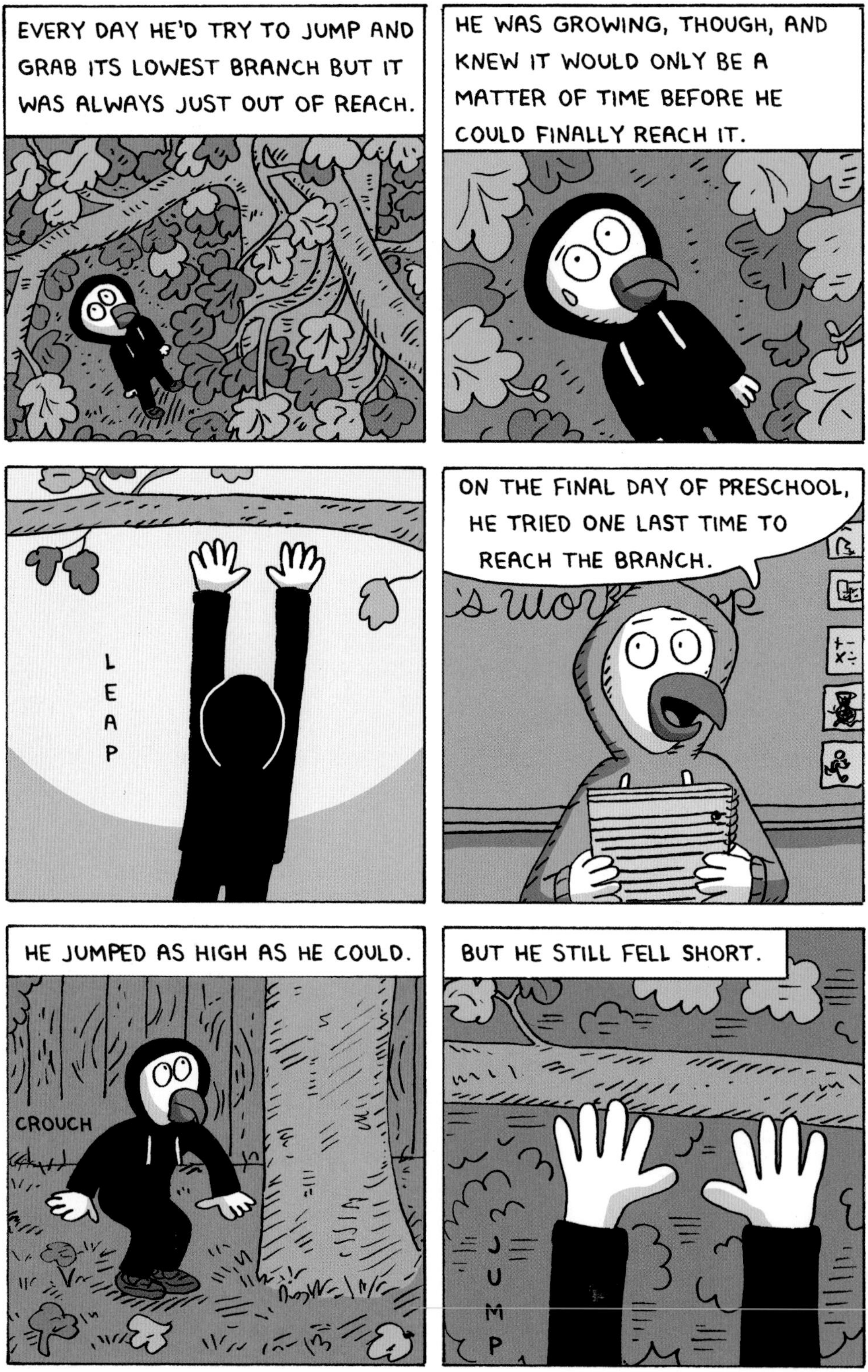
EVERY DAY HE'D TRY TO JUMP AND GRAB ITS LOWEST BRANCH BUT IT WAS ALWAYS JUST OUT OF REACH.
HE WAS GROWING, THOUGH, AND KNEW IT WOULD ONLY BE A MATTER OF TIME BEFORE HE COULD FINALLY REACH IT.
LEAP
ON THE FINAL DAY OF PRESCHOOL, HE TRIED ONE LAST TIME TO REACH THE BRANCH.
HE JUMPED AS HIGH AS HE COULD.
CROUCH
BUT HE STILL FELL SHORT.
JUMP

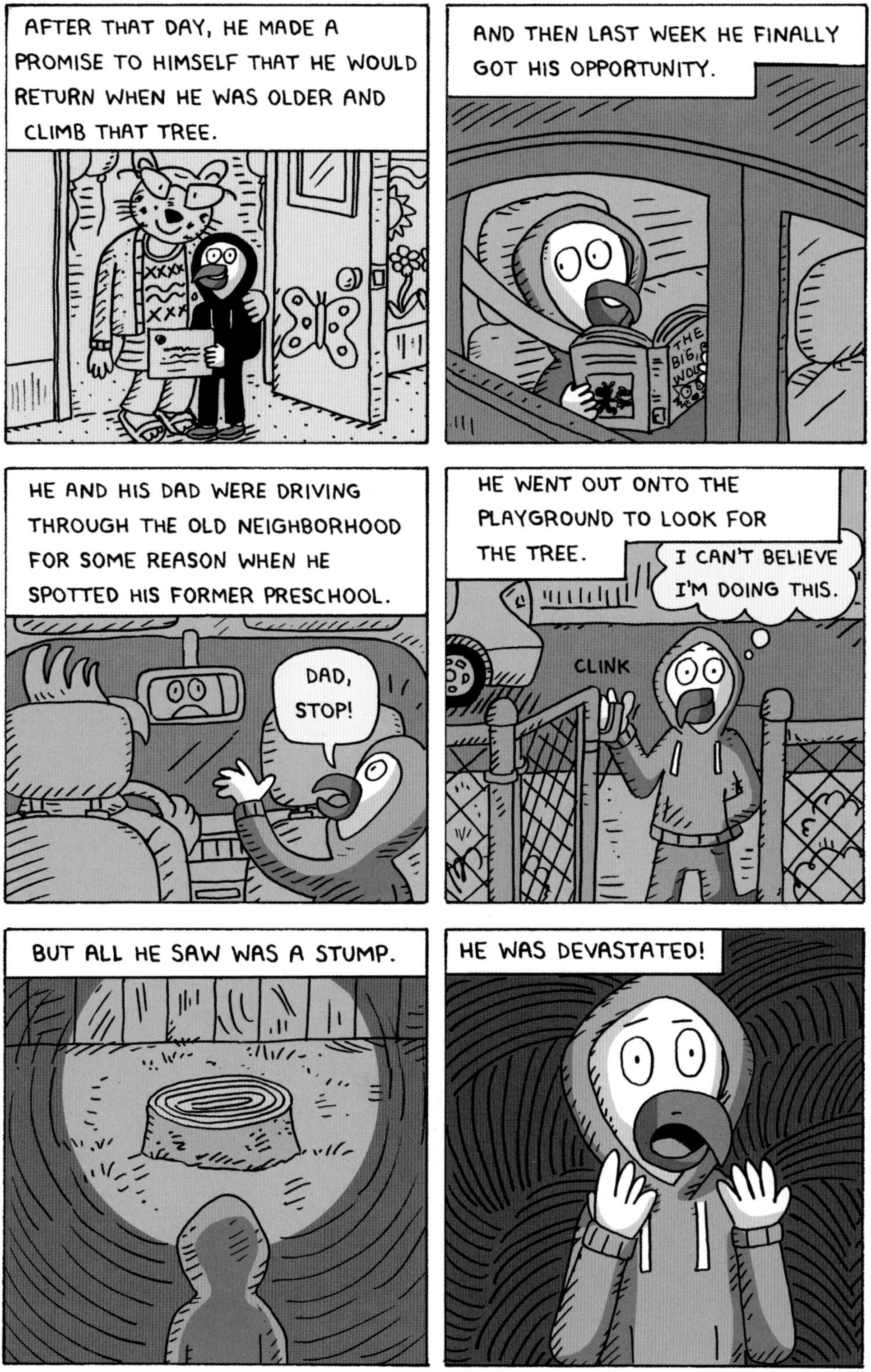
AFTER THAT DAY, HE MADE A PROMISE TO HIMSELF THAT HE WOULD RETURN WHEN HE WAS OLDER AND CLIMB THAT TREE.
AND THEN LAST WEEK HE FINALLY GOT HIS OPPORTUNITY.
HE AND HIS DAD WERE DRIVING THROUGH THE OLD NEIGHBORHOOD FOR SOME REASON WHEN HE SPOTTED HIS FORMER PRESCHOOL.
DAD, STOP!
HE WENT OUT ONTO THE PLAYGROUND TO LOOK FOR THE TREE.
I CAN'T BELIEVE I'M DOING THIS.
CLINK
BUT ALL HE SAW WAS A STUMP.
HE WAS DEVASTATED!

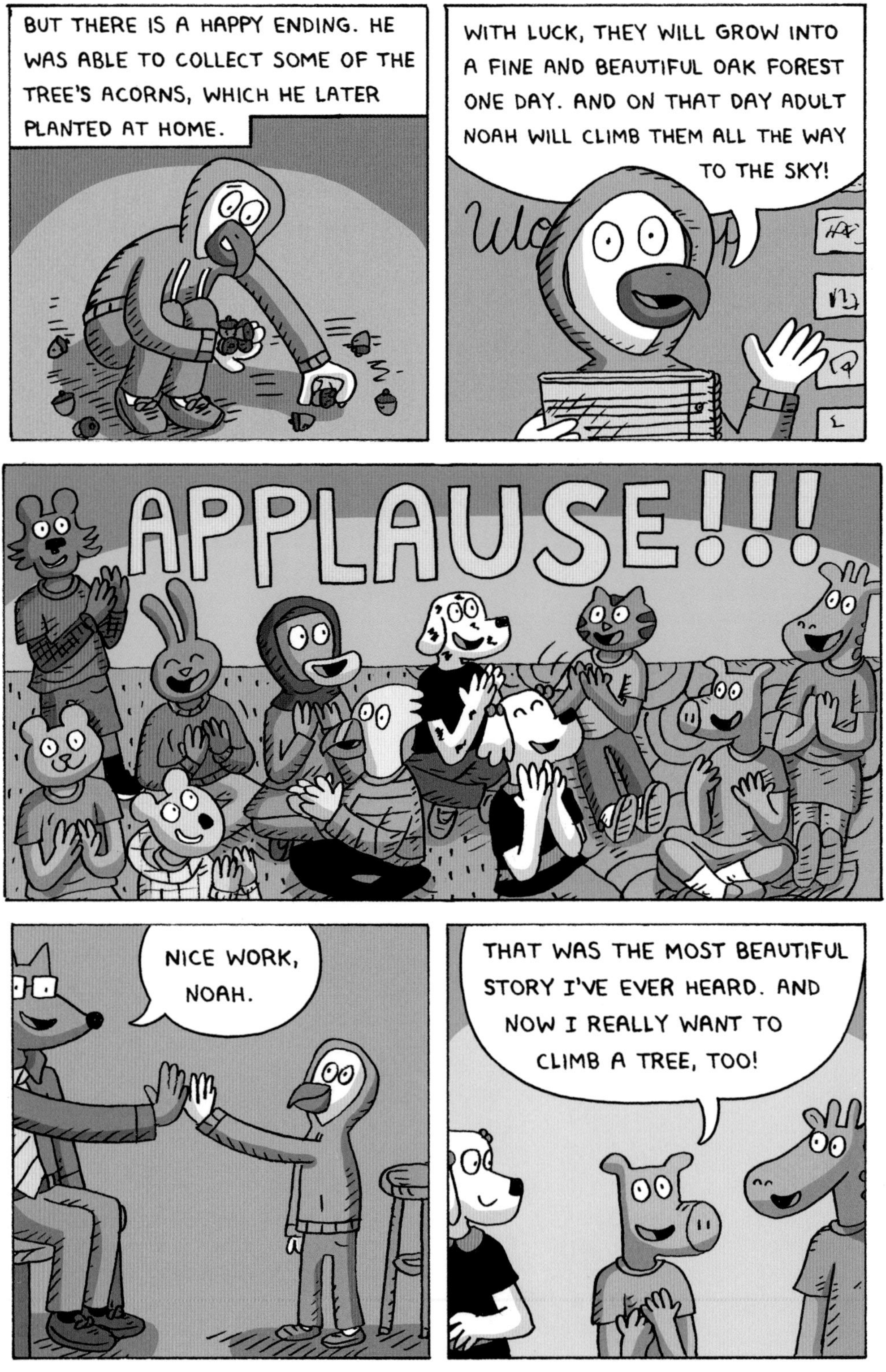
BUT THERE IS A HAPPY ENDING. HE WAS ABLE TO COLLECT SOME OF THE TREE'S ACORNS, WHICH HE LATER PLANTED AT HOME.
WITH LUCK, THEY WILL GROW INTO A FINE AND BEAUTIFUL OAK FOREST ONE DAY. AND ON THAT DAY ADULT NOAH WILL CLIMB THEM ALL THE WAY TO THE SKY!
APPLAUSE!!!
NICE WORK, NOAH.
THAT WAS THE MOST BEAUTIFUL STORY I'VE EVER HEARD. AND NOW I REALLY WANT TO CLIMB A TREE, TOO!

CHAPTER SEVEN
A New Perspective

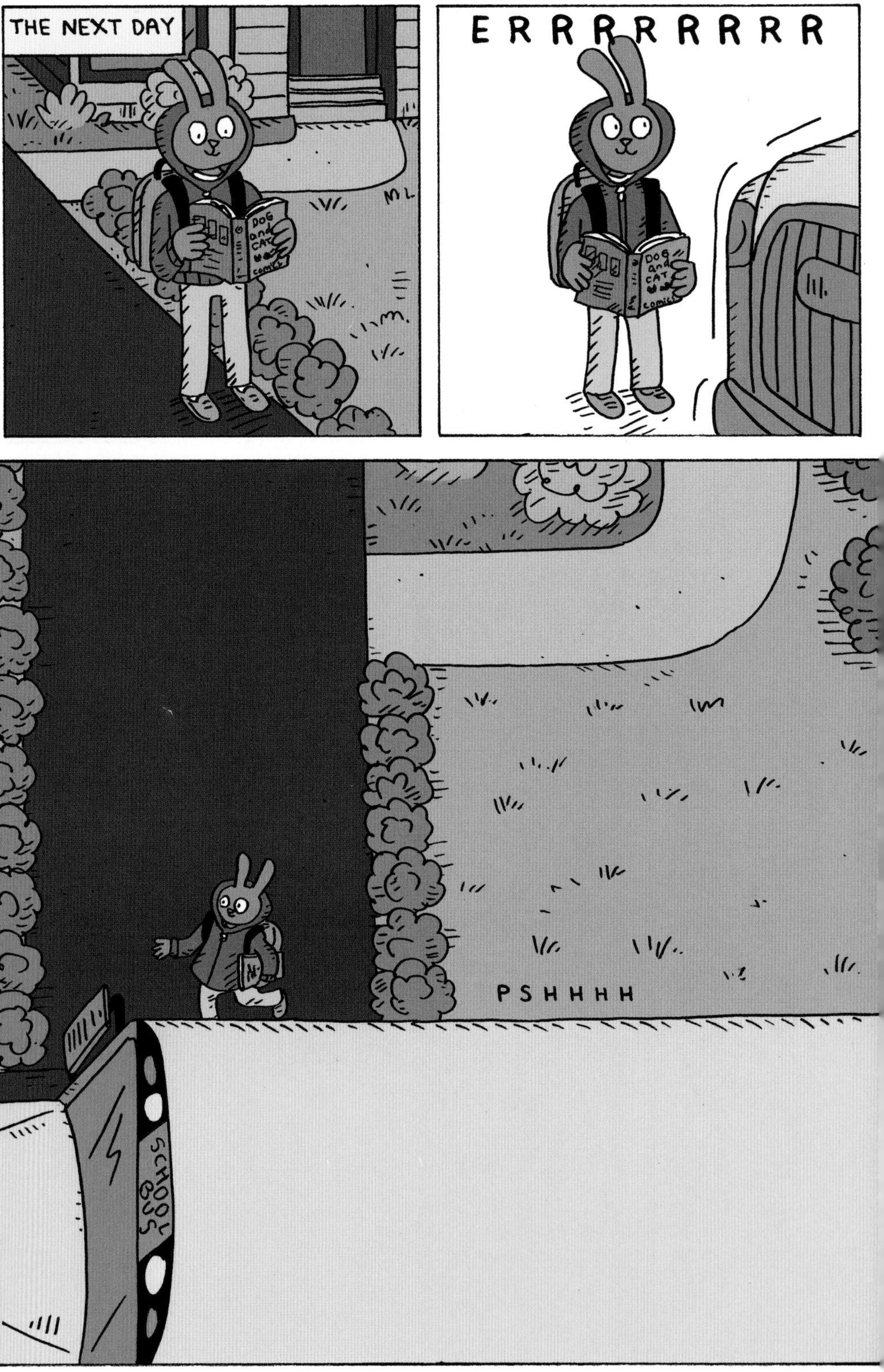
THE NEXT DAY
DOG and CAT comics
ERRRRRRRR
PSHHHH
SCHOOL BUS

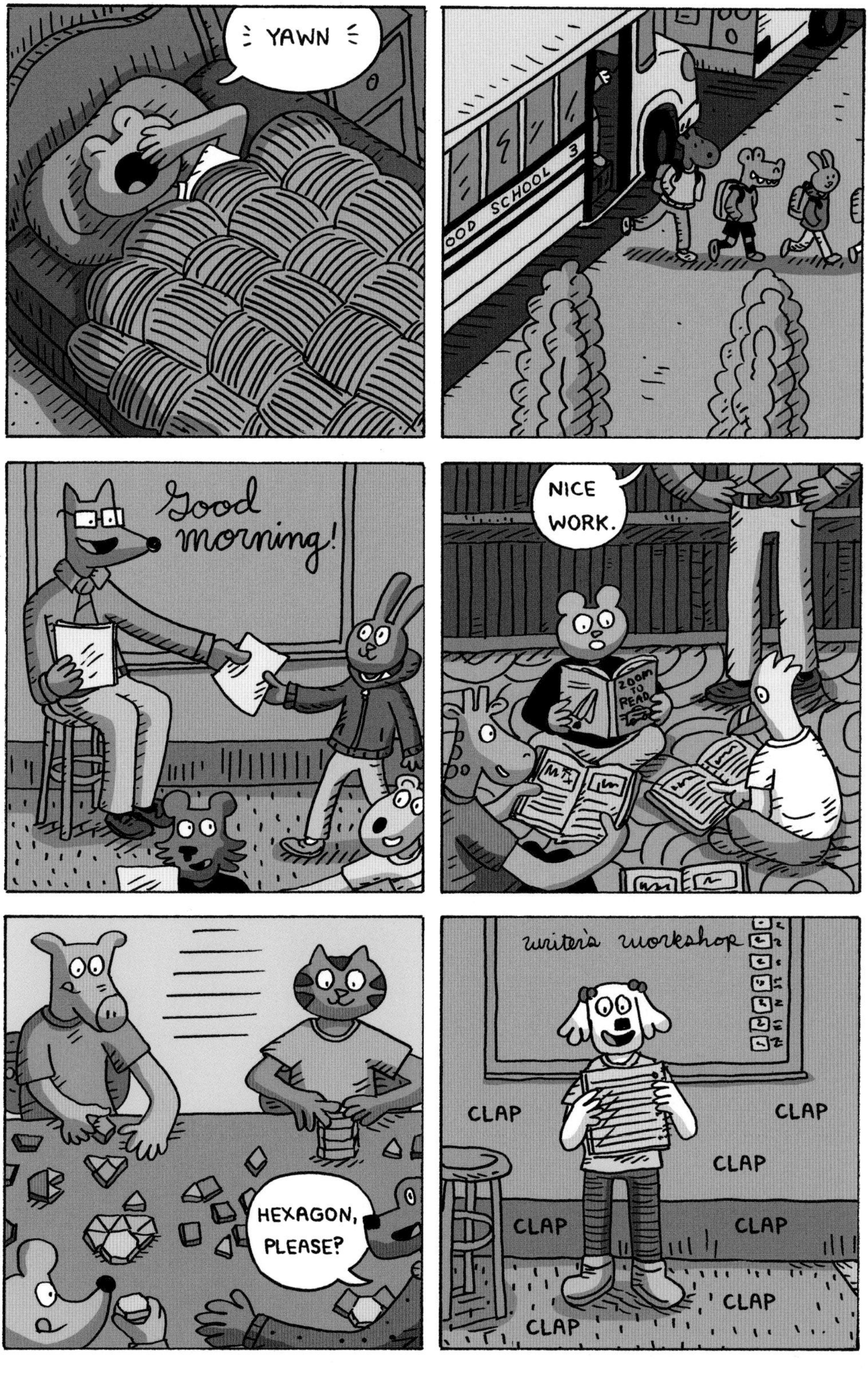
YAWN
OOD SCHOOL 3
Good morning!
NICE WORK.
ZOOM TO READ
HEXAGON, PLEASE?
writer's workshop
CLAP
CLAP
CLAP
CLAP
CLAP
CLAP
CLAP

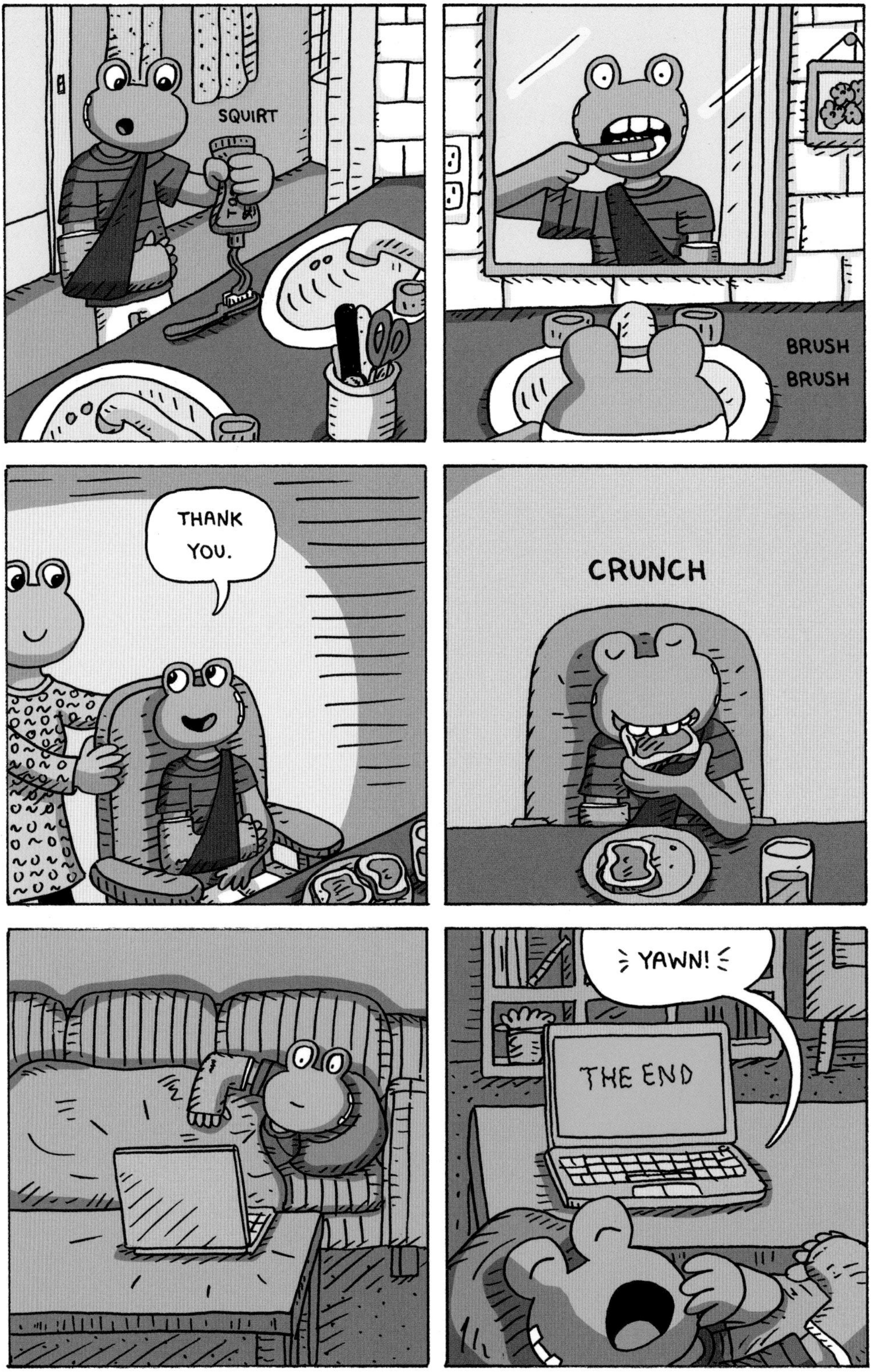
SQUIRT
BRUSH
BRUSH
THANK YOU.
CRUNCH
YAWN!
THE END

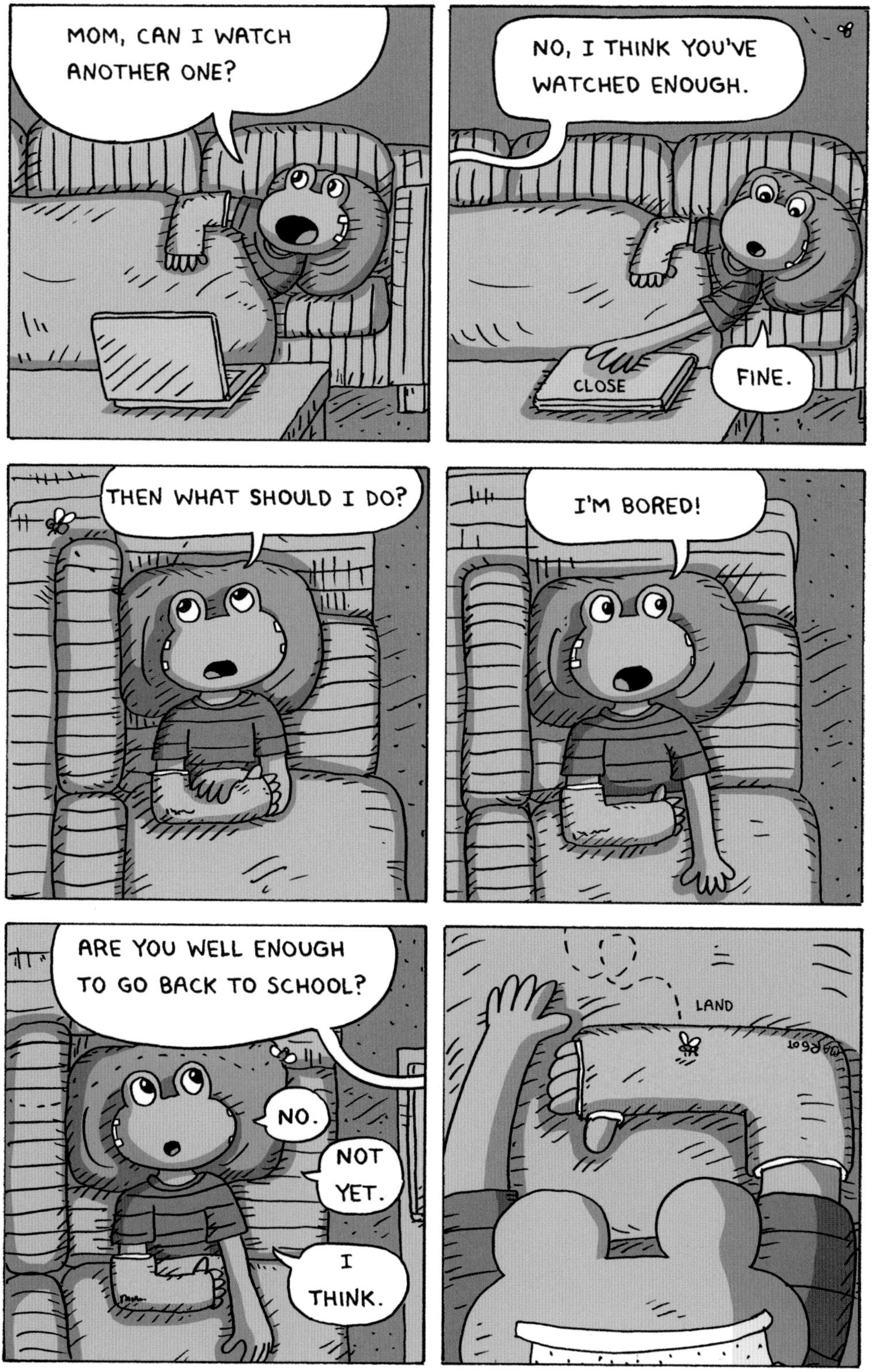
MOM, CAN I WATCH ANOTHER ONE?
NO, I THINK YOU'VE WATCHED ENOUGH.
CLOSE
FINE.
THEN WHAT SHOULD I DO?
I'M BORED!
ARE YOU WELL ENOUGH TO GO BACK TO SCHOOL?
NO.
NOT YET.
I THINK.
LAND

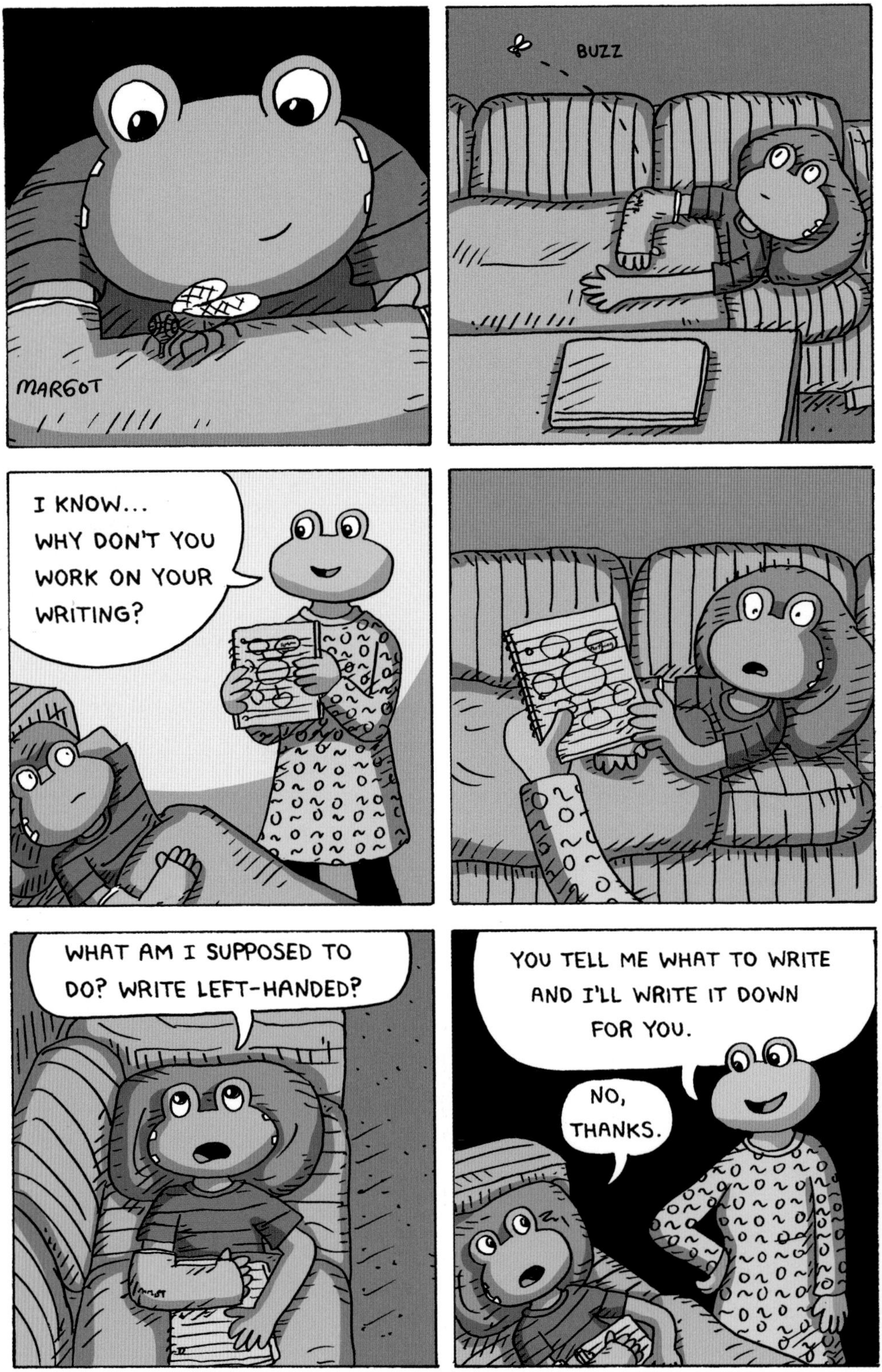
MARGOT
BUZZ
I KNOW... WHY DON'T YOU WORK ON YOUR WRITING?
WHAT AM I SUPPOSED TO DO? WRITE LEFT-HANDED?
YOU TELL ME WHAT TO WRITE AND I'LL WRITE IT DOWN FOR YOU.
NO, THANKS.

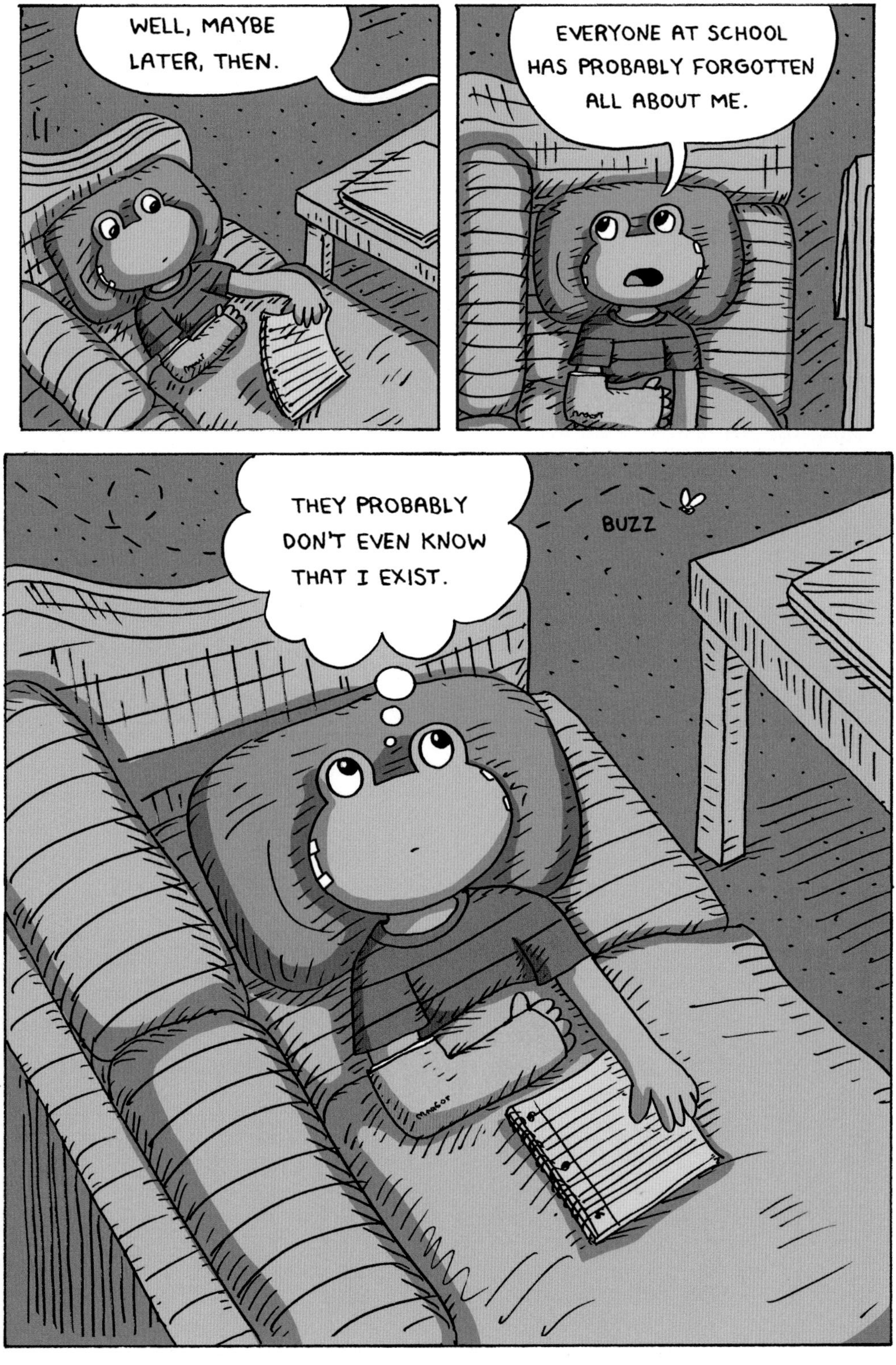
WELL, MAYBE LATER, THEN.
EVERYONE AT SCHOOL HAS PROBABLY FORGOTTEN ALL ABOUT ME.
THEY PROBABLY DON'T EVEN KNOW THAT I EXIST.
BUZZ

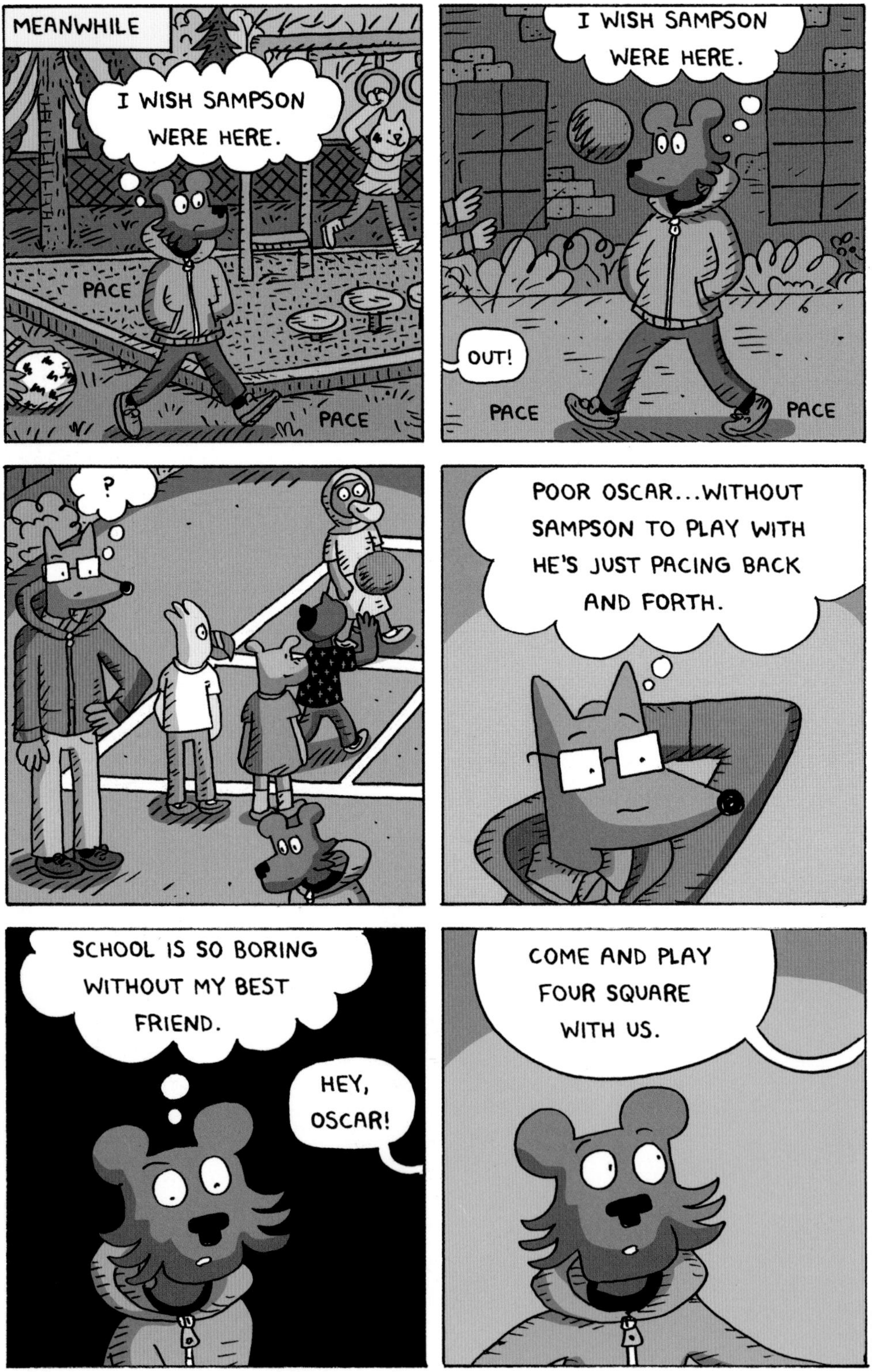
MEANWHILE
I WISH SAMPSON WERE HERE.
PACE
PACE
I WISH SAMPSON WERE HERE.
OUT!
PACE
PACE
?
POOR OSCAR...WITHOUT SAMPSON TO PLAY WITH HE'S JUST PACING BACK AND FORTH.
SCHOOL IS SO BORING WITHOUT MY BEST FRIEND.
HEY, OSCAR!
COME AND PLAY FOUR SQUARE WITH US.

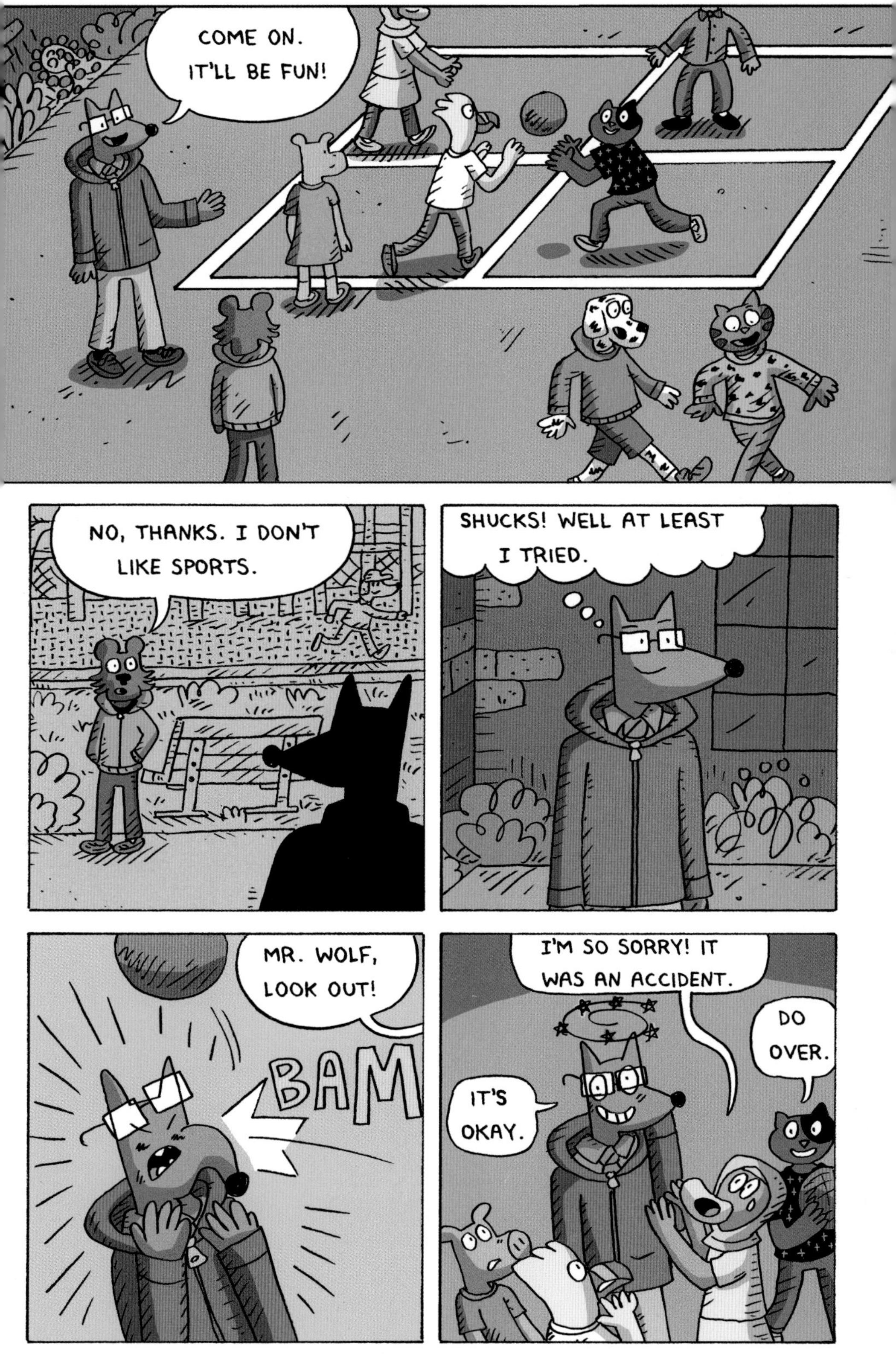

COME ON. IT'LL BE FUN!
NO, THANKS. I DON'T LIKE SPORTS.
SHUCKS! WELL AT LEAST I TRIED.
MR. WOLF, LOOK OUT!
BAM
I'M SO SORRY! IT WAS AN ACCIDENT.
IT'S OKAY.
DO OVER.

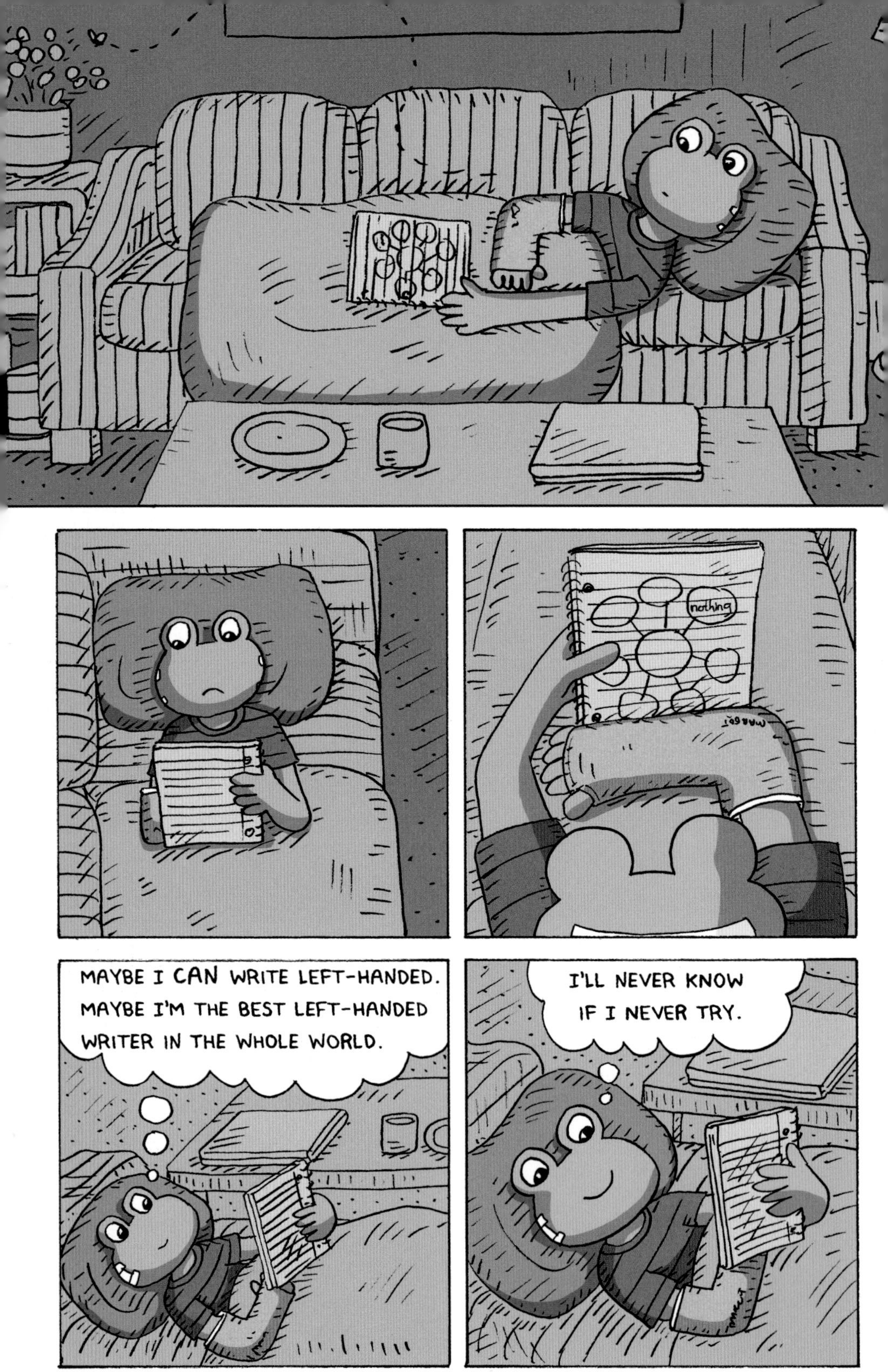
nothing
MAYBE I CAN WRITE LEFT-HANDED. MAYBE I'M THE BEST LEFT-HANDED WRITER IN THE WHOLE WORLD.
I'LL NEVER KNOW IF I NEVER TRY.

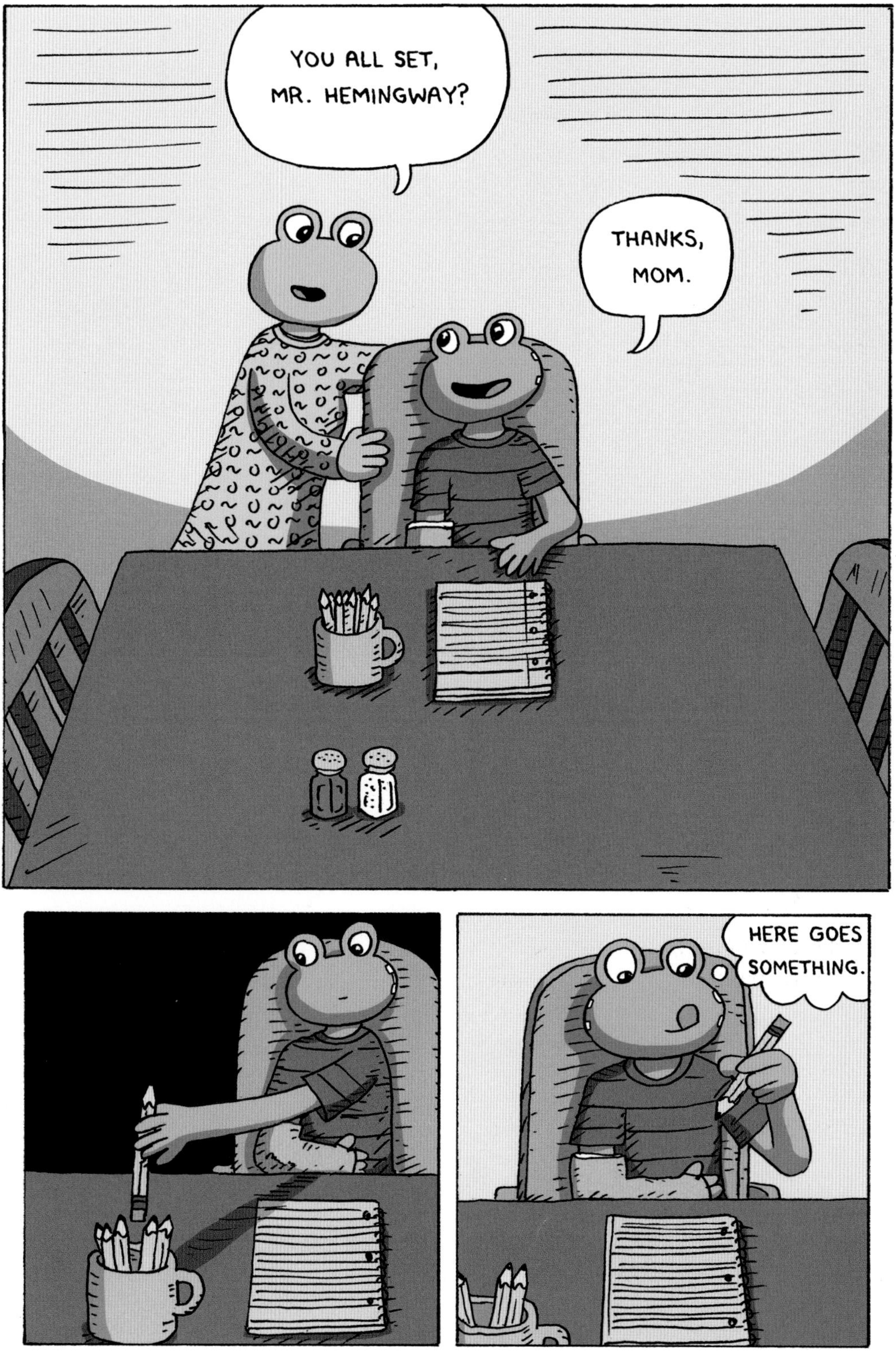
YOU ALL SET, MR. HEMINGWAY?
THANKS, MOM.
HERE GOES SOMETHING.

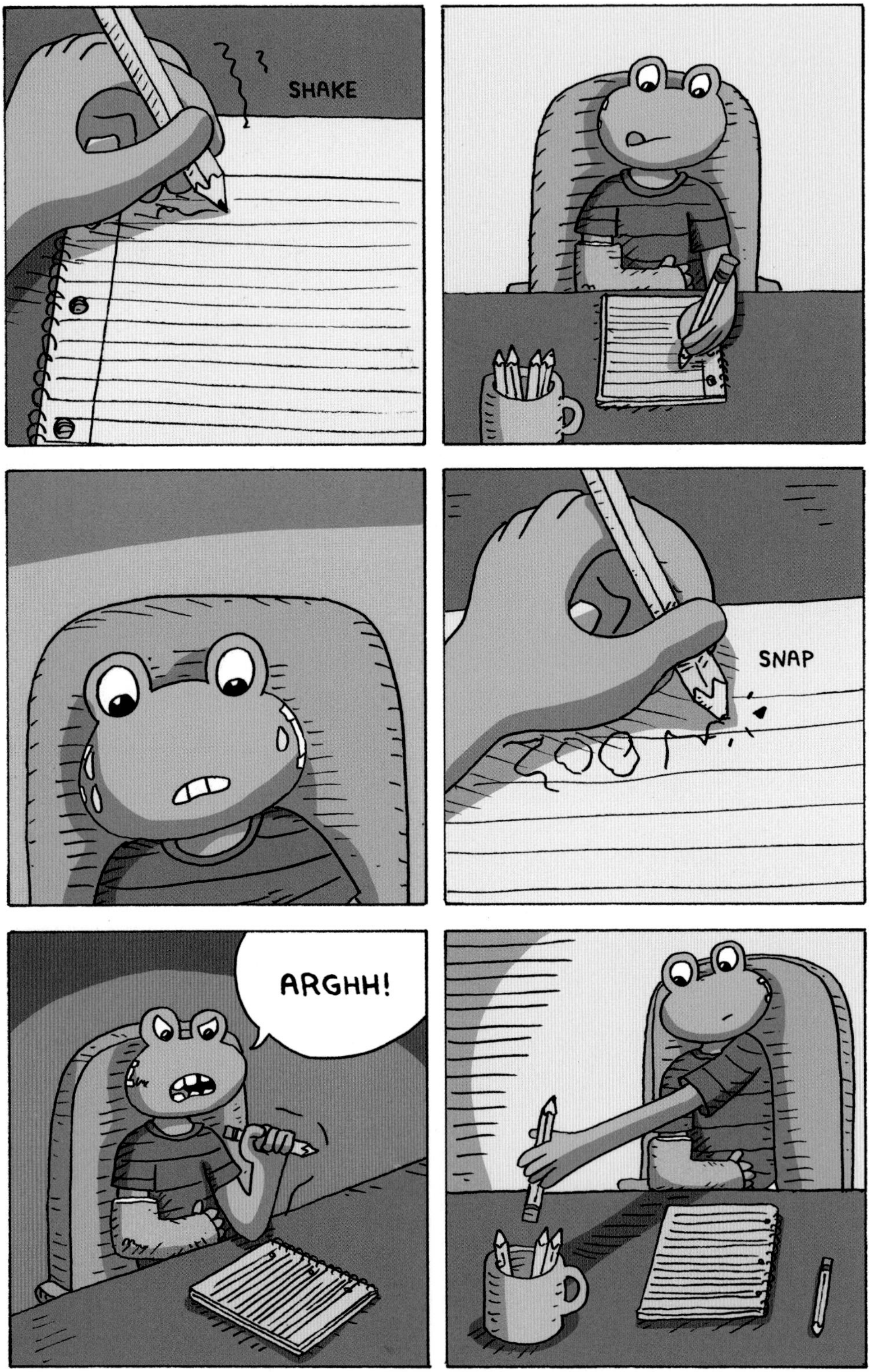
SHAKE
SNAP
ARGHH!

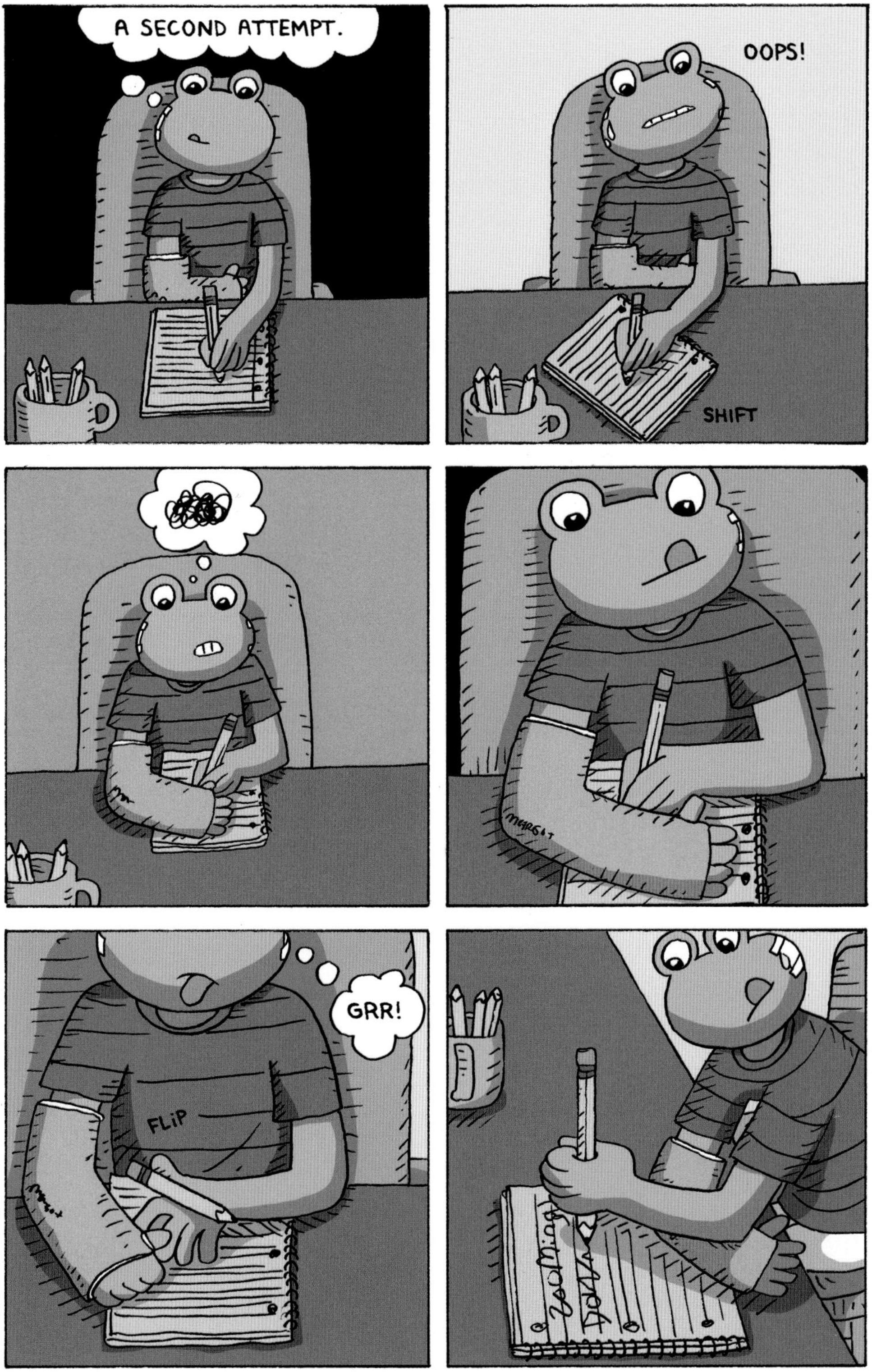
A SECOND ATTEMPT.
OOPS!
SHIFT
GRR!
FLIP

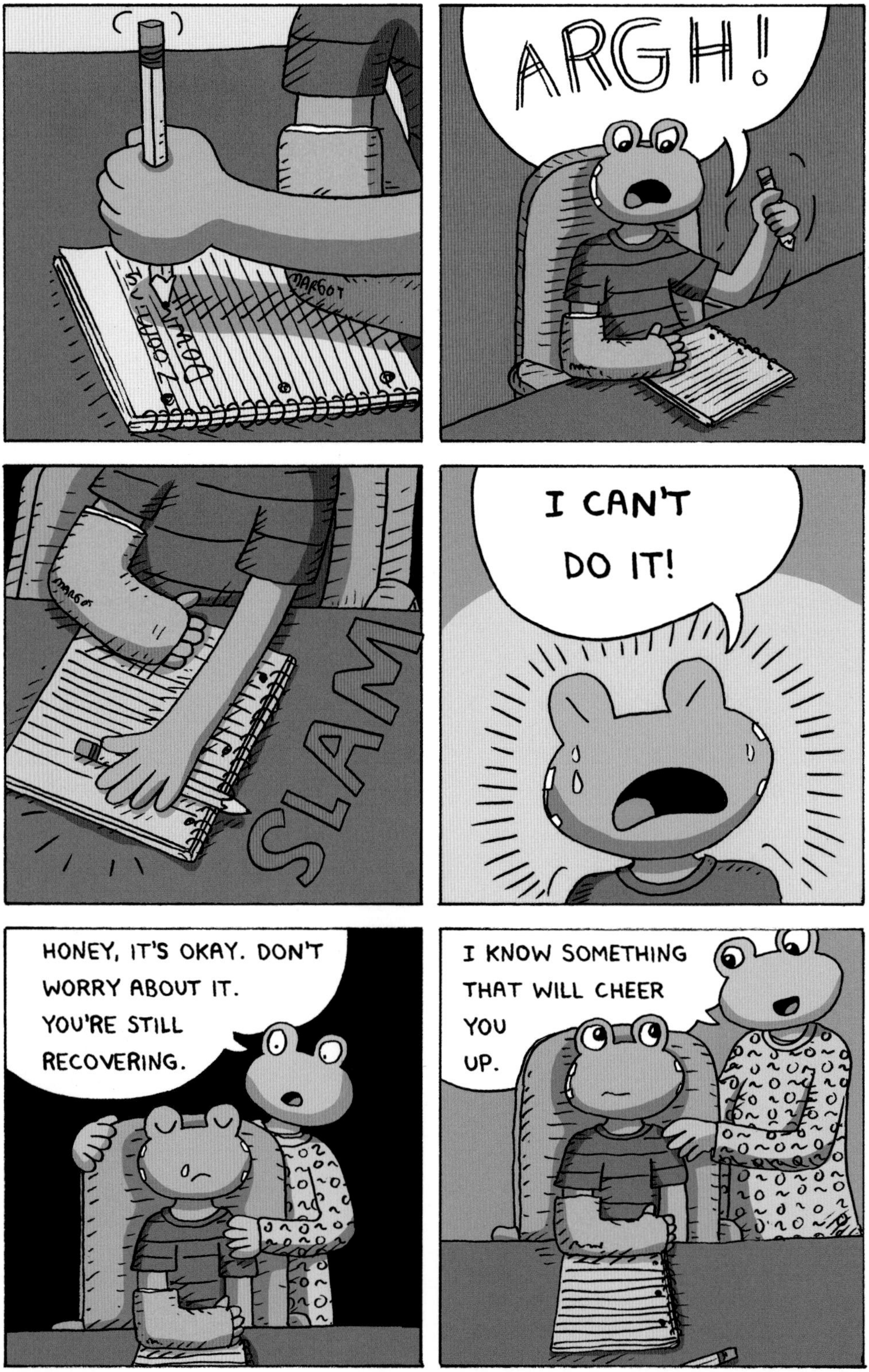
ARGH!
SLAM
I CAN'T DO IT!
HONEY, IT'S OKAY. DON'T WORRY ABOUT IT. YOU'RE STILL RECOVERING.
I KNOW SOMETHING THAT WILL CHEER YOU UP.

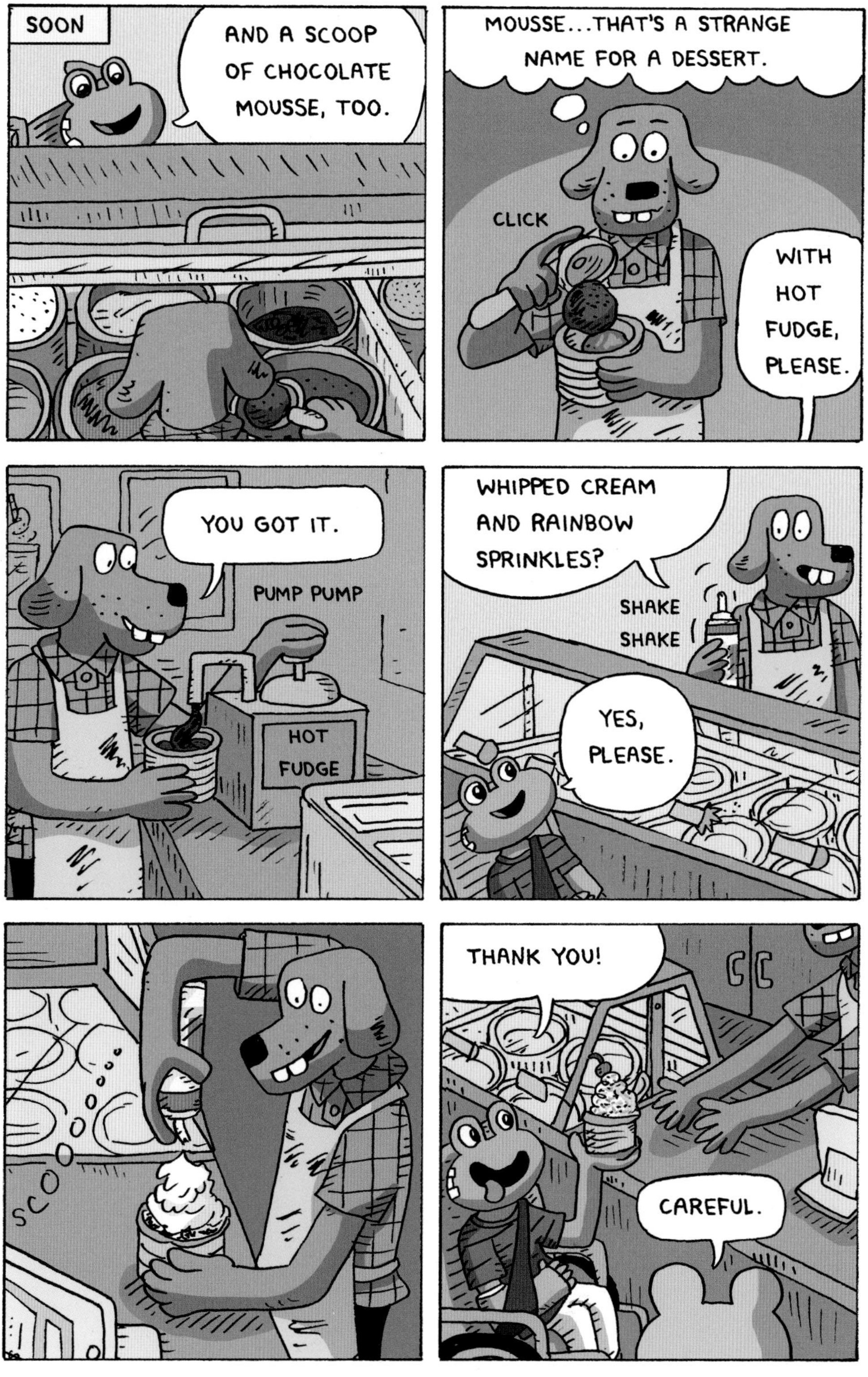
SOON
AND A SCOOP OF CHOCOLATE MOUSSE, TOO.
MOUSSE...THAT'S A STRANGE NAME FOR A DESSERT.
CLICK
WITH HOT FUDGE, PLEASE.
YOU GOT IT.
PUMP PUMP
HOT FUDGE
WHIPPED CREAM AND RAINBOW SPRINKLES?
SHAKE SHAKE
YES, PLEASE.
THANK YOU!
CAREFUL.

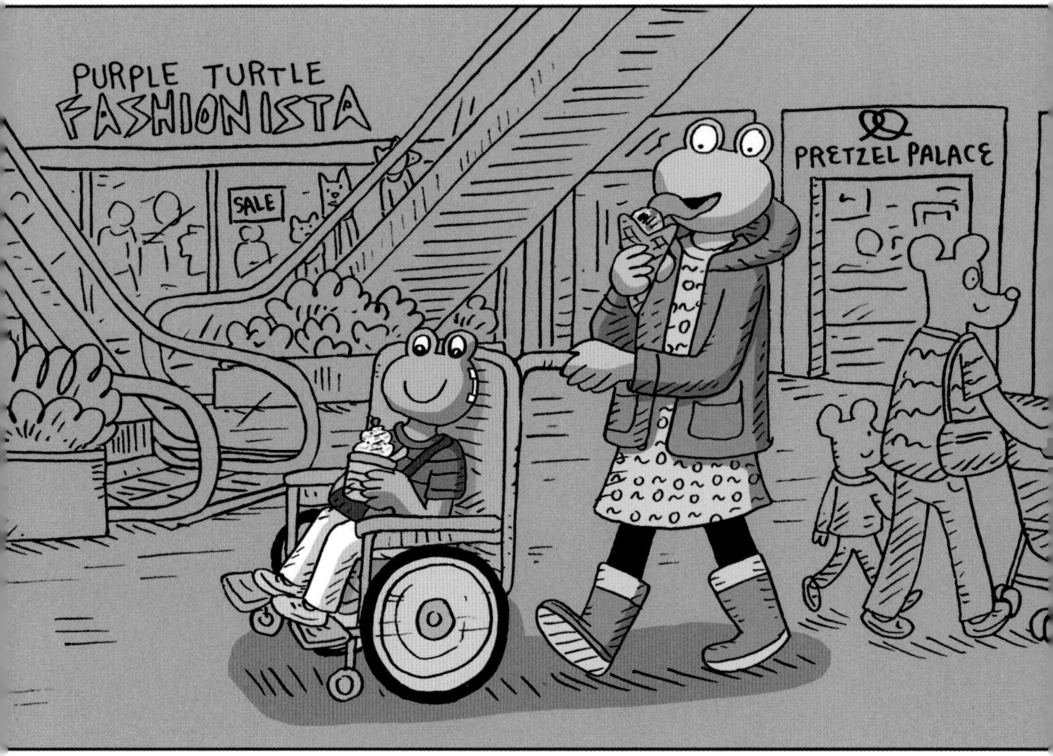
PURPLE TURTLE
FASHIONISTA
SALE
PRETZEL PALACE

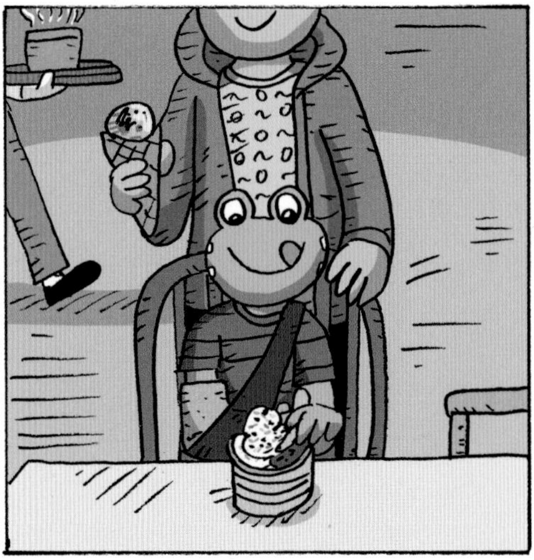

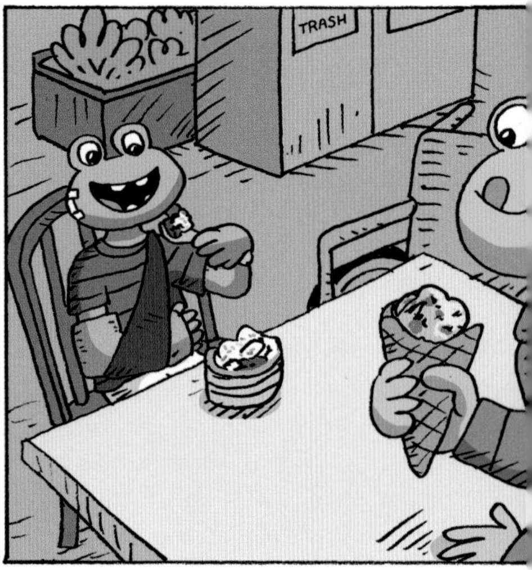
TRASH

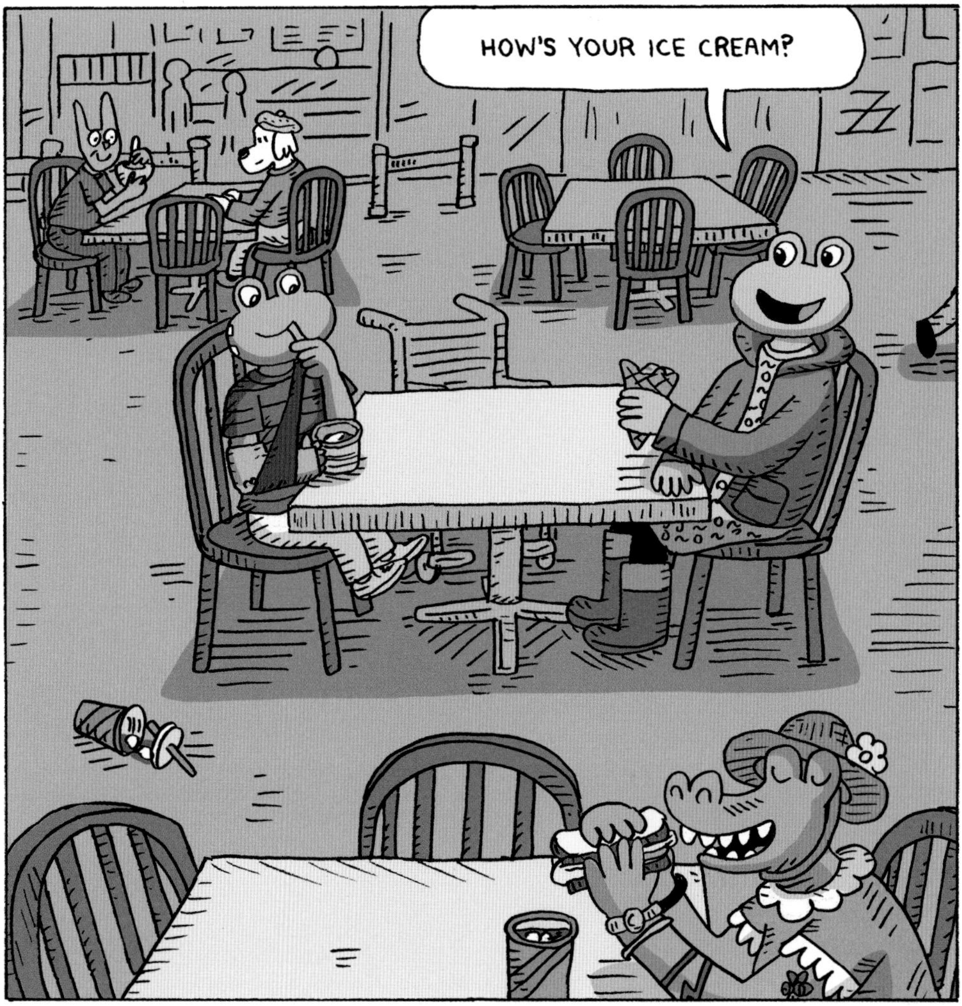
HOW'S YOUR ICE CREAM?

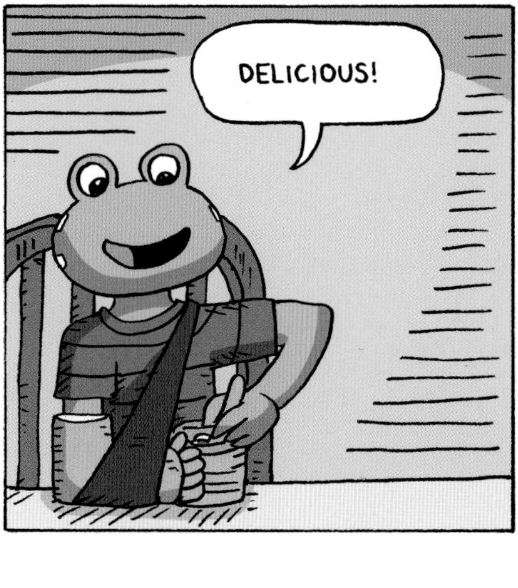
DELICIOUS!

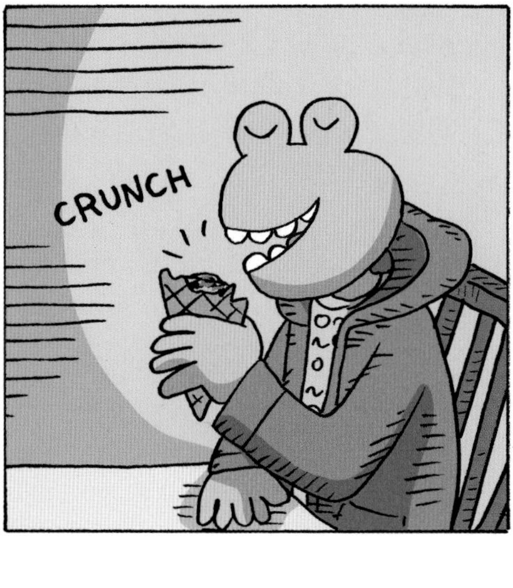
CRUNCH

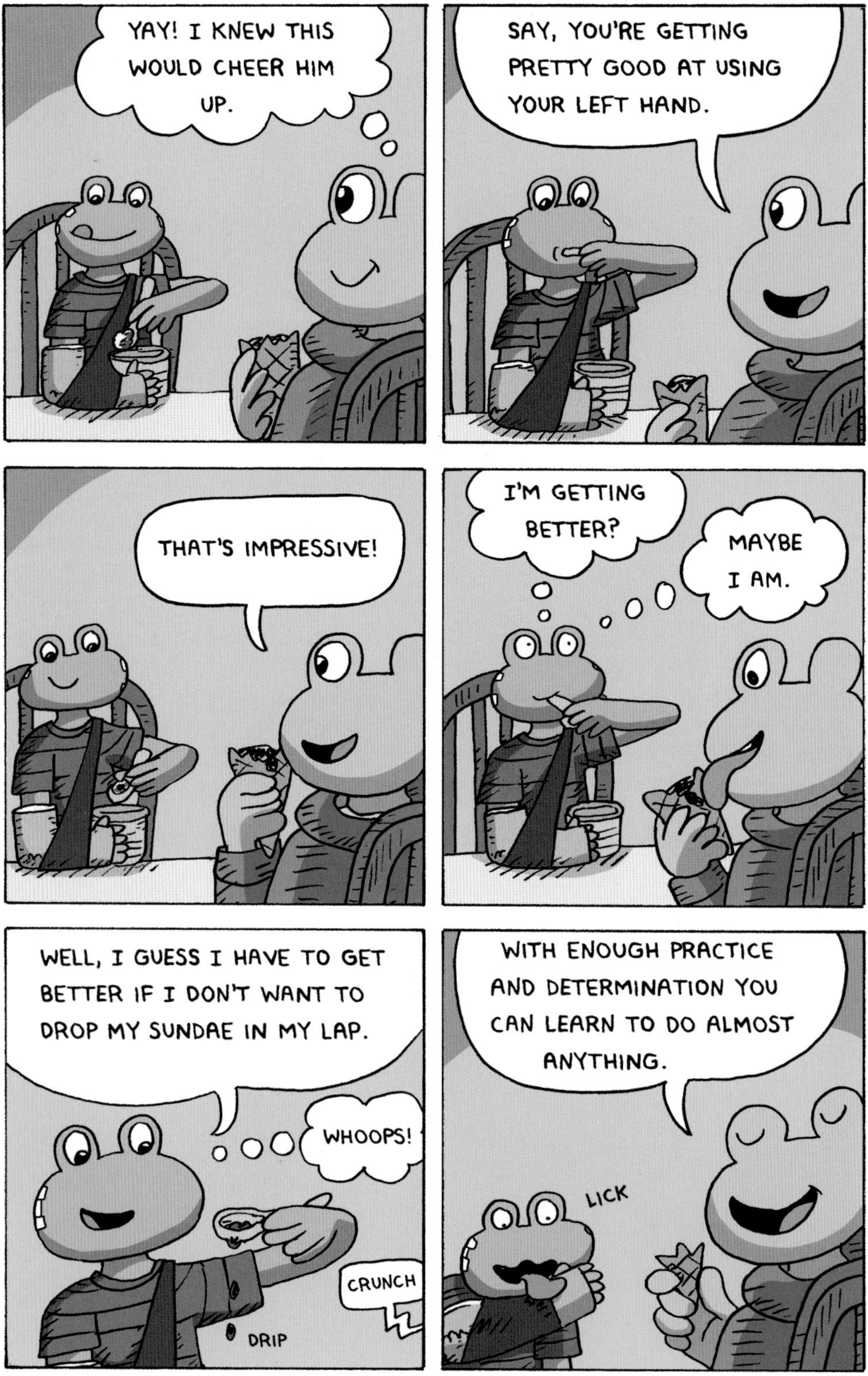
YAY! I KNEW THIS WOULD CHEER HIM UP.
SAY, YOU'RE GETTING PRETTY GOOD AT USING YOUR LEFT HAND.
THAT'S IMPRESSIVE!
I'M GETTING BETTER?
MAYBE I AM.
WELL, I GUESS I HAVE TO GET BETTER IF I DON'T WANT TO DROP MY SUNDAE IN MY LAP.
WHOOPS!
CRUNCH
DRIP
WITH ENOUGH PRACTICE AND DETERMINATION YOU CAN LEARN TO DO ALMOST ANYTHING.
LICK

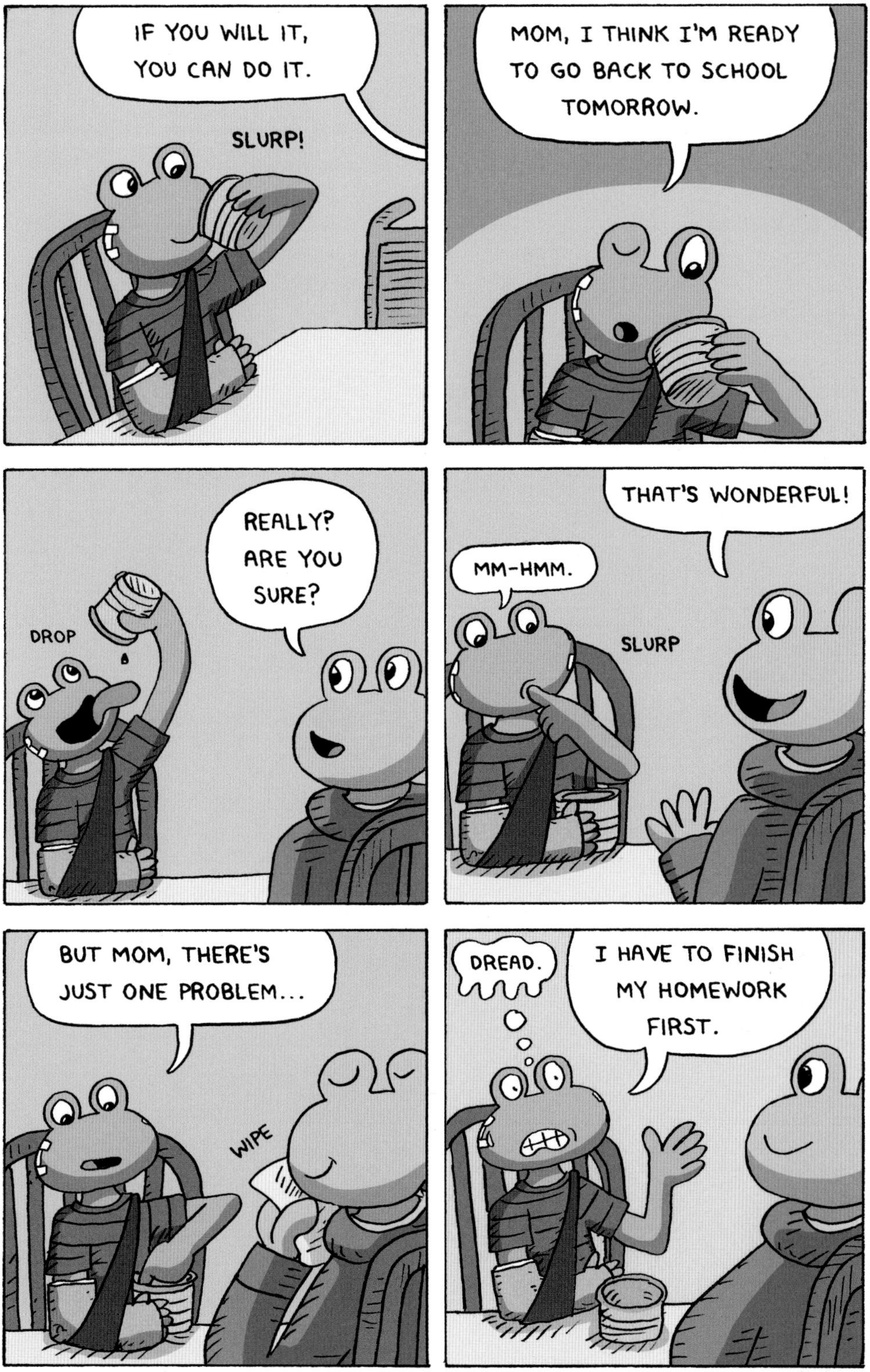
IF YOU WILL IT, YOU CAN DO IT.
SLURP!
MOM, I THINK I'M READY TO GO BACK TO SCHOOL TOMORROW.
REALLY? ARE YOU SURE?
DROP
MM-HMM.
THAT'S WONDERFUL!
SLURP
BUT MOM, THERE'S JUST ONE PROBLEM...
WIPE
DREAD.
I HAVE TO FINISH MY HOMEWORK FIRST.

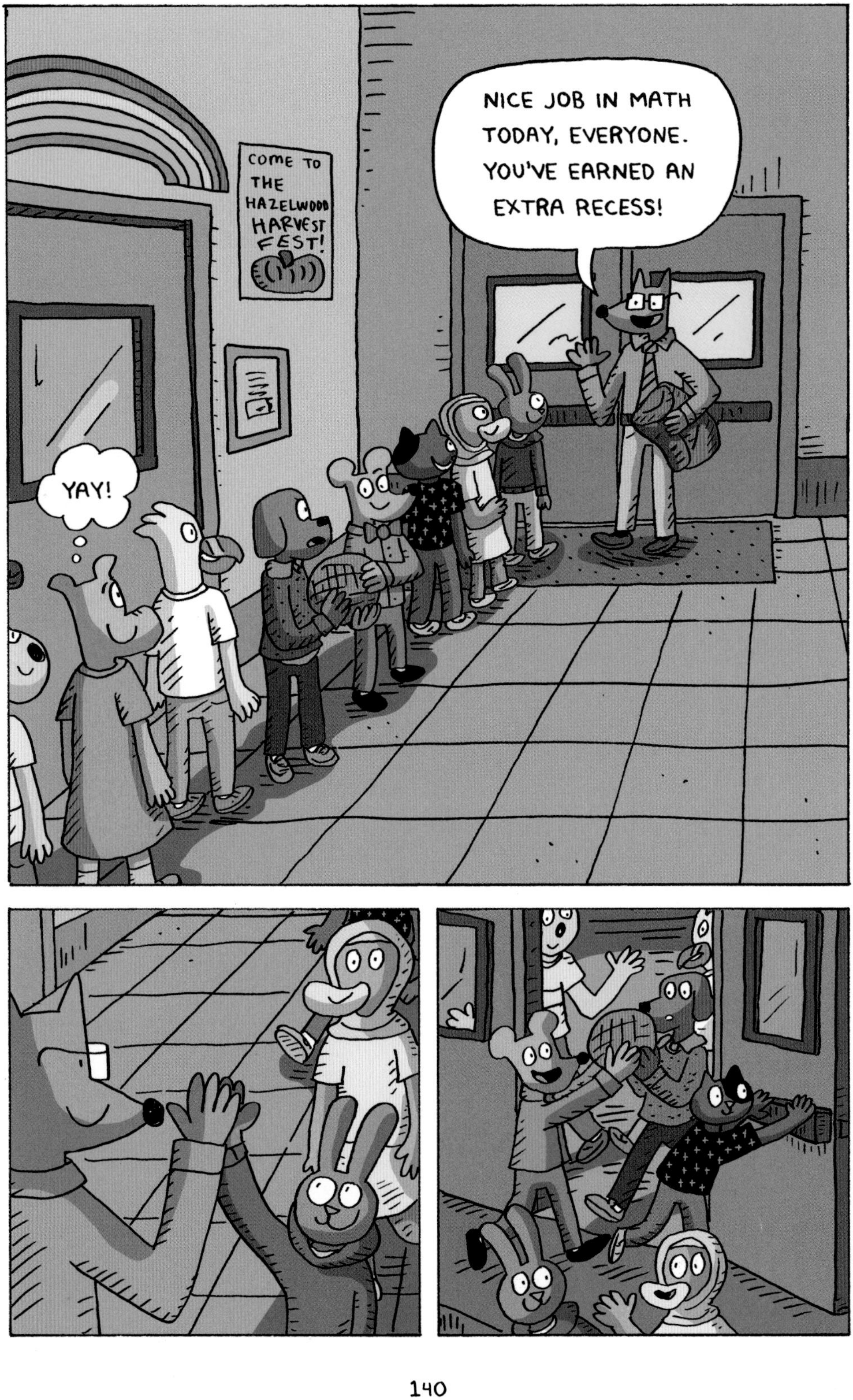
NICE JOB IN MATH TODAY, EVERYONE. YOU'VE EARNED AN EXTRA RECESS!
COME TO THE HAZELWOOD HARVEST FEST!
YAY!

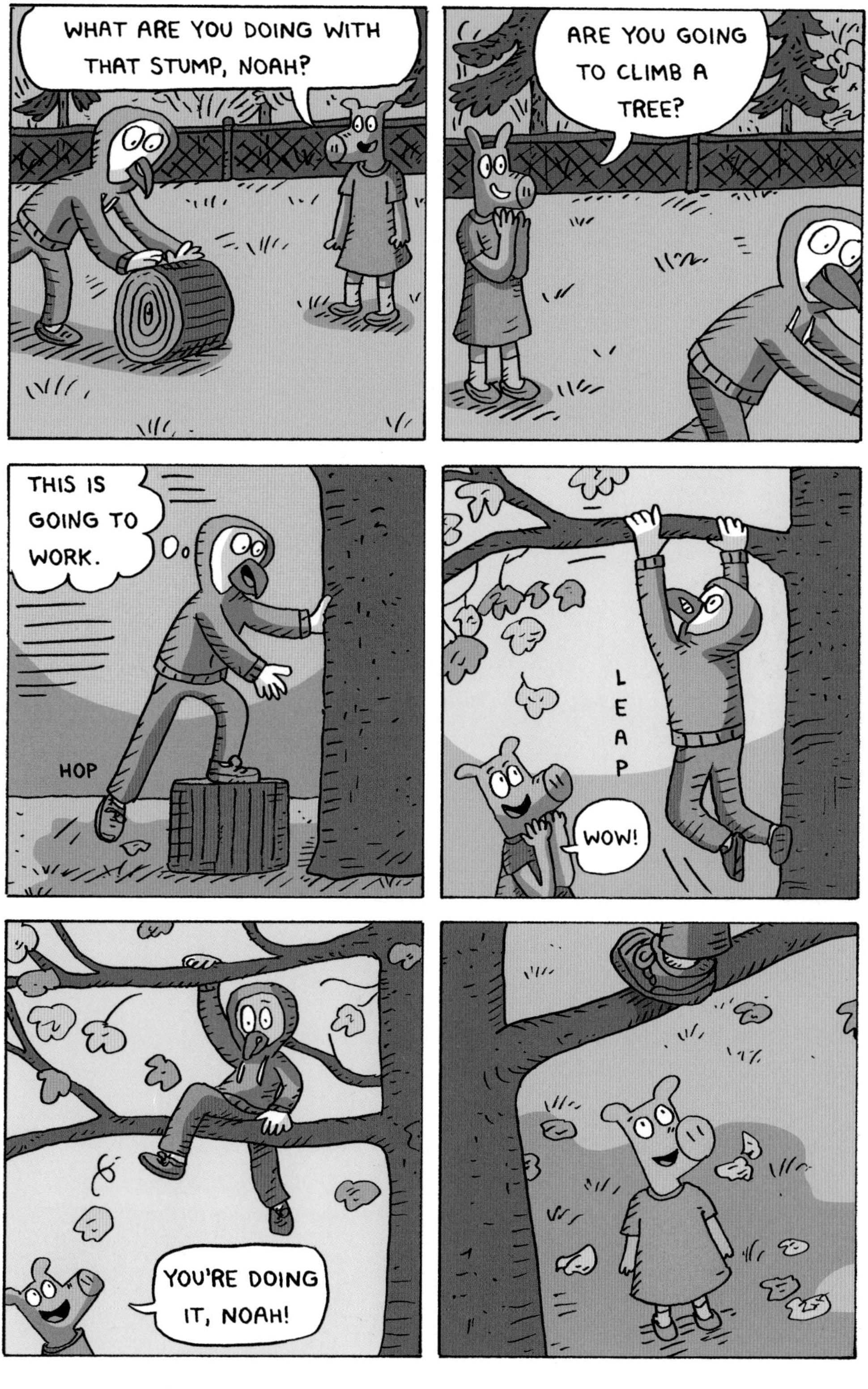
WHAT ARE YOU DOING WITH THAT STUMP, NOAH?
ARE YOU GOING TO CLIMB A TREE?
THIS IS GOING TO WORK.
HOP
L E A P
WOW!
YOU'RE DOING IT, NOAH!

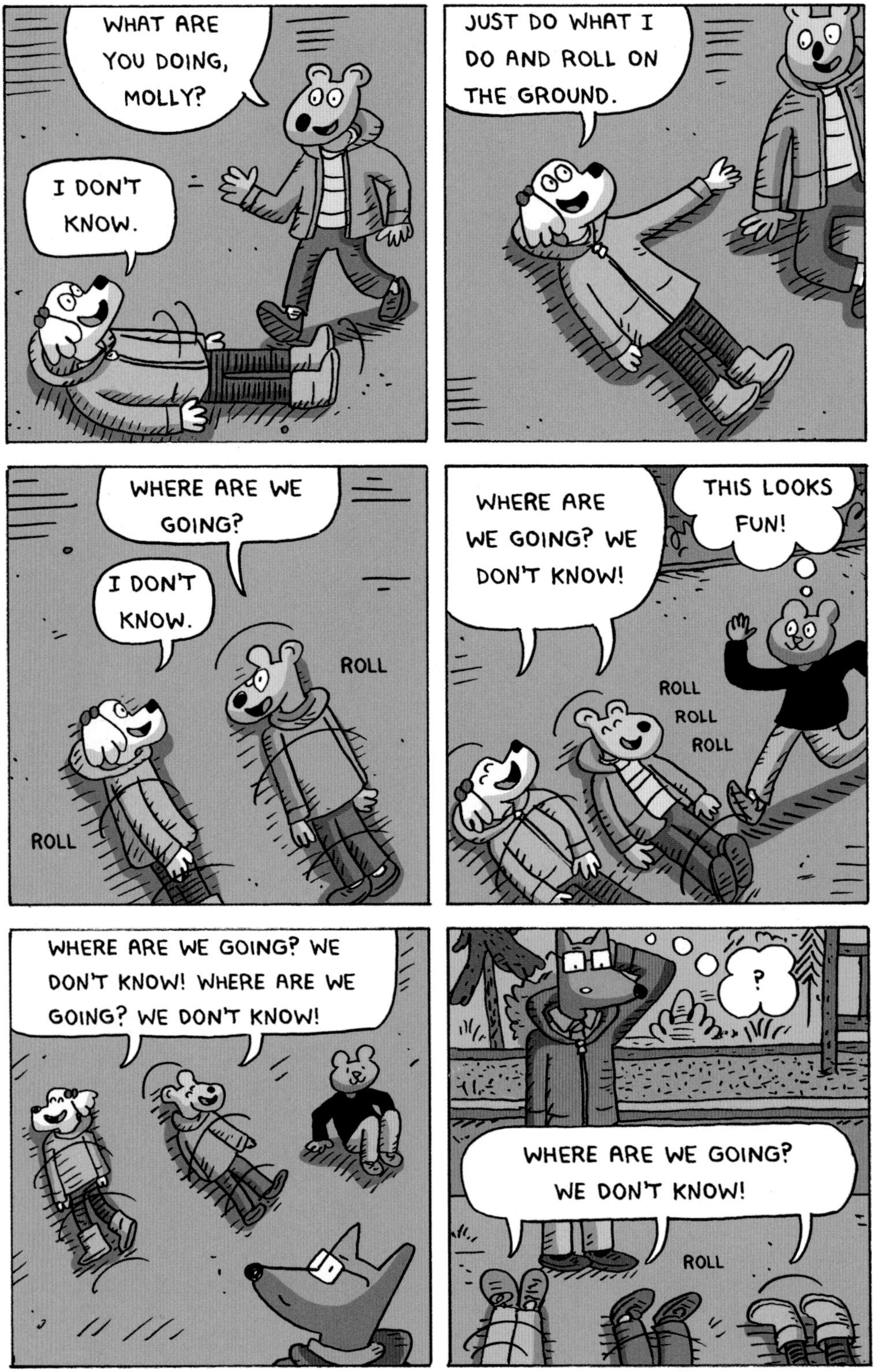
WHAT ARE YOU DOING, MOLLY?
I DON'T KNOW.
JUST DO WHAT I DO AND ROLL ON THE GROUND.
WHERE ARE WE GOING?
I DON'T KNOW.
ROLL
ROLL
WHERE ARE WE GOING? WE DON'T KNOW!
THIS LOOKS FUN!
ROLL
ROLL
ROLL
WHERE ARE WE GOING? WE DON'T KNOW! WHERE ARE WE GOING? WE DON'T KNOW!
?
WHERE ARE WE GOING? WE DON'T KNOW!
ROLL

MR. WOLF, LET ME INTRODUCE YOU TO OUR NEWEST BOARD MEMBERS.
SAY HELLO TO MR. ROSE AND MS. WAX.
HELLO... NICE TO MEET YOU.
I WAS SHOWING THEM HOW HARD WE'VE BEEN WORKING TO KEEP STUDENTS SAFE ON THE PLAYGROUND.
PRINCIPAL WILCOX, SHOULD THE CHILDREN BE ALLOWED TO CLIMB TREES?
!
I DID IT!
OH MAN!
SORRY, KIDS.

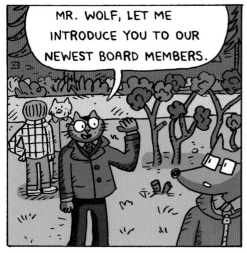

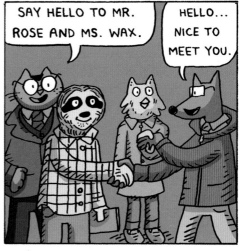

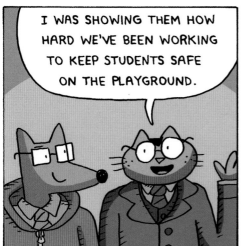

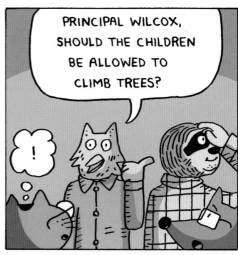

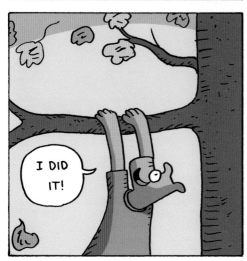

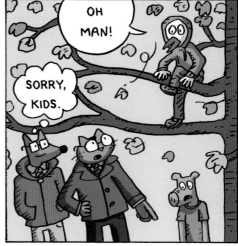

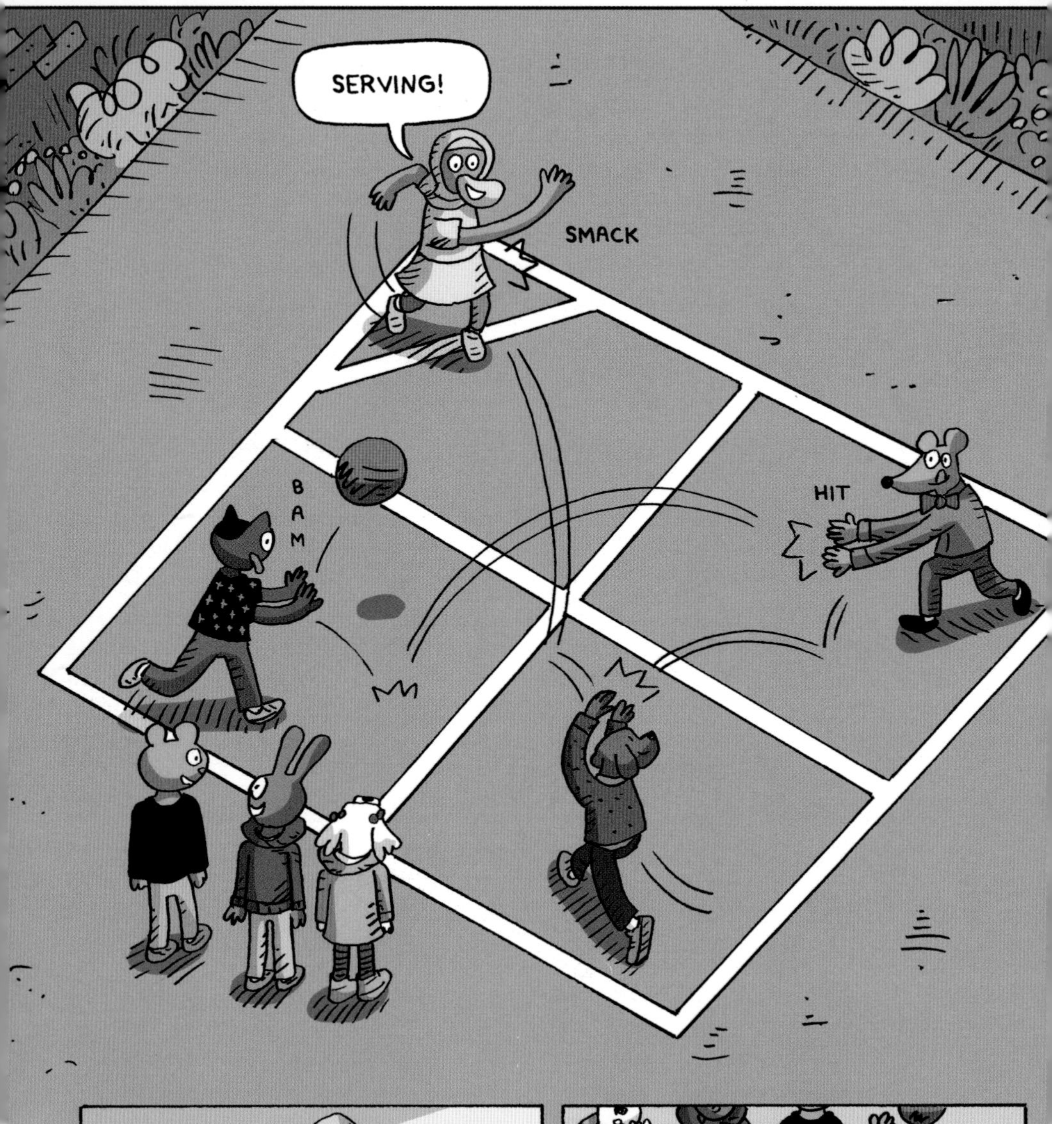
SERVING!
SMACK
BAM
HIT

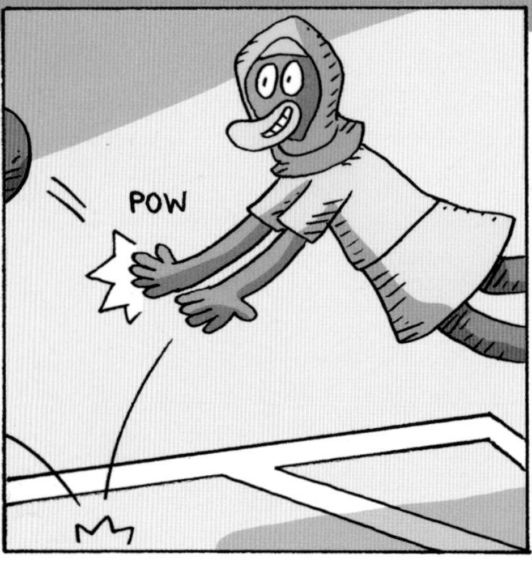
POW

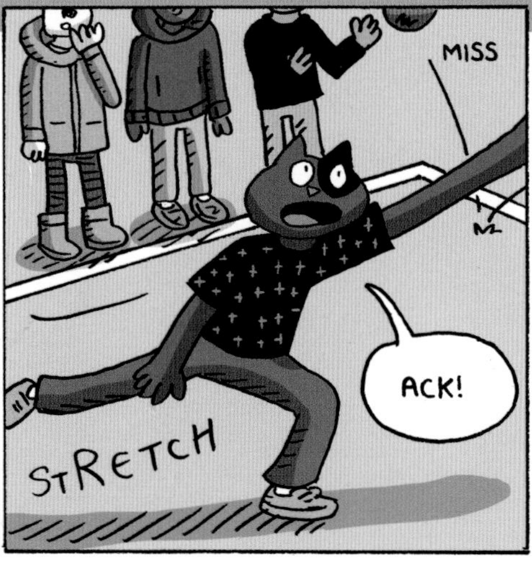
MISS
ACK!
STRETCH

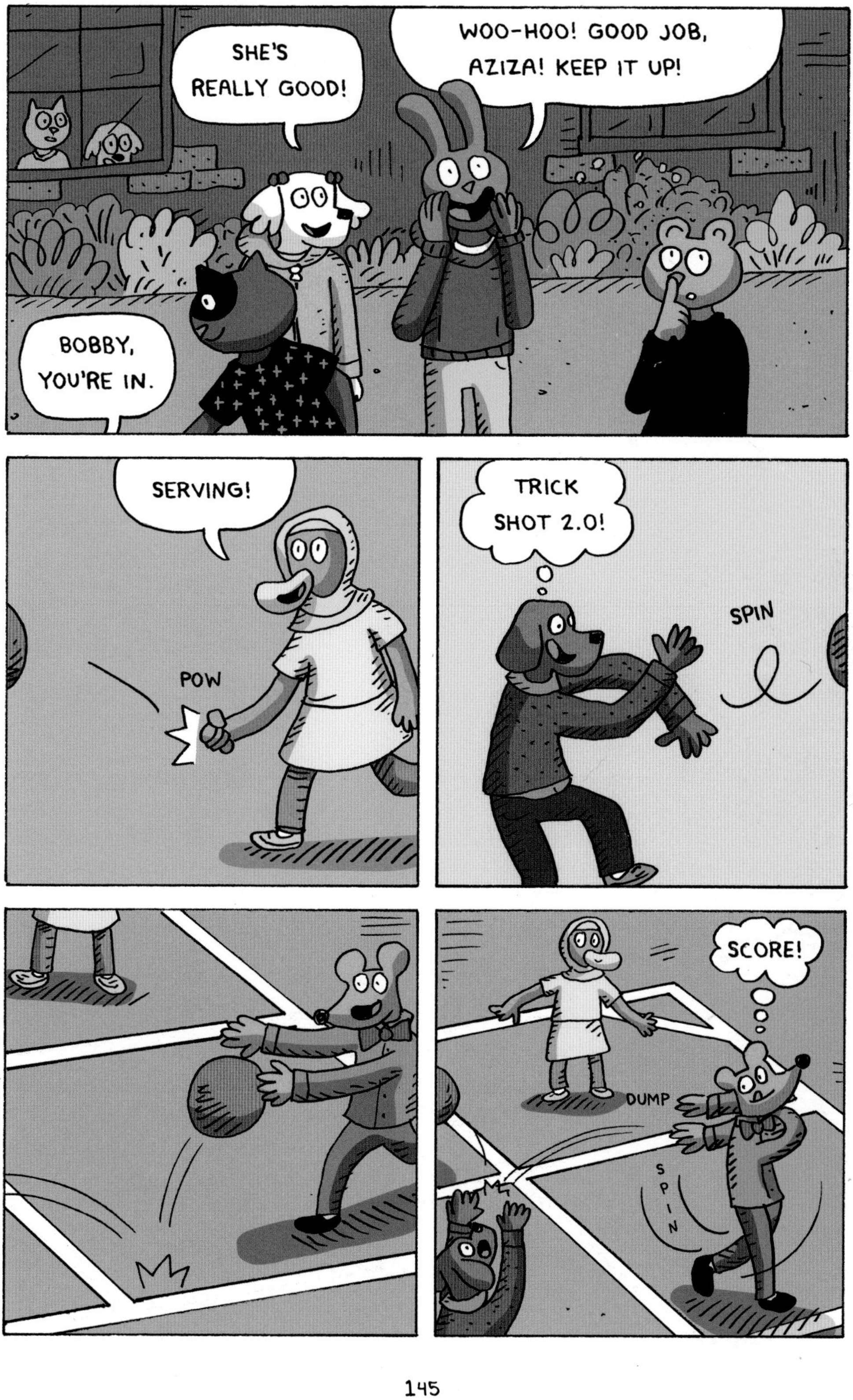
SHE'S REALLY GOOD!
WOO-HOO! GOOD JOB, AZIZA! KEEP IT UP!
BOBBY, YOU'RE IN.
SERVING!
POW
TRICK SHOT 2.0!
SPIN
SCORE!
DUMP
SPIN

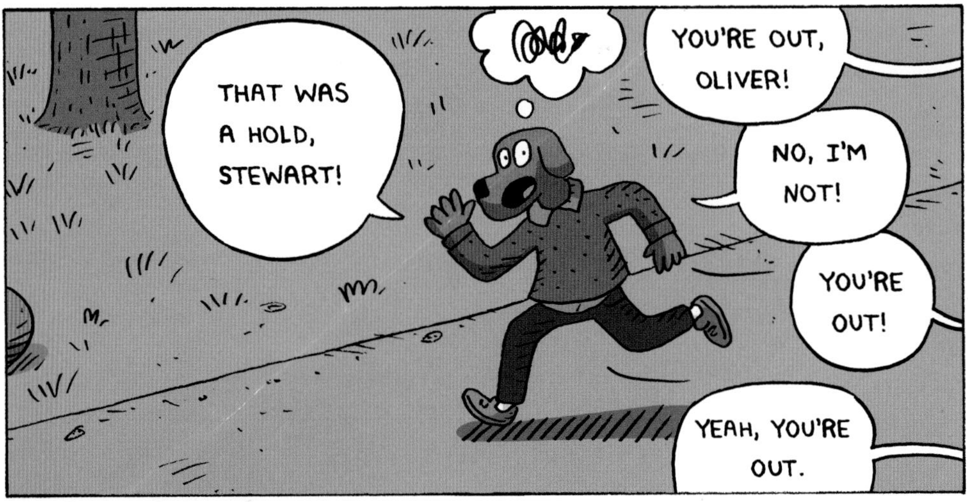
THAT WAS A HOLD, STEWART!
YOU'RE OUT, OLIVER!
NO, I'M NOT!
YOU'RE OUT!
YEAH, YOU'RE OUT.

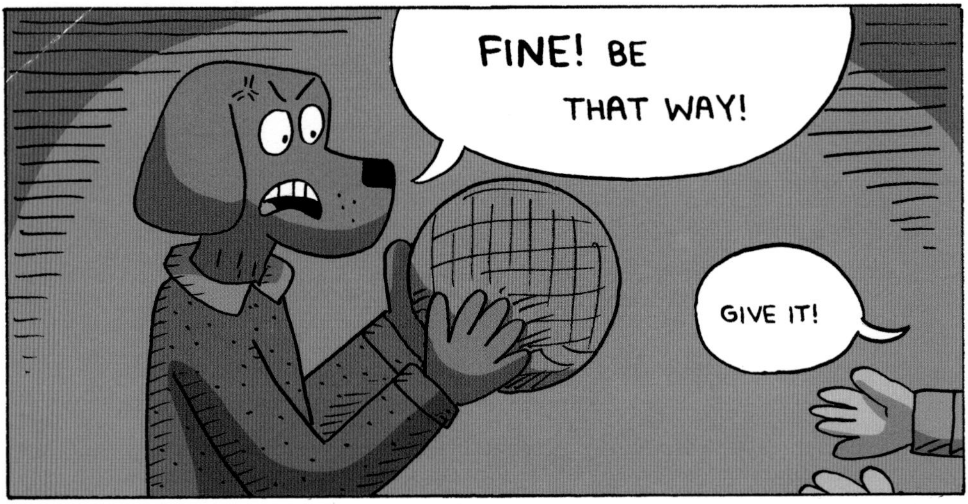
FINE! BE THAT WAY!
GIVE IT!

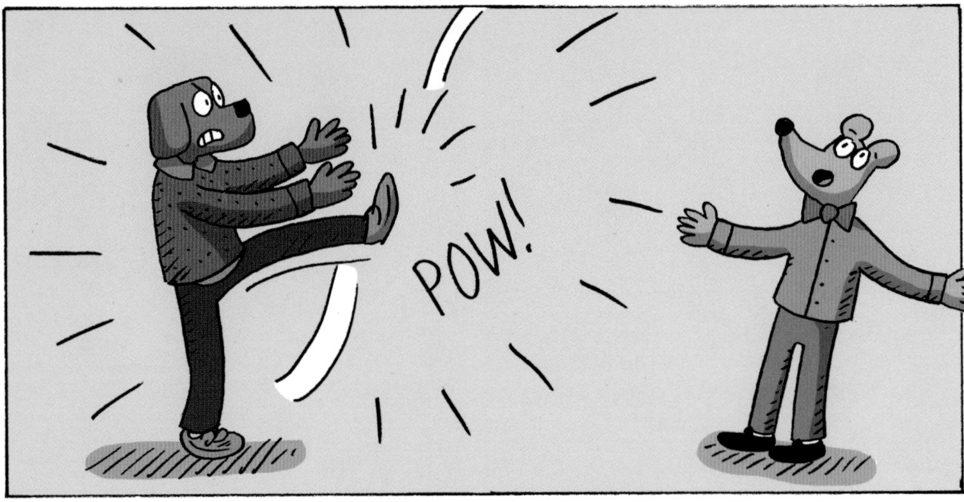
POW!

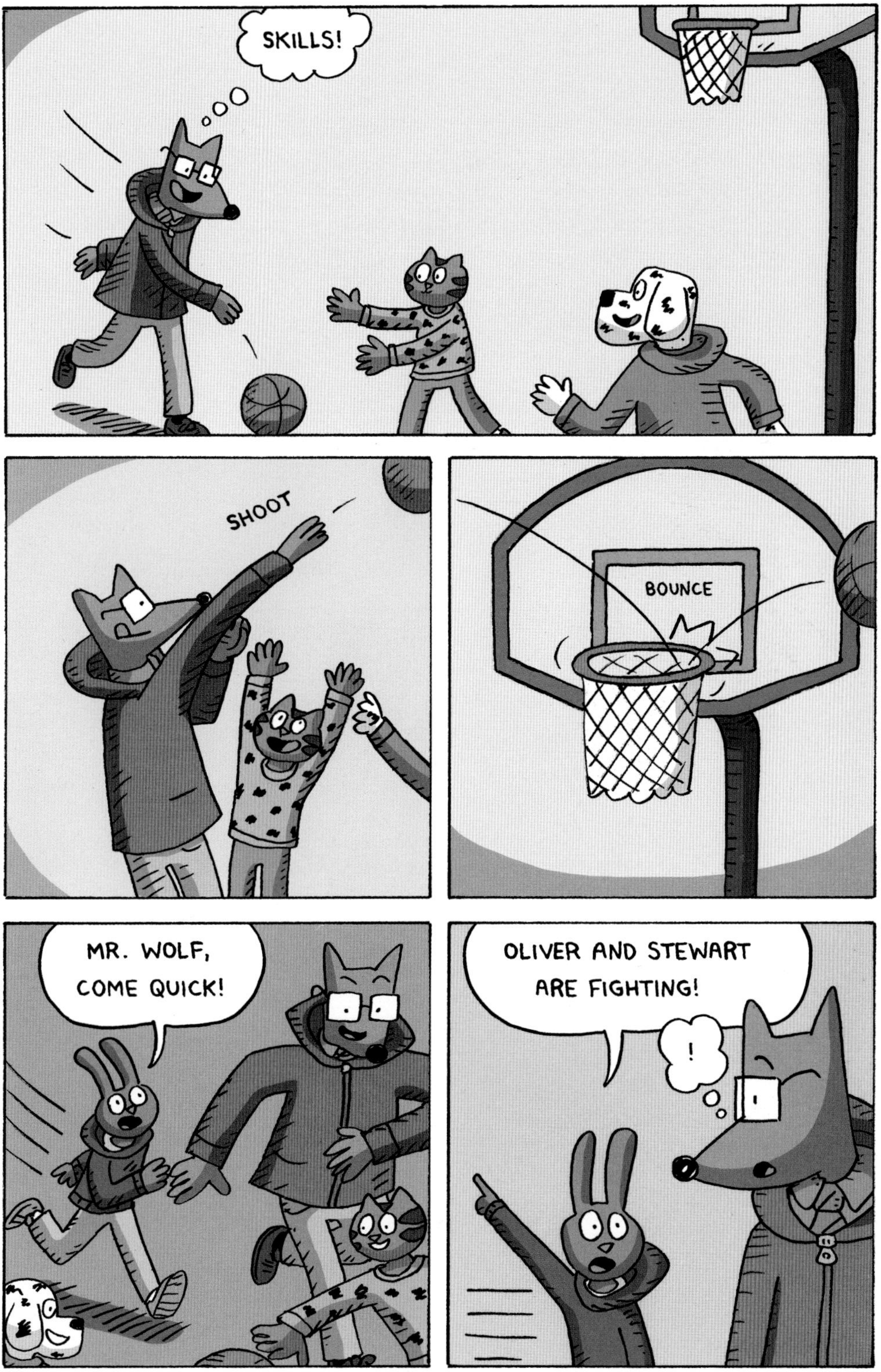
SKILLS!
SHOOT
BOUNCE
MR. WOLF, COME QUICK!
OLIVER AND STEWART ARE FIGHTING!
!

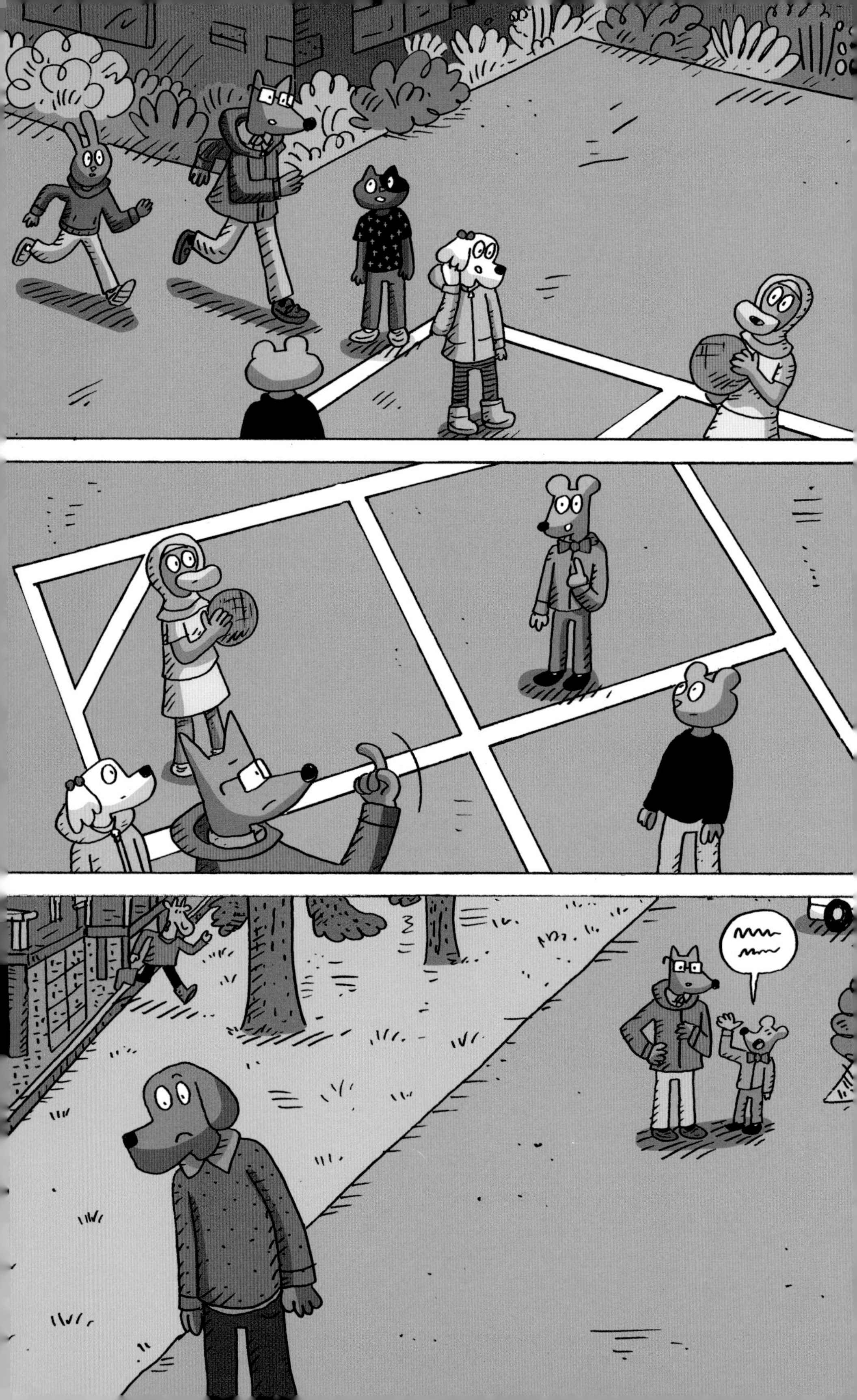

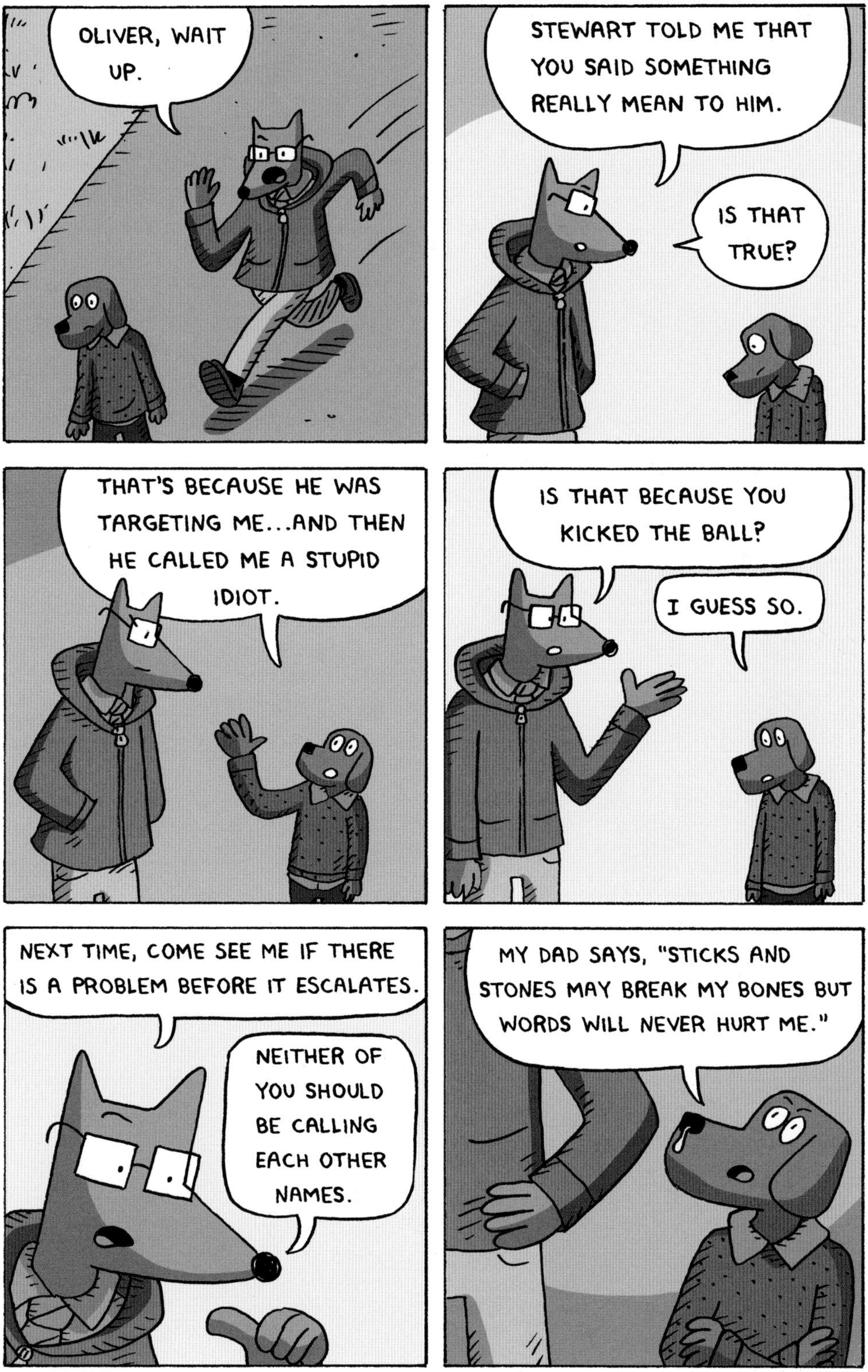
OLIVER, WAIT UP.
STEWART TOLD ME THAT YOU SAID SOMETHING REALLY MEAN TO HIM.
IS THAT TRUE?
THAT'S BECAUSE HE WAS TARGETING ME...AND THEN HE CALLED ME A STUPID IDIOT.
IS THAT BECAUSE YOU KICKED THE BALL?
I GUESS SO.
NEXT TIME, COME SEE ME IF THERE IS A PROBLEM BEFORE IT ESCALATES.
NEITHER OF YOU SHOULD BE CALLING EACH OTHER NAMES.
MY DAD SAYS, "STICKS AND STONES MAY BREAK MY BONES BUT WORDS WILL NEVER HURT ME."

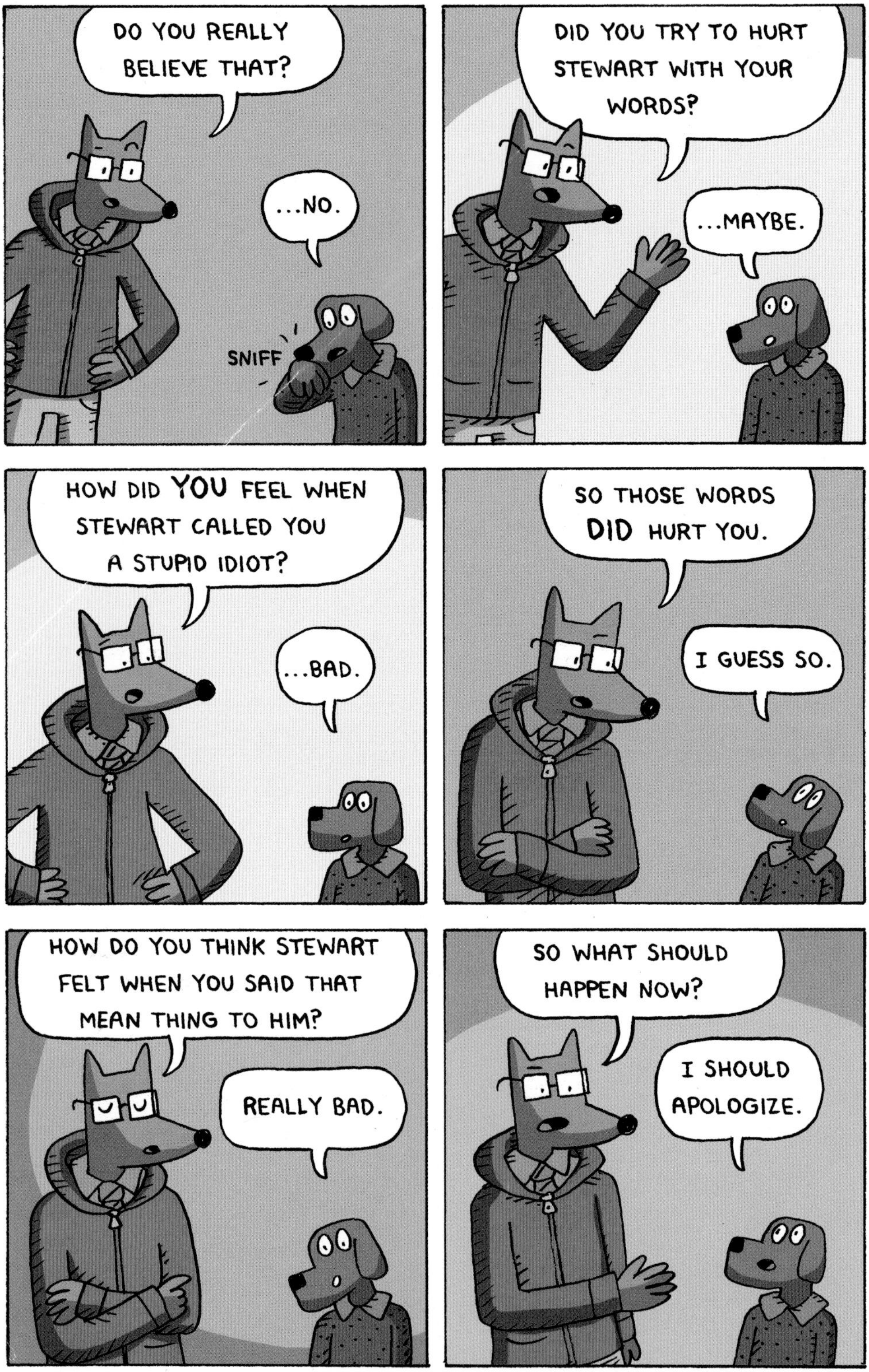
DO YOU REALLY BELIEVE THAT?
...NO.
SNIFF
DID YOU TRY TO HURT STEWART WITH YOUR WORDS?
...MAYBE.
HOW DID YOU FEEL WHEN STEWART CALLED YOU A STUPID IDIOT?
...BAD.
SO THOSE WORDS DID HURT YOU.
I GUESS SO.
HOW DO YOU THINK STEWART FELT WHEN YOU SAID THAT MEAN THING TO HIM?
REALLY BAD.
SO WHAT SHOULD HAPPEN NOW?
I SHOULD APOLOGIZE.

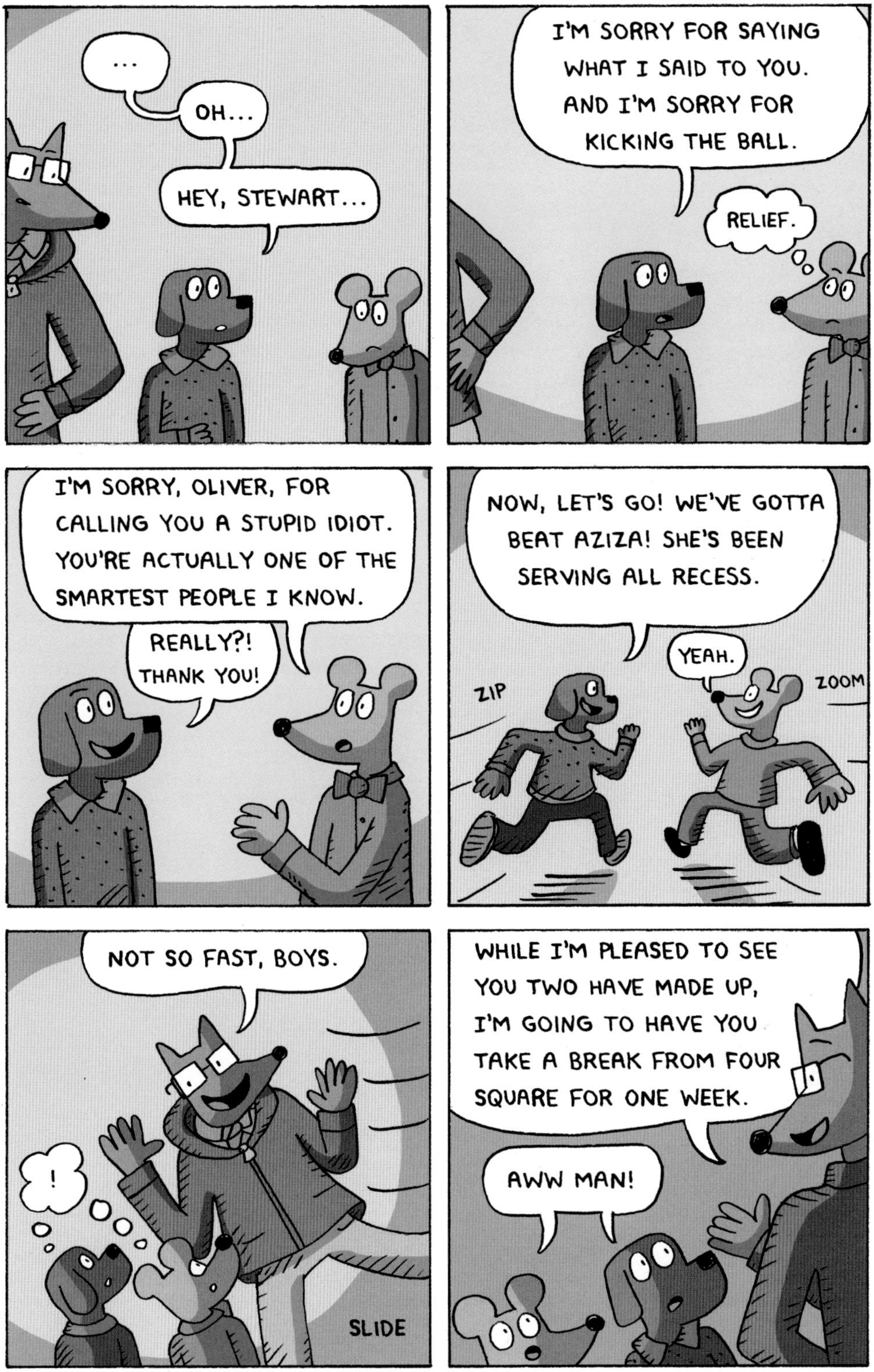
...
OH...
HEY, STEWART...
I'M SORRY FOR SAYING WHAT I SAID TO YOU. AND I'M SORRY FOR KICKING THE BALL.
RELIEF.
I'M SORRY, OLIVER, FOR CALLING YOU A STUPID IDIOT. YOU'RE ACTUALLY ONE OF THE SMARTEST PEOPLE I KNOW.
REALLY?! THANK YOU!
NOW, LET'S GO! WE'VE GOTTA BEAT AZIZA! SHE'S BEEN SERVING ALL RECESS.
YEAH.
ZIP
ZOOM
NOT SO FAST, BOYS.
!
SLIDE
WHILE I'M PLEASED TO SEE YOU TWO HAVE MADE UP, I'M GOING TO HAVE YOU TAKE A BREAK FROM FOUR SQUARE FOR ONE WEEK.
AWW MAN!

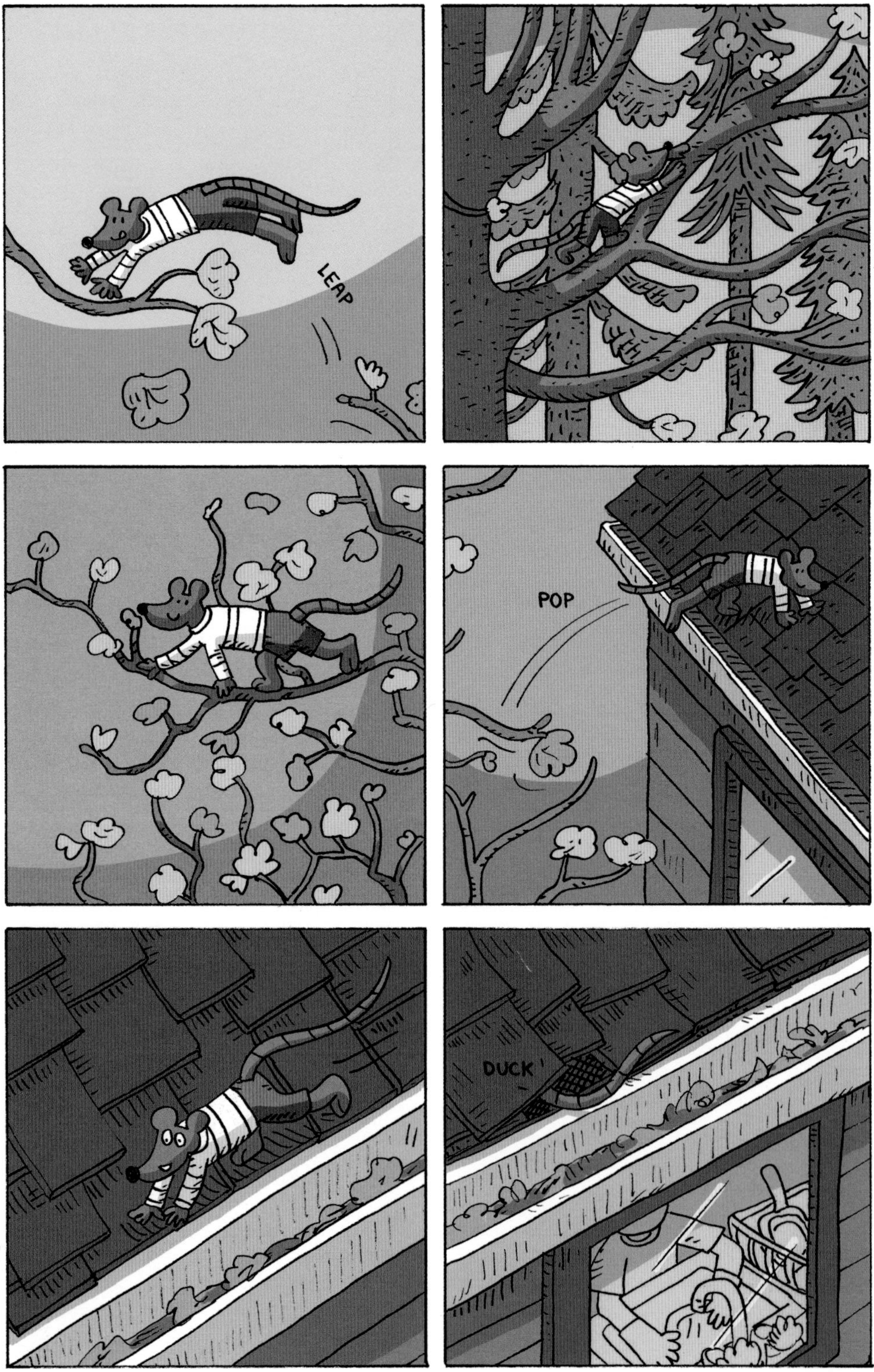
LEAP
POP
DUCK

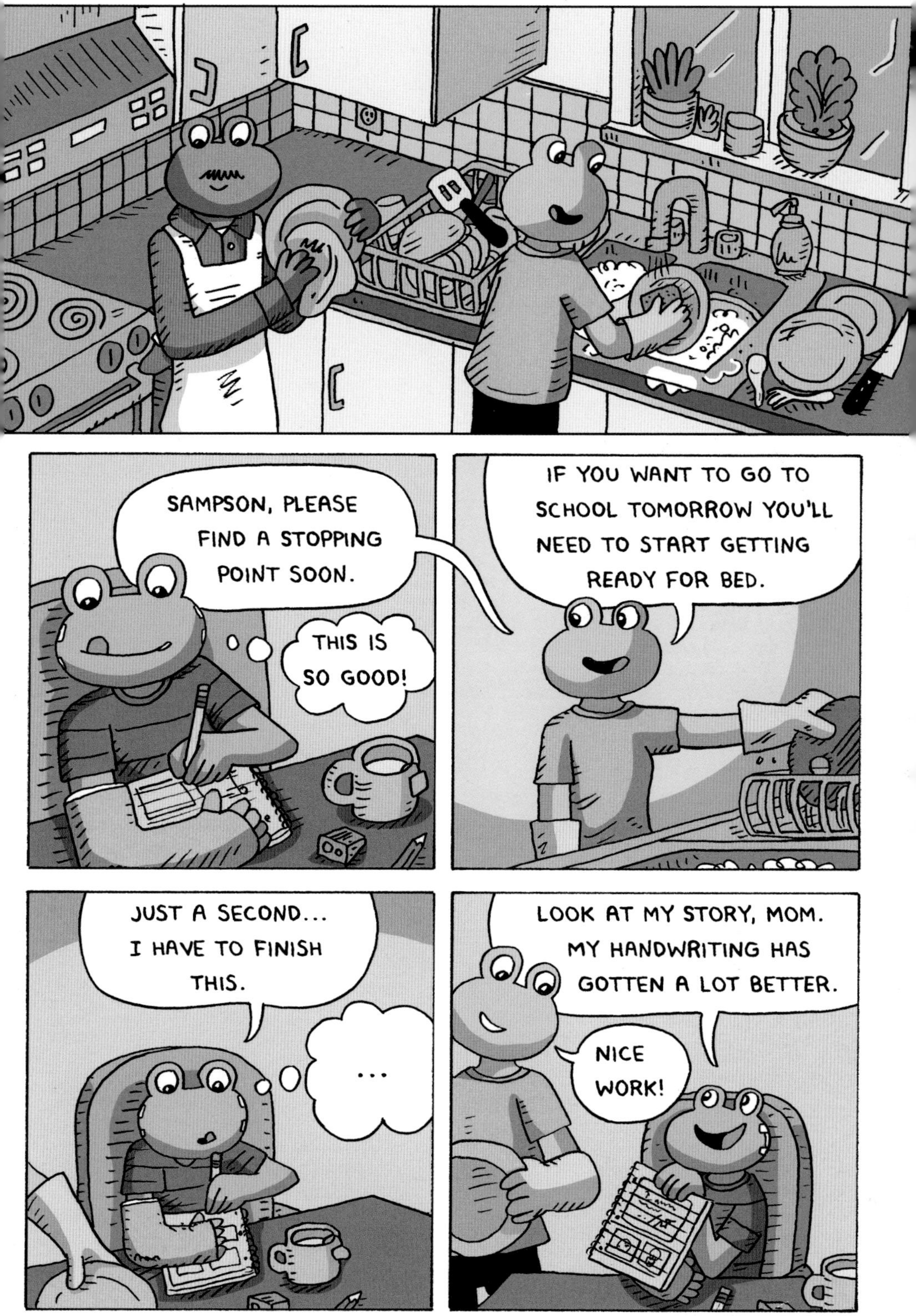
SAMPSON, PLEASE FIND A STOPPING POINT SOON.
THIS IS SO GOOD!
IF YOU WANT TO GO TO SCHOOL TOMORROW YOU'LL NEED TO START GETTING READY FOR BED.
JUST A SECOND... I HAVE TO FINISH THIS.
...
LOOK AT MY STORY, MOM. MY HANDWRITING HAS GOTTEN A LOT BETTER.
NICE WORK!

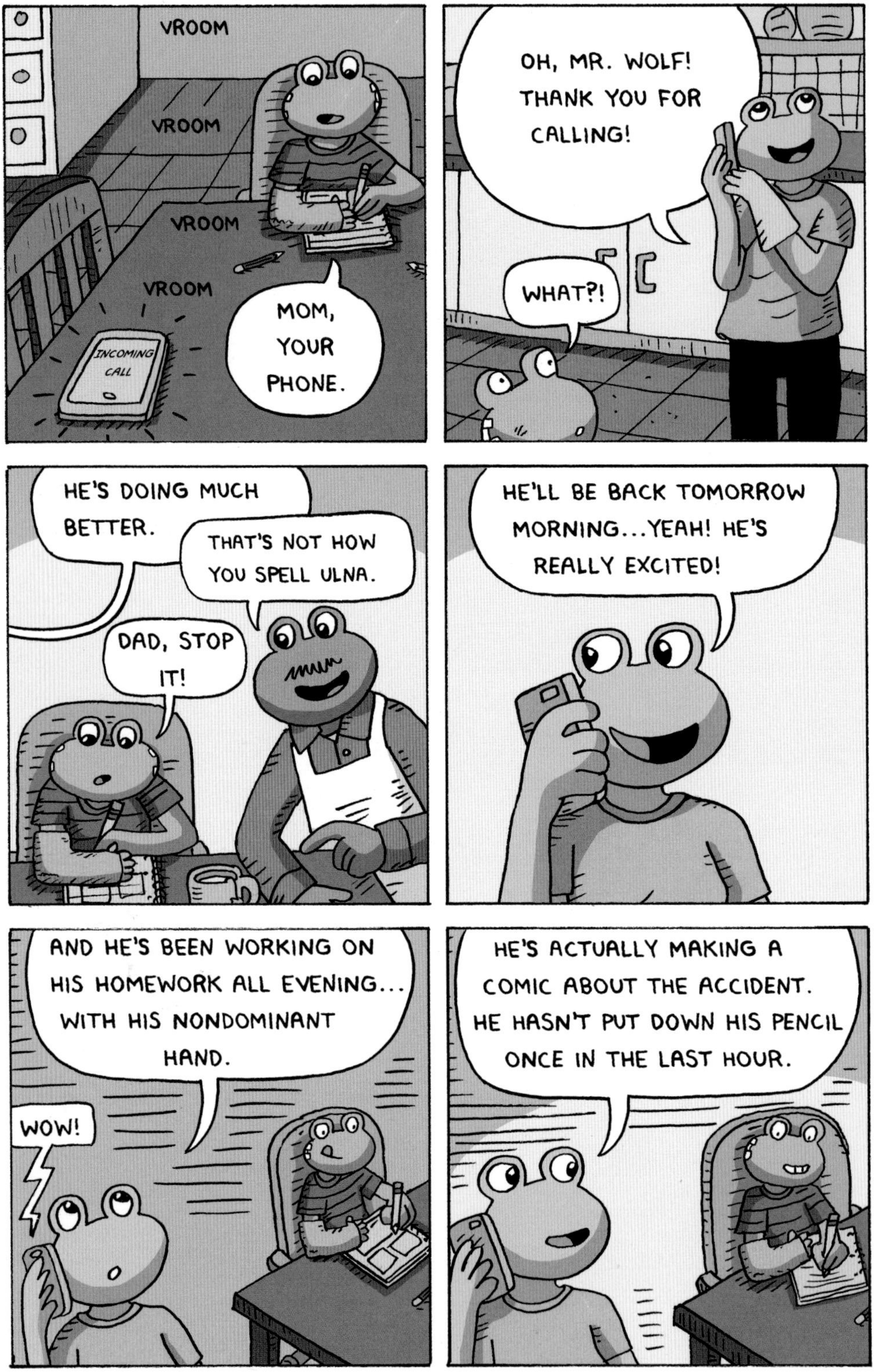
VROOM
VROOM
VROOM
VROOM
INCOMING CALL
MOM, YOUR PHONE.
OH, MR. WOLF! THANK YOU FOR CALLING!
WHAT?!
HE'S DOING MUCH BETTER.
THAT'S NOT HOW YOU SPELL ULNA.
DAD, STOP IT!
HE'LL BE BACK TOMORROW MORNING...YEAH! HE'S REALLY EXCITED!
AND HE'S BEEN WORKING ON HIS HOMEWORK ALL EVENING... WITH HIS NONDOMINANT HAND.
WOW!
HE'S ACTUALLY MAKING A COMIC ABOUT THE ACCIDENT. HE HASN'T PUT DOWN HIS PENCIL ONCE IN THE LAST HOUR.

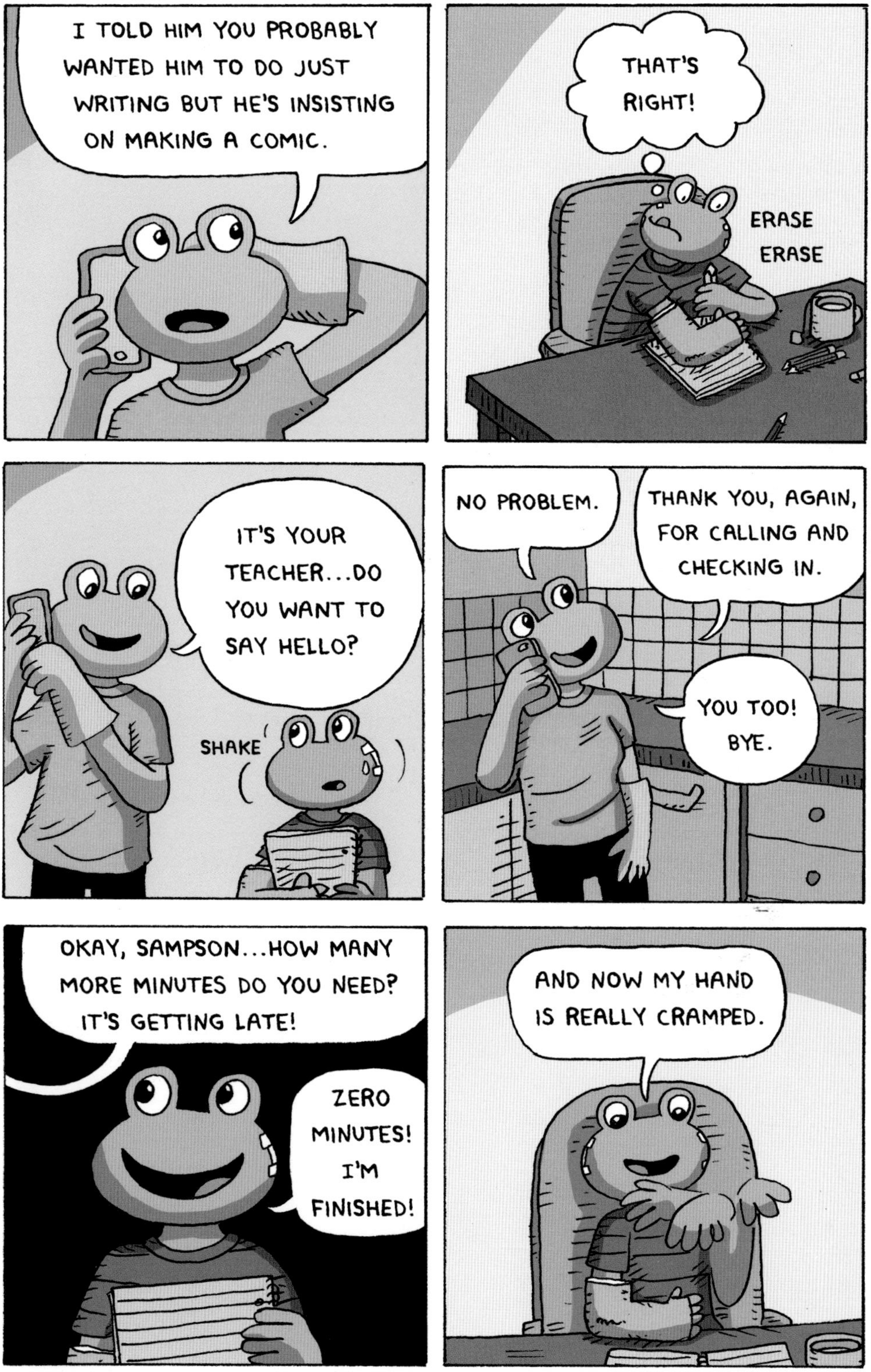
I TOLD HIM YOU PROBABLY WANTED HIM TO DO JUST WRITING BUT HE'S INSISTING ON MAKING A COMIC.
THAT'S RIGHT!
ERASE ERASE
IT'S YOUR TEACHER...DO YOU WANT TO SAY HELLO?
SHAKE
NO PROBLEM.
THANK YOU, AGAIN, FOR CALLING AND CHECKING IN.
YOU TOO! BYE.
OKAY, SAMPSON...HOW MANY MORE MINUTES DO YOU NEED? IT'S GETTING LATE!
ZERO MINUTES! I'M FINISHED!
AND NOW MY HAND IS REALLY CRAMPED.

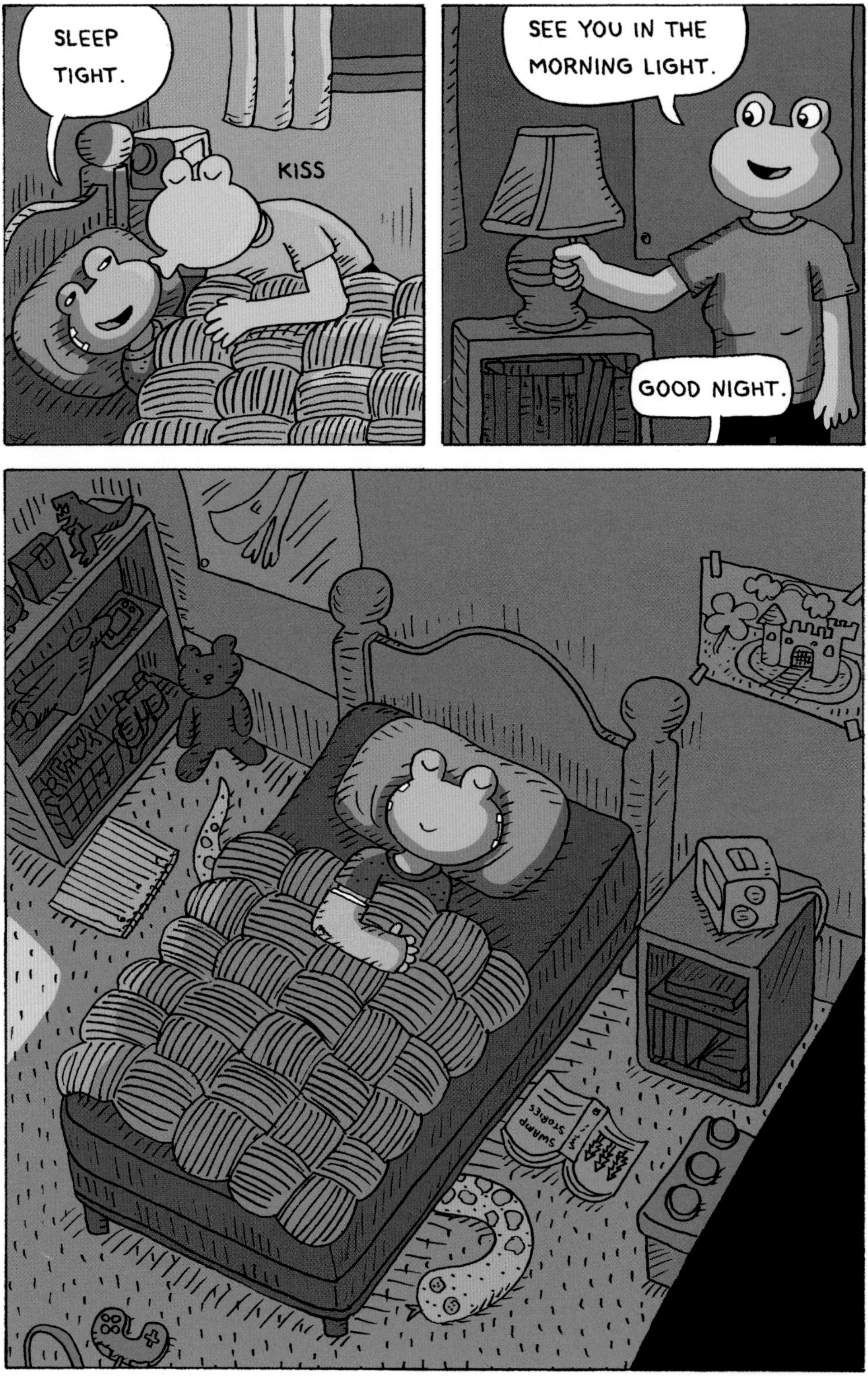
SLEEP TIGHT.
KISS
SEE YOU IN THE MORNING LIGHT.
GOOD NIGHT.
SWAMP STORIES

CHAPTER EIGHT
Sampson's Return

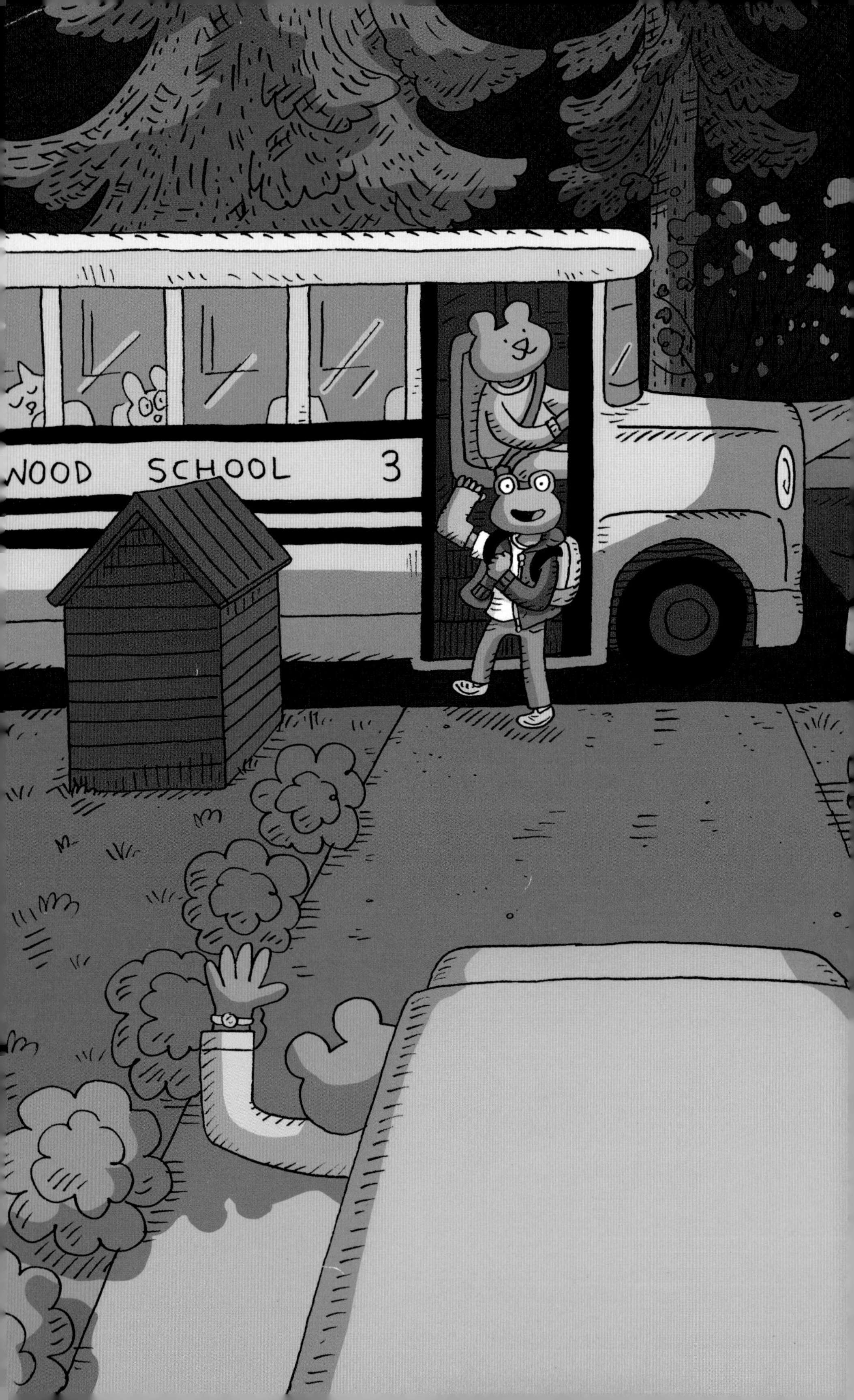
WOOD SCHOOL 3

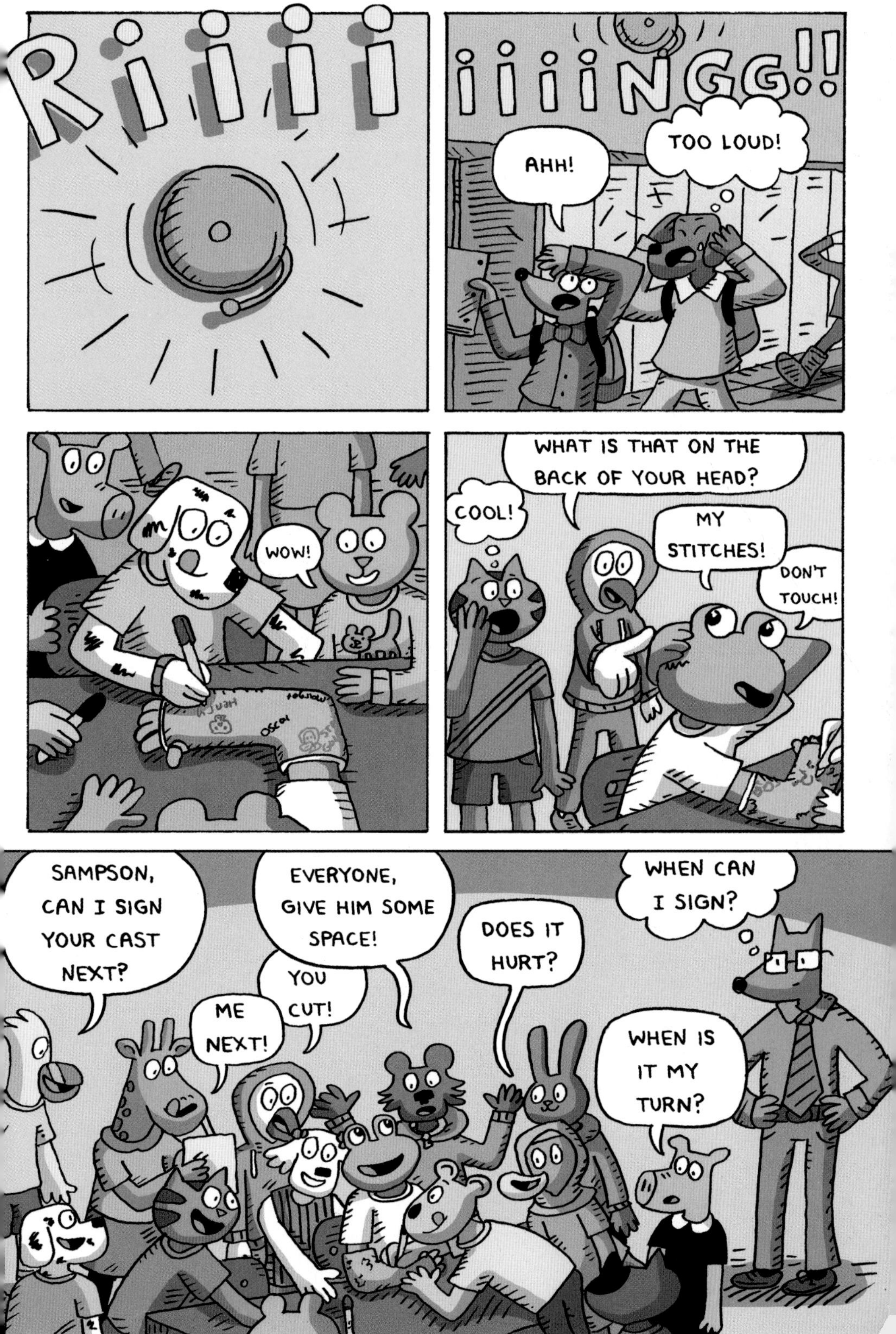
RIIIIIIIINGG!!
AHH!
TOO LOUD!
WOW!
WHAT IS THAT ON THE BACK OF YOUR HEAD?
COOL!
MY STITCHES!
DON'T TOUCH!
SAMPSON, CAN I SIGN YOUR CAST NEXT?
EVERYONE, GIVE HIM SOME SPACE!
YOU CUT!
ME NEXT!
DOES IT HURT?
WHEN CAN I SIGN?
WHEN IS IT MY TURN?

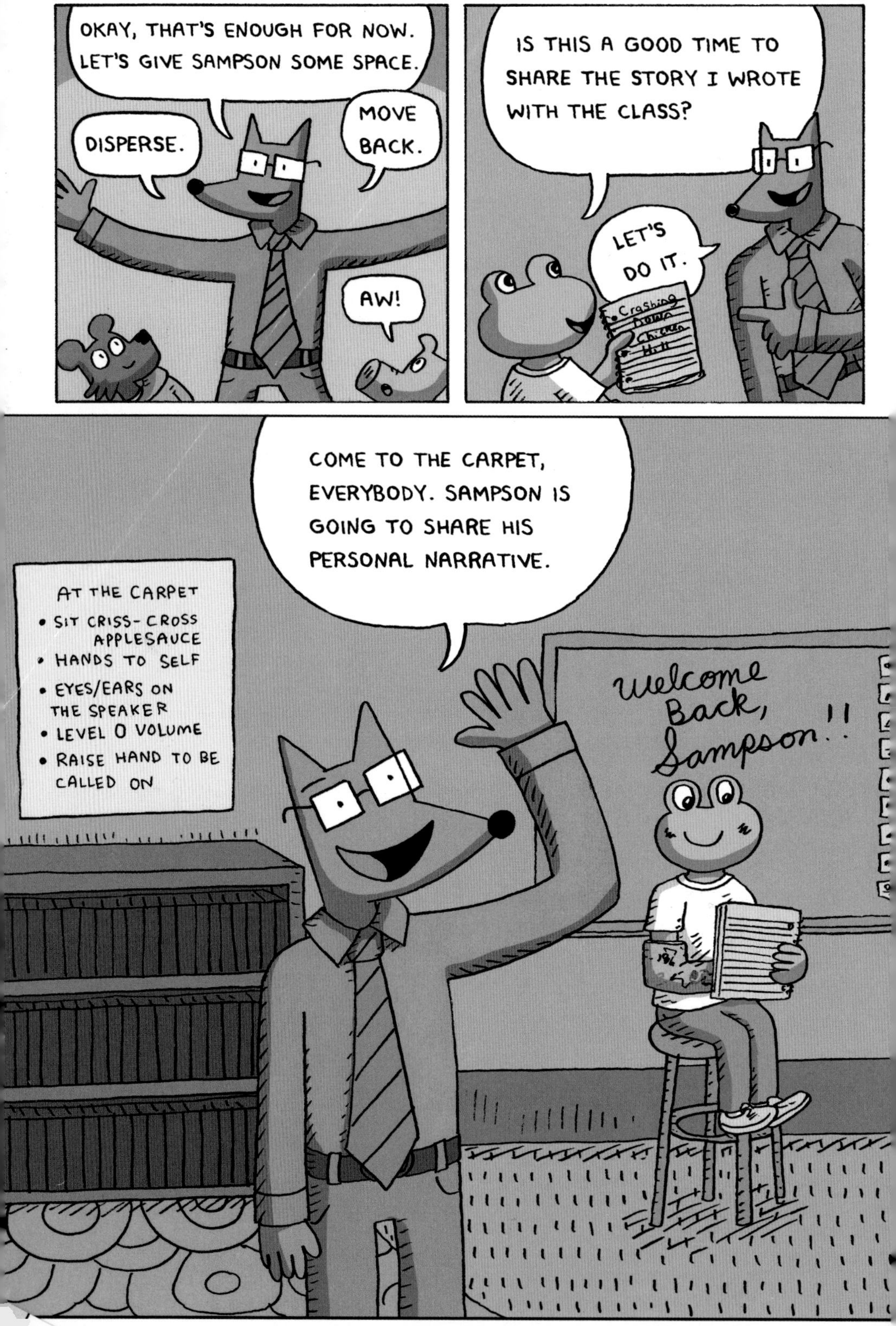
OKAY, THAT'S ENOUGH FOR NOW. LET'S GIVE SAMPSON SOME SPACE.
DISPERSE.
MOVE BACK.
AW!
IS THIS A GOOD TIME TO SHARE THE STORY I WROTE WITH THE CLASS?
LET'S DO IT.
COME TO THE CARPET, EVERYBODY. SAMPSON IS GOING TO SHARE HIS PERSONAL NARRATIVE.
AT THE CARPET
• SIT CRISS-CROSS APPLESAUCE
• HANDS TO SELF
• EYES/EARS ON THE SPEAKER
• LEVEL 0 VOLUME
• RAISE HAND TO BE CALLED ON
Welcome Back, Sampson!!

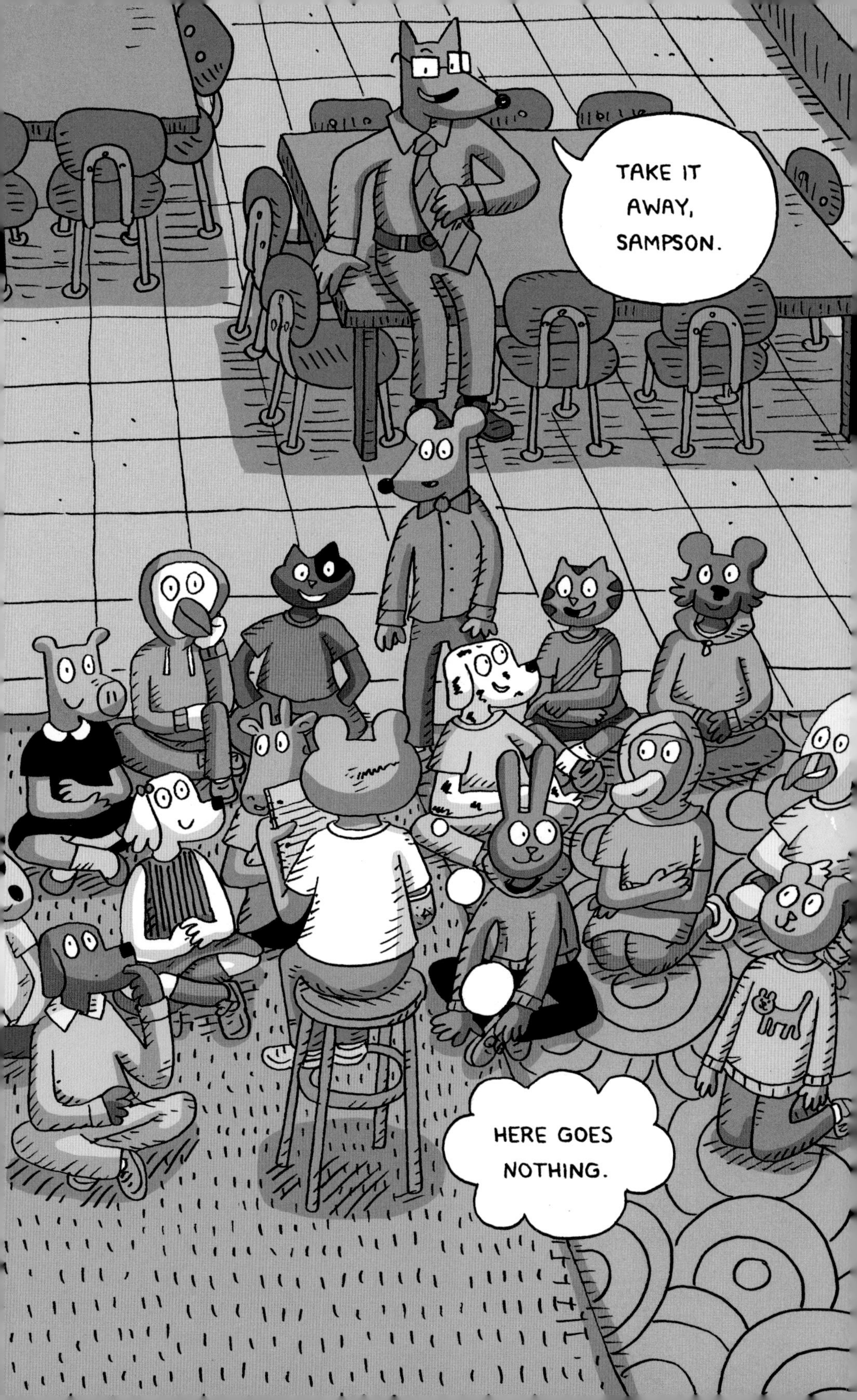
TAKE IT AWAY, SAMPSON.
HERE GOES NOTHING.

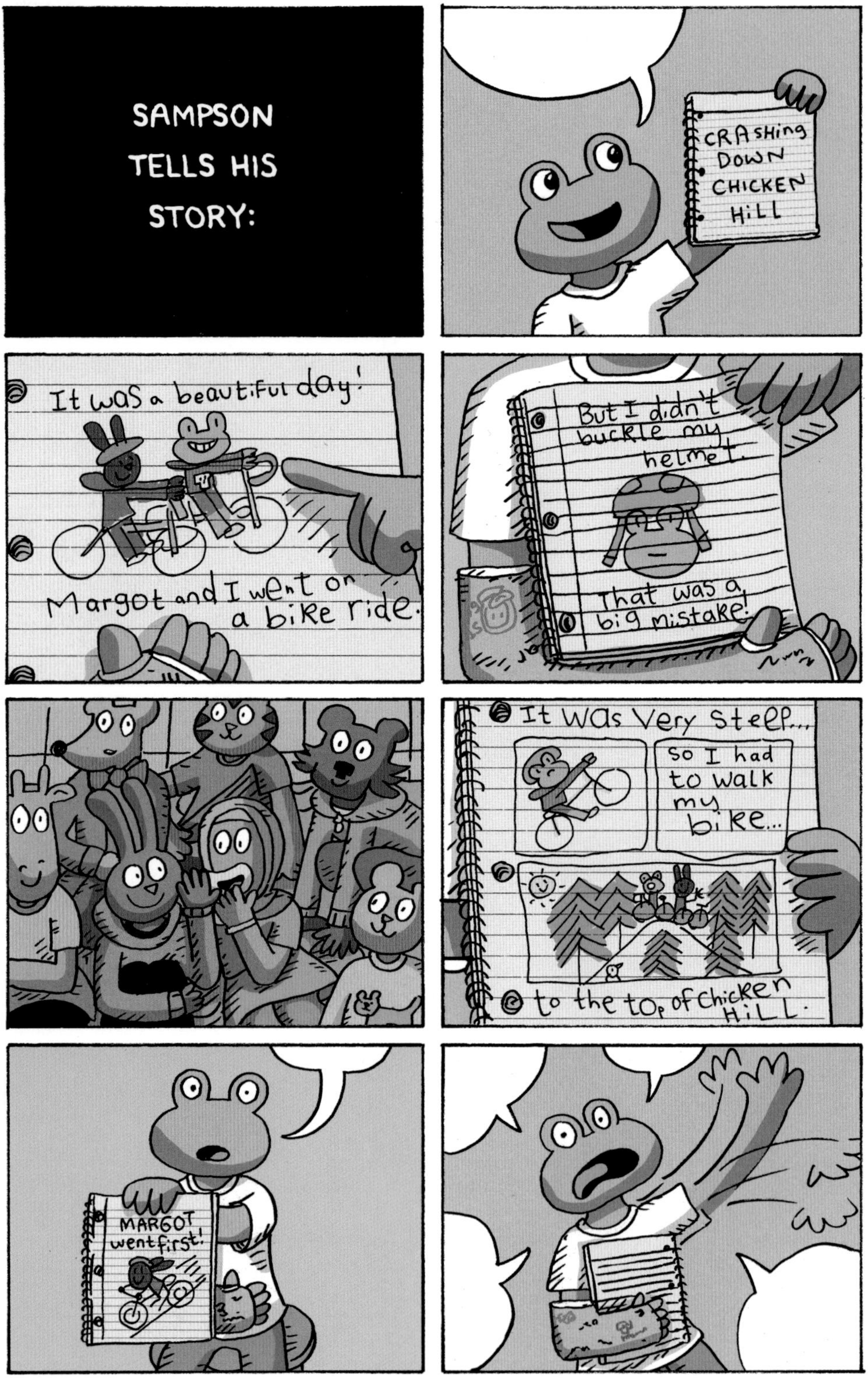
SAMPSON TELLS HIS STORY:
CRASHING DOWN CHICKEN HILL
It was a beautiful day!
Margot and I went on a bike ride.
But I didn't buckle my helmet.
That was a big mistake!
It was very steep...
so I had to walk my bike...
to the top of Chicken Hill.
MARGOT went first!

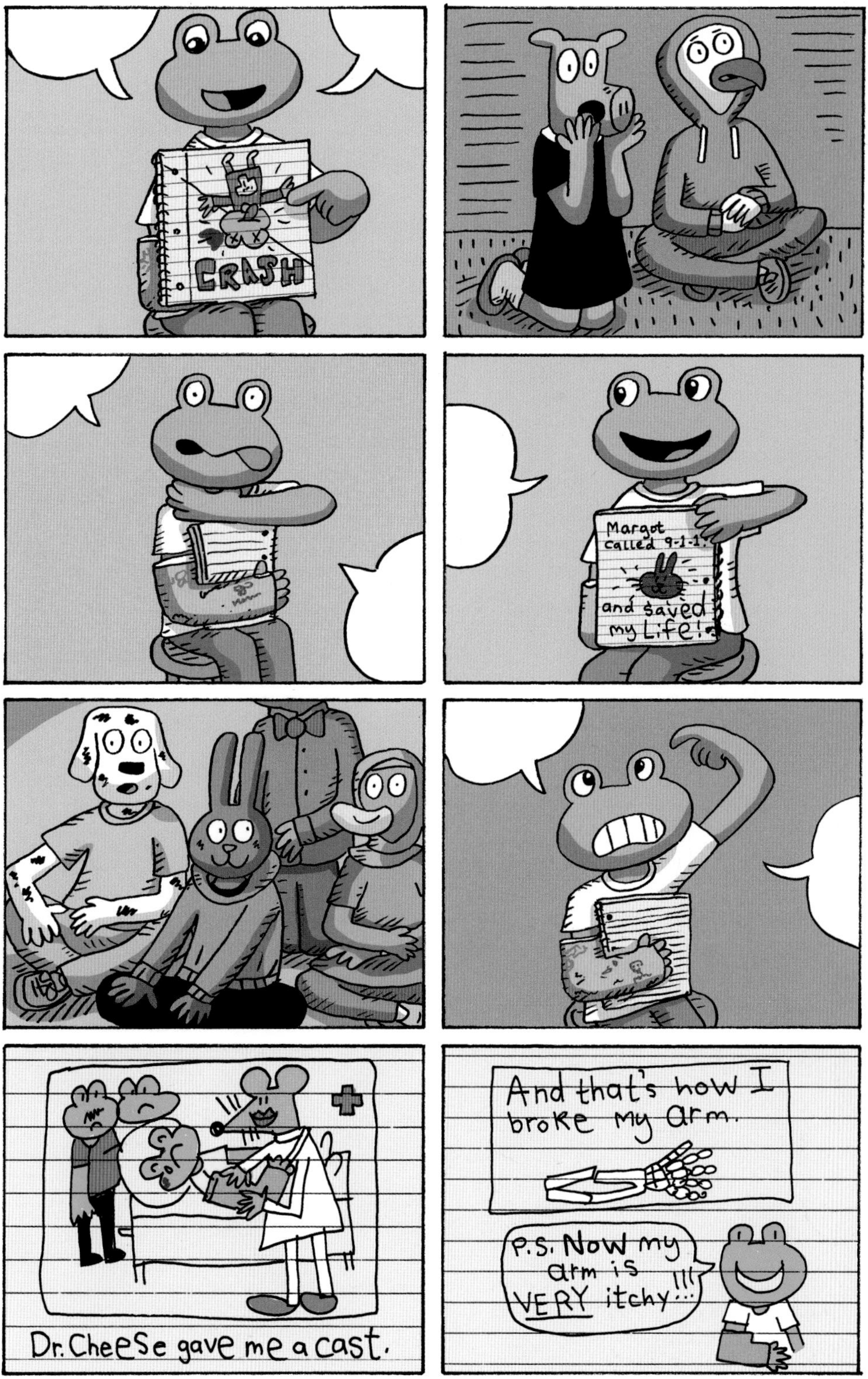
CRASH
Margot called 9-1-1.
and saved my Life!
Dr. Cheese gave me a cast.
And that's how I broke my arm.
P.S. Now my arm is VERY itchy!!!

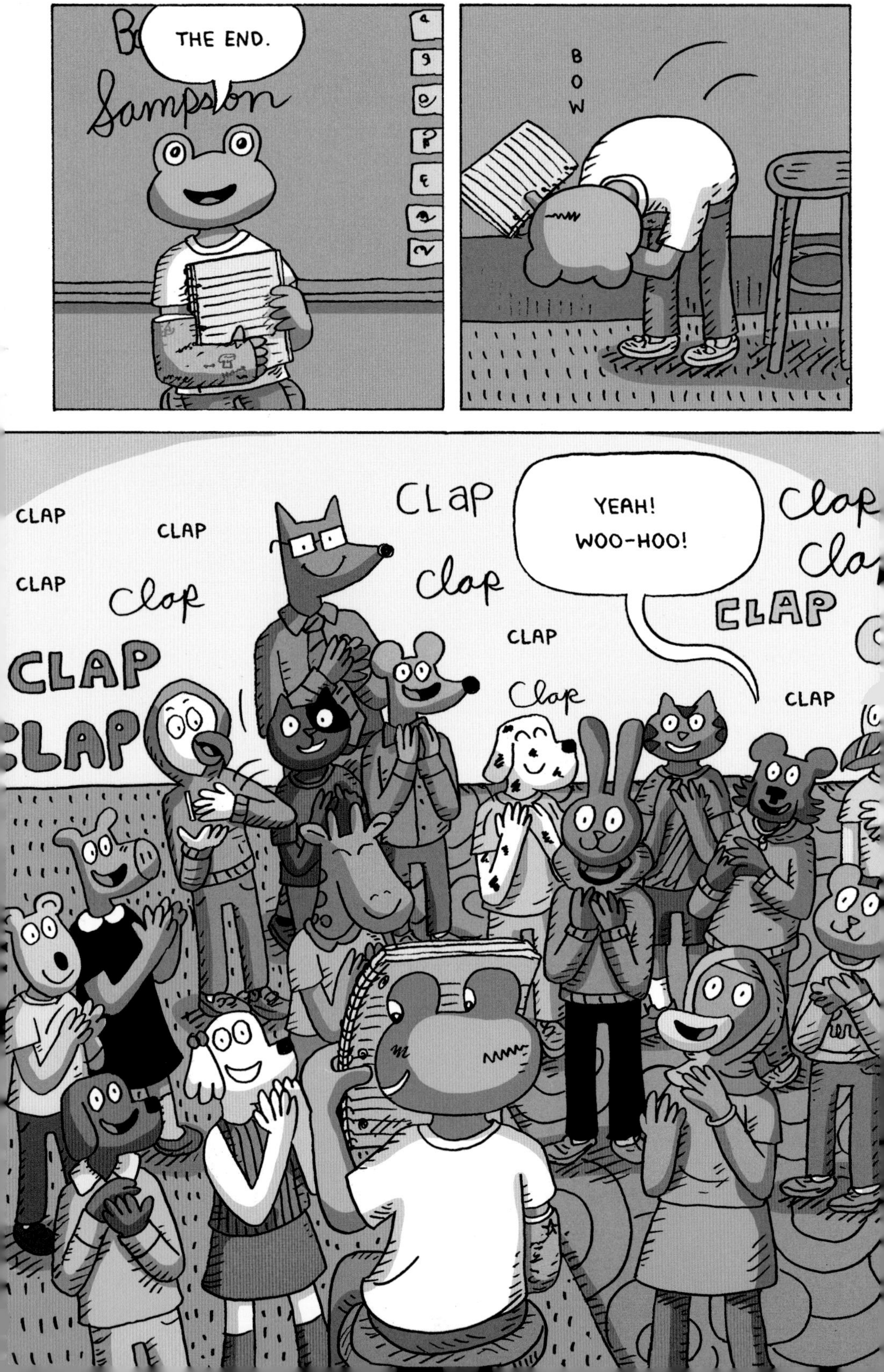

THE END.
Sampson
BOW
CLAP
CLAP
CLAP
Clap
CLAP
CLAP
CLap
Clap
CLAP
Clap
YEAH!
WOO-HOO!
Clap
CLAP
CLAP

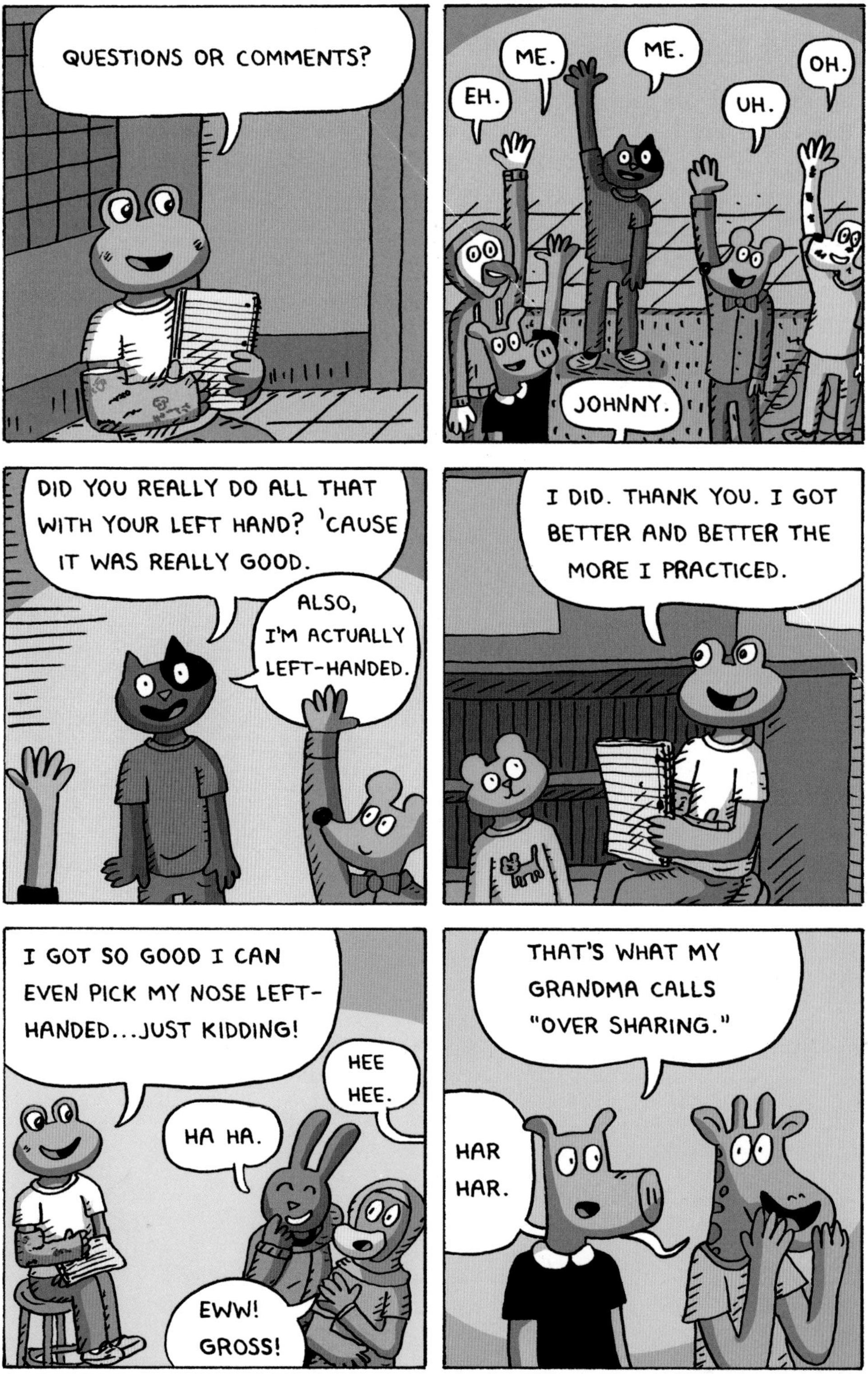
QUESTIONS OR COMMENTS?
EH.
ME.
ME.
UH.
OH.
JOHNNY.
DID YOU REALLY DO ALL THAT WITH YOUR LEFT HAND? 'CAUSE IT WAS REALLY GOOD.
ALSO, I'M ACTUALLY LEFT-HANDED.
I DID. THANK YOU. I GOT BETTER AND BETTER THE MORE I PRACTICED.
I GOT SO GOOD I CAN EVEN PICK MY NOSE LEFT-HANDED...JUST KIDDING!
HA HA.
HEE HEE.
EWW! GROSS!
THAT'S WHAT MY GRANDMA CALLS "OVER SHARING."
HAR HAR.

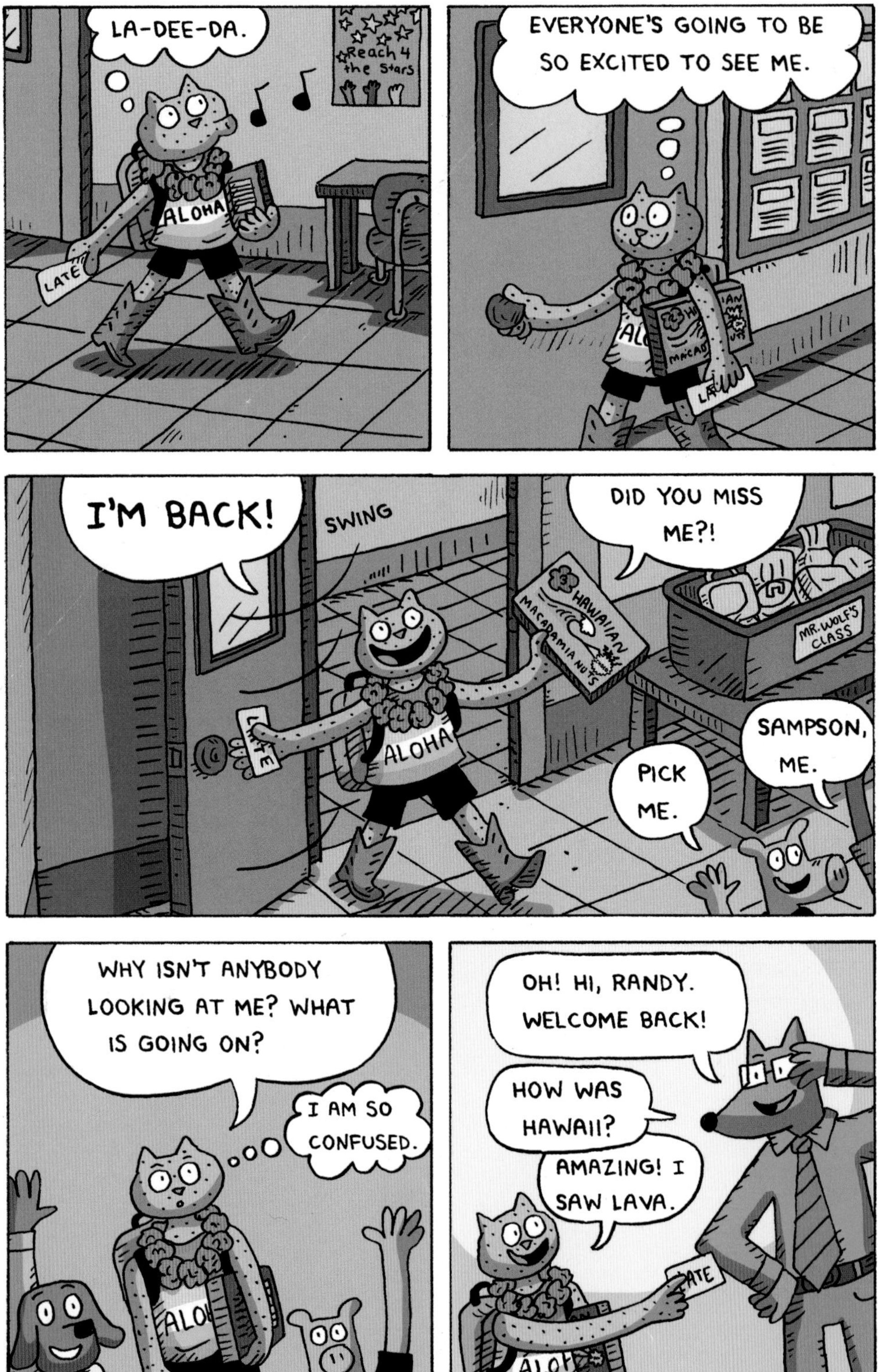

LA-DEE-DA.
Reach 4 the Stars
LATE
ALOHA
EVERYONE'S GOING TO BE SO EXCITED TO SEE ME.
I'M BACK!
SWING
DID YOU MISS ME?!
HAWAIIAN MACADAMIA NUTS
MR. WOLF'S CLASS
LATE
ALOHA
SAMPSON, ME.
PICK ME.
WHY ISN'T ANYBODY LOOKING AT ME? WHAT IS GOING ON?
I AM SO CONFUSED.
OH! HI, RANDY. WELCOME BACK!
HOW WAS HAWAII?
AMAZING! I SAW LAVA.
LATE

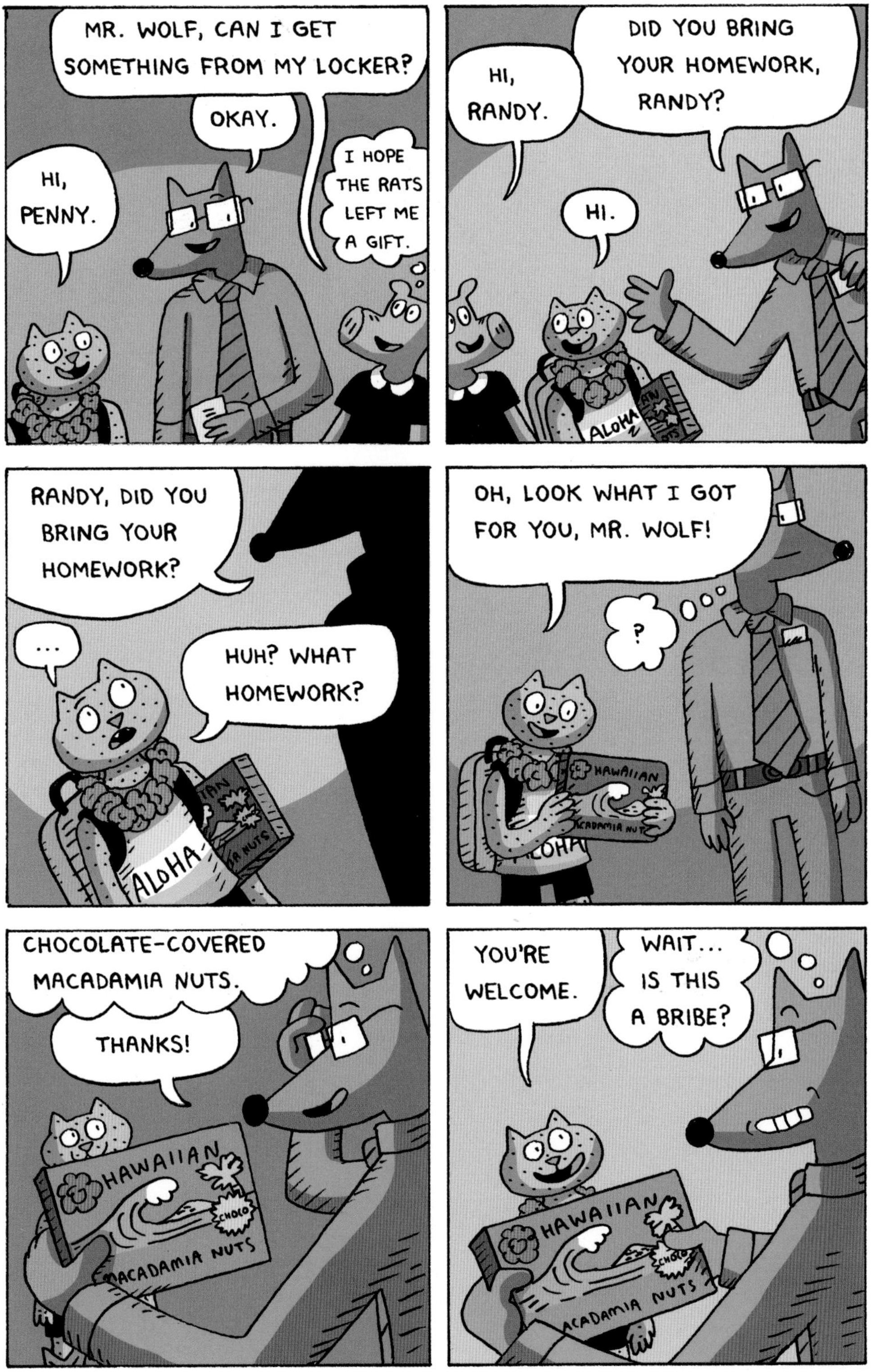
MR. WOLF, CAN I GET SOMETHING FROM MY LOCKER?
OKAY.
HI, PENNY.
I HOPE THE RATS LEFT ME A GIFT.
HI, RANDY.
DID YOU BRING YOUR HOMEWORK, RANDY?
HI.
ALOHA
RANDY, DID YOU BRING YOUR HOMEWORK?
...
HUH? WHAT HOMEWORK?
ALOHA
OH, LOOK WHAT I GOT FOR YOU, MR. WOLF!
?
HAWAIIAN
CHOCOLATE-COVERED MACADAMIA NUTS.
THANKS!
HAWAIIAN
CHOCO
MACADAMIA NUTS
YOU'RE WELCOME.
WAIT... IS THIS A BRIBE?
HAWAIIAN
CHOCO
MACADAMIA NUTS

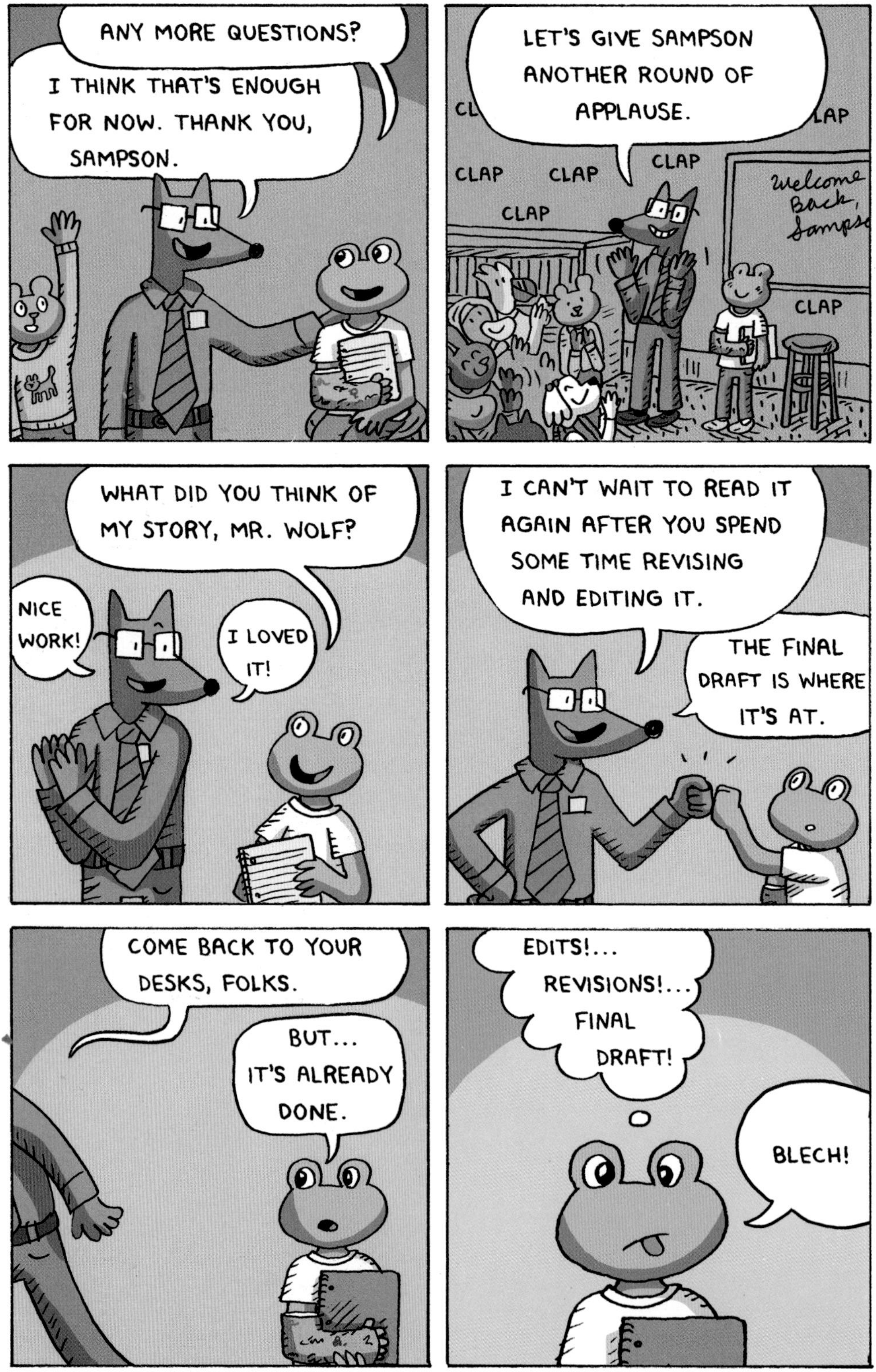
ANY MORE QUESTIONS?
I THINK THAT'S ENOUGH FOR NOW. THANK YOU, SAMPSON.
LET'S GIVE SAMPSON ANOTHER ROUND OF APPLAUSE.
CLAP CLAP CLAP CLAP CLAP
Welcome Back,
WHAT DID YOU THINK OF MY STORY, MR. WOLF?
NICE WORK!
I LOVED IT!
I CAN'T WAIT TO READ IT AGAIN AFTER YOU SPEND SOME TIME REVISING AND EDITING IT.
THE FINAL DRAFT IS WHERE IT'S AT.
COME BACK TO YOUR DESKS, FOLKS.
BUT... IT'S ALREADY DONE.
EDITS!... REVISIONS!... FINAL DRAFT!
BLECH!

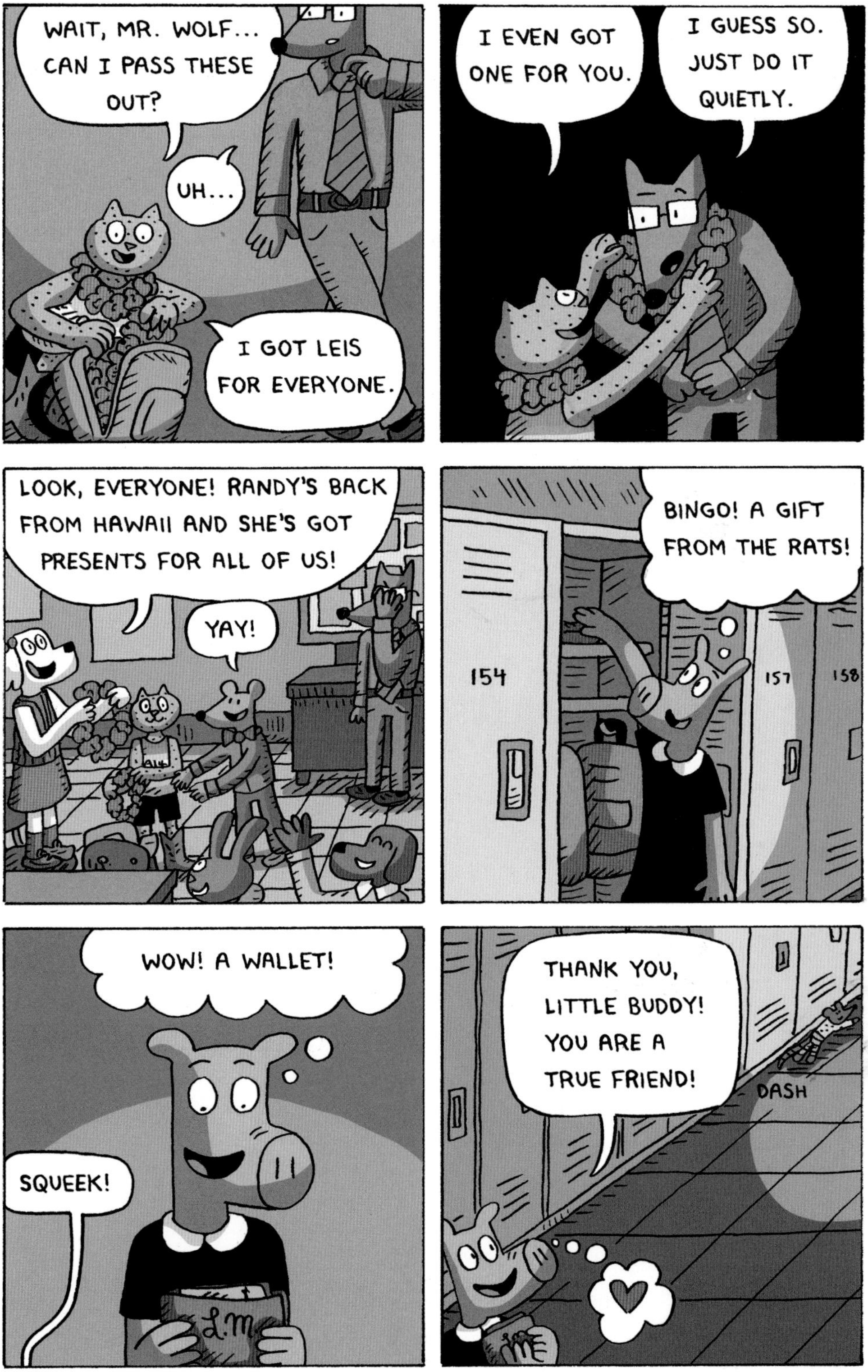
WAIT, MR. WOLF... CAN I PASS THESE OUT?
UH...
I GOT LEIS FOR EVERYONE.
I EVEN GOT ONE FOR YOU.
I GUESS SO. JUST DO IT QUIETLY.
LOOK, EVERYONE! RANDY'S BACK FROM HAWAII AND SHE'S GOT PRESENTS FOR ALL OF US!
YAY!
BINGO! A GIFT FROM THE RATS!
154
157
158
WOW! A WALLET!
SQUEEK!
L.M.
THANK YOU, LITTLE BUDDY! YOU ARE A TRUE FRIEND!
DASH

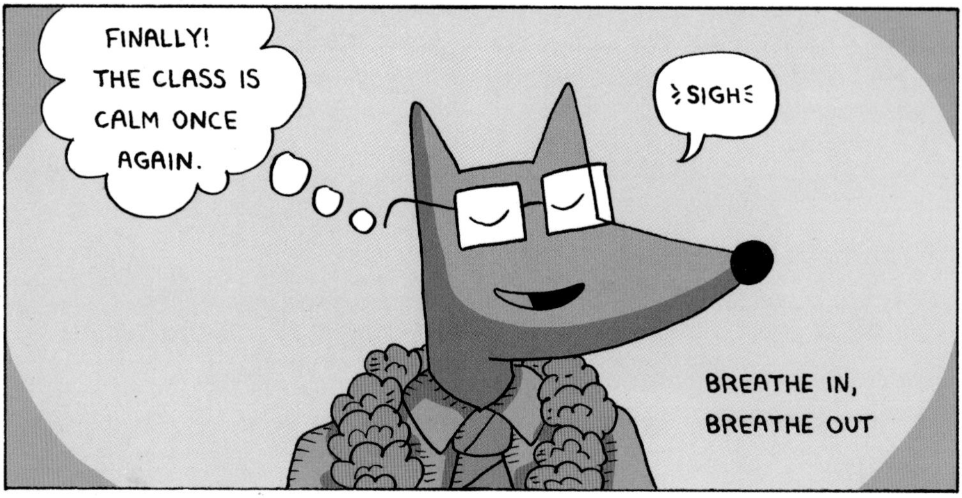
FINALLY! THE CLASS IS CALM ONCE AGAIN.
SIGH
BREATHE IN, BREATHE OUT

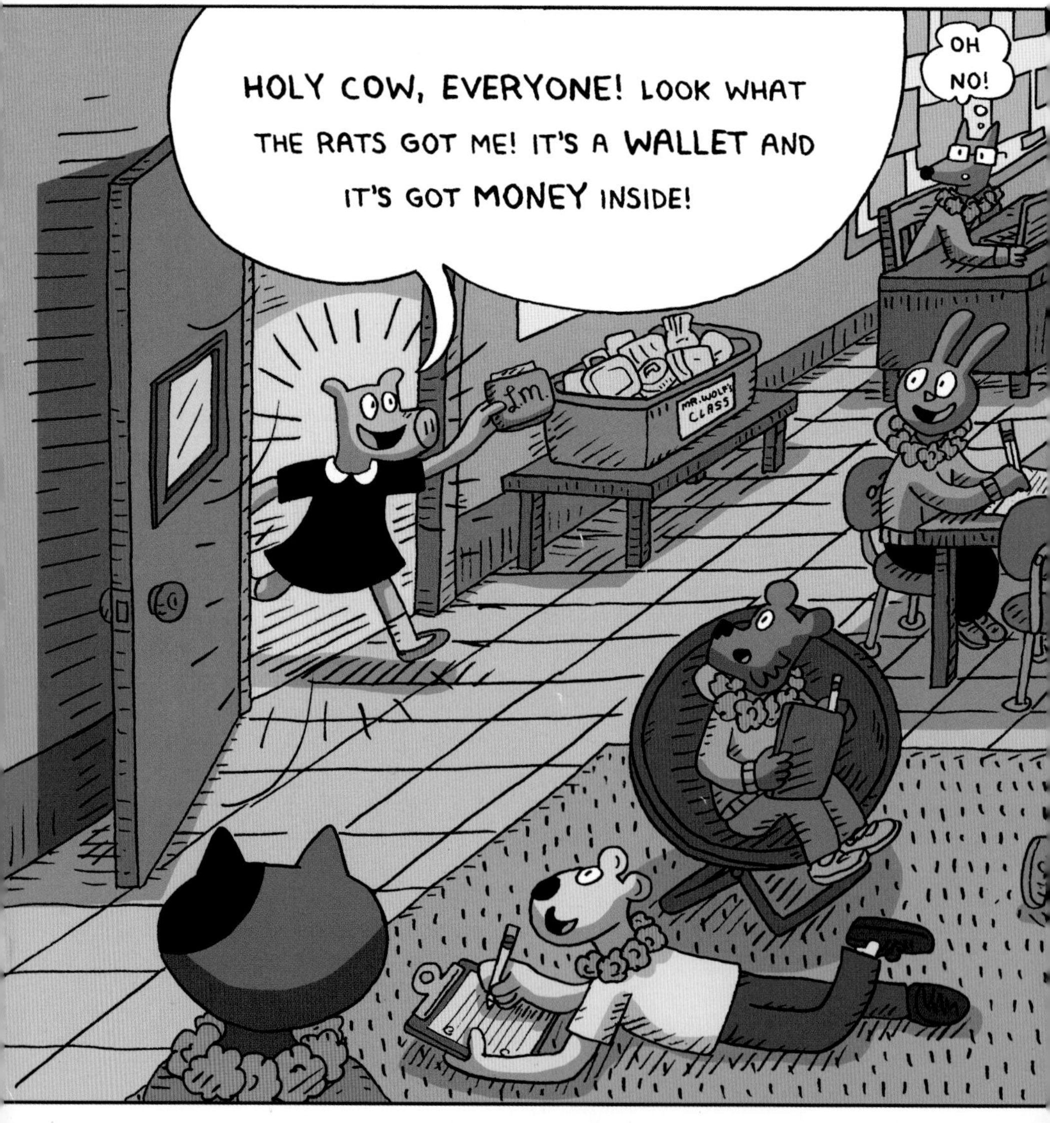
HOLY COW, EVERYONE! LOOK WHAT THE RATS GOT ME! IT'S A WALLET AND IT'S GOT MONEY INSIDE!
OH NO!
MR. WOLF'S CLASS

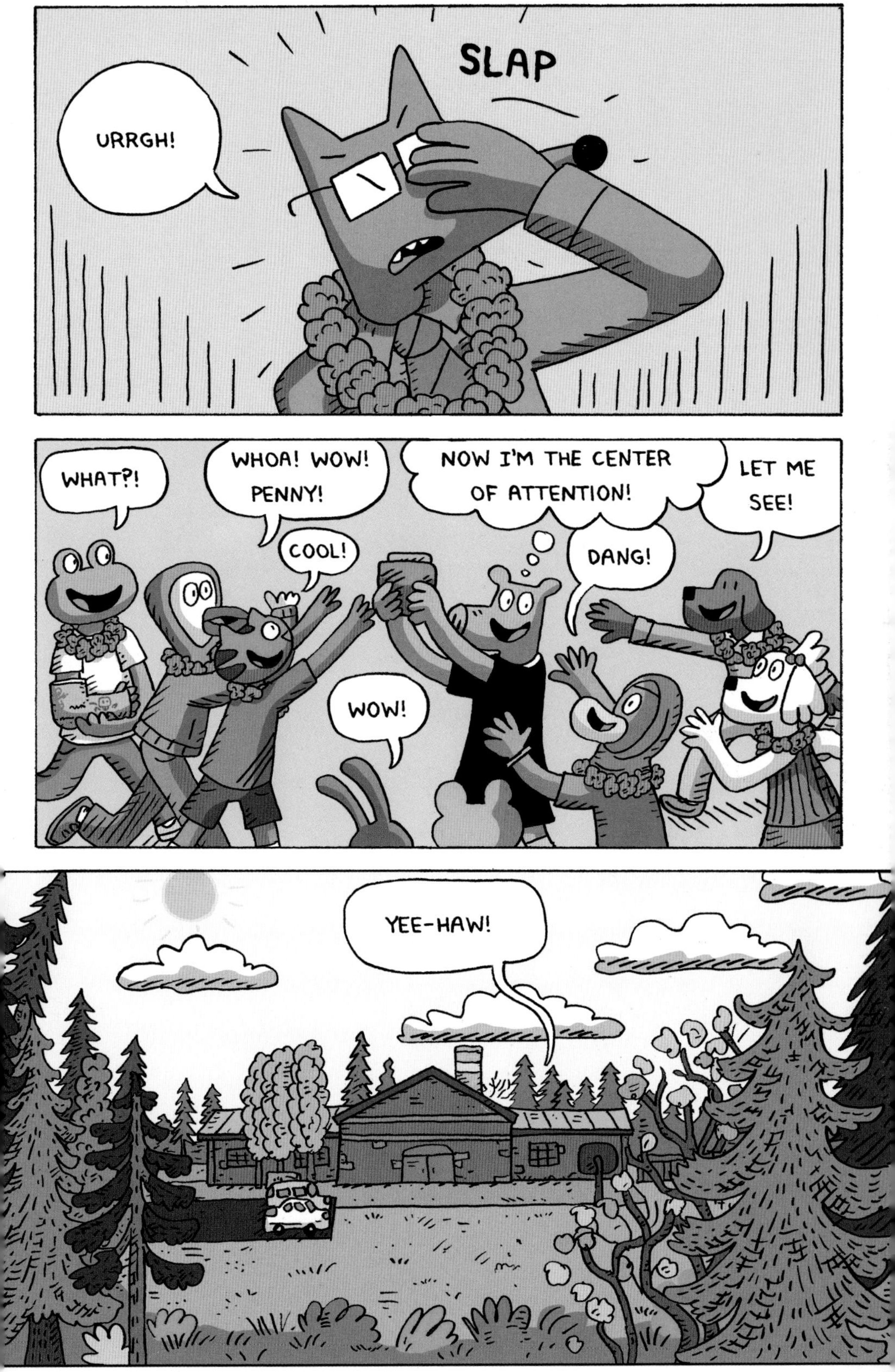
SLAP
URRGH!
WHAT?!
WHOA! WOW! PENNY!
COOL!
NOW I'M THE CENTER OF ATTENTION!
DANG!
LET ME SEE!
WOW!
YEE-HAW!

Thank you to . . .

Judy Hansen, Cassandra Pelham Fulton, Phil Falco, David Saylor, Jordana Kulak, Emily Heddleson, Judy Newman, Matt Poulter, Michael Strouse, and everyone at Scholastic and Graphix who helped this book make it into your hands.

To Ariel, Marlen, Don, Alona, Lisa, David, Ed, and the rest of my family.

To my students, who always surprise me year after year with their creativity, curiosity, and compassion.

To Alex Chiu, Barry Deutsch, Jonathan Hill, Lark Pien, Raina Telgemeier, Jarrett Krosoczka, Andy Runton, Alec Longstreth, Kate Messner, John Schu, Michael Ring, Greg Means, and Gene Luen Yang for your help and support.

Thank you to all of the small and independent bookstores that have supported me throughout the years, as well as a huge thank-you to school and community librarians who are doing the good work.

To Inez, Jack, Finn, Viola, Connor, and all the kids on the block.

And of course, thank you, dear reader, for spending time in Mr. Wolf's class.

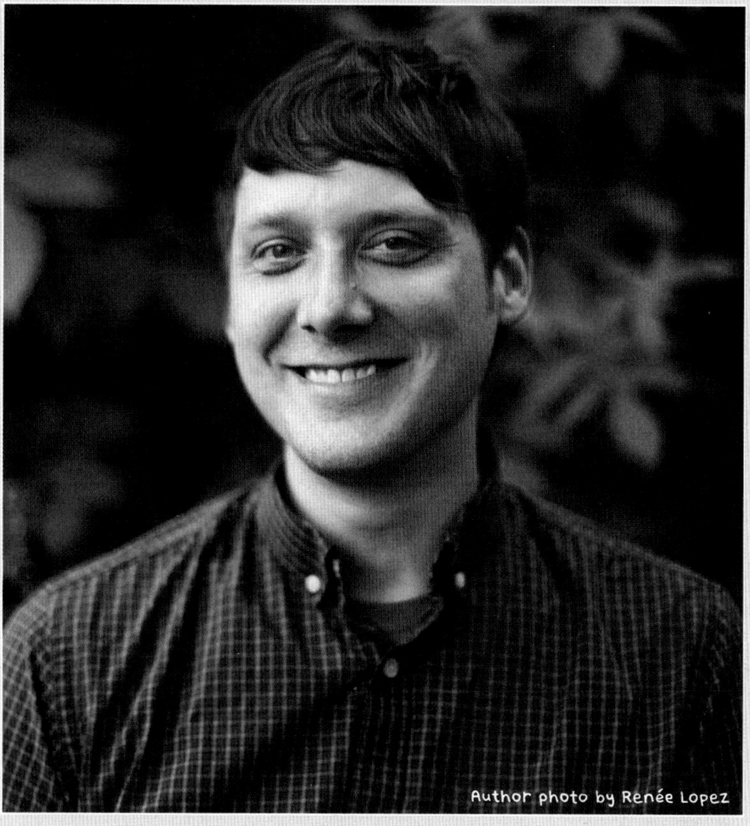

Author photo by Renée Lopez

Aron Nels Steinke is the Eisner Award–winning creator of the Mr. Wolf's Class series, and is the illustrator and coauthor, with Ariel Cohn, of *The Zoo Box*. One summer day back in 1988 when Aron was seven years old, he had a bad bike accident that left him with a broken arm and unable to walk for two weeks. He wasn't wearing a helmet and considers himself very lucky that his injuries weren't more serious. Once they had healed, he quickly got back on his bike and hasn't stopped riding since. If you're in Portland, Oregon, you might find him riding his bike to his other job, where he teaches fourth and fifth graders.

Don't miss the other adventures in Mr. Wolf's class!

From the Eisner Award-winning author
ARON NELS STEINKE
MR. WOLF'S CLASS

From the Eisner Award-winning author
ARON NELS STEINKE
MR. WOLF'S CLASS
MYSTERY CLUB

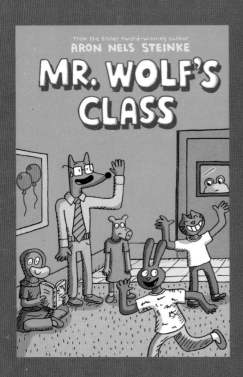

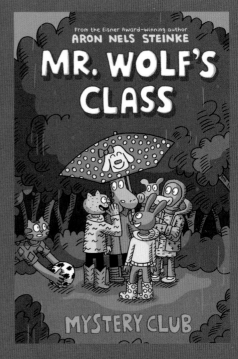